Heavy
Weather

A Carolina Coast Novel

Heavy Weather

A Carolina Coast Novel

Normandie Fischer

Sleepy Creek Press
Gloucester, North Carolina

Sleepy Creek Press, PO Box 114, Gloucester, NC, 28528
www.sleepycreekpress.com

Publisher's Note: This is a work of fiction. Names, characters, places, and incidents are a product of the author's imagination. Locales and public names are sometimes used for atmospheric purposes. Any resemblance to actual people, living or dead, or to businesses, companies, events, institutions, or locales is completely coincidental.

Book Layout ©2013 BookDesignTemplates.com

Cover Design ©2015 Normandie Fischer, with Sarah Thompson at www.sarahthompsondesign.com Cover photo credits, www.unsplash.com, Dominik Martin; background painting by Andreas Achenbach (1815-1910)

Scripture from the New American Standard Bible, Copyright© 1960, 1962, 1963, 1968, 1971, 1972, 1973, 1975, 1977, 1995 by the Lockman Foundation. Used by permission

Ordering Information:
Quantity sales. Special discounts are available on quantity purchases by corporations, associations, and others. For details, contact the "Special Sales Department" at the address above.

Heavy Weather/Normandie Fischer -- 1st ed.
ISBN 978-0-9861416-0-7

Dedicated To

Ariana, my strong and valiant girl:
a warrior for the hurting, talented and beautiful, my daughter, my
friend. I couldn't be prouder of you—or more thrilled at the mother you've
become to our precious Ella.
(Ariana, from the Greek: holy one; from the Welsh: silver. Oh, yes!)

Also dedicated to any who have faced abuse and found the courage to
fly free. To the wounded, to those ravaged by longing for what cannot be
... may you find peace and joy in the beloved.

A TOAST TO FRIENDSHIP

*Yes'm, old friends is always best, 'less you can catch a new one
that's fit to make an old one out of.*
−SARAH ORNE JEWETT (1849-1909)

*It is one of the blessings of old friends that you can afford to be
stupid with them.*
−RALPH WALDO EMERSON (1803-1882)

COMFORT FOR THE BROKEN

...He has sent me to bind up the brokenhearted, To proclaim
liberty to captives and freedom to prisoners; To proclaim...the day
of vengeance of our God; To comfort all who mourn ...Giving them
a garland instead of ashes, The oil of gladness instead of mourning,
the mantle of praise ...
−ISAIAH 61:1-3

*...Weeping may last for the night, But a shout of joy comes in the
morning.*
−PSALM 30:5

1 ANNIE MAC

Blood oozed between Annie Mac's fingers from the gash in her cheek. She huddled by the refrigerator, shivering, praying Roy's knuckles wouldn't rip up more of her flesh.

She couldn't focus. But she could hear. Oh, yes, she could hear while pain sliced like knives through nerves she hadn't known existed, scraping her raw inside and out, blades sharpening themselves on her flesh.

Roy's rants of "Where is she? Where'd you hide my girl?" echoed in his wake as he demolished the living room, the bedrooms, probably the bathrooms, but other words played over and over in her head. *Please help my babies, please.*

Her prayers hit the ceiling and flattened, spreading out so they covered her but didn't fly high enough to reach heaven. *Auntie Sim, I need. I need.*

She'd always needed, hadn't she? From the beginning, as far back as she could remember.

A clomping sounded across the hardwood floor, becoming a scuff and shuffle on the kitchen linoleum when Roy came for her again. His curses filled the room, screams of anger louder than any she'd heard from him before.

She shuffled backwards, raising her arms to ward off another blow, but his steel-toed boot kicked her legs clean out from under her. Her buttocks took the fall. Before she could curl onto her side, his fist smashed into her temple, slamming her against the wall. She bounced back to the floor. This time, the pain brought on the shakes and the surety that she'd never escape. Never.

Red morphed to gray shadows in her mind. She tried to slow the panicky rise and fall of her chest. In and out ... slowly ... in and out. Surely, he'd broken a rib. And more.

"What have you done with my girl?" He grabbed her shoulders, hefted her to spitting level. "Where'd that fool boy take her?"

She shut her eyes against the sight of him and against the crippling pain. He lashed once more with his boot into her shin and threw her against the wall. Her leg crumpled. This time the scream was hers.

2   HANNAH

The half-light of pre-dawn lit Hannah's way from the bathroom back to her big, comfortable bed and her sleeping husband. But before she could pull up the sheet, a cold nose nudged her thigh, and there was Harvey, tongue lolling out the side of his red snout, waiting. She caressed one floppy ear and pointed to his pillow, but he was having none of it. She was up. He was up. And, honey, that meant outside *now.*

She slipped on jogging shorts and a tee shirt, hurrying so the Irish Setter wouldn't forget he was house-trained. Ahead of her, he dove down the stairs, his nails clicking on the floor. "Leash," she called. The word brought him to a momentary halt, and she fumbled to attach the clip before he started dancing at her feet. And then they were off.

The sun began its slow ascent over Taylor Creek, showing off tendrils of mauve and pink and yellow. The dog trotted at her side, all a-quiver with tail swishing as the salt tang and the scent of plough mud hit. The marsh was home to birds and critters that livened a setter's world.

Wasn't she fortunate to have only a dog binding her to ritual? A dog and a husband who adored her—and who gave her freedom to be and to do what she wanted? She had time to work on her pottery, a shop in which to sell her craft, and, glory be, she had a best friend coming home. Life couldn't get any better.

A heron screeched, and Harvey's head snapped toward it. He tried to bolt toward the water. "Heel," she said, pulling him down a side street, but as soon as the heron's cry subsided, a man's angry yell took its place. Ahead, a truck rattled to a start and tires squealed around a corner.

Her heart did a little tup-tap at the shouts and at that revved truck. Those poor folk, living with such fury. As she drew closer to the house where the truck had been, Harvey lunged toward a big vine-covered bush.

"No, you don't. We're not going into anyone's yard."

The dog reared on his hind legs when the leash grew taut. She sighed, dropped the leash, and gave him his head.

His nose dug under the vines, and his tail slapped her leg. Imagining he'd sniffed out a squirrel, she whispered, "Come back here. Now."

Harvey was having none of it. And then a small squeal came from inside the bush. She spread aside the leaves and peeked behind them. Two frightened pairs of eyes stared back at her, their whites reflecting what light she'd let in.

"Oh, my," she said. "And what are you two doing out here at this hour?" She crouched to their level. "This your house?"

The girl sucked on her thumb. The boy took a moment before nodding.

"And your parents? They inside? I bet they're worried about you. Shall we go see?"

The little girl tucked her face against the boy's chest. He held her close. "It's okay, Katie."

"Katie. What a pretty name. And what's yours?" Her smile felt twisted, lopsided, instead of the soothing she'd hoped for.

The boy's glance darted from her to Harvey's sniffing nose. One hand continued to pat Katie's back. "Tyler Rinehart," he finally said. "Ty."

"Well, Ty, don't you think we ought to find your parents?"

Ty watched Harvey. "I'm supposed to take care of Katie. Mama said."

"Oh. Well. That's good." Hannah tried for calm, as if finding children under a bush at dawn were a normal occurrence, and glanced at the dark house.

Harvey wiggled his way in until he nudged the boy's hand. Tentatively, Ty touched Harvey's snout and ran his fingers across the dog's head to pull at the drooping ears. Katie whimpered.

"Harvey, stop that." Hannah grabbed for his collar.

"It's okay," Ty told his sister. "See, he's only trying to make friends."

The little one broke suction long enough to say, "Mama." Her pitiful little voice made Hannah want to scoop the child up.

Ty repeated his "It's okay," then peeked through the vines. Glancing back at Harvey, he seemed to take courage. "Maybe we can go see Mama now."

"Daddy?" Katie said.

"Roy's gone. Remember, he gave up and went off in his truck?"

Oh, my. She should have connected the dots. These poor children were hiding from that angry voice. "Were you waiting for him to leave before you went inside?"

Ty nodded.

"Well, why don't we go see if we can find your mama now?" She held out her hand.

Ignoring her, Ty nudged Katie and backed with her out the other side. He hesitated when they got to the porch steps, glancing up and down the street and then at his sister. Hannah tried to guess their age. Maybe eight and four?

She grabbed Harvey's trailing leash. Whatever was going on here was way out of her league. Way out. But she was the adult, the one who'd have to suck it up and put on her big-girl pants. "You want me to go first? While you stay with your sister?"

"Yes, ma'am."

"Watch Harvey for me?" She held out the leash. He took it and marched Katie to the stoop, where they scooted up against the wooden railings, Harvey at their feet, his tongue hanging out one side, his head cocked.

No one answered her knock. "Ty, honey, what's your mama's name?"

"Annie Mac. Annie Mac Bingham." He shook his head. "No, I forgot. She fixed it back to Rinehart."

Hannah turned the knob and swung the door open to reveal ripped cushions, broken glass, and knocked-over lamps. She stood rooted. Then she felt for a switch and flicked on the ceiling light. She said to Ty, "You keep your sister out here while I find your mama. You hear?"

Ty's eyes widened, and he nodded.

"Oh, God, please," she whispered. A lump shot right up her throat and filled her mouth with the sour taste of bile.

In the silence, she imagined a madman's curses ricocheting off the walls. She wasn't fanciful, not really, but as she tiptoed through the breakage, she pictured specters hovering behind closed doors.

She stepped around an overturned lamp. At the kitchen doorway, she grabbed the framing with one hand and peered around the separating wall. "Oh, no." She covered her mouth to stifle her cry and clamped her eyes shut.

"Open your eyes, woman," she told herself in her best imitation of take-charge and in-control.

The mother of those babies lay in a pool of blood, one leg awkwardly twisted beneath her, her arms flung wide as if she'd clutched at air on her way down.

3 HANNAH

Hannah knelt and inched her fingers over the woman's neck until she traced a faint beat. "Thank God."

Her words tumbled into a prayer that she'd find a phone. Above her, wires spilled uselessly from the wall. She dashed through the rest of the house, scanning the living room, the bedrooms, checking under tossed pillows and behind upended tables. "Come on!" she said, as if that might conjure an extension. There had to be one somewhere. Her house had five.

Why had she left her cell phone at home? Fool, fool.

There, in a corner near a double bed, a boxy black phone lay half hidden beneath tossed pillows. It took way too long for the dispatcher to answer, way too long for Hannah to figure out the cross streets. "No, I can't stay on. And I don't know the house number. I'll be outside, waiting. Just get someone here. Now!" The children's mother could be dying, and they had to be scared to death, and they couldn't come in and see their mama like that.

It was hard not to gag at the smell of the blood and the sight of splattered eggs and spaghetti dripping down the wall, the tomato sauce just shades lighter than the blood's red. He'd even pulled the sink from the wall, though at least the pipes didn't seem to be leaking. She imagined a Goliath of a man.

She felt again for a pulse. "I know. I should have taken that First Aid class." Touching the woman's shoulder, she said, "You'll be fine. The ambulance is on its way. Oh, and your children are with Harvey, my dog. He won't let anyone get near them, so don't you worry. Whoever did this to you is long gone, but the police will find him. He won't hurt you any more."

A moan escaped the swollen lips, startling Hannah so that she nearly sat back on the glass-strewn floor. "Don't move," she said. "Someone will be here in a minute. My name is Hannah. I've called an ambulance."

Another moan, a strangled, "My ... my babies."

Hannah bent closer. "They're fine."

"Please?" It came out a whisper.

Blood congealed on one closed and swollen eye. Half that cheek lay open in an ugly, bloody mess, and bloody red hair caked around her face, glued to her cheeks and that gash. Hannah wanted to press the skin closed to stop the bleeding, but she was afraid to touch anything, afraid she'd make it worse. Annie Mac's other eye stared up at her, and a tear escaped.

"My dog is watching," Hannah said. "No one will get them."

Another tear. One hand clutched Hannah's arm. "He. Will. Oh, God, he *will*." The woman's nails dug in at the last word, and then her hand fell to the floor as if she'd depleted all her reserves in reaching out.

"No, he won't. Harvey won't let him."

The eye pled. Hannah tried to exude confidence when what she wanted was to run out the door. Flag down the ambulance. Anything but stare at that eye.

Another whisper. "You?"

Hannah squinted. "Me, what?"

A pause, then a gravelly, "Hide my babies. Please. Please."

"You want me to take your children? Take care of them?"

The woman's eye blinked.

"So he won't find them?"

Another blink. A sound that was neither moan nor cry came just before another pathetic "Please."

Sirens approached. Thank God. "Help is coming." That was the best she could manage, wasn't it? Finding help. Getting the children into a safe home.

"No ... foster." The last word seemed to ooze on a wave of pain. "He'll ... oh, God, he'll take them."

"The ambulance." She stood and began to back away. "I'll go flag it."

A sort-of sob followed her through the living room and out the screen door. Two blond heads flashed around to stare up at her.

"It's okay. Your mama will be fine, soon as we get her some help. You two wait right there." She headed toward the sidewalk with her arm raised. "Here comes help." At her words, an unmarked Jeep with a flashing light—a *Jeep*?—turned the corner and skidded to a stop at the curb, followed almost immediately by a Beaufort patrol car and then the ambulance.

She turned back to the children. "See? Here we go."

Ty started toward the front door. She called to him, nodding toward his sister. "Ty, honey, why don't you take Katie and Harvey up to the porch, and you two can sit on that nice swing? Can you do that? Keep out of everyone's way so these good folk can take care of your mama?"

"I want Mama!" Katie's lips trembled, and tears welled in her eyes.

"I know you do, sweetie," Hannah said. "See these nice men." She motioned toward one of Beaufort's finest and then nodded as Lieutenant Clay Dougherty, a plain-clothes detective she'd known since third grade, climbed out of the Jeep. "And the ambulance people? They're going to take care of your mama so you can be with her again."

Ty helped Katie onto the swing. "This lady is going to help us."

"Hannah. My name is Hannah."

"Miss Hannah is gonna help Mama," Ty said, reaching out to pet Harvey and bring him close.

Hannah's heart caught as she watched the blond children and the red dog. "Don't you worry," she told them. "I'm here."

She waited while the ambulance crew collected their equipment. Was she crazy? I'm here? As if she had the power to fix anything. Lord, help her.

Still, the idea of foster care? She'd heard stories. They all had.

Mercy, but look at them.

Okay. Maybe she wasn't qualified, maybe she couldn't do much, but the folk wielding power would have to flatten her if they wanted to pawn Ty and Katie off on Social Services.

She shot up another prayer and backed out of the way.

The uniformed officer held the door for the EMTs and followed them in. Clay looked from her to the children and back. "Hannah."

"Clay. I didn't expect to see you here. Not yet."

"I was on my way to the station when the call came. Let me see what we've got, then I'd like to talk to you."

Hannah followed him into the house, stopping close enough to the kitchen entrance that she could see the EMTs bent over the woman. Clay surveyed the scene, spoke to the medics, and turned back to her, lowering his voice. "What do you know?"

"Not much. I heard a man yell and then a noisy truck screeched off. The kids were hiding under a bush, scared half out of their wits."

An EMT spoke softly, accompanied by groans from the floor.

"You happened by?" Clay glanced at his watch, brows raised. "At this hour?"

"Harvey needed a walk." She shrugged. "And I couldn't sleep. Good thing he sniffed out the children." When Clay didn't comment, she continued. "No telling how long they'd been hiding there. Seems the boy, Ty, was protecting his little sister from someone named Roy. Ty said it was Roy in the truck. That's their mother, Annie Mac."

The younger of the two EMTs spoke over his shoulder. "Married to Royce Bingham." He lifted a really nasty needle.

She turned away. She and needles were not friends.

"You know him, J.T.?" Clay extracted a notepad from his jacket pocket.

"From Blackbeard's Cave, over on the beach. My buddies and I sometimes hang out there. Roy did too, until he started one too many fights. I gotta tell you, this isn't the first time he's tossed Annie Mac around, but it sure better be the last. Your office must have a file on him."

"I'll check."

Clay approached the bent figures. Hannah didn't let that long, ugly needle keep her from easing into the kitchen in Clay's wake.

Gauze now covered Annie Mac's gaping cheek. She raised a hand as the other medic strapped a cervical collar around her neck, and her lips moved. Clay bent forward. Hannah craned close enough to hear.

The woman's whisper had weakened, but she pointed toward Hannah. "Tyler. Katie. Her." And then, as if something more were required from her, she said, "Friend."

The tears continued to leak. And then—

"She's out," the older EMT said. "Need to stabilize that leg."

Clay herded Hannah into the living room, out of earshot of the front porch. "What was she talking about?"

"Her children. She wants me to take them."

"You know I need to report this to Social Services."

"Not if the mother asked for me. As a friend."

Clay stared hard at her.

"You probably want to talk to the boy," she said. "To Tyler. But I think Katie is pretty traumatized."

"Maybe they have other family. Someone other than you who can look after them. Hang on." He poked his head into the kitchen, asked J.T. what he knew.

Hannah looked out the window. Ty had settled Katie on the porch swing, but he leaned against the rail with his shoulders hunched, hanging onto Harvey's leash.

Clay came up beside her. "Used to be a great aunt, name of Sim MacKensie. She left the house to Annie Mac. Seems Annie Mac is really Annie MacKensie Bingham—"

"Rinehart," Hannah said. "Her son told me she went back to Rinehart."

Clay scribbled something in his notes. "Anyway, the woman works as a substitute teacher while she waits for a full-time job to open up."

"Really? A teacher and she married this Roy character? You think he left her for dead?"

Clay threaded his fingers through his hair, looking out toward the children. His words, though softly spoken, showed his disgust. "I can't imagine anyone that angry would have wanted her reporting it."

"He tore up the whole house. Even the kids' room."

"It happens." His sigh sounded as if it weighed a ton and seemed to flatten the air around him. "But it sure is hard to swallow."

"Where do men like that come from?"

This madness had existed only blocks from her own house. In sleepy little Beaufort. Comfortable, familiar Beaufort, North Carolina. How had no one known?

She waved at Ty, who stared back. "Listen, Clay. Annie Mac asked this of me. Aren't you supposed to respect that? A mother's wishes? There isn't any kin for these children as far as we can tell, and you know how big my house is. Besides, I promised I wouldn't leave them."

This time his sigh seemed not quite so stressed, as if it held remnants of that almost-grin. She pointed at his chest. "Clay Dougherty, you are not going to give these scared, helpless children to any social worker where, like as not, that man could track them down and come after them. Don't you even imagine it." And then she remembered the clincher. "Besides, if you run into any red tape, there must be records from when we tried to adopt. We got approved. Only, you just keep in mind, I'm doing this as her friend. That should count for something, even in these days of government interference in the minutiae of our lives."

"Minutiae?" A twinkle banished any semblance of the stand-up-straight policeman. "Big word there. Bigger than you normally use."

"I'm not as dumb as I look." She huffed in an effort to appear haughty, but his attention shifted to the boy and the girl and the dog.

"Harvey the new dog Matt brought home?"

"He is."

"Well, seems to me like Harvey wants the children, and they'd probably be real glad to be with him."

And if that didn't just feel like him handing over a gift instead of the responsibility for two very sad children. Maybe she could do them a little good. Feed them for a few days at least.

J.T. came out of the kitchen. "We're taking her now."

"Is she stabilized? I'd like to question her when she wakes."

J.T. lowered his voice, but Hannah picked out the words "internal bleeding … can't know … earlier injuries."

"I'll be right along," Clay said. The uniformed officer stepped from the hallway and signaled to Clay. "What?"

"You might want to see this, Lieutenant."

Clay excused himself and followed the officer. When he came back out, he didn't look pleased. "Looks like Mrs. Bingham's been self-medicating. Seems she has pain meds as well as tranquilizers. Prescriptions from two separate doctors."

"Maybe she needed them." A woman married to a man who hit her? Yeah, Hannah could imagine needing both tranquilizers and pain meds.

Clay, it seemed, could not. "And maybe she's an addict."

4 ROY

Roy gripped the steering wheel and tried not to bite clean through the side of his lip. Teeth on skin helped a guy focus, so he gnawed until he'd got the top layer off.

But no more than that. You had to know when to stop so you didn't bleed or make yourself hurt. That'd just be stupid.

What was the word? Meant the opposite of somebody who got off on hurting folk. The fingers of his right hand beat out a rhythm. Tara-tatat, tara-tatat.

Began with an m. Maso-something.

The word wouldn't land. Well, who cared? He wasn't it—or the other thing.

Self-control, that's what mattered. It's how you got ahead in this world and how you got behind when you lost it. He had his back now. Yeah, sure, he'd lost it for a few minutes back there, but he'd reined in at the end, and from now on out he'd maintain that edge.

He kept to the back roads, 101 toward Havelock, across the Neuse River high-rise bridge and on up Highway 17, aiming for the country, thinking maybe he'd take a little detour on his way back to Rachel. Move fast and far, but not so fast he'd draw attention to himself. Keep to the speed limit and no one would take notice, not of this old truck moseying through farm country. Not of him either. He fit. Looked like any other good old boy.

He picked up his cell phone, punched in her number. "Hey, darlin' girl," he said when she answered. "Sorry to be calling so early."

He heard the sleep in her voice, like she was stretching awake. He pictured her sprawled on their bed in that frilly gown she had.

"You rescue Katie?" she asked. "You bringing her home with you now?"

"Tried, honey. But the boy took her and hid. I told you what Annie Mac and that kid of hers are like. We won't worry ourselves about them right now, 'cause I should be with you in a couple more hours. Unless I run into trouble."

"Trouble?" Her voice hiked.

He worked at soothing her. "Nothing much. Just a little disagreement with Annie Mac over my girl."

"It's not right, her trying to keep you from your daughter."

"That's it. I'm pretty sure she'll sic the cops on me for asking to have my baby. She lies every time she opens her mouth, you know?"

"I'm so sorry. Well, you just come on home. I miss you so much."

He smiled. Oh, yeah, his Rachel missed him. Well, he missed her, too. "I'm gonna have to go back and fetch my baby later. She needs us, honey. Needs her daddy."

"You think she needs me, too? You think she'll like me?"

The catch in Rachel's voice brought a smile to his. "You two are gonna be perfect together."

And he could see it. Rachel had so much loving in her, ready to pour it on his baby like she did on him. Lordy, but he'd never had trouble with Rachel. He just wished he could give her a baby of her own.

"Gotta go now," he said. "I'll see you soon as I can, okay?"

"Love you, Royce."

"Love you, too, darlin'."

He'd been a sorry fool to have ever put Rachel aside. But live in Alligator, North Carolina? A crossroads township named after one of the nastiest reptiles on the planet?

"You get that?" he asked the rearview mirror.

And now look at him, headin' right back up there. Him. Royce T. Bingham.

The truck hiccupped. Roy slammed his palm against the dash and looked hard at the gas indicator to see where it registered after his slap. Hard to tell, but it was probably speaking to him.

He pulled into a gas station once he got into Bridgeton, filled up, took a leak, and came away with a six-pack and a bag of chips to tide him over. Next county up, he'd stop for a good meal, take his time, relax. He remembered a place where a man could get himself a good plate of grits, eggs sunny-side up, a mess of bacon, and toast slathered with butter.

The pines didn't canopy the highway up here. Better that way. You could see what was around the next bend. Up here, folk had plowed a lot of the land, but the houses were mostly left over from sharecroppers like his daddy's folk, who'd started down in Carteret County. Roy just bet that's what had made Pop so mean. Mean, stingy boss meant mean, angry workers, didn't it?

Weren't many who still worked the land that way. No sir. Everybody'd gone off to get a better job. And them that couldn't? Well, they didn't even bother trying. They just took. And the fellow in the White House made it real easy for the takers. Real easy.

Roy spat out the window. He'd better stop thinking that way. He let his mind wander to how easy some folk had it and he'd get riled. The system worked for some. But for men like him? Never. Not even once in all his thirty-four years.

"You know, it didn't have to be this way," he said to the image of Annie Mac that flashed into his angry zone. "We could have shared, you, me, and Rachel."

But no, Annie Mac wanted none of it. Her choice. All along, it had been her choices that got her where she was.

5 ANNIE MAC

Annie Mac felt the light before she saw it. One of her eyes wouldn't open at all, and the other was rimmed with sand and weighted down with two pounds of lead, but at least the lashes on the functional one parted enough that she could recognize the white and green of a hospital room. Voices and shuffling noises filtered from the hall. Machines beeped. Phones rang.

And at least she hurt. Pain meant she wasn't dead—certainly a happier state than she'd imagined when Roy's last blow had connected. Surely, he had meant to kill her.

But her babies. Thank God for that woman.

And then a moment of panic hit. What if the woman hadn't actually taken them to a safe place?

Tears pooled in her good eye, and she prayed her little ones were far from Roy. Because he would come back to finish the business. To go after Katie.

Maybe he was already hunting her.

Annie Mac's right hand had a needle poking into it, connected to an IV. Raising her left hand, she brushed away the wet as her throat constricted. Gauze covered part of her face. Breathing sent glass shards into her lungs. Fire coursed down her right leg, flaming skin and scorching bone. She couldn't lift it.

Maybe they'd strapped her down because they thought she was crazy. They wouldn't be the first. And they wouldn't be altogether wrong.

Roy had come because of those divorce papers. No telling what he'd do now, but one thing was certain—he wouldn't stay gone. Not when he didn't have Katie.

The pain hit inside her skull like plunging knives, severing her thoughts from the now of this room. She screamed. Voices closed in, and her guts came up her throat and out.

Just before the black shrouded her in nothingness, she called silently to God for Ty. For Katie. For life.

6 HANNAH

Hannah extended a towel to Matt as he stepped out of the shower. He swiped it down his face and lobbed back a grin and a brow wiggle, reaching toward her for a wet embrace.

She dodged his hands. "We have visitors."

"At this hour?" He worked the towel over his chest, down his arms. She tried not to stare at its progress, especially when he lowered it to work on his legs. She really liked the hard strength of those legs.

"Well, yes. Harvey and I found two children hiding out front of a house up past Pollock."

His startled expression was comical, but instead of laughing at it, she gazed at the curtained window as she described the scene.

"None of that explains why you brought them here." Matt stepped into a pair of maroon silk boxers she'd bought to celebrate his weight loss.

Again, she focused away. She would not think about that silk or the swish of it. This time of month made her crazy, absolutely crazy, and Matt knew full well what he did to her during her hormonal surge.

But it was so not happening. There were children downstairs.

"Shouldn't Clay have taken them to Social Services?" Matt said, forcing her unruly thoughts back into line.

"Their mama asked for my help."

"Why? You don't know her."

He was right, and yet Annie Mac's big eye and the tears spilling from it would have melted the hardest heart. "If you'd seen her .... She was so scared, so certain that the man who beat her would find the children if they were in the system. I couldn't say no."

"You shouldn't have gotten involved." His voice had morphed to cool, unlike him. "Not more than was absolutely necessary to get the ambulance there."

"How can you say that?"

"Think about it. You put yourself smack dab in the middle of a domestic abuse case. A violent one." Cool became cold. He glared. She stiffened. "How long," he asked on his way past her into the bedroom, "do you propose to keep them?"

She balled her hands into fists and spoke to his back as he opened his closet. "They are my guests."

"How long?"

"A week? Two maybe. Until their mother can leave the hospital."

"I'll talk to Clay."

He acted as if she'd let a mosquito in the door and all he had to do was slap it back—or slap it dead. What was wrong with him? Normally, no one was more generous. No one.

So, why the attitude?

"You do that," she said stiffly. "Call Clay. But first come down and meet Ty and Katie. Who are small children. Who are our guests." She loosed the last word with enough force to let him see the mad she had brewing.

She hurried down to the kitchen, pasting on a smile that didn't seem to do anything for the two mute figures sitting where she'd left them. She reached into the refrigerator. "Orange juice?"

Ty nodded, pausing a moment before he offered a reluctant "Thanks."

She filled two small glasses and slid one in front of each child. Katie's thumb remained stuck between her lips, and Ty continued to stare. It was a long moment before he reached for his juice.

When Matt's footsteps sounded on the stairs, she braced herself.

"Good morning." His tone had gentled since his snit upstairs. "I'm Matthew Morgan." She gave him one point for trying and another when he said, "I hear you'll be staying with us for a few days."

"We're so pleased to have you, aren't we, Matt?"

Ty just stared, probably because Matt's assent wasn't either loud or enthusiastic. Frustrated again, Hannah sliced a bagel, popped it in the toaster, and handed Matt his travel mug to fill with coffee. He added a dollop of cream while she pulled out the bagel, slathered it with cream cheese, and wrapped it in a napkin.

"You go on to work," she said, ushering him toward the entrance hall. "We'll be fine."

"I can stay."

"You'd better not." She wanted him gone, taking with him the lingering odor of his you-shouldn't-have-done this attitude. She had enough doubts of her own. Who needed his?

He followed her to the front door, set his breakfast on the hall table, and drew her close. "Hannah, honey, I'm sorry. But you've got to admit, this has the makings of a disaster. What if that man finds out those two are here and comes after you?" His big hands slid down her back. "I couldn't bear it if someone hurt you. You're my world."

Ah, that was better. "Silly man." She freed a hand to touch his cheek. "Nothing's going to happen to me or to any of us. The condition he left her in? He's long gone by now."

"You can't know that."

"No. But I do know Clay's good at his job."

"I'm going to call him. In the meantime, don't you go walking in town with them, hear?"

"I hear."

He picked up his cup and bagel. "And lock the doors."

"Go on now."

"The locks."

"Yes, sir. The locks." She shooed him out with another quick kiss, closed and locked the door, and leaned back against it, gazing at nothing as she gathered her wits.

Lord, have mercy, but she had to go do this thing she'd agreed to. Only, how? Those two children weren't plastic dolls from home-ec class, and her only role model for mothering had been Elvie Mae during those early sleepovers at Tadie's. She sure hadn't learned anything good from her own slap-happy nanny. Or from her air-kissing mama, who toot-a-looed her way out the door every single day and most nights, too.

"They won't be here long," she whispered and pushed off toward the kitchen. "You can do anything for a week or two."

Ty and Katie hadn't moved, unless you counted Katie's lips working hard on that thumb. Except for their stillness, they looked like ordinary children in need of clean clothes and a bath. But that could wait until they'd eaten and the clothes she'd gone back in and collected from their demolished room had finished washing. Normally, she and Matt would have shared this time now that he'd hired a business manager and had learned how to relax a little.

She stirred the dry ingredients for pancakes in a big bowl. "Either of you want to help mix this?" She glanced around. "Or maybe man a spatula?"

Katie didn't move. Ty finally said, "Don't know how."

Hannah broke two eggs and began to whisk them.

"I can try if you need help."

She mustered enthusiasm to fill the void in his. "Okay!"

She moved aside to bring Ty between her and the bowl as she demonstrated how to beat the eggs. Handing him the whisk, she poured the eggs into the measure of milk and oil. "Don't stir too hard, or it'll spill." His arm slowed so most of the milk mixture stayed inside the bowl's rim.

He picked up the wooden spoon and mixed in the dry ingredients while she slowly added the liquid. "That's got it." When the griddle was hot, she showed him how to oil it, then how to spoon on three small circles of batter. "Watch for bubbles on the surface. That's the baking powder doing its thing."

Ty leaned forward.

"Not too close." She handed him a spatula. "Okay, slip that under each pancake and turn it over so the other side cooks. That's it, right there." It folded on itself and the middle oozed out. "Oh, well, that one doesn't count," she began, but Ty had dropped the spatula and backed away, panic evident in his eyes.

"I'm sorry," he said. "I'm really sorry, I didn't mean ..."

She swallowed hard. Oh, my. Did he think she'd yell at him? Or hit him? What had that woman done to them? Or that man? "Hey, don't worry about it." She tried to keep her tone light. "Come on and try again. I never get the first one right. I should have warned you that the first one is always a practice pancake to see if the griddle's hot enough." She picked up the spatula and waved him forward. "Here, let me help you with this one." She waited until he edged back to the counter before placing her hand over his.

Together they flipped the pancake. "Excellent. See? Just takes a bit of practice. Now you do the third."

He did that one well and went on to fill three plates, a grin beginning to light his face when he turned to the table. She pulled out a chair across from them. "How about saying grace before we eat?"

"Auntie Sim used to say grace," Ty said, setting his fork back in its place.

"Do you remember what she said?"

"Un-unh."

"Well, why don't we start by giving thanks for the food?"

"Can we pray for Mama?"

Katie's thumb popped out. "Mama?"

Ty patted her hand. "We're gonna pray for Mama. You remember what Auntie Sim taught us?" Katie shook her head. Ty clasped his fingers together under his chin and said, "Like this." Katie mimicked his gesture. "Then you shut your eyes and bow your head." He glanced over at Hannah. "That right?"

"That's fine."

As soon as she'd finished the short prayer, Ty focused on the plate in front of him and on the fork moving swiftly toward his mouth, reverting to normal boy when he inverted the syrup bottle a second time until the sugary flow pooled around his pancakes. Katie's hands were too small to tip the bottle. Hannah did it for her.

Searching for clues as the children focused on their food, she kept her voice casual. "You have any grandmothers? You know, that you visit sometimes?"

Ty's look said she was stupid for asking. She sipped her coffee before trying again. "What about any other family besides your mama? I know you had a great-aunt, but is there anyone else?"

"You don't mean like Roy."

"No, not like Roy. An uncle or aunt?"

Ty stirred a bite of pancake around in the flood of syrup still on his plate. "Maybe an uncle."

"Oh? And where is he?"

"Dunno. Never seen him."

"Ah." An uncle he'd never met. Why not? "Is he your mama's brother?"

Ty nodded. "Found a picture once."

"Oh?"

"He was a kid."

"You mean in the picture? Did he have a name?"

The boy chewed, swallowed, speared another bite, then paused long enough to say, "Kev."

Hannah lengthened her own pause to keep pace with Ty's, hoping he'd relax enough to share more information. She couldn't help comparing him to Tadie's Jilly, who'd been Miss Chatterbox last time she'd been home. "I wonder where Kev is these days? I bet he'd like to see you."

With a quick glance and then a shrug, he said, "Dunno. Don't much care."

Which was about as untrue as anything Hannah'd ever heard.

After breakfast, she set the dryer for another ten minutes. "Bath time," she said, marshaling the children upstairs.

Her studio door stood ajar. She pictured little hands reaching for the mugs that lined her drying shelves, and closed the door. Another thing to remember, she decided as she pointed Ty toward the guest bathroom. "You can shower in there."

But he stepped in front of her when she took Katie's hand. "Where you taking her?"

Hannah clamped down her surprise. "I thought I'd help your sister bathe in my big tub."

While Ty stared hard at her for several moments, Hannah tried to maintain the sort of calm, trustworthy demeanor she might use in traffic court. This was not the moment to let embarrassment win.

Finally, Ty shifted his gaze to his sister. "You okay with that? She won't hurt you."

Levity vanished in an instant. "No, I certainly won't hurt either of you."

He waited until Katie nodded. "Okay. But I'll be right where you can call me. Hear?"

Hannah got Katie all the way into her bathroom before she heard Ty close the door to his. Gently, carefully, she helped the little girl slip her nightie over her head, fearful that there'd be bruises or scars to explain Ty's worry.

The little girl's skin appeared clear. Once she got her in the tub, Hannah handed Katie a washcloth for her front and tackled her nubbly back. Were all those protruding bones normal on a little girl?

"Sweetie, how old are you?" Hannah finger-combed the fine blond hair, leaning closer when the girl hunched into herself.

Katie trained her long-lashed blue eyes on Hannah's face and slowly held up four fingers.

Such soft little fingers. Soft innocence. Soft ... "Oh, my, what a big girl you are. Imagine."

Splashes sounded from the hall bath, and Harvey barked.

Oh, glory, wet dog meant wet floor and long red doggy hairs clinging everywhere. Harvey wasn't so bad if he really got clean. Merely wet? He stank. And getting those hairs off the cabinets?

The dryer's timer dinged. Hannah regarded the four-year-old in her tub. Four wouldn't drown if left alone for a second, not in five inches of water.

"Sit tight, honey. I'll be right back. I'm just going to get the laundry, okay?"

Katie ignored her.

Fine. Hannah dashed past the hall bath, calling, "You'll find rag towels on the bottom shelf for drying the floor and the dog. Try to catch him before he shakes water all over the place if you can."

"Yes, ma'am!"

She was back in minutes, out of breath and with her arms loaded. Tossing the clothes on her bed, she hurried back to help Katie, who still sucked her thumb and twirled water.

"Ah, wonderful, look at you. You ready to get out?"

The child stood obediently while Hannah dried her and, still draped in the huge towel, let Hannah help her into the bedroom.

"Shall we find you something pretty to wear?"

No answer.

Hannah separated out Ty's clothes and left Katie staring at her piles while she set Ty's outside his bathroom door. "You've got clean clothes out here, Ty," she said. "Don't let Harvey get them wet."

"Yes, ma'am."

Katie still stared at the clothes on the bed. "Okay, Katie. Which shorts do you want?"

The child pointed to a yellow pair and to panties with lace edges. Hannah helped her step into each.

"What about that pink and yellow top to go with those pretty yellow shorts?"

Dressing halfway seemed to have energized Katie, who grabbed a tee shirt with horses on the front and red trimming around the neck and arms.

"That's a fun one. I like horses, too."

The hall door opened and closed, but not before Harvey's collar jingled, meaning water had gone flying. Scuffling sounded from behind the closed door.

Ty appeared. "I'm sorry," he said. "Harvey was faster than me."

"Than I," Hannah corrected automatically as she surveyed an unrepentant Harvey. Dog etiquette definitely needed to go on the agenda, or Harvey would glom onto more bad habits in the short time these two were here. More bad habits she'd have to fix.

But when she inspected the bathroom a few minutes later, a slow smile stretched her lips. Ty's bath towel hung on the bar, and the two rag towels lay neatly spread on the tub. Only a few splatters remained on the counter, and both the bath and hall floors appeared reasonably dry. The few stray dog hairs attached to the leg of a hall table and stuck to the bathroom cabinet were nothing.

"Why don't you two take Harvey downstairs while I finish straightening up here?"

The phone rang as she was wiping out her bathtub. It was Clay, calling with a report on Annie Mac.

"I saw her right after they'd sedated her and set her leg. She's a mess, but we knew that, didn't we?"

"What about internal injuries?"

"You know what I know, which isn't much. But it looks like she'll be okay. Here are my notes. They said she had no orbital fracture or jaw fracture, which I guess they were worried about. They did have to stitch up her cheek and part of her scalp."

"Poor thing. And the other?" She didn't want to say it aloud, the word Clay had used when he mentioned the drugs.

"No answer yet from the lab. They said she had brief periods of lucidity when she kept repeating her children's names, asking about them. I'll stop by tomorrow, see if I can get more from her. I'll also try to get permission for the children to see her once she's awake enough."

"Do you think that's a good idea? Seeing their mama like that?"

"I'm pretty sure it would be good for her. Fretting isn't going to help her recover."

"Well, do what you think best, but it needs to be what's best for all of them, you know? Maybe you should talk to Rita."

Clay paused. "Rita Levinson?"

"I bet she'd help. With the legal issues at least." And Rita'd know counselors. "Everything else working out at your end?"

"Just trying to find Royce."

"Ty said there is—or was—an uncle," Hannah said. "His mother's brother, but he's never met him."

"Did you get a name?"

"Kev. So probably Kevin."

Clay promised to dig around.

So many unknowns floated out of reach. Hannah preferred orderly progression, which Matt provided in most areas of her life. Only, in this he couldn't help her.

She folded a pair of shorts and added it to the pile of Ty's clothes. Harvey's tags jiggled from the doorway. Next to him stood Ty, his face drawn, his bottom lip caught between his teeth.

"That was Lieutenant Dougherty. He said your mama's going to be fine." She could almost feel him release a held-in breath as his teeth let go.

"She didn't get beat too bad?"

Hannah figured the truth mattered. "Nothing that can't be fixed. Your mama has a broken leg and a few other injuries, but they've got her on lots of medications so she doesn't hurt."

Ty nodded. Katie came from behind him, her doll caught under her arm. She stared at Hannah's face before lifting the doll. Ty said, "Mama's gonna be okay. You hear?"

"What's your dolly's name?" Hannah asked.

But the thumb was back in place. Ty answered for her. "Agatha."

"Ah." Bending toward the child, Hannah touched the doll's head. "Hello, Agatha. I've never known an Agatha before."

"Agatha is a lady in a book Mama found for Katie. About geese that wanted their feathers back. You know, from pillows and things."

The thumb popped out. "Noffing comes from noffing."

"What do you mean, Katie?"

Katie glanced over at her brother. His expression softened as he touched her shoulder. "It's what Agatha said in the book. 'Nothing comes from nothing.'"

And wasn't that the truth?

Hannah let a barking Harvey in the back door and called up the stairs where she'd sent Ty to change his already grungy shirt for their trip to the grocery store. "You almost ready?"

"Yes'm!"

She found Katie sitting stiffly on the hall bench, dressed in the pretty dress they'd selected after the child spilled juice on her first outfit. Harvey skidded to a halt and sniffed. Katie whimpered.

It hadn't occurred to Hannah to insist on another bathroom visit. She bent over the child and wiped at her tears. She shouldn't have made assumptions, thinking four old enough to speak up. Forgetting that Katie wasn't an average child living in normal circumstances.

"Oh, dear. Were you afraid to tell me you needed to go?"

Ty tromped in, shoelaces dangling. "Sometimes when we couldn't make noise, she piddled. It wasn't her fault."

"Come on, honey, it's okay," Hannah said, scooping up the child and carrying her upstairs. "It was only an accident." But she took shallow breaths and pretended the wet wasn't seeping into her blouse. She'd tackle the puddle on the bench later.

Ty trailed along behind. "Roy used to yell real loud. Mama took to having us hide."

"Poor baby." She was too old to be potty training someone else's child, and the child was much too old to need it. She'd like to wring that mother's neck. "Let's get you washed up and into something else pretty, shall we? Then we can go get some goodies from the Food Lion. You'll like that."

In the bathroom, she seethed as she adjusted the water temperature, her indignation sharpening to anger at a mother who had allowed such a man inside her house. Annie Mac should have known better—and had the brute locked up years ago.

This had been going on four blocks away from here. Four blocks and in another world. She had no sympathy for a mother who let someone like Royce anywhere within a hundred feet of her children. Maybe the mother was the one needing handcuffs.

With effort, she refocused. "You want bubbles?" she asked, bending to pull some lilac-scented powder from under the sink. "I love a bubble bath. And you'll smell so pretty."

Katie didn't answer, but her tears stopped as the bubbles multiplied.

With Katie clean and dressed again, Hannah shooed the child downstairs to wait while she changed her own shirt and ran a brush through her hair, patting her cheeks when she'd finished. It was the first time since this morning that she'd really looked in the mirror, and her reflection caused a momentary panic.

She needed to hie herself to Lorraine's salon for more than just a trim. Which meant that Annie Mac needed to get patched up and home. Hannah couldn't imagine having to haul kids with her to the hairdresser.

The phone's ring made her jump. She picked up the bedside receiver.

It was Clay again. "Ginny over at Carteret just called. They put Mrs. Bingham—no, make that Ms. Rinehart—on a life flight to Vidant Medical Center in Greenville." His level tone didn't keep the words from hurtling Hannah's heart into overdrive. "She lost consciousness again and is exhibiting signs of a closed head injury."

"You mean, she could die."

"She could. I'll keep you posted." Clay disconnected.

Hannah didn't move. She could hear Ty's voice from downstairs, but up here the air seemed to change, sucking out oxygen.

Annie Mac might actually die.

7 CLAY

Laughter and ringing phones buzzed into the back office like a deer fly looking for a tasty bit of skin. Normally, Clay didn't even hear station sounds, but today he wanted to grab a fly swatter to silence the grating noises.

He needed another cup of coffee, but that would mean leaving the office. Not another soul in this place cared if they swilled muddy rotgut. Two or more complaining and they might force a change. On his own? The guys just laughed at him. And Stella said it didn't make no matter to her what came out of the coffee pot. "Tea," she said. "That's the only drink for decent folk." And she didn't mean English Breakfast or Earl Grey. She meant sweet iced tea, morning, noon, and night, brought in a plastic gallon jug from home.

Clay pulled his chair in closer and jabbed at the keyboard, but the report on the drug dealer they'd arrested was the last thing he felt like doing. He kept seeing that kitchen, the holes in the walls made by someone wielding more than a fist, the old, stand-alone sink loosened and a gaping mess behind it. And those two blond heads, unlike their mother's blood-darkened red.

Paperwork and reports should be outlawed while Royce Bingham was still out there and would be guilty of more than abuse if Ms. Rinehart died. Her condition certainly upped the ante. Yes, Clay had found the earlier file. Too bad it hadn't contained charges hefty enough to have locked the man up before he'd escalated to this extent.

Chief Bradley stepped into the doorway. Clay swiveled his chair to face him. "Chief."

"Thinking about that Bingham woman?"

"Rinehart, she says."

Avery Grainger, the young detective who shared Clay's office, excused himself to the chief and leaned in. "Clay, you may want to pick up line two."

Clay lifted the handset, answered.

"You the detective in charge of hunting up Royce Bingham?"

"Clay Dougherty. What can I do for you?"

"This is Steve Marshall, Belhaven Police. One of ours just came back in, swears he saw a stranger exiting Fish Hooks this morning who looked a lot like your suspect. The man bent his head at the approach of my guy so, naturally, Officer Cramer checked out the man's face before seeing him climb into a rusty Ford pickup. The license plate wasn't easy to read, but he got three numbers. Soon as he returned here, he saw your printout. Numbers matched what we could find in the system."

"Your man know which way the suspect was headed and when?"

"He said west on 264. Hold on."

Clay waited.

"It was just after the café opened at nine."

Clay checked his watch. Less than an hour ago.

"Appreciate the call."

"No problem. Let us know if we can help."

Clay disconnected and turned to the chief, including Avery with a nod of his head. "Bingham was headed west out of Belhaven on 264 about an hour ago."

"Find out where he's from, where's he's lived," Chief Bradley said. "Where he might be trying to hunker down. Update Highway Patrol."

"I'm on it," Clay told the chief's back.

Avery grabbed a well-used coffee cup from his desk. "You want a refill?"

Clay glanced at his mug and tried to add hopeful to his expression. "Heading out to the coffee shop?"

Avery laughed. "You, my friend, are way too much of a snob."

"Not possible."

"I'm gonna step out back for a minute. You find anything about Bingham, let me know."

Clay waved him away. "Go get lung cancer. I've got work to do."

He called the state troopers, gave them the latest, then, starting with the information he'd already accessed, he searched the databases. Dots began to connect. And when he hit pay dirt, he picked up the phone to call the Tyrrell County Sheriff.

Yes, sir. The Internet was a glorious thing.

8 ROY

Roy felt the surge that only came when he neared home and Rachel. She'd be up now, waiting for him. Probably would have called in sick from work so they could spend the day together. He pictured her sitting in her chair, maybe knitting. She'd have that sweet smile on her face. Her fine brown hair would be braided down her back.

He'd loosen it, let it flow over his fingers. A smile spread as he imagined the scent of honeysuckle he'd rouse as he played with her hair. She kept it so clean with that herbal shampoo she said she'd picked up just for him. Oh, man.

Maybe she'd be wearing that new blue dress with the flowers he'd bought her when they'd gone to Walmart last. She really liked that one. 'Course, her legs not working and all, she couldn't run right into his arms, but his arms would find her. No doubt about that.

Making Rachel happy took hardly any effort. So different from Annie Mac, who had her nose so high in the air she could drown in a rainstorm.

That lady helper of Rachel's would have come and gone by now, expecting Rachel to head off to work and not need her until the afternoon. They'd have some time together, him and Rachel. He couldn't wait to pick his gal up and hold her close, feel her lips on his, have her make him forget the mess in Beaufort.

She could do that. No one knew better how to smooth out the aches, ease him into that place he only got from loving her. She had fine hands, that woman of his. Fine hands and a cool-easy heart.

He passed the country store, took the paved road a mile or so back through the trees, then turned into the rutted lane, bouncing along past Rachel's dad's brick one-story. Rachel's brother and his wife and kids lived in what used to be the grandparents' old farm house, and Rachel's cottage lay just past a copse of sweetgums.

He dodged a washed-out trough, approached the copse, and saw a Crown Vic. Quicker than he could spit, he braked hard, backed his truck into the field, and headed right out of there. Lord have mercy, but he sure hoped the noise of his tires spitting oyster-shell chunks hadn't attracted attention from anyone belonging to that sheriff's car.

His heart was beating fit to kill, but he didn't stop until he was heading north again and could pull off behind an old barn. Out of sight, so he could think.

Raking his hands through his hair, he tried to puzzle it out. They had to be there because of him, but how had they found out about Rachel? And linked him up with her so soon?

Far as anyone knew, he hadn't lived up here for more than five years. The work he'd done since coming back had all been under the table. His cell phone was a throw-away from Walmart, his truck still registered in Carteret County.

Rachel would be beside herself, police coming to her house. Made him sick to think about it, her big brown eyes round and scared. She'd be bound to weep for him. Worry herself sick.

He sure hoped they didn't tell her what he'd done back in Beaufort. He hadn't meant to go at Annie Mac like that. It had been an accident on account of her making him so blamed mad by hiding his little girl.

The thought of Rachel hating him made his gut squirm until he felt like he was gonna toss it up. He grabbed a beer and yanked the tab off, then swilled enough to settle his stomach.

Only thing to do was keep moving. Get himself far away from this town, and yes, from this state. It was nothing but trouble for him. Always had been.

He'd head to West Virginia. Maybe Tennessee. Hadn't his mama said something about cousins in Chattanooga? All he had to do was find them. Then he could send for Rachel.

Rotten, stinking cops. They took it all away from a man. Every last time.

He'd get it all back, and take care of Annie Mac, too.

9 HANNAH

Hannah woke to whispered voices in the hall and Harvey's nails clipping down the stairs. She squinted at the bedside clock as it flipped to 6:22. Way too early to be up, but, if she remembered correctly, that's what children did. They woke up at the crack of dawn until they hit their teen years, and then they slept until well past noon. She stretched and slipped out of bed.

It would have been Harvey if it hadn't been the kids. Dog, kids, not much difference.

Matt flung an arm wide as if her rising had liberated it. She tiptoed into the bathroom and stared down at her blood-spotted gown as words from an old gospel song about blood's wonder-working power flipped through her mental juke box. Too bad she couldn't just insert a quarter and remember them all.

Or maybe not. Maybe forgetfulness was better. Because, honey, there wasn't any life and power flowing from her womb today. Or ever again. All the supposed-to-bes in the world wouldn't turn her monthly bloodletting to more than a reminder of death.

She washed herself and ran water over her silken gown. She would not cry. She'd suck those tears right back where they belonged. She was happy. Tadie and that pretty boat—and the family Tadie had married, plus the soon-to-be-born addition—were coming home. Tomorrow. Or the next day.

"Depending on the weather," Tadie'd said. Because cruisers tucked out of the way of storms.

No storms today, only air that dripped humidity like a fine mist. You couldn't escape wet on summer days this close to the ocean.

She was fine. Really. It was all about recognizing the problem and fixing it. She had kids downstairs who needed her and a husband who would cuddle her. That thought made her grin: Matt wiggling his brows, his eyes getting that gleam in them. That man held a foolproof prescription for her soggy moods, and he didn't care what time of the month it was. See, that's why her life was so perfect, just the way it was. Who could want more?

Not Hannah Morgan.

By the time she'd changed into shorts and a tee shirt, the rattle of Matt's snores accompanied her across the hall to check on Katie's sheets. Ah, yes. Well. The wet had meandered past the pad she'd laid down last night. She collected the soaked linens, the mattress pad, and Katie's nightie and panties from the floor. Ty must have made his sister change. Good for him. She didn't want to imagine urine migrating to her good furniture.

Harvey never peed on her cushions. Dog, kids … the dog scored on that one.

Downstairs, she found Katie propped on the couch, dressed in shorts and a shirt, clutching Agatha and smiling around her thumb as Harvey played tug of war with her brother. Harvey's teeth held better than Ty's hand, but the dog quickly plunked the damp rope back in front of his new playmate.

"Good morning," Hannah said. "You guys ready for breakfast?"

Katie nodded. Ty spoke. "Sure."

"I'm thinking you might want to see where we keep things around here. That way, you can fix yourselves a snack if I'm not around. What do you think about that?"

Ty's eyes rounded. "Really?"

"Really." Giving them access seemed like a good idea, but Hannah couldn't help second-guessing herself as she waved them into the kitchen. On the positive side, she wouldn't have to leap out of bed at first light if they could get something on their own, especially if Ty would let Harvey out back to take care of business. On the negative, she'd lose control and perhaps be opening a Pandora's Box.

Her big kitchen was all white-painted cupboards and a few fixtures that had been there since Hannah first entered as a bride. Matt had offered to replace everything, to let her redecorate, but other than having a new wood floor put in and the cupboards repainted last year when they'd added new countertops—oh, and a new dishwasher to replace the one that died—she hadn't needed anything. The refrigerator was huge. Maybe it used more electricity than the modern ones, but it had a pull-out drawer for a freezer and tons of room. The stove was a wonderful old gas unit that worked like a charm—yes, they'd replaced the knobs, but why get a new one when the old worked?—and the porcelain sink had barely any nicks. She had space for anything she wanted, and the old pine table was one she'd inherited from her grandmother. The room soothed her. Maybe it would do the same for these two.

She opened a long pantry cupboard and pointed inside. "Cereal is here. Milk's in the refrigerator, of course. Cookies, which are only for after a meal—or maybe in the middle of the afternoon, but *not* right before dinner—are in that jar on the counter. And only one at a time." She led Ty toward the bowl of fruit, lifted it to show Katie.

"I try to keep this stocked with good things, and you can have an apple or banana any time you want."

"Really?" he asked again. Katie stared with as much enthusiasm as her brother at all the lovely food.

"Fruit is good for you, so absolutely. Now, what shall we fix for breakfast this morning? I have eggs, oatmeal, cereal, French toast, muffins."

"Fwench toast!" Katie said, bouncing up on her toes.

"What about you, Ty? Is French toast okay with you?"

"Mama makes great French toast."

"Well, why don't we fix some, and you can think about her while you eat it. I bet she'd like that."

"Mama," Katie said.

"That's right. Your mama makes it. And I bet she'll make it again as soon as she gets all patched up and home from the hospital." And Hannah spoke silently to the heavens. *You're seeing to that, aren't you?*

She let Katie stand on a chair to break eggs into a bowl. Ty manned the spatula again, while Harvey watched from the doorway, not moving even when they sat down at the table.

"Harvey, go. No one is going to give you a treat here."

Ty glanced over his shoulder. "Aw, Miss Hannah. He looks so hungry."

"His bowl of dog chow was filled last night. I don't want him learning to beg at the table."

"Can I give him some after?"

"It's not good for him."

Ty stared down at his plate, but he didn't argue.

"Okay. A tiny bit." The boy's head jerked up. "But in the mudroom," she said, "once you've finished." Another bad habit she'd have to break once she had the house to herself again, but this one seemed like such a small thing in light of the joy on that child's face.

After breakfast, she sent them outside to play with Harvey while she fixed a plate for her now-showered-and-shaved husband. Matt didn't dawdle. After downing one slice of French toast, he filled his travel mug with another cup of coffee.

"Meetings today," he said. "Plus, Clay said he'd get me access to that house. See if I can help. Seems Bingham really did a number on it. You gonna be okay?"

"Why not?" She accepted his kiss at the door, which he opened quickly and as quickly closed against the heat already steaming off the front stoop. Thank God for air conditioning.

This time she didn't have to calm herself before heading back to tackle the kitchen mess.

Of course, there was the spilled food Harvey had missed. Oh, and look at that, a spot of something gooey on the rug.

Grabbing a rag and rug cleaner, she spritzed the area and scrubbed out the ick. The vacuum took care of crumbs folded into red dog hairs at the rug's edge. She tried not to mind that she'd done this day before yesterday. Vacuuming was supposed to be a once-a-week chore, in spite of Harvey's hair balls. She should have brushed him yesterday. And kept the children in the kitchen when they snacked.

And bought more laundry detergent. Who knew?

Occasionally, she glanced out the back window at the children and Harvey chasing each other around the yard, dancing and playing as if they hadn't a care in the world.

Harvey was the first to wilt from the heat. His tongue lolled as he followed them into the cool house.

"I've lemonade for you. And I'll put on a National Geographic video."

Ty paused on his way to the den and stared down at an open newspaper Matt had left behind last night. Coming up behind him, Hannah noticed the picture of a movie-theater bombing. She nudged the boy's shoulder. "Come on. Let's see what's happening under the sea."

When she'd settled them, she tucked the paper into the waste bin. There was so much to remember with kids in the house. What else had she forgotten?

Four-year-olds and poisons. Right.

She backtracked to the kitchen and pulled all the cleaning agents from under the sink. What didn't fit in the laundry-room cupboards would have to go outside. Oh, yeah, and the bathrooms ... more toxic chemicals. And no high cupboards there.

What did real mothers do? Organize, she decided. They made space, which she did by moving extra towels from the top shelf in the linen closet and tucking them under the sink in place of the chemicals.

Proud of herself, she loaded more clothes in the washer. When the doorbell sounded, she turned the dial to start, wiped a sticky dribble of detergent off her hands, and opened the door.

Rita Levinson fluffed damp tendrils off her neck with one hand. In the other she carried a briefcase. "Hey, Hannah."

"Lands, girl, look at you. Come in and cool off." Hannah waved her to the kitchen table. "Lemonade? I just made it."

"Anything. Hope this is a good time for you."

"Of course. You have a meeting or something, all dressed to the nines?" She filled two glasses and passed one across the table. "That lemony color suits."

Rita glanced down at the loose silk blouse. "Martin's mama sent it with him yesterday. She said she thought it would set off my skin." Running her fingers under its front and over her pregnant belly, she smiled. "I had to wear it."

"It works. You, all caramel-toned."

"Well, I think more dark honey this time of year."

"Like your mama. Poster women for the born-in tan."

"Not so long ago," Rita said with a humorous glint in those lovely eyes, "they called it something different. I remember."

"Yes, well." To change the subject—because Rita's truth embarrassed her, even if the guilt weren't personally hers—Hannah patted her cheeks. "Now, me? I go from peach to freckles in an afternoon."

Rita laughed. "You've been saying that long as I can remember, Hannah Morgan, and I've yet to see more than a couple of beauty spots dotting your face. Maybe a few freckles on your arms and nose, but they just enhance your lovely skin."

"Hah. I suppose I should just say thank you."

"You should. And you should tell me about these two you've got staying." Rita angled her head toward the den. "They in there with Harvey?"

"They've bonded, all three of them. I'll introduce you soon's you cool off. You want a refill?"

Rita waved her off. "No, thanks. You ever think what being pregnant in summertime does to you? I used to see church ladies fanning themselves like mad and didn't have nearly the sympathy I should have."

"I had winter pregnancies."

"Oh. Yes. I'm sorry." Rita shifted in her seat, brushed her curly dark hair away from her face, and let out a long sigh. "You've been having an exciting time here."

"You could call it that. You think you've got someone at the Women's Shelter who can help them? Imagining what they've seen makes me want to weep."

"I'll ask. See who's best with troubled children. When do you think their mother will be up for a visit?"

Hannah traced drip trails down the side of the glass and wiped the wet on a corner of her baggy shirt. "Clay didn't tell you? They had to life-flight her to Greenville."

"Oh, Hannah. Why?"

"Some sort of head injury. Clay didn't know much more."

"What are you all going to do?"

"You mean, if she doesn't make it?"

Rita looked away momentarily, her hands returning to her belly. "If she dies, they'll need a guardian, one appointed by the court if family can't be found."

"The boy, Ty, said there's an uncle. Or at least there was one."

"Is Clay looking for him?" At Hannah's nod, she said, "I'll talk to the children, but if they become orphans, my hands will be tied. Unless you're granted custody."

Hannah turned to get her cookie tin and slid it across to Rita. "Oatmeal raisin. Harris Teeter's own."

"Thank you. I'm always hungry these days. Hope I'll be able to drop the pounds once the baby comes."

"You're fine. Skinny as you've always been."

"So," Rita said, opening the tin and lifting out a cookie, "you plan to file for custody if the uncle doesn't show up and there's a need?"

Hannah drew the tin closer but kept her hands on its rounded outside. "I don't think that would work. Not for the long term."

"Right. You and Matt decided against adopting, didn't you?"

The cookies had a nice color to them. Not too brown, crisp bits of raisin and walnut. But Hannah broke off a piece instead of biting into it.

Yes, they'd decided not to adopt. And for very good reasons that still seemed valid. She nodded, unable to answer with words.

Hannah checked the time. She'd left Rita and Ty in the den when Katie needed to go to the potty. Then she'd brought the little girl into the living room to read her a story and had watched her fall asleep, but she hadn't wanted to intrude on whatever Rita had going on with the boy. It just seemed odd. Ty wasn't much of a talker.

Was he?

She slid a sleeping Katie off her lap and onto the couch. The thumb stayed tucked with Agatha snuggled under the child's other arm. Brushing a loose hair off the soft cheek, Hannah felt a thirst that was more than a longing for lemons and water. As she couldn't slake it with anything she knew about, she went for another glass of lemonade.

Rita came in alone. "I turned the video back on so Ty could finish it."

"Thanks. Katie's out for the count."

"Precious children, but I've got to say, a ten-year-old on the brink of adolescence had better get help fast before he replicates what he's seen."

"Ten? I thought Ty was younger. He's awfully small, isn't he?"

"Hard to tell if he'll stay that way." Rita tucked her pad back in the briefcase. When she straightened, her hand rested on her rounded belly as her fingers beat a light tattoo. "He may stay small, or he may shoot up in a few years," she said, but her eyes seemed focused elsewhere.

Hannah stared again at the water drops sliding down the outside of her glass. "His mama's pretty tiny. Maybe he takes after her."

"He has quite a vocabulary, which makes me think he must be a reader. I was surprised at how well he could verbalize when he let his guard down. Of course, his mama being a teacher might account for it."

Hannah picked at a hangnail. She ought to squirt on some lotion and then get out the polish. And weren't those newly formed age spots on the back of her hands? Should she even have age spots? She wasn't yet forty, for crying out loud. Maybe they were large freckles, mutating together.

"She's been substituting."

A teacher who didn't have a real job. Then again, maybe they didn't need much to live on if she owned the house outright. But food, clothes, insurance, taxes could mount up. "Ty hasn't told me much of anything."

Rita probably knew the questions to ask. After all, Rita was the lawyer. What did a potter know?

"Well," Rita said, "I got him to tell me what life was like before his step-father came to live with them."

"Really?" Too bad she'd left the room with Katie, because information was important, wasn't it? Knowing more about them might help. For the short time they'd be here. She straightened. "How old was he when his mama remarried?"

"Going on six. He and his mama lived with her aunt. Or maybe great-aunt. I don't think he knows his father."

"Maybe the father doesn't know about him. I mean, you hear about women doing that, getting pregnant and not saying anything."

Rita nodded. "She could have had her reasons."

"I guess, but she did bring an abuser into their life and let him stay."

Factual. Real. Rita needed information, too, didn't she, if she were going to recommend a counselor for the children?

"I'll see what Clay can find out," Rita said. "If Ty's father doesn't know he has a son, he might want to be involved in his life, especially if something happens to the mother."

"Oh, but there's Katie."

Why hadn't she connected the dots? Katie left alone? Ty off with some unknown father? Not a good idea.

"We'll figure that one out if need be." Rita sounded unconcerned.

Which made Hannah push back her chair and carry the glasses to the sink. Damp had seeped past the skinny napkin on the table, so she grabbed a sponge and mopped it up. Rita backed away to give her room.

It wasn't until Rita bent to get her briefcase that Hannah stopped fidgeting. She tossed the sponge in the sink and leaned back against the counter. "You'll talk to Clay?"

"I'll let you know what he says. You'll do the same for me?"

"Sure."

"I can ask around at the center, but I told you, my hands are tied until someone with authority over those kids asks for help." Rita headed down the hall.

Hannah worked on her smile as she followed. "How're your folks? Elvie Mae and James doing okay? And is Martin still liking life in the slow lane after doctoring in Raleigh?"

"Everybody's fine. I'll tell them you asked. And you get Matt to call Martin one day. Maybe they can do another round of golf."

"Sounds good. He's always looking for someone to brave the course with him."

"Too hot for my taste."

Hannah laughed. "Amen. Working under that sun just to follow a little white ball? No thanks."

"Lord, love 'em." Rita stepped out into the heat and suddenly pivoted back. "Can't believe I almost forgot. I'm supposed to tell you Daddy's picking up Tadie and her crew when they get to the New Bern dock this afternoon. He didn't want you thinking you'd have to bother. You know him. He considers it his place to do for Tadie, like he did for her daddy and Miss Caroline."

"Okay. Right. Thanks," she said to Rita's back.

While the children ate lunch, Hannah shifted clothes from washer to dryer. When they went out to play, she shuffled up the steps to her pottery studio, hoping for distraction. But even with bowls waiting on the drying shelf to be glazed, she found herself contemplating colors and nothing more.

Back downstairs, she got out the mop to scrub out the spot where Harvey sometimes hunkered down under the kitchen table. Too bad she couldn't scrub out the hurt from Rita's last words, which lodged like a burr in her throat.

She picked up a dust rag and wandered around flicking specs off surfaces that didn't need it. When she got to the hall mirror, she stared at her reflection. "Here's the thing," she told that other face. "I don't like someone else, anyone other than Tadie, telling me the whens and wherefores of my best friend's coming. It just feels wrong."

She turned away, closing her eyes for a moment before swiveling back to face the mirror. "I know. I'm a wretch." She leaned closer and wiped at a smudge with the tip of her finger. It didn't go away. "Still ..."

She knew perfectly well that Tadie had a cell phone on board the *Nancy Grace*, and wasn't that her own blue one, sitting right in front of her on the counter? It was set to speed dial Tadie's number, as hers was on Tadie's phone. They were each #3, right after Matt or Will, who naturally got #2 on their respective phones. If she remembered right, #1 dialed 911. They each had the same ring tone for the other: an excerpt from "When the Saints Go Marching In." The two husbands got a smattering of "The Hallelujah Chorus." They used to tease each other about their heart rate increasing when one or the other of those pieces popped up on the phone.

She should hear those saints marching: a simple call to say when the boat would dock, when Tadie would get to Beaufort. It was fine, James fetching them. He'd been driving Tadie's family around since Mr. Samuel first hired him on account of having wretched eyesight.

No, the driving part didn't bother her. She just needed to get the word in the right order from the right person.

She was being absurd, but hurt was hurt, wasn't it? And didn't a person get to feel a little bit left out when a best friend failed to call? When that best friend asked another person—even if that other person was a friend, too—to pass the word?

She harrumphed as she opened the dryer door, pulled out the clean clothes and dropped them in the laundry basket to take to the kitchen table for folding. She'd finished the sheets. And the towels. Normally, she only had to do laundry once a week. Now look at her. A housemaid.

Perhaps Clay would locate their uncle. Hannah wouldn't think about an absentee father for only one of them. No. Annie Mac would recover so that she could provide a home for these two. She'd grow physically and emotionally healthy. Soon. And life here could get back to normal.

Rita's hands sure had flitted around, hadn't they? Those tapered fingers—not at all like her own unmanicured and clay-ravaged ones, and how had that happened without her noticing?—had fluttered over Rita's rounded form, initiating that secret, inward-gaze pregnant women took on. Rita hadn't meant anything by it.

Hannah lifted a small pink shirt from the basket—so tiny—and smiled at the white unicorn decorating its front. Smoothing it flat, she matched up the little puff sleeves just so. Next came a yellow one with a ruffly neck. She traced the ruffle with her fingertip. Oh, my.

Sighing, she reached for Katie's nightie. The grass stain hadn't come all the way out, not even with two washings, but at least it was clean. And there'd be no more hiding under bushes for those two if Hannah could help it. She drew the gown to her nostrils and breathed in the scent of fabric softener. What? Had she expected to smell little girl?

She folded it in half, then again, smoothing the thin cotton under palms that imagined the childish skin. Closing her eyes, she forced back a choke in her throat. Good thing they would leave soon.

A very good thing.

But weren't those children the cutest things?

She sure wished...

No. Stop it.

She blew a stray hair out of her face, trying not to feel as if she'd been forgotten. Again.

See, that's what she hated, thoughts like that. She had a wonderful husband, a sweet, intelligent man who adored her. She twisted her wedding band. She'd almost lost him two years ago. Now he was healthy again. And they were happy. And look at the house they owned. It was a great house, full of beautiful things, with lots of rooms, including her studio. They had friends and good health and more of everything than nine-tenths of the world's people. They were contented. She was contented.

And, during this short interlude in her comfortable life, two very sweet children needed her.

Not for long, of course. But having this house and this life made it possible for her to help them. She was doing something good. It should be enough.

It was enough. Really.

She just had to be very careful. Because they would go.

She straightened her legs and flexed her calf muscles. She and Harvey hadn't taken a walk since the children had come. Maybe that was her problem. That and the time of the month.

Tadie would be home soon. Tadie and Jilly and Will. A pregnant Tadie and, very soon, another Merritt to enjoy. Her godchild. She couldn't wait to snuggle that little one close.

All was—would be—well. She had so much to look forward to. To be thankful for.

The air conditioner cycled on, ruffling the sheers so they fluttered over the back of the rocker. As if the years hadn't created a gap in time, she pictured herself in that chair, humming. The childish melody echoed, tinny ghost strings that warbled in her head. "Here comes Peter Cottontail, hopping down the bunny trail." Twice upon a time, she and Matt had stood over an empty crib and wound the music box, taking comfort in the colorful figurines that bobbed at the end of fish-line strings. Twice, they'd dreamt of their soon-to-be-born child's legs kicking, baby eyes lighting at the sight of swinging plastic bunnies, a baby voice gurgling, tiny hands grasping. But twice that mobile had been stilled by death, the music box rendered silent. Why did she hear it now?

She'd experienced it often enough, this sense of being out of sync in a world that assembled lottery winners yet never even told her how to buy a ticket.

So what? Maybe her grown-up self still felt as if she'd been an accident her folks had worked around by patting the top of her too-fine hair and handing her off to the housekeeper for all the mundane things of life, like feeding and clothing and bathing and loving. But there hadn't even been loving, had there? Just the caretaking. And the back of a hand when she'd been imperfect, disrespectful. Bad.

She scooped up the folded clothes and carried them upstairs. Really, she had to get over herself. She was a grown woman, staring forty in the face, for heaven's sake. She was loved and happy, and no one in her house hit anyone else. Ever.

10 HANNAH

The saints marched on Hannah's cell phone that evening, dashing her messy thoughts and making her feel guilty when she heard the exhaustion in Tadie's voice.

".James mentioned you'd taken in strays," Tadie said. ".Jilly's over the moon to see you all, but it's Harvey she particularly wants. She talks of little else."

"Harvey outranks her Auntie Hannah?"

"Will has tried to explain that a dog on a boat isn't a match made in heaven, but that hasn't stopped the broad hints and occasional begging."

"You'd think she'd be satisfied with a baby."

"I'm not sure she believes I'll ever give birth. I'm not sure I do, either."

"Cute thing. You go on to bed now, and we'll see you in the morning."

Hannah felt a smile play on her face as she helped the children bathe and get ready for bed. Matt was working late again tonight, but she'd promised him a dinner for two at seven. It was a quarter to now.

"You two may read for a little while," she told Ty and Katie after they brushed their teeth. "I'll be back to check on you soon."

"Yes, ma'am," Ty said.

"Yeth, m'm."

Downstairs, Hannah made a spinach salad topped with sliced peaches, strawberries, and walnuts and set these at two places in the dining room. She reheated the spaghetti sauce and tossed in the noodles left over from the children's meal. From the refrigerator, she took out the grated parmesan.

She was about to open a bottle of merlot when the phone rang. She checked caller ID. It was Clay.

"Two pieces of news that should please you," he said with a lightness in his voice she hadn't heard since this mess started. "First, Royce Bingham ran a stop sign up in Grayton County and is now in custody."

"Grayton? Where on earth is that?"

"A few counties west of here and up near the border."

"Oh, Clay, I'm so glad they caught him." She heard the front door open and Matt's keys land on the hall table. "Hey, honey, talking to Clay," she called and then turned back to the phone. "What was the other news? Annie Mac?"

Matt leaned in to kiss her cheek, releasing what remained of his particular limey scent, overlaid now with wood odors from their lumber yard and something she didn't recognize. She'd have liked to sniff more, but Clay had begun to speak again.

"She's holding her own. They've got her in a medically induced coma with a breathing tube while her head heals. And our other concern? About those pill bottles? No drugs were in her system when she was brought in. She's in the clear for substance abuse."

"You're just brimming with good tidings, aren't you? I can't wait to hear all the details, but I've got to feed this starving man."

"Enjoy your meal. Tell Matt I'll be in touch."

She disconnected and accepted the glass of wine Matt offered. "It seems that Royce is a new resident of Grayton County Jail."

"Isn't that good news? And did I hear Clay say that the mother should be okay?"

"It sounds like it."

He lifted his glass. "A toast. To good news all around."

They clinked glasses and sipped. "Dinner's ready. Are you?"

"Starving."

She plated his spaghetti and carried it to the table.

"What about you? Aren't you eating?"

"I'm having salad now, with you. I sat down with the children earlier."

He scowled. "I suppose you said grace with them too."

"That won't stop me from joining in again."

But Matt just picked up his fork and began twirling noodles around the tines. She purposefully bowed her head, but that's all she did. Not a single God-thought slid past her frustration with his pouting. Two children in the house were enough. She didn't need a third.

Pulling her salad plate closer, she tried to ignore Matt's sulking as silver clinked against china. When the noise of her own swallowing echoed in her ears, she couldn't stand it. "It's not forever, you know. They'll be gone soon."

His hand stilled in the process of lifting his glass. "I just want things back the way they were," he said, reaching toward her.

Which, of course, drained the anger right out as that big hand wrapped around hers. "I know. And they will be."

"I got some of the guys working over at their house."

Her eyes filled. "Oh, Matt, you darling."

"Well, what's the good of owning Morgan's if I can't use some of our building supplies to help out?"

"You think she has insurance to cover the workmen?"

"Probably not. If we find out different in the end, that's fine. But I figure the sooner their place is ready, the sooner Mrs. Bingham—"

"Rinehart. She's been using her maiden name."

"Okay, the sooner Ms. Rinehart will be able to get back there with her children."

Hannah swirled wine in her glass and studied it before taking a fortifying sip to help her speak without choking on tears. "You're the best husband in the whole world. You do know that, don't you?"

"Well, I'm pretty certain I'm the best one for you." He wiggled his brows suggestively. "And I've been thinking. We ought to take a trip after they leave. A vacation for us both."

She batted her lashes and tilted her head, trying for seductive. "You mean, like to Europe?"

"Well, no."

Of course he vetoed long-distance travel, just as he'd done since she first asked if they could go abroad. In the beginning of their marriage, it had been business issues tying them to the East Coast. Then, those pregnancies. Those losses. With a sigh, she waited for him to describe the trip he supposed she wanted.

"I was thinking perhaps a weekend in New York," he said. "I know how much fun you had with Tadie, but you never did go to a play on Broadway. I could get us tickets to whatever you'd like to see." He looked so hopeful, the dear. So ready to give her anything except the trip she coveted, far from home.

"It sounds like fun. Thank you." She gave his hand a quick pat. "And that reminds me. Tadie called. They're back."

"Ah, no wonder you had that sparkle in your eye when I walked in the door. Having Tadie and Jilly around will help you pass the days until the children's mother can take care of them again."

"It will. Though boredom doesn't seem to be an issue."

"No? Then tell me about your day. Did you get any studio time?"

Knowing he wouldn't really want to hear about the many loads of laundry, she described Rita's visit and how easily Rita had picked Ty's brain. "I wish it had been me he'd told," she admitted. "I mean, it's fine, really. At least we know more."

"Doesn't sound like you know much more at all. It seems to me you've only uncovered more questions."

"You mean like Ty's missing father."

"And uncle. Not to mention the state of their mother's emotional health, which plays into their safety."

Hannah stabbed a slice of peach and took her time chewing it. "I hate this."

"I know. You like answers, and you want them yesterday."

"Neat rows. You know me."

"All except in your studio." He winked at her over his glass.

"A girl has to break loose somewhere."

"Amen." Matt glanced around. "Did you get everyone to sleep already? It's awfully quiet."

"I told them I'd be up to turn out the lights soon. Eight seems like a good bedtime, don't you think?"

"As if I'd know."

Right. They were both winging it here.

She checked her watch. "I should just dash up and check on things."

"You go ahead. I've almost finished."

At the door to the children's room, she stopped. Katie lay curled on her side, thumb loose on her lips and Agatha's head sharing her pillow. Ty had fallen asleep with one hand draped over Harvey's neck.

She ought to shoo the dog off the bed, but she couldn't bring herself to upset the tableau of dog and boy. Blond boy and red dog. Blond girl and dark-haired doll. Asleep in her house.

She tiptoed near enough to touch. But she kept her hands to herself as she backed out and turned off the light.

Downstairs, Matt had loaded their plates in the dishwasher and was hand-polishing the wine glasses. He turned to her. "They asleep?"

She nodded.

He reached out and drew her close. "You smell mighty good, Mrs. Morgan."

She wanted to respond, really she did. She knew exactly what his body meant when he traced his fingers down her neck and followed with his lips. But she was suddenly exhausted. Much too exhausted to make love to her husband tonight.

She pulled away. "I'm so tired, I think I'll go take a hot shower and climb in bed with a book."

He sighed and turned back to the sink. "You go on ahead then. I'll wash this last pan and perhaps catch something on television."

That got her. "Why don't you come join me? The shower may be just what I need to revive this old body."

"Maybe later." But he didn't look at her, and she could tell she'd hurt him. Not because she was too tired. Too tired came with living, didn't it? And they'd been married a long time. He felt hurt because their house was full of folk who had nothing to do with him, folk who stole her attention and her energy.

She'd make it up to him. Soon. Ty and Katie would be gone, and her house would return to its well-oiled routine and to the joy of having sex whenever the mood struck either of them.

11 HANNAH

Hannah loved Tadie's big old house with its huge yard and beautiful views across Front Street to Taylors Creek and Carrot Island. How many summer days had they spent crabbing from Tadie's dock or sailing on her little boat to the islands, sometimes all the way to Cape Lookout? Now, *Luna* bounced in the wake of a passing trawler.

She pressed against the porch floorboards with a sandaled foot to set her rocker moving. The creak of wooden runners soothed her. "Doesn't get much better than this," she said, setting her glass of sweet tea on the slatted table between her chair and Tadie's.

Her friend's rocker kept time. "Not much."

Hannah counted gulls on the dock pilings. Squawking things, always after something, but they made a pretty picture out there, all five of them busy preening or waiting for food to show up. About as pretty as the sight of Katie and Ty squealing and laughing as they cavorted with Tadie's step-daughter and the dog. What a contrast between this and their earlier trembling silence.

Town was so busy during the summers, what with all the foot traffic from visitors: women in floppy hats, men in sandals, kids dashing ahead or lollygagging behind, folk lining up for boat rides to the cape. Everyone spent money, of course, which she and Down East Creations appreciated, thank you very much. But it was still a slow place, where only the occasional hotrod irritated pedestrians.

In this very yard, she and Tadie had played jacks or hopscotch, read romantic novels in the hammock, whispered secrets and giggled. They'd climbed out on that live oak's huge branch to watch the boats, making up stories of travelers from afar and dreaming of being on board—well, that was mostly Tadie—and sailing to distant lands. Hannah preferred the idea of flying off, but they shared the dream of travel. Tadie had gone to Europe, and Hannah had married Matt. It had been right in this house that they'd practiced putting on make-up and polish. Speaking of which …

She glanced at her sandaled foot. She'd been so preoccupied, she hadn't noticed her toes were almost as naked as her fingers. She wiggled them, catching Tadie's attention.

"Haven't done mine since forever," Tadie said. "Can't reach."

"You have an excuse. Though you could get Jilly to paint them for you."

"That'd be a hoot. She'd want to put smiley faces on each one."

Hannah held out her hands. "Look, starting to crack. I usually do better than this, in spite of always sticking them in clay." When she wasn't washing and scrubbing up after children. She glanced up at a shout from the yard, Katie squealing over something. "I bet those little girls would enjoy painted nails."

"Paint Katie's, maybe she won't suck her thumb so much."

"I'm not messing with that." Hannah smiled to herself as she watched Katie chase after Jilly, giggles erupting from each. "Seems to me, it gives her comfort."

They rocked in silence until Hannah continued the thought. "I read somewhere that thumb sucking wasn't so bad if they quit before their big teeth come in. Time enough."

"And someone else's worry."

"There's that. Look how she's taking to Jilly."

"Seems to like Jilly's hair."

"Probably because her mama's a redhead, too."

"Interesting that neither of her children got that gene."

After Jilly untangled her legs from Harvey's long leash for the second time, she ran up to the porch and bent forward, hands on her knees. She caught her breath, straightened so her pigtails danced next to her cheeks, and asked, "How come Harvey has to be tied up?"

"We don't want him running into the road to chase a gull," Hannah said.

Jilly's thin arms circled Harvey's neck. "You be good, hear? No roads." Then she took off to chase after Ty.

"They're beautiful children," Tadie said. "Especially that Katie, though her brother has incredible eyes, doesn't he?"

Hannah kept her focus on her friend, not on the children. Or their eyes. "He does."

"What will happen to them if their mama doesn't recover?" Tadie's voice sounded distant as if she were thinking private thoughts.

"I don't know. Clay's checking to see if there's more family. You should have seen Ty's expression when I told him his step-father was in jail."

"The thought of anything happening to either Jilly or this baby has me in knots."

"Jilly really is yours now, isn't she?"

Tadie's expression eased into a smile. "We were talking about that recently, the three of us. Jilly asked if the baby would belong to me more than she did."

"Belong. That's a heavy word."

"I think that's what we all want more than anything else in the world. To belong to someone. And to have someone who belongs to us."

"Like I do with Matt."

"And he's enough."

Hannah nodded, but she focused on a motorboat easing down the channel and didn't speak.

"I don't think I ever really knew belonging until I married Will. Oh, I had Mama and Daddy and Bucky, and, of course, Elvie Mae and James, but this is a whole new level, isn't it? Having Will and Jilly be mine and being theirs. And now this one," Tadie said, rubbing her belly. "God's supposed to be enough, but I didn't even get that before Jilly taught me to trust. My life feels so full now. You know?"

"I do," Hannah said, watching the side-yard antics. "Speaking of husbands, Matt suggested we go to New York as soon as Annie Mac gets out of the hospital. Get away together for a few days."

"Won't that be fun?" Tadie took a slow sip of tea and asked casually, "Is he feeling threatened by having his home invaded?"

"We've just been the two of us for so long. We have a good life."

"I know you do. And you'll have it back before long."

"Yes. Yes, I will. We will."

Tadie kicked off to get her chair moving. "Tell me more about the mother, Annie Mac. That's her name, isn't it? How on earth could she let herself be victimized to that extent? Especially with two children to protect."

Katie tried an overhand throw and didn't let go soon enough. And there was Jilly, running to help her. So precious.

Tadie continued. "Hard to imagine circumstances that could make any woman endure a beating after the first time. Once, she might be taken unawares. Twice? She'd have to be crazy not to have him locked up."

"I get so angry thinking about it. I mean, I'm supposed to have compassion, but it's hard. Do you realize all this was going on just four blocks from my house? Four blocks."

"Abuse happens, but you're right. It's hard to imagine it happening here." Floorboards creaked, and a quick expression of worry flickered in Tadie's eyes. "Isa. You remember? Her husband had money and position. He was even a church elder. She had no inkling he was anything but what he seemed to the world when she married him."

Hannah winced. "Ouch."

"At least she freed herself, and it did bring her down here. That's still working out? You and Isa?"

"She a marvel. I think being part owner of the shop has given her a new perspective, inspired her to come up with really creative ideas. All I have to do is make my pots, but I tell you, we miss your constant supply of jewelry. You doing any work lately?"

"None. And I promised Isa I'd get busy. It'll be easier here than on the boat."

Hannah was about to comment when Tadie groaned. "What? You okay?"

"Your godchild's going to play football—or soccer. He thinks my stomach is the ball."

"Really? Let me feel." Hannah laid a hand beside Tadie's. "Oh, there, my goodness. Rambunctious baby, isn't he? Or do we want a she? Though maybe not if football's the game."

"I don't care. I just want it to be soon. I want to quit feeling like a blimp with a basketball jutting out front. And don't say it. I know I'm mixing my metaphors. But you've seen the waddle."

Hannah's hand tingled as it felt another kick. "Were you sick much?"

"Soon as that zygote started multiplying cells."

"Oh, Tadie."

"I sure never wanted to see anything green, which meant I didn't eat well once I finally let food down my throat. That made me bloated and swollen, then all crabby, to the point where I wondered who'd taken over whom."

Hannah removed her hand and pushed off against the floor. The movement settled her stomach. "Is Will much help?"

"Amazing that he even kept a sense of humor. Mine must have drowned in the amniotic fluid." Tadie fluttered a hand and grinned. "Glad I can sometimes laugh at myself. Landsakes, Hannah, you should have seen me yesterday, sitting in the head, moaning because I was so hot and I kept having to pee and I just felt too fat to move. I'd reverted to thinking of the wasteland my prayers must inhabit. You know the ones we pray when things are lousy? Like when I was throwing up my guts or blossoming in varicose veins everywhere, including my breasts." She pointed toward them. "Yep, striped melons, that's what I've got."

Hannah tried to smile. "It happens." She twisted her ring and sped up her rocking because she was not going to bring up the scars from her own pregnancies. She wasn't going to think about them. Nope. She shut her eyes momentarily, pushing her thoughts outward toward laughing children and bouncing balls. And the dog.

Tadie seemed focused on the memory. With one hand resting on her belly, the other continued its flutter. "I felt so ridiculous. Sitting there, and all of a sudden, I saw my words in some cartoon script, you know, with exclamation points flung after every sentence: 'This was supposed to be fun! I'm in love! I'm Jilly's mama! I get to go sailing!'"

Hannah stilled her movement. "I can see it." It was so Tadie. "Then what?"

"Then I peeked between my fingers at the floor's teak grating and knew I was losing it." Tadie's laugh finally teased her into a smile. "Poor Jilly," Tadie said. "She piped up from the salon to ask if I were okay. There's absolutely no privacy for tears. I couldn't even fall apart in peace."

"Speaking of privacy, what about...?"

Tadie held up a hand, but her eyes still glistened. "Don't even start."

"Not fair." There were only so many feet between the cabins on the *Nancy Grace*, and the doors had open slats for ventilation. Envisioning the lack of personal space when you couldn't even cry without the world hearing, she tilted her head. "How do you know what I was going to ask?"

"You think I don't?"

"A person can't help wondering."

"Yes. A person can."

"Can manage or can refrain from wondering?"

"Both. Either. Anyway, trust me, there's space and privacy enough, or I wouldn't have this belly full, would I?"

"Got me there." Her laugh sounded like a bark. She coughed to cover it.

"Let's get everyone together tonight when Will gets back from the boat. I'd love to see that man of yours."

"I'll bring something. Fill in what you don't have."

Tadie grinned. "Like old times."

It had been a good afternoon. The children had played in her studio, while she'd demonstrated wheel technique and thrown a couple of mugs. Katie giggled as she held up a snake she'd rolled, and Ty practiced kneading the mud-like mess to make it elastic and ready to use. When a design idea fixed itself in her head, Hannah tucked it away until she had quiet and time to concentrate.

And at dinner with Tadie and hers, there'd been laughter and good food. Now, Hannah's palms itched. Her wheel beckoned.

She stepped into the children's room to check on them. Harvey sprawled on the cool floor within reach of Ty's hand, while Katie snuggled up with Agatha and her thumb. Good. They were both asleep. She could work.

She would not let herself be drawn toward those beds. Well, except to cover Ty with the sheet he'd kicked off, exposing his thin hips and his knobbly, little-boy knees. Harvey snuffled in sleep. Images of Ty's frightened eyes, along with his staunch defense of his sister, hit her, and she whispered, "Enough," before heading downstairs.

Matt muted a BBC mystery program when she entered the den. "I'll be at the wheel for a while, if you need me for anything," she said.

He waved her away and clicked the volume back up.

When the first bowl grew cleanly, she threw another. But they didn't satisfy her. With her eyes closed, she tried to bring her earlier vision to the forefront so her fingers could replicate it. They lifted and thinned, lifted and thinned the spinning clay.

She didn't hear his footsteps or know he was near until Matt placed a steadying hand on her shoulder. "You plan on coming to bed soon?"

Leaning back against him, she smiled. "A few minutes more."

"Don't go exhausting yourself. Those two get you up early." He bent to kiss her full on the lips and let his hands smooth back her hair. She loved the feel of him, both of his lips and of his hand caressing, stroking her scalp. Tingles slithered down her spine, but her hands were deep in goopy clay.

"Love you," he whispered, giving her shoulder one last pat.

Lord, but she loved him right back. Maybe tomorrow night she'd show him how much.

She feathered the lip of the vase until it lapped in ripples like the edges of a flower. Appreciating the effect, she replicated it in a smaller version, which didn't work quite as well. Two more tries, and she had it. By then it was after midnight. She cut the smaller vase off the wheel and set it with the larger version on the drying shelf. After cleaning up, she flipped off the light and pulled the door closed.

Her refection glared back as she slathered lotion on her face. Had a whole batch of new wrinkles cropped up that day? It sure looked like it.

Vanity didn't mix with aging. She held up her arms to see if the upper part jiggled in spite of her exercises. At least they remained firm. And she knew her backside was still taut, thanks to walking all over town. But what was she supposed to do to keep her eyelids from drooping and her cheeks from jowling?

Pregnancy suited Tadie. Well, of course it did. Everything suited Tadie.

"What is wrong with you?" She stuck out her tongue at her unnice self. Tadie was everything a best friend should be. Why had she suddenly begun imagining inequities, as if there were a scale and she sat on the high, light end? As if—heaven help her—as if she ought to have more than she did just to even up the scales.

She squeezed her eyes shut so she wouldn't have to look herself in the face, because, honey, there was pure meanness lurking there. How had it hidden from her all these years?

Up to now, she'd imagined herself as okay. Not as smart as Tadie, but okay. If she'd compared the two of them, it hadn't produced a minus, mostly because she had Matt and their life together, while Tadie had stayed single all those years. She'd felt

NORMANDIE FISCHER

blessed back then. Wanted the same for Tadie. She'd been thrilled when Will had swooped Tadie off her feet.

She yanked a brush through her hair and pulled on her nightgown. If a scale existed, she would have to live with her portion and get her mind focused on the positive again. She knew how to do that.

And wasn't Isa going to be thrilled with the new vases?

She stiffened when Matt turned over and tried to pull her close. "Hannah?"

"Shhh. Go on back to sleep."

"You're all wound up, babe." His long fingers roamed over her back.

"A long day, that's all."

He edged away so his hands could ease over her tight muscles and his thumbs could knead the lumps out from under her shoulder blades. When he squeezed the jitters from her lower back and turned her so he could work her legs, she purred.

"You doing too much these days, what with the kids here and all?"

She wasn't sure she had the energy to answer as his hand slid down her arm, then picked up the other one to begin on it. Her voice turned languid, as liquid as her body felt. "Not... much."

"They're not taking too much out of you?"

"Good... kids."

"I know they're good. But I don't want you getting too attached, you know?"

"Mmm."

"You falling asleep on me?"

He chuckled as he pulled her back against him and tucked an arm around her, sliding from her breast to her belly. "I love you, Hannah Morgan."

"Mmm. Love you." And the last thing she felt before sleep took her was the warmth of his breath sliding across her neck and the comfort of his large hand cradling her.

12 ROY

Roy bided his time. The fat deputy didn't seem to be thinking much about the job at hand. Country music blared loud enough to deafen the idiot and everyone within ten feet of the car. Roy might have liked the tune in another place and at another time, but now? With that deputy hunched over the wheel, batting it with his fingertips and singing along like he had a voice? Fool couldn't even carry a tune.

They'd zipped through New Bern and were on the outskirts of Havelock, heading down 101. No traffic this time of morning, with the sun just sneaking up over the trees. Roy figured he'd wait 'til closer to the old store up near Harlowe before he did anything. Had friends back in the woods a ways. Pete. Pete's brother. They'd help. Leastways, Pete would.

He had to get out of this mess, grab Katie, and then move on. They'd probably ruined things for Rachel and him, rotten, lousy cops. He couldn't go back to Alligator, and who knew if he could convince her to run away with him. It'd be too hard, what with her legs not working.

Oh, Lordy, but the guilt washed over him again. Sweet, sweet Rachel. If only he'd seen that other car in time, stopped it from hitting Rachel's side.

He needed to talk to her once more. All he'd been able to say when they gave him his one call was that he loved her, but he wouldn't be able to see her for a while. She'd promised to find him a lawyer.

Well, he wasn't going to stay caught long enough to need a lawyer.

He shifted in his seat, trying to make the handcuffs sit more comfortably. Should be against the law, against some civil liberties code or something to cuff a man and make him practically sit on his hands for so long. Wasn't like he could do much, not with that metal screen between the seats. He ought to bring a lawsuit against the government. Reckless endangerment. It wasn't like he was a convicted felon. And he wouldn't ever be, not if he could help it.

They'd just passed the bend in the road. Clear place coming up. He needed to get the deputy to pull over soon.

"Hey, I gotta take a leak," he called through the screen.

"You can wait." The deputy opened his window to spit, closed it, and turned the radio louder. "We ain't stoppin'. I got orders," he shouted over the noise.

"Hey," Roy yelled back. "Said I gotta take a leak."

The deputy turned slightly. "And I said you can wait."

"Fine. I piss in this here car, ain't gonna bother me none. Might get you in a heap of trouble, though. You not being willing to stop, ruining the seat. Making a mess like that. Hell, it's gonna stink something awful before we get to Beaufort. You want to explain that? Cruel and unusual, it's called."

The deputy cursed but then peered ahead as if looking for a place to pull over.

"Can't hold it much longer." The place he had in mind was up the way, and he wanted to give the fellow plenty of incentive to pick that one. Wouldn't be far from there to the road he needed.

The deputy was stupider than he ought to be. It fairly disgusted Roy, seeing how the man could be so easily manipulated. This was gonna be a piece of cake.

He chuckled to himself as the car veered off the road and onto gravel. The deputy parked, eased his bulk out, pried his gun from its holster, and opened the back door. He motioned Roy toward the ditch.

Roy struggled to climb out so he'd appear weaker than he was, more awkward. "Can't very well take a leak with my hands behind my back. You gonna open my fly for me? You like to do that?"

"You sick or something?" the deputy asked, grimacing. "All right. I'm gonna unlock one hand. I'll have this gun pointed right at you, so don't you try nothin'. I won't mind shooting you. Not one bit. You hear?"

"Yes, sir, I hear fine. Just do it. I can't wait no more."

The deputy fished out the key and then put it in the left-hand lock. Roy didn't wait for him to stand up straight or to get his act together. In that split second of being free, Roy swung that dangling cuff at the deputy's face, knocking him off guard before he even had a chance to aim the gun. Roy used his knee next, then his foot. Before that fool knew what had happened, the gun was out of his hands, he was down on the ground, and Roy was pointing the muzzle between his eyes. The deputy stared up at the weapon, his jowls sagging.

"You were gonna shoot me, you said?" Roy let his voice hiss, delighting at the round, petrified look he got back.

"I wouldn't. No. Never," the oaf sputtered. "I was just sayin' so. Didn't mean a thing."

Roy thought of just hitting the fellow and tying him up in the trunk. Rachel would say that's how he ought to handle it. She'd tell him to go on to jail and trust his lawyer, but no way was that happening. Lawyers were for rich folk, not for someone like him. The system never helped a guy who'd had a few bad breaks.

If he stuffed the deputy in the trunk, the fool would probably wake up and start kicking up a ruckus before Roy got properly hid. A car slowed on the opposite side of the road. They were shielded by the open door and the car and by the not-quite-full daylight, so he wasn't surprised when the gawker sped up and left. He lifted his head for a quick scan of the area and grinned. Then he squeezed the trigger.

"Sorry, fellow, but you didn't help me none, so I can't help you," Roy said as he dragged the body to the ditch. There were rules. Do good, get good. Do bad, get bad. He knew the laws of nature—and, on the whole, he tried to follow each and every one, minus a few incidents he was sorry for. But he'd apologized for those. In his book—and Rachel's—an apology counted, sort of struck out the bad. She said it was in the Bible, talked about forgiveness and slates wiped clean. Soon as she said it, she'd held onto him something fierce.

He scuffed his boot across the gravel to cover the trail of blood from the bullet's exit wound and set the gun aside while he fiddled for the deputy's keys. After he unlocked the other cuff, he took what cash he could find in the fool's wallet and rolled him into the ditch. Next, he hid the patrol car in the back lot of a nearby church.

That was good thinking. Nobody'd see that car until Sunday.

Speaking of Sundays. He'd be missing out on Rachel and her hugs for who knew how long, so he glanced up where he figured

God was. "You take care of her, hear? I mean, I get that you don't pay me no mind, but she's a good woman. A deserving woman."

Yeah, fine, his daddy never gave out a single *sorry* in his whole blamed life. But Roy'd said his sorries, and those should have satisfied Annie Mac. Kept her from signing that paper to take away his baby.

So, it seemed reasonable that all this could be laid on her plate.

He dashed across the road from the church and hugged the edge of the woods when a vehicle passed, slogged through ditches when the coast was clear, and finally arrived at the side road to Pete's. He had a gun now and what looked like a hundred or so in cash. He'd find transportation. After that, he'd find Katie.

Should have been able to grab hold of her 'fore he left. He would have, if Annie Mac hadn't distracted him. And if that stupid boy of hers hadn't taken his baby girl off to who knows where.

But he'd get her, yes, he would. He'd save his girl from those sorry folk.

And maybe, just maybe, if things went well enough, he'd be able to get them settled and could send for Rachel. Once he had a good place for her with a ramp and all.

He trudged along, wiping sweat from his brow, glad they'd let him keep on his jeans and shirt instead of being stuck in some jail-house scrubs. Imagine if he'd been hiding behind trees dressed in bright orange.

Grayton must have the dumbest cops this side of hell.

"Coming, baby girl." He'd fetch her if it was the last thing he did.

Yeah, he probably shouldn't have shot that deputy. Rachel wouldn't like it and neither would Katie. Both his girls were such sweet, loving little things. And didn't Katie just get all excited, watching the birds with her daddy?

But the fellow'd been ready to shoot *him* and would have, given half a chance.

Besides, looking at it from a different perspective—and it always paid to look at things from all sides—he'd done the gene pool a huge favor by eliminating someone so dumb. Daddy always said there weren't room enough in the world for all the fools inhabiting it.

Roy sighed and ducked into the woods as a truck approached. Might have been friendlies, but best not take the chance.

He'd be looking forward to a shower by the time he got to Pete's. And some dry shoes. He remembered the place as being a tad primitive, but it did have hot running water and an old shower stall. He'd be forced to use an outhouse, God help him, but he could keep himself clean, dry, and fed.

"Look at that, will you?" he said, glancing up with a hand shielding his eyes. "A red-tailed hawk. Isn't he a beaut?" He paused as the bird swooped to catch something at the edge of a field. Then, singing softly to himself, Roy stepped back into the mud at the edge of the ditch.

13 CLAY

It was just coming on dawn down east when Clay's legs propelled him to the kitchen. He couldn't think and he sure couldn't talk until that strong brew hit his brain.

His French press offered a minimalist approach to espresso-strength coffee. Minimalist worked. The whirring grinder released an aroma that woke his taste buds, bringing at least one part of his body to high alert.

When the kettle whistled, he poured the boiling water—fine, the purists said the water should be just *at* the boil—over the grounds and set the timer for four minutes.

What could be simpler?

Four minutes gave him time to start his omelet. By rote.

But he was waking. Awake was good. Might keep him from slicing off a fingertip or scalding himself.

From the refrigerator, he removed eggs, mushrooms, a block of cheese, and two green onions and set about chopping and grating.

While he whisked the eggs, the vegetables browned. A dash of salt and pepper, and this morning—his fingers hovered over the spice rack—a pinch of thyme.

Big doings at the station today. Royce Bingham would be delivered into his hands. Oh, yeah.

Yep, this was the way it ought to be. Easy-peasy. Gave Clay time to put up his feet, take a nap if he wanted. Get out of the office for a decent cup.

Who wanted to play politics or wear body armor just to get the job done? To flash guns at folk—or even, for heaven's sake, have guns flashed at him? Not this policeman. Beaufort was the place for him. Kept the heartburn down and the angst elsewhere.

The timer buzzed. Clay pressed the plunger and poured the dark, thick brew into a mug.

Oh, man.

Sipping, he sighed, then sipped again as the caffeine hit brain cells that badly needed zapping.

Okay. Vegetables out, eggs in. He used a wooden omelet fork to froth the eggs. Added the cheese and vegetables, folded the mixture, slid it onto a plate, and headed outside.

Nothing better than living alone with no responsibilities. He could eat what he wanted, when he wanted, and where he wanted. Mornings like this, when barely a breeze rippled the creek, he could spare a half hour for breakfast on the deck. Let town messes recede.

Oranges, pinks, and purples striated the sky and found a perfect reflection in the mirror-like creek. The sight caught him. That was another good reason for being on his own. He didn't have to choke down emotion and pretend at someone else's idea of manliness. He wanted to sing, he could sing. He wanted to let the view get to him, he could let it. Nobody here to say differently, was there?

And there was his dock, outlined dark gray against the pewter of in-shore water where the waking sun hadn't yet lit things. It needed only a skiff tied to its pilings for zipping across the creek to buy seafood straight off the boats. The lights of a trawler rounded the channel marker, and its diesel engine chug-a-lugged across the water. "Wonder what their catch is."

And, yes, he was talking to himself again.

So what? Sometimes a person needed to hear a voice. Was that a crime?

"Right. Didn't think so."

He settled back to finish his coffee. Pelicans and gulls kept a watch out for jumping fish. The cacophony from the night—frogs croaking, crickets sawing, and owls hooting at one another—broke into bird calls. A heron or two often wandered this way in the early morning hours.

This was his creek, bay, whatever you wanted to call it. Sure, other houses fronted it, but they were acres away, and his long lane kept out folk who liked to drop by and get into a person's business. In town, the doorbell would ring too often for comfort.

He checked his watch, figuring he'd better get a move on. He did the dishes and gathered the stack of papers he'd studied last night. See Royce, make sure Ms. Rinehart was doing well, check in on Hannah and those kids. A good day all around.

Once settled at his office desk, he lined up folders in a neat stack. There'd been some delay in getting Royce here. He'd called the sheriff's department up in Grayton. Their man was on his way but must be out of cell phone range. No worries.

Clay flipped back through Bingham's file. He was supposed to be detecting, helping build a case against the man.

Instead, he admired his new screen saver that flashed pictures of sailboats, all of which were bigger than his Sunfish. Lusting, that's what he was doing. What sailor wouldn't?

Maybe a thirty-footer, a weekender he could launch over on Harkers Island and take to the Cape for a few days. He imagined the waves lapping against the hull, the gulls cawing at him as he sipped a sundowner on deck. He'd snorkel over the rays, head to the breakwater on the ocean side, spear a fish for dinner, and then barbecue that fish on a rail-mounted grill. Oh, yeah. His mouth watered at the thought.

He might even get back into racing.

Pie in the sky dreams, that's what those were. He clicked on his email program just to get temptation off the screen. Avery had the afternoon off. Clay only wished he did, too, because it was drop-dead gorgeous out there. A sailor's day.

What good was detective work without new murders or thefts to detect? He hated to wait on other folk. And he was tired of typing.

It was quiet around town. Clay didn't trust the quiet, not when he knew rot existed just under the surface in parts of this sleepy little place.

As much as he enjoyed the low-key aspects of his job, he got antsy without a challenge or two. He'd nailed a major drug dealer—though he still had to find the kingpin—and wife-abuser Royce Bingham would be here any moment.

Tyrrell's sheriff had talked to that woman, Rachel Saunders, who seemed to be the girlfriend. Too bad about her. The sheriff said she seemed real sweet on Royce, that she painted a completely different picture of the man from the one Ms. Rinehart had married.

No accounting for taste, of course, but it made a person wonder about relationships and why a man would beat up one woman and be loving to another. Maybe it was Miss Saunders' condition that did it. Or maybe Ms. Rinehart had provoked the response.

But then, if Royce had been the loving man Miss Saunders depicted, he would have left a wife who riled him instead of hitting her to the point of near-death. Wouldn't it be interesting if Royce were a victim of multiple personalities? Clay'd never dealt with anything like that, but he remembered some case histories from his psych classes in college.

Maybe the interview with Royce would provide a clue about how the man thought. He just bet the court-appointed attorney would call in a psychiatrist.

When were they supposed to wake Ms. Rinehart from that coma? Four days? That'd be tomorrow. Come on, Royce. Get here.

He pictured those two children over at Hannah's. It seemed as if they'd bonded reasonably well with Hannah and extremely well with her dog. And Hannah? If she weren't close to losing her heart to that boy and girl, he was blind, deaf, and dumb. He sure hoped she wouldn't regret her decision to get involved.

At least that was Matt's worry, not his.

Chief Bradley yelled from his office. "Clay, get in here."

That didn't sound good. Clay got in there. "Sir."

"We've got a situation. Grayton County just called. They lost their prisoner."

Clay stepped all the way into the office. "You've got to be kidding."

"Don't I wish."

"So, where did they lose him?"

"Off 101. Seems the Grayton office got concerned when they didn't hear anything. Called here. 'Bout the same time, Highway Patrol got word from some church over near Harlowe. A deacon said he was closing up and happened to notice an out-of-town police car parked out back. It was there when they started their meeting, but he didn't think anything of it until afterward. That's when he became suspicious."

"Bright fellow."

Chief Bradley snorted. "The Highway Patrol went by, called Grayton. They verified it was the car that Royce Bingham had been in and notified the Craven sheriff's department. Dogs are on it now."

"They find anything yet?"

"The deputy, about a mile past, face down in a ditch."

"And no Royce Bingham," Clay said.

"This has gone way beyond assault. We've got a murderer on our hands."

The manhunt eventually involved three sheriffs' departments and one police force. Clay knew the Grayton County boys would be out for blood. Craven and Carteret County deputies would line up right behind them, with state troopers mounting an air search with one of their military surplus helicopters. Clay could picture it now: dogs barking, lights flashing, a sense of urgency. Bingham had that dead deputy's gun and no reason at all not to use it again.

It was late. Chief Bradley leaned against the door frame of the back office, his arms crossed, his face sagging with exhaustion. "Sheriff Randall sounded completely disgusted, though maybe with himself for not sending someone who could keep Bingham in that car. There's a ditch had water in it. Seems he must have walked along in it. Hopefully, the dogs will pick up the scent some place."

"Can of worms, isn't it?

"You said it," Chief Bradley agreed, pushing himself away and leaving Clay to worry on his own.

Clay stared at the computer screen and listened to the loud voice of one of the officers out front. Those on duty itched to be in on the chase, but if they all took off for Craven Country, there wouldn't be anyone here to fight whatever crime raised its head.

Evil existed. Real evil, the black-and-white kind without any gray, where a man lost his humanity and acted as if he'd signed on the devil's dotted line. It seemed that Royce Bingham was one of those.

It made Clay wonder about motivation and upbringing. What made someone as mean as this? Turned him from a man who'd maybe had a hard life but was working on it into a man who took out his anger on others? One who would beat his wife and kill someone in cold blood?

Wasn't that an apropos phrase? In cold blood? Because a man's blood had to run cold to turn him into a monster. Human blood was warm. But evil seemed like a pervading cold trying to freeze the humanity out.

Clay had felt it. Sensed a fog-like cold that had tentacles reaching out to choke and blind. He'd been in the presence of evil during interviews in the men's prison, when cuffing a dealer whose meth sales had sent a teen to his death, when standing at the scene of a suicide pact.

Maybe Beaufort was a sleepy little town. And maybe its sleep covered dark-of-night workings that needed stopping.

Clay's father might not have been a lawman, but he'd taught Clay right and wrong. He'd insisted that good people fight to defend those weaker than they and to stand up for justice. That's what had driven Clay into law enforcement. And that's what kept him here, in spite of being lazy, liking comfort with his feet up, and wishing he could go off sailing and forget about messes.

He could own up to his faults. But maybe the only way to find comfort was to fight the bad guys who wanted to steal that comfort—from him and from others. Because his daddy always said a man isn't a man if he doesn't do for those who can't do for themselves.

Clay fingered his holster. He had a badge and a gun, and he knew how to use both to do what had to be done.

14 HANNAH

Matt leaned against the counter, draining his allotted glass of red wine while Hannah loaded the dishwasher and finished telling him about her day. The children were in their room, in bed and reading—or pretending to—in order to wind down from all the excitement of having Ty's best friend, Andy, come for a visit.

"Andy's mother's almost completely deaf, but she reads lips. And he's such a sweetheart. I mean how many boys that age would be kind to a friend's little sister?"

"Not many."

"I wish you could have seen him. He lisps through a cracked tooth and has a grin almost too big for his face. A lot like his ears that stick out of all those curls. Such a cutie."

Matt reached for the ringing phone. "It's Clay," he said, drawing her close enough to listen and then steadying her as the story unfolded.

"He may lie low until things quiet down," Clay said. "Or he may come looking for the children."

Pulsing blood whooshed past her ears, making her lightheaded. "Heaven help us, Royce Bingham is loose nearby with a *gun*?"

"Does he have transportation?" Matt asked.

"He didn't take the cruiser," Clay said. "I don't know if he has friends back in those woods or a way to get a car. We're doing our best to track him."

Matt tightened his hold. "Was Hannah's name on the original police report? Can he find out she was there or that the kids are with us?"

"No and no," Clay said. "Calm down, both of you. The only way he'll know where they are is if they're seen with you. So, Hannah, just make sure you keep them inside or behind the fence."

"My van has tinted windows," she said.

"Good. He's not likely to be wandering the streets of Beaufort, but I don't want you taking any chances."

"What about Annie Mac?" She circled her fingers around Matt's and drew the phone closer. She had to know, because it would kill those kids if something more happened to their mama now. "Is she safe in Greenville? Can Royce find her?"

"I don't see how. Even if he found out where she is, he'd never gain access to her room."

"This is awful, Clay. Can you imagine how she's going to feel when they tell her?"

"As far as I know, she isn't awake yet," Clay responded. "I'll try to check on her in the morning. Meanwhile, y'all just lie low. Gotta go."

"Thanks for calling," Matt said, but Clay had already disconnected.

As she turned her head into her husband's chest, she noticed a pair of small bare feet in the doorway. She sucked in a breath and then worked up a smile, trying for a light tone as she disengaged from Matt's embrace. "Hey, there. Did you need something?"

Ty did not smile back. "I heard."

When she didn't answer, because how could she, Matt said, "Then you know Royce escaped."

"My mama?" His glare was for Hannah. "You told me she was getting better, not that she went someplace else and isn't even awake."

Oh, my. She longed to reach out to fix this for the barefoot boy in front of her who'd already seen so much.

"I'm sorry," was all she could manage. Because how do you burden a young boy with something as scary as a life flight and surgery? Her own tears edged toward the surface.

He swiped at his face with the back of his hand and spoke with a hitch in his voice. "Is she dying?"

"No, she's not dying." Matt crouched at Ty's level and rested a hand on the boy's shoulder. "They put her to sleep with some medicine. It's something doctors do sometimes to help a person get better. They took your mama to Greenville because they've got really good doctors there. Vidant Medical Center is one of the best with plenty of doctors who know how to fix heads that get banged up like your mama's did. And letting her sleep will help her head heal."

"When's she gonna wake back up?"

"Lieutenant Dougherty said he'd check on her tomorrow, so we should all know more soon." Matt stood and pressed Ty toward the stairs. "Okay, back to bed with you. I know this isn't the news you wanted, but it's all going to work out. You and your sister are safe here with us until your mother can take care of you. And she will be okay. It's just going to take a little longer than we first thought."

"I'll take him up," he told Hannah. "You finish here."

That was a first. If nothing else went right tonight, having Matt soothe Ty was a big plus.

A scream woke her. She tossed back the sheet and dashed into the children's room. Harvey stood next to Ty's bed, licking the boy's face. Katie whimpered as she huddled around her doll.

Hannah eased down on the bed next to Ty. "Sit, Harvey," she said as she brushed the boy's damp hair off his forehead. "It's okay, honey. It's okay. It was just a dream."

He gulped on a sob. "He got her. Roy got Mama."

"No, he didn't. He won't."

His fists dug around his eyes, and he hiccupped as the tears continued. "You can't know for sure. He hurt her. You saw. And now he's out there."

Katie climbed out of bed and stepped on the far side of Harvey. "Ty had a bad dream."

"Yes," Hannah said, hoisting Katie onto her lap. "It was just a dream. He'll be okay."

"Mama?"

"Your mama's going to be okay, too."

Katie snuggled against her, and Hannah breathed in the sweet scent of the child's strawberry shampoo.

"And until she comes home, you're both safe here with me and Mr. Matt. We won't let anyone hurt either of you. Just like Lieutenant Dougherty and his men will protect your mama."

Hannah hoped that was true. She certainly wanted it to be, and she was positive that Clay would do his best. He was a good man. But the police were the ones who'd lost Roy.

No wonder the boy was petrified.

"Mama," Katie said again before plugging up her mouth and pressing closer. Hannah felt a tug in her breasts.

She crooned sweet nothings and continued to stroke Ty's head with her free hand. His sobs lessened, and eventually he curled toward her.

Curled. Toward. Her.

Oh, dear God.

Just like that, Hannah Morgan fell down the rabbit hole into love.

15 HANNAH

She almost fell off the ladder when her cell phone jangled in her pocket with Tadie's distinctive tone the next morning. She climbed down, placed the new light bulb on the counter, and answered. "Hey, sleepyhead."

"Sorry, my eyes were glued shut when you called earlier."

"Will said my godchild kicked and squirmed all night."

"Too true." Tadie sighed. "Plus, I was having another pity party."

"You worried?"

"Some. Maybe. Will's so cavalier about this whole thing, and he *laughs* at me so much, sometimes he drives me crazy." Tadie huffed into the phone. "I lost it. Completely. I was downright mean to him and scared poor Jilly half out of her wits. Lands, Hannah, I even wanted to scream at Nancy, and she's dead."

"You didn't. At his dead wife?"

"You see why he laughs. I'm absurd."

"Just be glad he laughs. He could do a lot of other things."

"Will told me about Royce."

"Clay says not to let the children out front or take them walking around town. At least our back's fenced, but it's going to be pretty confining."

"I'll bring Jilly over."

Tadie's switch to bright and cheerful meant she was in her let's-fix-this mode. Good. Hannah needed someone else's creativity to kick in.

"Or," Tadie continued, "they can play inside here, have the run of the attic. Jilly loves our duck-under rooms, but she hasn't had much chance to enjoy them. You bring those two, they can play like you and I used to."

"Hide and seek?"

"Or dress up in the old clothes."

"Maybe not Ty, then."

"Right. I don't think we have any pirate garb, but they can search the old trunks."

Hannah glanced out the window to check on the kids. Ty's head hung low as if the ground were more interesting than his sister or the dog. "I don't think Ty really believes in good things happening. He had a nightmare last night."

"Poor thing. Well, right now, Jilly and her daddy are out on *Luna*, but maybe we could get them all together when they get back?"

"Call me."

She went back to changing the light bulb and had just finished putting the ladder away in the closet when the kids followed Harvey inside. "Hey. Y'all thirsty?"

Katie nodded, but Ty just said, "Can I use your computer?"

"You know how?"

He merely stared back. Of course he knew how. Probably better than she did.

She settled him in front of it, wondering what he had in mind. She didn't have any games on the thing—at least, none she knew about. "Is there anything in particular you want to see?"

"I figured it might be something to do. You know, on account of not having the one from school."

"Have at it. Katie and I will go in and fix us all a snack."

Katie skipped ahead. Instead of rousing at the mention of food, Ty remained fixated on the computer. Thank goodness she'd be able to distract him later with a visit to Jilly's.

Maybe playing inside wasn't as fun, but with a murderer out there, safe was a whole lot better.

16 HANNAH

Hannah woke to snuffling noises from the children's room. Opening her eyes, she checked the clock. It was almost seven. She slid her feet into slippers, pulled on a robe, and opened the children's door. Harvey bounded past her and down the stairs. Why hadn't Ty let him out?

The boy's bed was empty. Across the room Katie was awake and curled on her side.

Harvey barked. Hannah knew that bark and hurried to let him out. Then she checked the rooms for Ty. He wasn't in the den, the downstairs bath, the upstairs bath. Katie had gotten up and stood in the middle of the floor, naked, her wet panties and gown draped at her feet.

Ah. Yes.

"Where's your brother?" Katie shook her head. Hannah slid open a dresser drawer, trying for calm as she pulled out a fresh pair of panties, a shirt, and shorts, and led Katie to the bathroom for a quick wash.

Helping the child dress, she tried again. "You don't know?"

Katie just stared at her, the thumb tucked between her lips.

She longed to shake words from the child, but she schooled her face and spoke gently. "Well, sweetie, why don't you play in your room for just a few minutes while I talk to Mr. Matt?"

As she crossed the hall, a scream wanted out, but she muffled it and shook Matt's shoulder. "Wake up! Ty's gone."

Her husband rolled toward her and opened his eyes. "What do you mean, gone?" His voice still held hints of sleep. He cleared his throat, pushed to a sitting position, and threw his legs over the side.

"I don't know what I mean. Just that I can't find him in the house. He didn't let Harvey out or get his sister changed."

"Does he normally do that?"

"Every morning."

"Good boy." He grabbed his robe. "Did you notice anything strange yesterday? Any hint that he might be planning something?"

"No. He was still upset, but he did fine at Tadie's."

"There must have been something. Think."

"I'm thinking!" She hated when he used that tone, as if she were one of his underlings.

And then she remembered Ty in the den before they went to Tadie's. "He used the computer. Said he was bored."

Matt stopped at the top of the stairs. "Why don't you feed Katie while I check the browsing history."

She didn't bother to ask what a browsing history was but called to Katie. "Sweetie, let's go down and get some breakfast."

She held the child's hand on the stairs and then spoke with a lightness she was far from feeling. "Will you open the back door and let Harvey in? I'll pour you a bowl of cereal." Because cold cereal would have to do for anyone who had an appetite for eating this morning.

Matt came out of the den, the phone in his hand, and waved her toward the hall as he punched in numbers. "Clay? Sorry to bother you this early. Oh, not early for you. Good. Anyway, Ty has gone missing, but it seems that he logged onto to our computer yesterday and searched for the hospital where his mother's staying. He also looked at buses and taxis."

She leaned in to hear Clay's question. "Do we have buses to Greenville?"

"No. But he could catch one in Morehead, change in New Bern, and be in Greenville in—" Matt checked his watch "—about three, three and a half hours."

"What time is the first bus?"

"Seven twenty-five."

"I'm just leaving the house. I'll call and get someone there right away, and I'll have New Bern meet the bus if we miss it at this end."

"Thank you. I'll stick around here in case I'm needed."

She leaned into Matt as he disconnected. "That poor boy."

"They'll find him. He'll be home soon."

But he wasn't. Katie was in the den in front of a video when Clay's call came an hour later. Matt put the kitchen phone on speaker.

"Morehead police missed the bus."

"Can't someone overtake it?" she asked. "Maybe the sheriff's department?"

"I spoke with them. They said they need more proof the boy is on board. They don't want to pull over a passenger bus on the basis of an Internet search record. You know how these things work. They figure he could just be hiding out around here. That he could have gone to visit a friend."

"But we know better," Matt said.

"Probably. I just interviewed the ticket agent myself. She said she thought she remembered a couple of guys, and, yeah, one of them might have been blond. But no lone boy bought a ticket."

"Maybe someone bought it for him."

"You don't think he's trying to walk there, do you?" she asked. "I mean from here to Morehead?"

Matt answered. "More likely a taxi. Probably found a local one in the phone book."

"Let's assume he caught the bus to New Bern," Clay said. "The Morehead and Beaufort police will be on the lookout for him, and the New Bern police have been alerted. I'm going to head on up to New Bern. I may not be in time to meet the first bus, but I should be able to catch him before he makes the connection. I'll bring him back."

She wanted to believe him. But patience wasn't a virtue she'd learned.

She left Matt to phone taxi companies that worked in Beaufort and went to start a load of laundry, hugging a pair of Ty's jeans to her chest before adding them to the mix. Oh, and that striped shirt he'd worn yesterday. She wiped at the brown blotches on its front and sniffed, but the cotton just held the boy smell that had grown so familiar.

God, please find him. Bring him back safely.

It would be at least an hour more before they could expect a call from Clay in New Bern, and the wait seemed interminable. She went looking for Matt to see if he'd heard anything.

He lowered the newspaper he'd been reading. "I called, but it's not like they can just walk outside to ask a driver if he's driven a kid anywhere. They'll make some calls, see if they can find out anything. It's a waiting game."

"I hate to wait."

He raised his brows. "Really?" But he said it with a humor that always disarmed her.

She'd go crazy if she didn't keep busy. "I'm going to throw some pots." She called for Katie to join her.

Katie had fun rolling clay. Harvey had fun watching Katie have fun. Hannah had no fun at all.

She kneaded, pounding out air with enough force to make the plaster-topped table wobble in spite of its heavy legs. She threw a mug, tore it down, built another, wetting her hands and pulling up on the clay as her wheel turned. Again and again what she made grew and fell, grew and fell.

Her empty stomach tied itself in knots that needed smoothing out like the stupid clay in front of her. She longed to scream, but she had to smile and soothe the child next to her.

At least Katie believed her when she said that Ty would be back soon. Katie did, but Hannah wasn't convinced.

Kids disappeared when you started to love them. Hers had, hadn't they?

And look what she'd gone and done. Begun to love Ty. Love Katie.

Lord, have mercy. She was a mess.

She had *known* better.

The creative failures returned to the barrel before she took the child downstairs to make a PB&J sandwich. Matt said, yeah, he'd eat. "One of your delicious quesadillas?"

So, she melted cheese on a flour tortilla and decided she'd better eat one, too. Katie shared part of it after munching through the middle of the PB&J.

"Have you tried calling Clay?" Hannah asked. It had been two hours plus.

"He'll phone as soon as he knows something."

She turned away. That was such a male answer. If she pushed, he'd do that downward motion thing with his hands that meant calm yourself, relax.

And she'd glare back.

How was she supposed to calm down? That sweet boy was out there all by himself. Probably heading off to play Galahad for his mother. Like he did for his little sister.

Lord, please...

But like Clay, God was silent.

Until she heard rain hit the windows, giving her a new worry.

When the phone rang, she was on it. Matt raised an eyebrow. She hit the speaker button.

"We seem to have missed him."

"What do you mean, *missed* him?" Her voice had climbed an octave, but she didn't lower it. "How could you miss him?"

"It's not a regular bus station here, only a market with lots of cars around, lots of people. All I can think," Clay said, "is that he saw the New Bern patrol car and managed to sneak off. Maybe he hid behind the seats until the patrolman went inside the gas station. I don't know. All I know is that the Greenville bus just left and Ty wasn't on it."

"But you're sure he was on the first bus?" This from Matt.

"The driver confirmed that a short blond boy got on in Morehead, but the driver didn't hang around to count the passengers getting off. Nature called, he said."

"And the patrolman didn't climb on board to look?"

"He followed the driver. To question him."

"Brilliant." She'd like to go punch someone. Punching wasn't allowed, but that didn't stop her hands from fisting.

"Ty had plenty of time to leave the bus unnoticed."

"But if he didn't get on the bus to Greenville, where is he? I assume it's raining there, too?" She relaxed one fist and reached for

Matt's hand as she pictured a bedraggled little boy, standing in the rain, wet and miserable.

"Pouring."

"Is there another, later bus?"

"There is. I'm going to circle the area to look for him, then come back to wait in case he tries to take it. He can't want to walk very far in this mess. I've sent the patrol car away. I don't think Ty will recognize my Jeep."

"He'll recognize you."

"He won't expect to see me. And there's a good place to park back near the car wash where I can watch the bus stop. I'll see if he boards."

"And in the meantime, he could be anywhere."

"He could."

"Oh mercy, Clay. It's not safe. He's just a little boy. He could catch cold. Get pneumonia."

"I know. I'm sick about it too."

"You want me to come up," Matt asked. "Help you search?"

Clay paused and then said, "Yeah, I do. The next bus isn't for two hours. It'll take you, what, forty, fifty minutes to get here? If I don't see him before then, I'll leave you to wait for the bus, and I'll head on to Greenville. We know he's trying to get there."

"Where would he get the money for all this?" Matt asked.

Hannah looked at Matt, stricken. The boy wouldn't, would he? She held up a palm, got a nod from her husband.

"Hannah's gone to check her purse and the envelope I keep in my desk drawer," he told Clay.

The wallet still held the hundred dollars she'd put in it three days ago. Bills were untouched in the desk.

"He didn't take any of ours," she said so Clay could hear as she walked into the kitchen. "So where would he have found enough money for this?"

Katie padded in behind her. "Mommy keeps a box of 'mergency money. I'm not supposed to know about it. But I saw."

She'd forgotten the child was in earshot.

"Does your brother know about the box?" Matt crouched down to Katie's level. "Would he have touched it?"

Katie shrugged, the thumb back between her lips.

"He must have," Hannah said. "He didn't take anything from us."

"Would it be enough to take a taxi?" Clay asked.

"That's the only way he would have gotten here to Morehead. I'm still waiting for a call back from the cab companies." Matt raked his fingers through his thinning hair. "It would be very expensive to get a cab all the way from New Bern to Greenville."

"It would," Clay agreed. "Let's assume he means to catch the next bus and go from there."

"I'm leaving now," Matt said. "Give me the address."

17 ANNIE MAC

Annie Mac vaguely remembered people coming and going, speaking, but never when she was lucid enough to find out much of anything. She didn't even know what day it was.

They'd come rushing in, hadn't they, doctors and nurses talking over each other? Because she'd thrown up? And then there'd been nothing except soft words when she woke again and soft hands touching her.

Her throat felt like sandpaper had rubbed it raw. As if she hadn't swallowed something all the way. Lord, what a mess. Typical, wasn't it?

If only.

She'd certainly collected a passel of if-onlys in her life, though the biggest had to do with Katie. Hadn't that been the biggest lie, the stupidest? When she'd told herself her silence would protect Katie? No more trauma for her baby, she'd said. Quiet was best, she'd said. Now look.

If only.

She blinked back the tears and was about to press the call button when a nurse approached and lifted her wrist to check her pulse. "A little more alert now, are you? Excellent."

Annie Mac didn't answer.

"Do you know what day it is? Where you are?"

She tried to shake her head. It didn't move without pain.

"You are in Vidant Medical Center, in Greenville. Can you tell me your name?"

She whispered it.

"How do you feel?"

How did she feel? How did they think she felt? Why wasn't she in Morehead? Why Greenville? But she didn't have the energy to ask.

Another form came to stand at the foot of her bed. The nurse acknowledged the visitor. "Don't exhaust her. You know the rules." And then to Annie Mac. "I'm about to go off duty, but Brenda will be in to check on you in a few minutes. Someone will be right outside your room if you need anything."

The man's deep, dark eyes watched her from a long face carved by the sun. His brown hair fell over his forehead. He ran his fingers through it, brushing it back.

She'd seen him before.

"Ms. Rinehart, I'm Lieutenant Dougherty."

He'd been there. At the house. Maybe he'd been here before, too. Something had registered through the fog, but not much.

He felt like a lifeline. She sipped a shallow breath and whispered. "My children?"

"With the Morgans. You asked Hannah Morgan to take them, and she did."

He came closer, draping long fingers over the rail as he spoke of the Morgans, Hannah and Matt. Oh, my. The woman wasn't really a stranger, was she? Mrs. Matthew Morgan, whose husband had fired Roy.

"We have another problem right now." He seemed to hesitate.

She didn't speak.

"Your son, Tyler, has run away. We believe he is on his way here, to you."

She reached toward the man but grabbed the rail instead.

The lieutenant continued. "Royce Bingham was being transported back to Beaufort when he overpowered a deputy and escaped, killing the deputy and taking his gun. We believe that Tyler thinks he needs to come protect you."

Her baby. Oh, God, her *boy*.

"How?" She had more words she wanted to say, more questions, but they wouldn't press past the hurt.

"From what we can tell, Tyler caught a bus out of Morehead this morning. We lost track of him in New Bern, but he may be making his way here."

"Why ... am ... I ... here?"

"You don't remember. I'm not surprised."

While he explained how she'd gotten here, all Annie Mac could do was think about Ty, alone, trying to save her. Her heart slammed where it should only have been ticking. She tried to slow her breathing, tried to keep her ribs still.

She closed her functioning eye and begged God to take care of her boy, to bring him safely to her. When she finally looked at the policeman again, he seemed to be waiting.

"Searching?"

"They are. Both in New Bern and on the road—well, roads—to here. Matthew Morgan is assisting the police in New Bern. I came here to see if Ty had arrived and to alert hospital staff."

"Can... I..." She tried to swallow. And then there was a straw at her lips. She sipped carefully. "Thank you."

"I've asked security not to stop the boy but to let me know if they see him or anyone like him." The lieutenant smiled slightly. "He's a very enterprising young man, you know. He found out where you are and how to get here by searching the Internet on the Morgans' computer."

She could believe that.

"But we're not sure where he got the money for the taxi or bus."

"Box…"

"Ah, Katie mentioned you had a hidden stash."

Her daughter knew?

"Would it have been enough to take a taxi from New Bern here? We don't think he got on another bus unless he caught one in Kinston, but that's an awful lot of navigating for a ten-year-old."

"Enough… if he…" But she couldn't say any more.

A new nurse nodded at the lieutenant as she entered. "How are you feeling?" she asked Annie Mac as she checked the IV drip. "You've been having a good long rest, haven't you? My name is Brenda, and I'll be taking care of you this afternoon. So, anything you need, you just let me know." Brenda held out a thermometer and stuck it in Annie Mac's mouth.

"How's the pain?" Brenda asked as she read the results and jotted a note.

"O-kay."

"Do you need a little something to make it easier?" The nurse scowled over at the lieutenant. "Your pulse is slightly elevated."

"Not… now."

"I want you to tell me before it gets really bad, okay?"

"I want to … be awake."

"That's fine, but you'll heal better if you can rest, and you won't rest if you're in a lot of pain." Brenda poured some ice chips in a cup from an insulated pitcher on the side table. "You suck on these. They'll soothe your throat."

Annie Mac slid a frozen chip onto her tongue and felt the cold bring immediate relief. "Mmm."

Brenda smiled. "I'll be back to check on you soon. Try to rest." She glanced at the lieutenant and left.

When they were alone, he approached the bed again. "Do you feel up to answering a few questions?"

She blinked her yes. If it would help, she'd do anything. Questions, self-immolation.

"I understand that you weren't living with your estranged husband at the time of the attack."

"A year. Threw him out." She let another ice chip sit at the side of her cheek, melting cool into her throat. "He wanted Katie ... after I filed." A pause, another ice chip. "Sorry." She waved at her throat. But she had to try. Had to tell him. "Told Roy, to stay away from Katie."

"He hurt your daughter, too?"

Annie Mac flinched at the barely banked anger in the man's voice. He must have noticed, because he took his hands off the rail and dragged a chair closer, which kept him high enough to maintain eye contact. When he asked, "What about Tyler?" his voice had gentled.

All she could do was turn so he wouldn't see her horror. "My babies."

He waited, but she didn't turn back. Finally, he said, "The children will need counseling. When you are well enough, Rita Levinson can help you find someone. She's a lawyer who works with the women and children's center in Morehead."

Maybe he'd go away if she kept her mouth shut. A lawyer would cost too much. A counselor would dig too deeply. The shame kept piling up. How could she say no to counseling? But how on earth could she say yes?

He waited.

"No money," she whispered. "No insurance. Bills."

"There's aid. And Rita can help you file the papers."

Annie Mac blinked. The tears threatened again. It shouldn't be this way. She shouldn't have let it get like this.

If the nurse came back in now, she could ask for a fill-up on that IV. Top it off, knock her out, bring on never-never land.

But, no, Ty was coming. She had to stay alert.

He slid a hand up and back on the bed rail. His fingers were long, slender. She watched them curl around the steel as if talking to her made him uncomfortable. Normally, she might have tried to make this easier. Now? She just wanted him out looking for Ty.

"I understand you have a brother. Kevin, is it?"

Kevin? Kevin?

She hadn't heard his name mentioned in years. She swiped at her cheeks to blot the tears that wouldn't stay hidden. "I had. Once."

"I'm sorry." He brushed his hands down the side of his slacks and cleared his throat. "I hate to ask this, but what about Tyler's father? I was wondering if you'd consider asking for his help."

She blinked, clutched the sheet. "He's gone."

What else could she say? How could she explain any of it?

"Okay. Well." He stood. "I'm going to leave you to rest again while I check on the search for your son. I'll be back."

"You'll tell me?"

He nodded and left.

She released another sigh, slowly so it wouldn't move too many muscles. Whatever it took—and the physical aspect of recovery seemed daunting—she had to get well and out of here to take care of her babies.

Please let them find her boy, her sweet, sweet boy, before Roy did.

The echo of her father's voice bounced against the walls of her hospital room. "Your sin's found you out, missy."

The hours—minutes—dripped like a leaky faucet, plink-plinking at the drain as she waited for Ty or for news of him. She itched everywhere she couldn't scratch. Her lower back cried for relief, but she couldn't shift off of it, not with her leg a solid lump below. She couldn't read or watch anything. All she could think about was Roy loose and hunting for her baby, Ty loose and vulnerable. Lost out there. Why didn't the lieutenant call? Hadn't he heard something?

Please, God, please help find my baby.

Noises in the hall, a visitor's heel tapping, a voice raised, sped her pulse again. When the nurse came to check on her, Annie Mac's "Oh!" startled them both.

"Do you hurt?" Brenda-the-nurse asked.

Annie Mac didn't tell her that thoughts of Roy and her babies, not pain, made her jumpy. "I'm … okay."

"Well, you let me know if that changes."

She shut her eyes. When had she last been okay?

Maybe she could excuse the first time she'd made a fool of herself. She'd only been sixteen, and the promise of that moon had rung true enough for her to close her eyes and let Danny Marker, the star quarterback and cutest boy in school, touch her in ways she'd been warned could lead to trouble. And had it ever. Nobody'd blamed Danny—who stomped off, claiming it wasn't his—when her belly got too big for her to stay in school. Nobody'd blamed Danny when he hightailed it off to State without a backward glance in her direction, then stayed in Raleigh with never a card, never a call, never a care for the son he'd helped create. Nobody had even suggested DNA testing or child support. Oh, no. Not for the likes of her.

Her parents hadn't been any better, believing Danny, not her. She could see them now, Mama murmuring, "How'm I gonna hold up my head with a daughter, my daughter, disgracing us so?"

Mama's lips had formed a straight line, jowl to jowl, while her eyes blazed into Annie Mac's soul, searing those days into her memory.

Mama had plucked at her apron, wiping and pulling as if she were the one who wouldn't come clean. Papa stood with his shiny banker's shoes planted firmly on the carpet, his eyebrows drawn together, his whole arm pointing her out the door. "You think you're all growed up, can do what you want, Missy? Well, you can just do it elsewhere. Not in my house." He paused to wave his arm so she'd see "his" house again, his showplace, the brick house he'd built after tearing down the old rambler his wife had inherited. He'd become a big man, branch manager of the local bank, and now he owned the fanciest house on the county road. He pointed to the door again. "This is a God-fearing house. Not a place for the likes of you."

His daughter, the harlot, hiked a couple of miles to the corner store, where she made a collect call to Auntie Sim. "Hang on, lovey," that dear voice had said. "I'm coming."

She swiped at another tear and reached for a tissue.

If it hadn't been for Auntie Sim tsk-tsking and holding out those loving arms, showing her a different kind of God, Annie Mac would have been an atheist by now.

Still, all of Auntie Sim's loving, all of her teaching and showing, hadn't kept Annie Mac from letting Roy sneak into their lives.

One thing was certain. No man would ever hurt her babies again. That was a promise she intended to keep. No matter what.

18 CLAY

With a sigh, Clay hit the *End* button on his cell phone and went back to watching the front of the hospital. The longer he waited with no news from anyone, the more he fought off images of what could happen next. It was hard to stay positive in a world full of madness. So he prayed.

The rain had let up some, but the hiss of tires through puddles reminded him just how much had fallen and how quickly. It flooded gutters and swirled at grates choked with debris.

He'd parked his Jeep where he wouldn't be the first thing a boy might notice and didn't pay much attention when a slightly battered station wagon turned into the hospital's front drive and stopped at the main entrance. An elderly man sat hunched over the wheel, a silver-haired woman beside him. Clay smiled at the picture they made—until a blond head shot up in the backseat. Tyler Rinehart, hidden until that moment, slid out of the car and followed the woman into the hospital.

By the time the old man had parked and turned off his engine, Clay had made it to the driver's side. He rapped on the glass and flashed his badge. The man opened his door. "You lookin' for the boy?" he asked as he climbed out, cane first.

"I am."

"The wife and I figured there was bound to be someone wanting him, nice boy like that. Scared to death about his mama." He held out a hand. "Johnny Lewis."

Clay shook it. "Clay Dougherty, Beaufort Police."

"The boy come all the way from there, did he? Enterprising young scamp."

Clay grinned. "Yes, sir. That's what I called him myself. Where did you find him?"

"Well, we was stopped at a McDonald's over in New Bern when this young fellow came in, all soaked and real unhappy. He ordered himself a burger and sat down across the way, but my wife, Goldie, she noticed that he'd wiped himself off with some of the napkins and instead of eating, the boy had tears running down his face. He was trying to hide his misery, but my wife seen it. A good-hearted woman, my Goldie, and no way was she going to let this alone. You know?"

"She's a grandmother?"

"Twelve times over. We've even got ourselves two great-grandbabies."

"She'd have to help him."

"Yes, sir. First off, he just kept shaking his head, saying he was fine. Goldie handed the boy another napkin but wouldn't let him get up. By the time she'd finished with him, she'd gotten most of the story out of him."

"I take it the key word is 'most.'"

Mr. Lewis seemed pleased with Clay's understanding. "You got it. Couldn't get a word out of him about where he come from or his last name. So we figured the best thing we could do was bring him on here. Let him see his mama and then find out who was worried about him."

"That would be all of Beaufort, Morehead, New Bern, and here." Clay shook his head at the thought and pulled out his cell phone. "I'd better let them know we have him safe."

Mr. Lewis nodded. "I'll go in with you when you finish. Want to meet this boy's mama."

They found Ty with his head on his mama's chest. She stroked him, cooing, and tears streaked her cheek. Mrs. Lewis sat in the room's one chair, looking quite pleased.

Annie Mac—Ms. Rinehart—stretched out her free hand to Mr. Lewis, her smile so big it lit her face in spite of the tears. "Thank you so much."

"You got a good boy there, ma'am," Mr. Lewis said. "A lovin' boy."

"The... the best."

Ty stood up, swiping at his eyes with the back of his hands. "Mr. Lewis," he said, his voice steadying as he spoke. "This is my mama. Her name's Annie Mac Rinehart. I'm sorry I wouldn't tell you before."

"We're glad to meet you, Mrs. Rinehart. Glad that we could help get your boy to you."

Ty turned to Clay, straightening his thin shoulders. "And, Lieutenant, I'm real sorry I scared everybody."

"We're just glad you left a trail we could follow from your Internet search for buses and taxicabs. Otherwise, we'd be knocking on every door in Beaufort, worrying someone had kidnapped you."

Ty hung his head. "I didn't think. I'm really sorry."

"I got the word out that you're safe. You can apologize to the others when we get back."

"Thank you, sir." He bit his lip and peeked up at Clay. "Do you have to arrest me? I mean, for making all this trouble?"

Taken aback, Clay paused a moment before crouching in front of the boy. "I ought to. There've been police officers from three counties hunting for you."

Ty paled.

"But if you promise never, ever, to do something like that again, I'll let you off this time."

The boy's head shot higher, and he brightened. "I promise. Oh, I promise. Thank you, sir. I won't ever run away again."

The Lewises took their leave, but not before writing down their address and phone number for Ty and extracting a promise from his mother to bring the boy and his sister to visit them once she was well again.

Annie Mac—Ms. Rinehart—nodded, but she couldn't seem to form the words. Clay took pity on her and escorted the older couple to the elevator. "Thank you again."

"Glad we were there, Lieutenant."

And wasn't he also? His stomach unclenched for the first time that day.

Back in the room, Ty leaned close to his mama, his head hanging low as she spoke too softly for Clay to hear. Ty's answer held enough of a whine that it carried. "I don't want to leave you, Mama. Not with Roy out there hunting you."

"I'm safe here, sweet boy. And Katie needs you."

"No one's going to get through security in this hospital," Clay said. "You think all those nurses and doctors will let Roy sneak in here even if he could find out where your mama is?"

"But he could sneak up on a guard and drag him in a closet and then steal a white coat and one of those things doctor's wear around their necks," Ty said, his voice rising with each word.

"Nobody would know in a big place like this. He could get right on past anyone."

Resting a hand on the boy's shoulder, Clay said, "No. He couldn't. You saw how you had to check in at the desk. Everyone has to be identified before they can come up. He can't just sneak in, Ty. You wouldn't have been able to either."

Ty didn't look convinced. "You don't know Roy."

"No, but I know hospitals like this one. Just because you've seen bad things happen in movies or on television," and here Clay raised his brows at Annie Mac, "it doesn't mean that they happen in real life."

Annie Mac hiked her own brows right back at him before shifting her gaze to her son.

Again, Ty ducked his head. "I watched at Andy's."

"Well," Clay said, trying not to let humor soften his tone or show in his eyes, "not everything you see or hear on television is truth."

"Yes, sir."

Time to get on the road. Clay clapped his hands together lightly, something he'd seen his dad do to rally the team. The gesture made him self-conscious. "Okay, then. Your mama's getting better all the time, but any minute these nurses are going to throw us out. Guests can only stay for very short periods, and you've gone way over the limit."

"But I just got here."

Annie Mac pulled the boy close. "Sweet love."

"Can't I stay?" he said into her chest. "Please?"

Timing is everything, they say, and the nurse's entrance couldn't have been better choreographed.

"And who's this young man?"

The boy raised his head. His mama smiled. "My son, Tyler."

"Well, Tyler," the nurse said, moving to change the IV bag. "I know how happy your mama is to see you, but we've got to let her rest. She's been through a hard time, and the only way she's going to get better is if she sleeps."

"But, if she's asleep—" Ty began.

"Now, don't you go worrying your head about anything. I promise you, no one's going to get past any of us to hurt your mama. You hear? We know all about how to protect our patients. Especially really nice patients like your mama here."

"One more hug," Clay said. "We'll come back for a visit real soon."

"And before you know it," the nurse said, "she'll be out of here and home with you."

Annie Mac held out an arm to Ty, keeping her IV line clear of his hands. "Love you bunches."

"Love you, Mama."

After leaving Ty with a grateful Hannah, Clay grabbed a burger and headed back to the station. His stomach raced his mind to see which could work faster. His stomach won.

The hospital had promised to be certain someone always maintained the security station, and Greenville police were going to keep their eyes open.

He'd never convince Ty his mama was safe. But Clay's responsibility was finding Royce Bingham, not protecting Ty's mama. She'd be fine.

He flipped through his notes. Notes that needed augmenting with more facts, more clues.

The problem was, those children felt like his assignment. Maybe if he'd insisted on handing them over to Social Services, they wouldn't sit so heavily on his conscience. That wasn't saying they'd be better off. They just wouldn't be under his nose.

He sighed. He'd spent the better part of a day worrying himself sick over Ty, and he'd let the boy get under his skin—as well as the boy's fears. So, he had a concern there. And maybe Ms. Rinehart could fill in the blanks in Bingham's file, help him figure out where the man might be hiding. She was bound to know something, even if she didn't realize it.

Okay. That meant her safety really *was* his part of his job.

Pulling a stack of cards from his desk drawer, he weighed his options, then snapped off the rubber band that secured them and flipped through toward the end. He hoped the guy he knew still owned that company.

"Brock's Security."

"This is Lieutenant Dougherty, Beaufort Police Department. Is David Brock around?"

"Hold on a sec. I'll check."

Finally, a gruff voice answered, "Brock here."

"This is Clay Dougherty. You remember? Ed's friend."

"Clay?" His smoker's laugh was gravelly. "You some fancy lieutenant these days? Son of a gun."

"How's the security business going? Still keeping you hopping?"

"Not bad. Not great either. More people going with electronics."

"Didn't we have this discussion about ten years ago? Ed wanted you to branch out, you said you'd run the company your way for twenty-five years and knew what you were doing?"

"Rub it in, why don't you? That guy drives up in his fancy Mercedes nowadays, reminds me who won that bet."

"So why don't you consolidate businesses?"

"He doesn't want this one. Says he's got all the work he needs setting up systems."

"Oh, well. No imagination."

"You got that right. Sometimes you need people, not just machines. I got the people."

"And I need one of them."

"Talk to me."

Another trip to Greenville hadn't been part of Clay's agenda for the day, but David Brock had found him a man who could start that night. Clay called the hospital administrator, saying only he'd found someone willing to do guard duty.

"Set everyone's mind at rest," the administrator said, obviously glad to have the security issue off his plate.

The rain had stopped, which made the drive relatively smooth. And Ms. Rinehart's relief when Clay introduced the security detail made him glad he'd done it. Not that he identified himself as the pocket providing the guard.

He stopped by Hannah's on his way home.

"Thank—thank you," Ty said, his thin shoulders visibly relaxing even as his lips quivered.

"You think you can trust she'll be okay now?"

"If you say this man can protect her."

"He can. He's a big man, and he's trained."

"Okay then."

"And, remember, there are a lot of people working to find Roy."

Which Clay sure hoped would net some results. The man had gone missing in an area full of woods and swamp and not much else. The stills that used to be there were probably meth labs now. There were certainly guns and folk who didn't mind using them, even against the sheriff. *Especially* against the sheriff and his deputies. Folk who thought they had a right to whatever they wanted. It was a free country, and nobody ought to go telling them any different.

Bingham should fit right in, unless he thought to sneak up on one of them before they got to know him.

Clay could hope for the best, that the meth dealers and Royce Bingham would take aim at each other and both hit their target.

That would take care of things neatly. Especially if one of the dealers happened to be the supplier whose identity eluded them. And as long as the bodies were found and identified and not lost to the gators, the big cats, or the wild boars—things that were more at home in the swamps or deep woods than any man. Draping kudzu, which had moved north to strangle too many trees, could hide decomposing bodies from prying eyes, leaving them to become scrap for scavengers.

19 CLAY

Clay woke with an itch just below his rib cage. He scratched. The itch spread. He flattened his palm against his skin—and opened his eyes. No, not an itch, but something irritated him. Maybe he just needed a good run.

At the end of two miles, the heat had become a steam bath instead of a sauna. He took his time in the shower and then sat on his deck while he ate a bowl of rolled oats and fresh berries moistened with almond milk. His next younger brother had turned him on to the stuff, and Clay had developed a taste for it even though he didn't have a lactose issue. He just liked the idea of drinking nuts instead of cow.

All he had to do now was figure out how he wanted to spend his day off. Napping or reading?

Of course, he could go check on Brock's man in Greenville. The day was fine for a drive, and just maybe that boy would like to see his mama again. The girl too. He imagined the mama would be pretty glad to see her two children. Might help her healing progress.

He changed into his favorite red polo shirt and a pair of khaki shorts, and was scraping his change from the top of the bureau when he caught sight of his new iPod, which brought to mind his old one, which took him to the drawer where he'd stuck it and then to his laptop.

In minutes, he'd cleared his old unit of its songs. His mama had started listening to audiobooks right after her eye surgery on that little iPod he'd bought her. The thought of loading things for Annie Mac—Ms. Rinehart—had him grinning. He bet the kids would get a kick out of it. Especially, Ty. Boys liked electronic stuff.

He played it safe with classics such as *The Scarlet Pimpernel.* He'd seen the DVD with his sister. The book might be fun. And *Pride and Prejudice.* Most women seemed to like Jane Austen. Couldn't go wrong with Jane Austen or Arthur Conan Doyle. It was the new stuff made him uneasy. You never knew with new books.

When he finished, he set off for Hannah's house, trying to suppress a smug smile by reminding himself this was just part of the job. He was merely putting the witness at ease so she'd remember and talk. No biggie.

And wasn't he the worst liar in the universe? Couldn't even tell a decent lie to himself.

Tyler answered the door and stared up with those deep, almost purplish blue eyes that had slightly up-slanted ends. Seems the boy had tucked whatever smile he normally used out of reach. Clay followed him to the kitchen, wondering what had set Ty's shoulders into a defiant thrust.

"Hey, Hannah," Clay said, eyeing the apple quarters and cookies on a plate in the middle of the table.

"You eaten?"

"I have."

"Well, you sit down and help me polish off those apples. We're a little late with lunch today, but those two are on cookie duty already." She poured a glass of tea and set it in front of him.

"Thanks." Clay set his briefcase on the floor and pulled out the chair next to Katie's. "You having fun with Harvey there?"

Katie's thumb popped out. "Ty feeds him."

"He does?" Clay picked up a piece of apple and bit into it.

"Yeth," Katie said, the thumb back in.

Hannah slid the plate toward Clay. "Harvey thinks he's died and gone to dog heaven, the way these two are spoiling him." She jerked her head toward the mudroom. "See? There he is, drooling in anticipation."

"Harvey likes apples?"

Hannah snorted. "Harvey likes anything. Especially if he sees people eating it."

"I was thinking about your mama today." Clay spoke casually as he looked from one child to the other.

Ty, who had taken one bite of his cookie, now sat still, not touching his food. Katie seemed interested only in her thumb.

"We talked to her on the phone this morning before church," Hannah said. "She sounded uncomfortable."

"Well, you know what?" Clay brought his briefcase to his lap. "She can't read or do much while she's lying there getting better, so I thought about how my own mama listens to books on her iPod."

Katie's head swung toward Ty. The boy said, "It's a little thing that plays stuff. Some of the guys at school have them."

"They do, huh?" Hannah said. "More new technology."

Clay grinned as he fished out the iPod. He fiddled with it until music sounded through small earphones that he extended toward the children. "I downloaded a few books and some music. Thought it might make the time pass faster for your mama."

"You're kidding," Hannah said. "That little thing holds all that?"

Clay laughed, catching the grin Ty finally let loose. "This is only an old one, but I tell you, it can hold more songs than you'd ever need. When their mama's finished with the books I have on it, I can add more."

"How do you do that?" Hannah asked.

"Internet," Ty said.

"Oh. The Internet. Of course."

Clay winked at Ty. "We obviously need to educate Hannah."

"Looks like it," Ty answered and picked up his cookie. Watching him, Katie bit into hers.

"Maybe we need one of those things," Hannah said. "Looks like a person could listen while she worked."

"Or while she walked the dog," Clay said.

At Katie's giggle, Hannah reached out to smooth the child's soft hair. "And maybe a couple of children could listen to books they liked."

Ty's eyes lit. "An iPod?"

"Can't let your mama get ahead of us in the technology department, can we?" She refilled Ty's glass and grabbed the pitcher of tea for Clay. "Katie, honey, you want some more milk?"

Katie nodded, though she still hadn't finished what was in her glass. Hannah pushed it toward her. "Drink this up, and I'll get you a refill." Obediently, Katie emptied her glass.

"You know, Hannah, I really love cookies, too," Clay said. "Never buy them though."

"Why not?" Ty asked.

"Well, I live alone, and I'd have to eat the whole pack quickly, or they'd end up going bad. Neither seems a good idea."

"Maybe you could bring the leftovers here. You know, so they wouldn't go bad on you."

"Now why didn't I think of that? Hannah, this boy is brilliant. When I shop next, I'll pick out my very favorite and separate out enough for me."

Katie looked interested in these negotiations. "What's your favorite?"

Clay paused. "I'm not sure. What's yours?"

"Oreos!"

He slapped his forehead. "You know what?" He bent toward her. "Those are mine, too."

Katie giggled again. "Ty likes 'Nilla Wafers."

"Well, isn't that an amazing coincidence? Those are my second favorite. You know, Hannah, this arrangement is going to work great. I'll get to eat what I want, and none of it will go to waste. Amazing."

"It certainly is. I don't suppose you would like to add chocolate chip to those favorites."

"For you?"

Her smiled broadened.

"I might. You never know." After downing the last of his tea, he slipped his chair back from the table. "I was thinking that I might take a run to Greenville to give this iPod to your mother so she won't be bored. Anyone want to go with me to see her?"

"Me!" Katie said.

Ty wiped his mouth with the back of his hand. "Me, too."

Hannah said, "After you finish that last bit of milk. You can take more cookies with you for the road." She filled a baggie and handed it to Clay, then turned back to say, "Oh, and, Katie sweetie, make sure you use the potty before you go with the lieutenant, okay?"

Katie finished her milk in two gulps and headed into the powder room to take care of business. Hannah turned to Clay. "What if they won't let Katie in?"

"I don't really think it will be a problem."

"The power of your badge?"

"It's got to be good for something. Besides, they moved her to a semi-private room."

"Sounds like progress."

The children followed them outside, where Hannah transferred the car seat from her van to the backseat of Clay's Jeep and helped Katie buckle in. "I do like this car of yours," she said, straightening. "Very sporty and pretty high-end with all these doors. You want to stop here for dinner when you get back? No sense you going home alone when we're going to have barbecued chicken."

"No sense at all. Thank you. Besides, I'd like to see Matt. Seems an age since we talked. I heard he's doing good things for Ms. Rinehart's house. Those carpenters and plumbers."

"He wanted to do his part to help out and make the house livable for them again. When it's time."

"Still, it's above and beyond."

Hannah shrugged, but the play of emotion across her face spoke of mixed feelings. Pride, maybe? Wistfulness?

Motioning him aside, she said, "Make sure Katie uses the bathroom before you leave the hospital, will you? Maybe one of the volunteers could help."

"That's an issue?"

"Seems like it."

"It's understandable, all she's been through."

"I suppose so. I wish I knew better how to handle it. I'm no expert."

Clay raised his brows.

Hannah's hand-flutter and expression reminded him of the girl from their childhood who liked to tease but didn't take it well when someone teased her back. He wondered how much of that old Hannah lingered.

She glanced over her shoulder. "Did you find out anything about their uncle?"

"He appears to have died. And Ty's father's not in the picture."

"I'm sorry. At least their mother will be out before too long." She paused as Clay headed to the car. "She will, won't she?"

"We can hope. It doesn't look to me as if she'll be in any shape to take care of herself real soon, let alone two kids." Clay climbed in the car and checked in his rearview mirror. "You two ready for an adventure?"

Ty nodded. Cute the way he tried to keep the emotion in check. Maybe he was still embarrassed about their last trip together and all those tears he'd let fall.

"A-venture!" Katie called.

"See you, Hannah. I'll call when we're ready to head back." As he started the engine, his cell phone rang. He checked the screen. Rita.

"Yes, ma'am, what can I do for you?"

"Hey, Clay. I'm thinking of heading over to Greenville to meet Annie Mac. Hannah said she's awake and able to talk, so I want to check in and get things started. See what we can offer her."

"You ready to go now? I've got her kids in the Jeep with me, wanting to see their mama, and we've room for a fourth."

"Really? Well, that would be great."

"While you're waiting for us, phone ahead to the hospital, will you? Let them know we're all coming."

"Done."

And wasn't this going to be interesting, all of them descending on Greenville? He wasn't likely to get much information from Ms. Rinehart with or without Rita there, but the iPod and kids might smooth the path for his next visit.

If nothing else, he planned to get her thinking. She was bound to know something he could use to find Bingham.

20 ANNIE MAC

Annie Mac woke slowly, still slightly groggy, and squinted into the lighted room. Yes, her wounded eye worked. Maybe not as well as she'd like, but Roy hadn't blinded her.

They'd promised to release her in a couple of days if she had some place to go and someone to help her. Someone to help her? How was she supposed to find—or pay for—that?

She held up the hand mirror to examine skin the bandages no longer covered. What stared back was a mottled, multihued face with stitches down one cheek and every shade of gray and yellow imaginable around her eye. They'd shaved hair from a patch of scalp that had needed stitches. She supposed she should be grateful they hadn't shaved her whole head.

Her ribs still needed to heal, and her leg would have to remain elevated when she wasn't trying to haul herself to the bathroom, which was a trick in itself. When she'd first used the bedpan instead of a catheter, the nurse—not Brenda—had acted as if she'd been a child in potty training, stopping just short of a round of applause. Annie Mac had wanted to pull the sheet over her head and hide for the rest of the day.

For her first trip to the bathroom, nurse Brenda had accompanied her.

"You gotta try, Annie Mac. You can't figure out how to get yourself to the bathroom, you're not going home. But I know you can do it," Brenda had said, as if Annie Mac weren't lugging a stiff leg that had to weigh a good thousand pounds.

Annie Mac stifled an unlovely retort and grabbed the bar above her head.

Yikes, it hurt. All of it. Her ribs, her lungs, her arms, her hips, her leg. The nurses were gentle, but that didn't stop her chest from screaming and the rest of her from moaning, if not audibly, at least loudly enough to convince Annie Mac she was going to faint.

"Swing your leg," Brenda said, showing her how to extend it over the side of the bed and then how to ease her L-shaped form to the edge where she could lower the leg and rise to vertical with a little help.

She closed her eyes against the wooziness.

"Hold on," Brenda said. "Give it a minute. You need to get your balance before you do anything else."

If Brenda hadn't been there to brace her as she clung to the bed with one hand and the walker with the other, Annie Mac would have face planted on the floor.

Still, Brenda got her to the bathroom and showed her how to lower herself onto the toilet. She fell the last few inches.

Yippee. And she was supposed to do this at home? Without grab bars? Without a strong nurse?

Finished—and she was past being embarrassed—she hobbled, again with help, back to the bed and reversed the process to get her body on board and recumbent.

She wanted it on record: She. Hurt. All. Over. She couldn't stifle the groans or stop the tears that dribbled down her face.

"I'm sorry," Brenda said, straightening the sheet over her legs and handing her a warm washcloth. "I know you're uncomfortable, but it will get better."

Of course it would. Things always got better. Eventually. But they expected her to go back to that mess of a house within *days*? Alone, crippled, and with two little children?

This sounded like a moment for a curse or two. She bit her lip so none would escape.

Her house probably still reeked. Roy had chucked spaghetti and eggs at the wall before he'd broken that chair for the last round. The food would be rotting now. Perhaps green slime patterned the walls.

And Roy was on the prowl, heading back to finish what he'd started. She couldn't go back there, not with her babies. Not like this.

The police weren't likely to stand guard at all her doors and windows. The one here made her feel safe, but that was here.

She'd like to sell her house, but if it sold—and no telling what would happen in this miserable market—where would they go? Besides, no bank would loan her the money for repairs. Banks liked regular payments. To make payments, she needed a job. To get a job, she had to be able to walk without crutches.

Six weeks. They said her cast could come off in six weeks. Would a bank give her that much time before they demanded her firstborn on account? How could she find a job—*any* old job—when she couldn't drive or walk? The old Ford needed new tires and a new exhaust before it could pass its next inspection even if she could drive. So, who would hire her? She couldn't go back to substitute teaching, not this way.

Her babies were staying with a rich lady who could give them all sorts of good things to eat and a big yard to play in. Ty and Katie would never be happy living in a small, poor place again, having to make do with what she could afford to feed them. A place without a dog. Where people could break down the door and almost kill their mama. Where bad things happened more than not, and their own mother hadn't been able—or hadn't tried hard enough—to protect them.

Maybe she ought to leave them where they were. Maybe they'd be a whole lot better off living in that big house.

She heard voices outside, the guard and someone else, another, and then her babies. Her babies...*oh, God, her babies.*

Katie clutched Ty's hand and peeked around him into the room. When she saw Annie Mac, she squealed and came running. "Mama! Mama!"

Clay caught up with her. "Hang on there, kiddo." He hoisted her up, raising his brows at Annie Mac, who smoothed a place at her side.

"My sweet loves," Annie Mac said, drawing her hand over Katie's soft curls as the child burrowed against her breast. With brimming eyes, Annie Mac smiled at Ty. "I had no idea you were coming today."

Clay waved a lovely toffee-skinned woman forward. "This is a group outing, Ms. Rinehart. I brought Rita Levinson to meet you. She's a lawyer with the women and children's center in Morehead, and she and Hannah have been talking over ways the center might be able to help you."

"Mrs. Levinson." Annie Mac looked from one to the other. "How, how... nice" was all she could manage.

"Rita, please."

Ty reached over the bed rail and handed her a small mesh case. "Open it, Mama."

"For me?"

Ty nodded. Katie raised her head, turned at her mama's side, and watched as Annie Mac unzipped the case and pulled out an iPod and earbuds.

"What...?"

"It's an iPod, Mama," Ty said.

"I see that. But why... I mean... where did it come from?"

"The lieutenant brought it to Miss Hannah's. He said we could give it to you."

She glanced over at the policeman and caught an expression that surprised her. The confident lieutenant could be flustered. Could even blush.

"I... I... really, it's nothing. Just an old one I had lying around."

"But for me?"

He shrugged, let loose a small smile as he indicated her leg. "I remembered when I was in the hospital and laid up. Drove me crazy. So, I just figured... I mean, my mama loves to listen to audiobooks on hers, so I thought.... Well, it seemed like it might help you pass the time."

"There's lots and lots of stuff on it. Books and music," Ty said, uncoiling the earplugs for her. "Katie and I heard some in the car. It's really neat."

Before any more words would come, she needed water, but with Katie on her lap, she couldn't reach. The lieutenant seemed to read her mind and a glass of water with a straw was on the way.

"Thank you." She sipped and smiled again at him.

He rolled her tray closer to her free hand so she could set down the cup with only a slight stretch. The stretch was probably good for her, even if it didn't feel great. She angled her head toward the iPod.

"That... is a very generous gift. Thank you."

"I wasn't sure what you liked to listen to, but it's not hard to add more."

"I can show you, Mama. When you get home."

"Speaking of which," Rita Levinson said, moving to the end of the bed, "have they said when you'll be released yet?"

Annie Mac let her gaze linger on Katie and Ty, before she sent a beseeching look in the lieutenant's direction. "Soon, I hope."

His large hand almost dwarfed her son's thin shoulder. "Ty, what do you say to us taking Katie to get an ice cream cone? I bet they've got really good ones downstairs."

Katie's thumb popped out. "I want Mama."

Annie Mac tucked strands of hair behind Katie's cheek. "You can come back. I should talk to Mrs. Levinson for just a couple of minutes. Okay?"

Her baby's lower lip trembled. That sweet little pouty lip. And those cheeks. It was all Annie Mac could do not to pull Katie back down and kiss every bit of that face.

"Come on, Katie," her brother said.

That was another thing that nearly broke Annie Mac's heart, seeing Ty square his shoulders and take responsibility. Be the grown-up—because she hadn't been.

Her throat choked up as she looked at him. And Katie, not daring to have a tantrum, docilely letting Ty help her off the bed.

She was a terrible mother.

When they'd gone, Rita Levinson pulled up a chair, setting her briefcase on the floor next to her. "I bet my mama would enjoy something like that iPod of yours. I should ask her, especially now that her magnifying lenses have gotten so heavy."

Rita was so beautiful, with that skin and the shirt flowing confidently over her pregnant belly. Annie Mac turned toward the ceiling. Staring at pebbly paint felt easier than making comparisons. Rita, her, Rita, her—pretty and successful versus a miserable ugly failure whose brain wouldn't shut up.

Get a grip, get a *grip*.

"I'm here to help you figure out a few things, if you don't mind."

"I'm grateful." Beggars couldn't mind, could they? She tried for a smile but didn't feel one happening.

"I've talked to Hannah and Clay, and we feel that your children will need some counseling after all this. You may want to talk to someone also."

"I can't afford... anything. I don't even know how to pay for this hospital."

"I can help you apply for aid. And our counselors work on a sliding fee scale. You don't need to worry about cost at our end."

Yep, digging a hole, climbing down into it, and sliding a cover on top seemed like a brilliant idea.

"I found a counselor I think will be good with both Ty and Katie," Rita said. "But she wants to wait until you are all together again."

Annie Mac tried to look pleased. Her lips stretched over her teeth but stuck on the dry enamel. She lifted them with her tongue and reached for her water.

Rita kept the words flowing. "You know about pets used in therapy? The counselor, Dr. Darian Evans, heard about how well the Morgans' dog is bonding with your children and feels that Harvey is helping them find a sense of security. She suggests that you might consider getting one when things stabilize in your life."

Annie Mac could do that. A big dog with teeth sharp enough to rip out Roy's throat. She pressed her clenched hands together. "You really think Katie's okay?" The talking still hurt, but she had to ask. "She's not too afraid of all these men she's meeting?" She hadn't intended to mention *it*—their skeleton—but the fact was that if no one knew, no one could protect Katie. She'd kept silent long enough.

Rita frowned. "Did Roy beat Katie, too? Should we be looking for some behavior in particular?"

Deep breath, slow release. She could do this. "The other. He touched her."

"Oh, no."

She grabbed another tissue and tried the breathing thing again. Slowly in, slowly back out. Her nose had clogged, so she opened her lips. The *out* whistled slightly. "I'm hope... hoping it was only what I saw, him touching her and showing himself. I walked in on them." The words croaked some, breaking in half, but even if she sounded like a whistling frog, she said it. She told. "I wanted to kill him."

Rita's jaw had gone slack, which surprised her, seeing as how Rita supposedly worked with abused women all the time.

"I imagine you did," Rita said. "He'd been messing around with a child of mine, I don't know what I'd have done. I'd certainly have wanted to break his neck. And probably cut off anything I could get hold of."

Annie Mac's lids closed on a whispered, "Yes," and when she opened them, she focused on a point beyond her visitor. "Once I recovered from the thought of what he'd done—or nearly done—I should have called the police." The memory hurt, the guilt. She couldn't stand how weak, how stupid her decision seemed from this place. Why hadn't it seemed so then? Her fingernails dug into her palms. She hoped they would draw blood.

"I told him to get out. Never come back. He stayed gone a year—until he got the divorce papers." She paused again, sipped, and again whispered, "It was so many months, I didn't imagine."

Rita laid a hand on her wrist, gently, but the touch was too much, and her tears started up. "I really am sorry," Rita said, "but I need to ask, for Katie's sake. Did he ever do more than touch that you know of? Or do it more than once?"

Annie Mac swiped at her cheeks, trying to swallow back the bile that rose and burned. "I don't see how. I never left her alone with him because of his temper. That day? He took her from the sitter's house before I got home."

"If you'd had proof, or if Katie had testified, the police could have held him. But you should have at least gotten a restraining order, especially as they had a record of him assaulting you. Not that restraining orders work all the time. I'm not saying someone crazy would pay one a lot of mind, but he'd have been on their radar for more than battering."

"I know. But she was only a baby. I couldn't put her through more. The added trauma. I was hoping she could forget." Another shallow breath, another pause, and she continued. "And I was ashamed. Ashamed I'd married him, that I'd taken him... back after he'd knocked me around that first time."

"All right. We've still got to consider what you're going to do when you get out of here. Are you sure there's no family who can come help you?"

"There's nobody." Nobody and no place. "How can I go back where he could find us? A loan maybe to fix my house and put it on the market?"

"Selling it might be a good idea. Starting over in a new place."

"If... if I could sell the house, maybe I wouldn't have to use aid. Pay the hospital bill myself."

"You could, of course, but you'd only have the balance left to work with after all these costs are covered."

Annie Mac felt herself grow colder, probably paler, too. What was left in her bank account had to be dwindling by the minute. Both her electrical and telephone would be debited this week, and there was that credit card bill coming due soon.

"Selling's a big decision," Rita said, "one you may not want to make lightly or right away."

"I can't work yet. If I sell, where do we go? If I don't sell, how do we go to that house with Roy out there?" She stopped. It wasn't just the hurt in her throat or the hurt in her body, but the hole in her soul that made her want to shrivel up and disappear. She sniffed back the tears. This was so embarrassing. "Lord, help me, I can't even get around without assistance, and I've no money to pay anyone."

The worry of it almost undid her again. She grabbed a tissue, dabbed with it, and busied herself tucking a few straggling hairs behind one ear, smoothing the messy bits on the other side. Avoiding the shaved spot and the stitches.

Rita's hands went to her belly as if to protect her unborn babe from the harsh realities of life. Annie Mac's realities.

"We'll figure something out." Rita picked up her briefcase, lifted her head, and stood. "I'll go out and call Clay. Let him know to bring the children back up to visit a few minutes. And don't you worry. I'll see what I can come up with and get back to you in a day or so."

Rita's promise sounded fine, her round lips saying what her eyes declared, but Annie Mac knew better. Maybe folk like Rita could offer and believe in promises, but *she* was the one who'd actually have to make things happen. She'd made the mess and let the bad rule for way too long. She was the one who'd have to fix it.

And didn't that just send her spiraling again. *Fix* it? From *here?*

21 CLAY

Clay raked his fingers through hair that fell haphazardly over his forehead as he headed to Morgan's Lumber. Matt better have a really good reason for making him miss his barber's appointment.

The young woman at the sales desk waved him through to the pine-paneled office where Matt held up one finger and concluded a phone call. "Glad you could come." Matt swiveled his big leather chair in Clay's direction. "Have a seat."

Clay did. "What is it you wanted to see me about?"

Matt twirled a pen. "I hear Rita and Hannah have been trying to settle on where to put those children and their mother when she gets out of the hospital. Rita seems to have hit a dead end, which you probably already know. It seems she also vetoed Annie Mac coming to our house, and all I can say is, she's absolutely right. It's not going to happen. Can you imagine Hannah having to tiptoe around the mother, who's bound to feel skittish, someone else taking care of her children—children who need help because of her mistakes?"

"It would be hard on her."

"Hannah's got herself too involved with them as it is. Best get them all moved on before letting go kills her."

Clay sighed. "It's not easy, is it? Wanting what you can't have?"

"I used to think she was okay about those babies we lost, once we figured out it was genetic and not from something we'd done." Matt rubbed his nearly bald head. "I thought we'd adopt, but somehow the time never seemed right ... or maybe we both got too comfortable, couldn't make the shift to adding someone else. Anyway, she seemed fine with just us. Busy with her projects. But here come Tadie and Rita, both in the family way. I've seen the pain she tries to hide, though she doesn't have a clue I've guessed. Now these two children? I wish I could have said no, but how?"

"Haven't a clue," Clay said, repeating Matt's phrase. It sounded apt. "You have any ideas for Ms. Rinehart? You did so much with that house of hers."

"Thinking to get her back in it and the kids with her. You couldn't convince her to give the place a go? With better locks and one of your men to drive by regularly."

"Didn't you see that back door?" Clay asked. "Bingham smashed right through it." The smell of the place, the mess. He tamped down the memory, tried to cover it by saying, "No way she and the children should be any place he can find them until he's locked up for good."

"I guess we could all pitch in and rent her an apartment," Matt said.

Clay leaned back with a sigh. "Tried that. Rita talked to the folk over at Hancock Realty. They handle rentals, most of the ones that aren't direct by owner. The agent knows of one or two small houses she wouldn't put her dog in, much less a couple of kids, and a number of pricey places none of us could afford. The couple of apartments they have are either upstairs or don't have enough bedrooms."

"Really?" Matt said.

"The problem is, Ms. Rinehart needs a ground-floor room, preferably handicap-equipped, in a safe place that Royce Bingham can't find, with room for someone who can help with the children and with cooking and cleaning."

"How mobile will she be?"

"Not very. Certainly not for a while. It's not only the leg. She's got broken ribs. Lots of bruising." Clay once again did a mental inventory of everyone he knew who might have room downstairs and the ability to help. His mama did, only she needed the downstairs space for herself since her knee had started giving her all that trouble.

"I can't think of anyone or anywhere," Matt said, echoing his thoughts. "Except your house. You've got room enough for the whole passel."

Whoa. Where had that come from? "Don't even go there. My house is no bigger than yours, probably not as big, just has more land around it. Feels open because of the fields and the creek."

"But you've got everything sprawled on one floor. I know you've got room."

"Matthew Morgan, what are you thinking? I'm just the policeman working the case. And a woman like that? Seems to me she'd be scared to death moving out to a man's house." And he'd be miserable having her and those kids invade his privacy.

"I bet it could work." Matt's gears clanged so loudly, Clay longed to shove an iron bar in to stop them. "You've got that little unfurnished room off the kitchen area," Matt said, "unless you've done something with it since I last saw the place. Put our rollaway or a single bed in there, hire a housekeeper. That's all we'd need to do, find you someone to come in and take care of Annie Mac and the children, some big, strong female to do the work. You're gone all day long. They wouldn't bother you all that much, now would they?"

"Can't do it, Matt."

"Why on earth not? You worried about the expense, I'll pitch in, and in a heartbeat. You'll be saving me from misery, which is what it would be, that woman and her kids staying with us, and in my den, too. And think of Hannah. Saving her from heartbreak. She could visit the children, but they'd be away from her mothering." He grinned at Clay as he swung his feet around and stood. "This is good. If Hannah gets all mopey on me once they're gone, I'll take her on that trip I promised. Maybe even to Europe. She's been pestering me to get her to Italy for years."

Clay glowered at the smile that spread across Matt's face. Matt obviously figured he'd saved his wife and his den, and that's all he cared about. Clay pushed back his chair as he prepared his defense, but Matt just stuck out his hand.

"Thanks so much for coming by and helping me solve this," he said, showing exactly how he'd gotten to be president of the local Rotary Club. "I'll have the ladies get right on finding someone to come in and help. You know they're better at it than men are. How does that sound to you?"

Clay stood and straightened to his full height, which he hoped gave his position more authority than he felt, and shook Matt's hand—only because he couldn't figure out how to ignore it. Trying to make his words at least as firm as Matt's had been, he said, "It's not going to happen, Matt. I'll talk to Rita, but my house is not an option."

"You do that. You talk to Rita. I'm sure the two of you can work something out that'll be agreeable all around." Matt slapped him on the back as he eased Clay out the door of his office.

Clay got in his Jeep and headed out of town, hiking his shoulders another notch. So, was this going to be a war of wills? There was no way on earth he'd ever agree to that absurd plan.

His thoughts slid all over the place, hunting up a solution that did not involve him in more than an advisory capacity. Rita couldn't have tried Morehead City if she'd come up empty. And what about Newport, Havelock, even New Bern? Jacksonville wasn't that far away. First-floor rentals had to exist someplace. This wasn't Outer Mongolia.

Matt seemed desperate to get his house and wife back, which meant he'd probably be willing to fork over a decent amount for rent. Okay, Clay could pitch some into the pot, too. All they needed was a garden apartment with three bedrooms that had good security.

His garage opened with the punch of a button. Ignition off, keys out, briefcase in hand, he entered his silent house. Too many voices scrambled for first place in his head, so he clicked on the CD player, then poured himself a glass of sweet tea and headed out to the deck, taking the phone with him.

Ripples from an outgoing shrimper's wake convoluted the otherwise still water, and its engine chugged in the distance. He sipped as he watched a couple of egrets glide to a roost on an old pine log near the marsh. A dog barked somewhere on the other side of the woods.

The dog brought to mind Hannah's Harvey with his tongue lolling to one side and his tail twitching. Which prompted thoughts of two blond children. He didn't want to have those thoughts, but they nudged their way smack-dab into his imagination.

He could see the two of them dashing down the creek bank, laughing while they hunted fiddler crabs at the marsh edge, dodging oyster shells. The boy would head out with him to gig flounder on moonlit nights, his wading shoes slurping up mud until they got to harder bottom. The slurps would make the boy giggle, just like they used to for Clay. He'd hold the lantern over the water and tow the skiff with a painter tied at his waist. In the skiff, they'd have a pot for those flounder and a basket for the crabs they'd stop from scurrying off sideways. He'd teach that boy how to scoop up those crabs, how to watch the bottom for a pair of eyes on top of an oval-shaped flounder.

He could imagine taking both of them out on the dock to demonstrate chicken-necking. He'd show them how to bait the crab lines with chicken necks and tie on sixteen-penny nails for weights. How to feel if a crab were nibbling, and then how to reel in the line, hand over hand, slowly so you didn't scare the critter off the bait. And, finally, how to set your net low enough so the crab wouldn't see it coming.

He pinched his nose because he didn't like where his head kept going, especially when he saw a pair of children dashing toward that little Sunfish, puffy with orange life vests. The boy would have his hand on the tiller, the little girl would be tucked in the footwell, maybe leaning back against Clay's shins while he taught that boy how to steer, how to pull in the sheet. In a few years, the girl could learn, too, and wouldn't that be a treat?

Of course, the children he saw were laughing in a carefree manner they'd probably never known in their short lives. But he couldn't change that. He wasn't qualified.

"You're a fool." Or maybe a masochist.

He'd just ignore Matt. And slam his eyes against the image of Katie's big eyes staring at him over that thumb of hers. Or of Ty trying so hard to be strong and capable. He'd never seen a boy who so badly needed to be let off the hook.

He glared at the phone, willing it to ring. Rita's first call had come while he was still at work, and since then they'd been playing phone tag.

Why on earth had that group elected him spokesperson for the humanitarian effort Rita and Hannah and Matt had cooked up among themselves? That's where he should have nipped this in the bud. He'd had nothing to do with it, other than hiring a guard for the hospital and supplying an outdated iPod. Why, now, was he being wrangled into coping with Annie Mac—*Ms. Rinehart?*

He had to quit thinking in terms of her first names. She and her children were part of a case. Period.

"Come on, Rita. Call."

The phone rang in the middle of his raging internal dialogue. "Yeah," he said. "Rita?"

"What's going on?"

Clay pushed back, settling deeper into his chair. "Matt's being difficult."

"What do you mean?"

"Oh, some ridiculous idea of placing Ms. Rinehart and her children at my house with a housekeeper. That's not happening, so I need you to figure something out. Doesn't the center have any safe houses available?"

"We had one I thought might work, but a boyfriend of one of the women got wind of it and busted right in. It's a small town. Hard to manage these things, especially with our limited resources."

"Did you try New Bern?"

"I did. And Kinston and Greenville. Even Jacksonville. Nothing available that will work and not cost an arm and a leg. She'd hate anyone paying for that. Frankly, I don't think she'd accept that sort of charity."

"So what are you going to do with them?"

"Annie Mac's certainly not going to let any of us pay her bills. But we're faced with her either selling her house or living in it." A pause, then, "Considering the amount of help she's going to need with her medical bills, we've got our hands tied. Medicaid will allow her to stay in her own home, but if she moves out, the house becomes an expendable asset, which has to be used in lieu of government aid."

"Limits her options, doesn't it? Matt may have to relent and let her have his den. The children love it there, and I just bet Hannah'd be tickled pink."

"It won't work."

"Why not? Hannah loves those two. Why can't she keep on loving them a little while longer? And I just bet Ms. Rinehart would like the place."

Clay was not going to be pushed into anything. He wasn't. He clamped his lips shut, and his grip tightened on the phone.

"Clay. Listen to yourself. You're a friend of Hannah's. I know you think Matt's being unreasonable, but he's just looking out for his wife. And besides her emotional issues, there's the problem of not enough bedrooms for the kids and a caregiver on the second floor, not with Hannah's studio up there. And she can't do all the lifting required, so a caregiver would be a necessity. Do you expect them to put a caregiver in the laundry room, maybe on top of the freezer? Or stick her on the couch next to Annie Mac in that den? You tell me, Clay."

He remained silent. A houseboat eased out the harbor and toward Brown's Island. He wouldn't want to be caught in a wind on one of those things, but he bet they were going to have fun at anchor.

More than he was, if this kept up. Still, he waited.

Rita cleared her throat. "You don't have anything to say?"

He hated the way women did that guilt thing. "What do you want from me?"

"How big is your place?"

"Not big enough. Even with Matt's hypothetical housekeeper."

"Figuratively or literally?"

He hesitated. He'd like to lie. "Not that it's any of your business."

"Clay, come on."

He spat the word into the phone. "Figuratively." All right, so he was being juvenile, but *was* it any of Rita's business?

"You're only worried that Annie Mac will be uncomfortable?"

"Well, yes. Mostly." Should he mention how miserable he'd be, giving up his privacy, his seclusion—having a big-eyed woman and her big-eyed children underfoot all the time? Not to mention some housekeeper. They were worried about Hannah's peace and well-being. Well, what about *his*?

"I hear you," Rita said, making Clay wonder if she really did. "Let me talk to Annie Mac. I'll see her in the morning and get back to you."

"Rita, no." Fine. He'd say it. Lay it out. "Why is it okay for me to be inconvenienced and not the Morgans? A caregiver could go to their house during the day, go home at night. I don't buy Matt's putting it all on me. I'm only the cop investigating the case, not the social worker."

"The cop who got involved."

"Not really. No more than anyone would."

"That's not what I hear."

He shifted uncomfortably. But he kept silent, trying keep some distance between him and Rita's words—and failing.

"It seems to me," Rita continued, "that our options are limited. One, Annie Mac and the children can return to her house with new locks, maybe an alarm system." He could picture Rita holding up fingers as she counted. "Two, they can squish into the Morgans' house with everyone miserable and Hannah left to take care of any middle-of-the-night emergencies. Three, they can try to find another place that's affordable, which isn't going to be much and will probably mean only one or two rooms—and who-knows-what kind of neighborhood. Four, we can forcibly move them into a place Matt subsidizes and ignore what that will do to her self-esteem. Or, five, they can move to your house for a few weeks."

"And where would you suggest I go while they're using my home?"

"Don't be ridiculous, Clay. You said you had enough room."

"There wouldn't be enough space even if I had ten bedrooms."

"Why, because you don't want company?"

"Yes." He huffed and drew in a breath. "And because I'm a man, and abused women tend to be petrified of men in general, especially one who isn't family."

"With a housekeeper living in? That should take care of those worries."

"Not likely," Clay said under his breath.

"What?"

"You ever heard of boundaries, Rita?"

"Come on. Let me try. No matter what you think, Hannah's house isn't an option. And Tadie and I both have babies on the way, which will mean no room at either inn. Do you know anyone else with even one spare bedroom, let alone three?"

"If I did, we wouldn't be having this conversation, would we?" He hoped sarcasm would work. He released a low groan and ran his fingers through his hair again.

This was the moment to show off that strong will he'd touted. But when he pictured himself telling them all just to leave him alone, he couldn't do it.

"Be a grump," Rita said. "If you're dead set against them moving in, it's a moot point, isn't it?"

"Look, I just don't want to put her in a difficult situation, and I don't want to be walking around on eggshells in my own house."

"How long would it be, realistically? I'll get a Realtor involved in selling her house for a reasonable price so it won't be on the market forever, and as soon as the cast comes off, she'll have options. Six weeks."

"Six weeks?"

"Eight. Max."

Clay felt himself slipping down a mountain of mud—on his butt. "Rita, I don't think I like you very much." And he sure wasn't going to like the result of today's work either—no matter what kind of daydreams he'd had. "All right. Two months. No more. But I'm not interviewing housekeepers, you hear? You women work this thing out. I'll stay out of your way."

"That's if she agrees to go to your place."

"Right. Maybe she'll prefer food stamps and a tenement."

22 CLAY

Clay dried his hands on a dishtowel and opened the door to Rita. "Here to rub it in, are you?"

She ignored the remark and followed him into the great room with a peek at the kitchen on the way. "Love this place. My, oh, my." At the French doors, she waved her hand over the vista. "Clay, you're a selfish man."

"That's not very nice."

"Wanting to keep all this to yourself." She tut-tutted. He didn't think he'd ever heard anyone actually make that sound. "Just imagine those children here."

Wasn't that what he'd been doing? If the children could be here without the mother—and with a housekeeper to mind them—he'd be game. Maybe not nice, not kind, but game.

Suddenly, he pictured his father. What would Coach Dougherty say if presented with this choice? Clay didn't comment, but he dipped his head, acknowledging the hit.

"Which way to the guest rooms?"

He led the way down the small hall off to their right.

"Wonderful. We'll need to install grab bars in the bathroom. Can you attend to that or do you want me to have Matt send someone over?"

Grab bars. Great. "You still haven't told me about your visit to Ms. Rinehart."

She grinned up at him. "You going to offer me a cold drink?"

"Sure. Water or water? I'm fresh out of tea."

"Can't do caffeine now anyway. Water would be great."

He filled a glass and handed it over, then ushered her to the couch. "So?"

"She's looking better, but she responded as we'd expected. Mortified at being under obligation to everyone and wishing she hadn't landed herself in this situation."

"She okay with coming here?"

Rita toyed with the glass for a moment. "She wasn't. But I told her what you said, that she'd be way on the other side of the house and that there'd be a housekeeper in between."

"And will there be?"

"There will. Mama and Daddy gave me a name, Becca Barnes, a woman from their church who takes care of folk since her husband up and lit out. Seems her lady just died and her daughter recently married. Mama says she's strong and eager."

"We had Bud Barnes in our jail a time or two before he, as you so eloquently put it, 'lit out' of Beaufort."

Rita smiled back and settled a hand on her stomach. "Becca's thrilled with the idea of having some children to look after and can live in for as long as you need her. I've got her number here."

"I told you to fix things. I'm merely the homeowner. Don't pay any attention to me."

Rita swatted his forearm. "You stop that right now. You may be older than I am, but you're acting like a mean-spirited child. This will be good for everyone."

Clay returned to the long windows. "Have you ever sailed?"

"Sure," Rita said, coming up beside him. "Tadie used to take me on *Luna* all the time."

"Then you know what 'sailing to weather' means."

"Heading into the wind?"

"And you know that trying to go into the wind is the hardest point of sail. You have to tack back and forth to get to the place you want, whether it's around the buoy in a race or back home after a day out. I've got to do that most of the time when I sail out of this creek, when the wind is like it is today." He pointed out to the mouth of the creek. "You see those markers, how the waves are coming straight in that narrow channel? When the weather builds, it's no easy trick to tack through that."

"What are you getting at?" She stared with him at water riled slightly by a southwesterly wind.

"I'm presenting you with a simile. All this finagling with my house and my comfort feels like being on a boat in big winds, pointing to weather. I'm thinking really heavy weather. We're slogging into some rough seas and fierce winds."

"That last was a metaphor."

"Rita."

She grinned. "Sorry."

"See if you can make the process relatively painless for all of us, will you? No wrecks?"

"I'm doing my best. Just tighten the lines, Clay. Your boat can handle it."

"You need to go home, girl."

She laughed as she reached up to give his cheek a quick kiss. "You're an old softie, you know that, you foolish man? It's going to be fine. More than fine."

23 ROY

Roy sat on Pete's miserable excuse for a bed and tossed an empty beer can in the direction of an overloaded bucket. It bounced off the other cans and rolled a few feet before coming smack up against a wall. He was sick and tired of this pigsty of Pete's. He'd been trying to come up with a plan to get into Beaufort unnoticed, but first he had to find out where they'd stashed Katie. Seems he hadn't finished off Annie Mac after all, but so far Pete hadn't been able to get any updates except she wasn't at the local hospital.

So, okay. Somebody had Katie, but who? It wasn't Annie Mac's old man or her sad excuse for a mother. Those two were a piece of work. He'd seen them one day when he, Annie Mac, and the kids had stopped for lunch at King's Barbecue in Kinston on their way somewhere. He didn't rightly remember where. Anyway, they'd come in, him prancing in a fancy suit, her all starched at his side. Annie Mac had pointed them out. And yeah, he'd tried to convince her to get on over to their table, introduce him and the kids. Make amends so maybe they'd share some of that banker's income with their only daughter. She was married now. She had a legitimate kid. Wouldn't they want to meet their grandbaby?

Annie Mac wouldn't hear of it. That woman was the stubbornest piece of flesh he'd ever run up against. And bossy? Wanted to take away his beer, make him keep his feet off the furniture, make him dress right, eat right, do right. He was well rid of her.

Roy's head fell forward into his palms. He was so tired.

But he had to fix things. He had to get Katie and then go to Rachel. Bring Rachel. Find Rachel. Hold Rachel.

Rachel had peace tucked up inside her, like a whisper on the wind. There she was. He could almost see her. He could hear her, "Shhh, it'll be okay. Okay..." Her croon came to him.

And he lay back on the bed and slept.

He woke stiff and sore a couple of hours later. Kicking off his boots, he pushed an old chair over so he could rest his feet. Phew! He'd better get those socks clean or find himself a new pair. If a man couldn't stand the stink of his own socks, they weren't fit to wear.

He'd better stop thinking about Rachel until he finished his business here. Dreaming of Rachel only made him ache, and aching was just a distraction.

Pete was a good man. He'd driven by Annie Mac's house, but there hadn't been any kids, only a plumber's truck, probably fixing that sink.

If Roy could figure out a disguise, he'd borrow Pete's car, drive around looking. They couldn't have gone far, not in a town the size of Beaufort. But it wouldn't do any good to go there and get himself caught.

A shriek curdled the night air. Roy shivered, remembering what Pete had said first time he'd questioned that horrific scream.

"It's only a cat."

"What kind of cat makes a noise like that?"

"Cougar. Lots to eat around here. You be real careful going out nights."

Roy had been. Real careful. Quick trips to the outhouse with a flashlight and his gun was all. Pete didn't stay much overnight, which, after his first night trying to sleep, Roy'd understood. He wouldn't hang here either if he had a better place in town.

That was the price of things, Roy figured. You had your fun and you paid the price. One good thing? He hadn't left Annie Mac fit for any other man. Nope, her getting it from anyone else was gonna be a long time coming. He couldn't help but grin at the mess he'd made of her face. She wasn't pretty no more.

But now he needed a plan. Too bad school hadn't started yet. What was it? A week of summer left? Maybe if he lay low for a while longer, he could snatch his girl during recess when she started at that school. The kids played right outside where you could see them. And he was pretty sure Annie Mac said she'd be sending Katie to pre-kindergarten this year.

That little sweetheart was going to be real happy to see her daddy again.

He wandered out to the front porch, kept the lights off, and listened. It was safe long as he stayed close to the house. Only you couldn't hear many birds, late like this. Sometimes an owl. Daytime though? Especially mornings? Rowdy things got the day stirring, they did.

Could make a fellow feel real good, hearing those birds chatter. He'd been leaving a bit of bread out, some seeds Pete had brung him, and he'd gotten a few eager ones to come near the porch. One day he'd have a big feeder again, a couple for him and Katie and Rachel. Wouldn't his girls be tickled pink when he set them up?

Pretty things, birds, some with lots of color, some plain, but smart and friendly, like the pair of doves he'd had back when he was a boy. Doves didn't turn on each other like Annie Mac had turned on him. No, sirree. He'd loved those birds, until the day he'd found them gone, the door open, their cage empty. Never did find out who'd opened that door.

The next morning, Pete showed up in his fancy car, followed by an old green Chevy. He climbed out, waved the Chevy's driver up next to him, and waited as the other man turned off the car, got out, and handed Pete the keys.

"Got you some wheels," Pete called. "Belonged to a fellow who couldn't pay his bills."

Roy walked down to meet his buddy. "That's real friendly of you. Might be able to do a little reconnoitering on my own this way."

Pete dropped the keys in Roy's hand, motioned the other man to the passenger side of the 'vette, and climbed behind the wheel. "Got enough gas for one trip. Figure you can manage to fill it up."

"Sure can."

Roy watched as Pete turned and sped out down the drive. Then he examined the Chevy. Yes, sir. He could find himself a little cash. After all, he had a gun.

He felt his smile grow. A little cash. A gun. And a way to get his baby.

Life was lookin' good.

24 HANNAH

It was one of those crystalline days when the silvered blue of the sky slid into the water with a light so intense it almost blinded Hannah. She hid behind her sunglasses and opened the van's storage area, pointing Tadie toward the creek. "You just go take a look at that water. I'll do the heavy lifting."

"Don't be silly. Give me that." Tadie took a bag of towels and headed toward the deck. "Lands, Hannah, can't you just see those two falling in love with this place?"

"They will. Anyone would."

Rita came down the deck steps. "I can carry something. You all come meet Becca Barnes. Mrs. Barnes," she called to the big woman following her, "that's Hannah and Tadie."

Mrs. Barnes patted her tight gray curls. "Pleased to meet you both." She reached for the bags Hannah carried, leaving her free to retrieve two more. "Where'd you hide those two babies?"

"With Tadie's husband and daughter. Want to get things ready first."

"Rita said you got toys and books they like. That'll be welcoming, sure enough."

"We've set up the second guest room for the children," Rita said, leading the way inside and down the short hall. In the bedroom, she pointed to the single bed on the left. "Fitted a rubberized mattress pad on that one."

"I brought some extra twin sheets," Hannah said.

"You all don't worry yourselves about that child." Mrs. Barnes took the sheets from Hannah and put them away in a closet. "A lot of loving, some peace, and she'll quit just fine on her own. My nephew? My sister got him some Superman trainers and said she didn't think Superman would want pee on him. Stopped the boy cold."

"Mrs. Barnes, you're a treasure." Rita grinned. "Come on, Hannah, I'll help you bring in the rest."

As they unpacked and tucked away toys, clothes, and books, Rita held up two new pairs of stretchy knit capris. "Good idea. Who thought of these?"

"I did," Tadie said. "They were comfortable when I started showing, so I figured a smaller size might work over her cast."

"You seen Clay's room yet?" Hannah asked.

Tadie crossed the large living space to check it out. "Whoa. Look at that bathroom, and he has access to the deck."

"Too bad the creek's got such skinny water, probably not much deeper than a couple of feet in places." Rita stared out the French doors. "But it would be good for kayaking and bird watching. And there's that dock for crabbing."

"He has a Sunfish," Hannah said. "I didn't know Clay sailed."

Tadie came up behind her. "I knew he used to race."

"Did you get a close look at this kitchen?" Rita poked into the cupboards. "The more I see of the place, the more interesting a person Clay becomes. Hard to picture a policeman living here by himself."

Mrs. Barnes worked in the background, putting away the food they'd bought, things Clay wasn't likely to stock, like cereal and peanut butter. "High-end living," Rita called Clay's larder, full of fine spices and condiments. "Seems the man likes good food, only not your run of the mill children's fare."

"Fine place this is," Mrs. Barnes said. "And my room's cozy, the way I like it. Miss Hannah, you thank your husband for the bed in there."

"Our rollaway?"

"No, ma'am. I got me a nice bed with a good mattress. Mr. Clay said that's where it had come from, your husband, so I just want him to know I'm grateful."

Tadie joined them. "Annie Mac has them reading some fun books, but if those two are anything like Jilly, those neatly organized shelves in their room will be chaos after one day." She spoke to Mrs. Barnes. "Do you have everything you need?"

"I do. And I've got it all tucked away so it won't bother the lieutenant none."

"He's being a bit of a bear about all this," Rita said, "but I think it's for show."

"We'll see." Mrs. Barnes wiped down the sink. "I aim to make them all happy."

Rita gave her a hug. "If anyone can do it, you can, Mrs. Barnes."

"Thank you, honey. Now, you all feel free to call me Becca. Anything you want."

Hannah nodded. "And you call us by our given names, too."

"Thank you, Miss Hannah."

"That's settled then," Rita said. "How do you want us to introduce you to the children?"

"You just go on as you did. Mrs. Barnes to start. It helps with politeness. The babies and I will fix things ourselves, once they get to know me. If I'm workin' for folk, sometimes it's best to stay a tad formal, you know what I mean? Works both ways."

It tugged on Hannah's heart to do so, but she took the children out to see the place after dinner. "You can't stay yet. But I thought you might like to check out your bedroom."

Ty kept his focus on the road. As Katie hummed something around her thumb, the words in Hannah's head kept time with the tune.

The kids will be fine. The world will be fine. You can do it, you can ... you can ...

She bit her lip to keep from speaking the mantra aloud. She just had to get through the leaving. Get through the next few days.

"Okay!" She kept her smile bright and her voice full of enthusiasm. "We're here."

As she opened the back door of the van, Harvey wiggled his way out.

"Whoa," Ty called, lunging after the dog.

Hannah caught Harvey's collar. "Definitely obedience school for you."

"Can I come, too?" Ty's eyes sparkled as he tightened up on the leash.

"May I. Remember?" She was probably wasting her time, trying to teach nuances to someone who wasn't likely to think of the difference ever again. Oh, well. What did it matter, really?

It didn't matter. None of it mattered.

She spoke to herself. "Repeat after me: it doesn't matter. It's fine. Everything will be fine."

The whispered words fell against the van hood as she circled to unhook Katie from her car seat. Still, Ty had heard. "What? Huh?"

Hannah waved behind her. "Nothing. Just hang onto Harvey, okay?"

"I'm sorry."

That stopped her. "Why?"

"'Cause I should have said, 'May I.' You know, may I come with you to train Harvey?"

This was killing her. Now she'd made that sweet boy feel guilty.

She lifted Katie out and turned her best smile in Ty's direction. "If you'd really like to help, I'd be thrilled, but it will be up to your mama. Harvey might mind you better."

"He does pretty good with me, doesn't he?"

"Yes, he does very well with you. Sometimes." There she went again, correcting him. Couldn't she get over herself and let well enough alone?

She glanced at him, but this time he didn't seem to notice.

Good.

Harvey barked when he heard footsteps and yanked Ty forward.

"Hey!" Clay bent to pet Harvey, whose hind end wiggled and whose whine showed how thrilled he was.

"You'd think we'd been abusing that dog," Hannah said, "the way he's going on."

Clay laughed. "He likes me."

"Obviously."

Clay offered his hand to Ty. "Glad to see you."

Ty hesitated only a moment before shaking the outstretched hand. "Yes, sir. Glad to see you, too."

"Hey, Katie," Clay said, though the child hid her face in Hannah's leg. "You want to come see my house?"

"Can ... um, may Harvey come inside?" Ty asked.

"I don't see why not. Let's go by way of the deck so you can take a look at the creek on the way in. The dock's off limits without an adult. You understand?"

"Yes, sir." Ty turned to his sister. "You hear, Katie? No goin' near the water."

"'kay."

Hannah and Katie followed a few paces behind the males. Katie didn't look nearly as excited as Ty, but that made two of them. "Look at the birds on the water, Katie," she said, with as much enthusiasm as she could muster. "And ducks. See the ducks?"

"Ducks." Katie took her thumb out long enough to enunciate and then plugged it back in, her free hand clutching Hannah's.

Hannah tightened her grip. Sweet little fingers. She felt a catch in her throat.

Harvey lunged toward the ducks. "Knock it off," Ty said, tightening the leash.

Clay laughed and patted his thigh as he climbed the stairs to the deck. "Come on, boy, up here." He ushered them inside where Becca stood at attention near the kitchen, waiting to meet them.

"Ty, Katie, this is Mrs. Barnes. She's going to be helping you and your mama when your mama gets out of the hospital tomorrow," Hannah said. "Can you say hello to her?"

"Hello."

"'Lo," echoed Katie.

"I'm mighty pleased to meet you both." The older woman's stillness surprised Hannah. Maybe it was that distance and respect thing. Or maybe she was waiting for the children to get used to her.

At Clay's nod, Hannah headed toward the guest rooms, keeping hold of Katie's hand as she showed off their mama's room. Two heads peered in and then up at her. It's okay, she wanted to say. It's okay to be happy. But she merely nodded and pointed to the second door. "And that will be your room."

Ty paused just inside. "Wow. My stuff's here." He dropped Harvey's lead and knelt on the carpet next to his bed to fondle the toys they'd salvaged and arranged, some action figures, a box of Legos. Katie let go of Hannah's fingers and sidled up next to her brother before wandering across the room to stare at her stuffed toys. Her patched-up doll's bed rested nearby. On the oval pine table between the beds, Rita had set up Katie's ballerina lamp. The mechanism for the ballerina hadn't worked since Roy's destructive visit, but with a new bulb at least the light functioned. Ty's lamp, a more masculine wooden one, had been too strongly built to break from a mere toss to the floor. They'd placed it on the desk at the foot of his bed. Katie climbed up and pressed her face into her stuffed animal collection. Ty stopped in the middle of making machine noises with his figurines to look around. "You got my books," he said and crawled over to finger them.

"You want more, we'll go back to the library," Hannah said. "Any time."

"Thanks. Thanks so much." The crack in the boy's voice went right to that overly sensitive spot in Hannah, the one that felt like a bruised rib.

She sucked it up and smiled at Clay who'd come up behind her. "Ty, as you can tell, likes to read." She edged out of the room. "Well, I think they'll settle in nicely. It's too bad Annie Mac isn't here tonight. I imagine they'd opt to stay if she were. Harvey, too."

She doubted Clay even noticed the melancholy she tried to hide. As he gazed past her, his face held the same rapt expression she was sure she'd worn many times since meeting these two. So, her loss, his gain.

The scales would balance. Surely.

Becca had coffee brewing and a pitcher of sweet tea on the counter. "What can I get you two?"

"Hannah?"

"It's too late for caffeine for me. How about water?"

"Tea for me, Mrs. Barnes. Thank you."

Clay accepted the tea and headed toward the French doors, where he stared out at the fading sun. He turned as Hannah neared. "You women did a marvelous job. I'm very impressed."

"Thanks. I think they'll be happy here. And far enough away from your end of the house that they shouldn't be a bother."

He took a long drink. "How are you dealing with it all? Matt seemed worried when we talked."

"I'm fine. Really. Oh, I'll miss them. It's amazing how quickly they found a niche in my heart." She ran her fingers up and down her water glass and concentrated on the motion and the wet. "I suppose foster parents go through something similar, don't you think? Whenever some child comes and then goes?"

"I imagine so."

"And you, Clay? You're not as aloof as you pretend."

He coughed. "Excuse me."

She waited.

"Aloof?" He kept his eyes on the pale sunset when he finally spoke. "No, I'm not. Which, frankly, is why I didn't want them coming here."

When the children complained about leaving their things to return to Hannah's for the night, Clay told them to imagine this as Christmas Eve and tomorrow as the day they got their gifts. He and Mrs. Barnes would pick up their mama from the hospital and bring her home, and Hannah would drive them over so they'd all be together again.

"Won't that be fun?" Hannah's sticky smile stretched her lips to hurting.

That night, they took their baths and climbed into bed without a fuss. After all, the sooner they slept, the sooner tomorrow would come.

She found Matt in the den, one foot resting on his knee, his shoes discarded on the floor, and a glass of something in his hand as he punched the remote control to change channels. Hannah sank onto the couch next to him.

"Whatcha watching and whatcha drinking?" she asked, settling close.

"I'm between shows. And this?" He lifted his glass in salute. "I'm on my fifth glass of water today. Tell me I'm a good boy."

She poked him in the side. "A very good boy. The doctor will be happy."

"As long as you are, love, I am."

"Well, aren't you the cooperative one?"

He drew her toward him and kissed the top of her head. "How are you with all that's going on?"

She draped an arm around his chest and snuggled into his embrace. "Well, after tomorrow, it will be just us two again."

"You okay with that?"

"Mmm. We have a good life, don't we?"

"Yes, we have. But you know, you want to make any changes, anything that will make you happier, I'm game. You know that."

Hannah couldn't help it, she started sniffling.

"Hey, I didn't mean to make you cry."

"I know. You're just so good to me."

"I love you, Mrs. Morgan. You mean the world to me."

"Oh, Matt, take me to bed, will you? I want you to make mad, passionate love to me."

"Honey, I'm your man." He laughed as he lifted her chin and kissed her soundly. "You hustle on up those stairs, and I'll turn out the lights down here."

She was showering when a hand reached in to push back the curtain. The hand was followed by a naked body. "Hello, there," she said with a grin of pleasure.

He took the soap from her and began rubbing it down her back, sending tingles of sensation wherever he touched.

"Twenty years and still going strong, eh?" Her voice held a slight tremor in response to his hands curved over her hips.

"Still thinking how beautiful you are. As lovely as the day I first saw you."

"Flatterer." She spoke in a mere whisper as his nimble fingers slipped to her breasts. "Ah, Matt, that feels so good."

"Age teaches a few things, doesn't it?"

The warm water beat down upon them. She turned in his arms. "And you, sir, have learned them well.

25 ANNIE MAC

The gravel crunched under the Jeep's tires as they drove down the lane leading to the lieutenant's house. Propped on pillows in the back seat, Annie Mac had felt each jolt like a pin in the voodoo doll of her body.

Mrs. Barnes sat up front next to the lieutenant. It pleased Annie Mac that the woman was so big and motherly, so protective. She hadn't said much on the drive from the hospital, but she'd been attentive, reminding Annie Mac of a queen-sized Auntie Sim with close-cropped, tight, grayish curls, oversized hands and feet, and a face that had seen a lot of laughter.

Annie Mac noticed the fields first, drying stalks of corn, some sort of bean ready for harvest, then pine woods, and finally a cedar-shingled house. Fronting this—or backing it, depending on how you looked at things—was a bay-like body of water. She couldn't quite believe the expanse of it and had trouble paying attention to anything other than the view as Mrs. Barnes and the lieutenant helped her out of the backseat and into a wheelchair with her leg extended in front. They hefted her up the deck steps, said it would be easier than coming through the garage or in the front.

So, he thought of the deck as being at the back of the house. Good to know.

"Be right back," the lieutenant said, dangling his keys and heading toward that front door.

"Oh, my," she whispered.

They were awfully close to that water, and her children didn't swim. She'd really have to trust Mrs. Barnes to keep an eye out because Ty was going to be mighty tempted by that little boat. Not to mention the dock.

Mrs. Barnes spoke from beside her. "It's something, isn't it?"

"I had no idea."

They wheeled her down the hall so she could look into what would be their rooms: the graceful bed with its tall posts and clean lines where she'd sleep, a hoist ready and waiting for her; the twin beds decorated with children's toys and stuffed animals, their books neatly organized. Someone had even thought to bring the lamps and comforters from their room at home.

"You ready to get in bed, Ms. Rinehart, or you want to go get in the lieutenant's big chair out there?"

"Do you mind if I spend some time in the recliner? There's so much to see, and I'm really very tired of beds."

Watching as the lieutenant gave last minute instructions to Mrs. Barnes before he returned to work, Annie Mac sighed. She couldn't believe she was actually here. In a place like this, which had absolutely nothing in common with the pictures she'd conjured of a policeman's home. The white walls showed off a hanging rug of some sort, bold geometrics in red and black with slashes of a burnt orange. It looked American Indian. A rug covered much of the oak flooring in a complementary pattern and colors, though it added blue into the mix. Earthy, beautiful. The bookcases were full, the furniture all man-sized and leather like this chair.

She ran her fingers over the tan hide, so soft it felt like velvet. A slight turn of her head and she could see out the glass windows and door. She'd even be able to watch the wildlife.

She wondered what sort of animals wandered through the property. Deer perhaps? Rabbits? Wouldn't it be fun to spot a fox? She'd never seen one except in pictures.

And what kinds of birds flew here? Maybe there was a bird book someplace so she could study them. She bet the lieutenant had a pair of binoculars.

And then another memory flashed of binoculars and birds and Roy. He'd loved anything winged. Really, it had seemed so endearing and had drawn her to him in the beginning, when he'd first taught her to appreciate things that flew. She'd loved watching him try to teach Katie birds' names when she was too little to say more than "birdie."

But that had been before.

And, no, she wasn't going to let thoughts of Roy keep her from bird watching. It wasn't the birds' fault he liked them.

She glanced around, checking the table tops and bookshelves, spying binoculars on the second shelf. Next time Mrs. Barnes came in the room, she'd ask her to fetch them. Maybe see if the chair could swivel.

The lieutenant had said he might have to work late, so they could go on and enjoy dinner without him. That was good. She looked across the great room, squinting at his door and gauging the distance from where she sat to where he slept. It really was on the other side of the house. *Way* past the fireplace and seating area.

She'd never been in a house with a room that opened up like this one, so you could see the view from everywhere instead of having rooms lined up off a hall like in most Beaufort houses. Auntie Sim's little house had one living room with a dining area off it, a small kitchen, three small bedrooms, and two bathrooms. It had been fine for them until she'd let Roy in.

This place? This was like going on vacation somewhere she'd never be able to afford. Maybe Auntie Sim had put in a good word with God for her, fixing it so they landed in such luxury. Only a couple of weeks ago, she'd been in the pit of hell, and now she was going to be here with her babies until she got well enough to move on. Had to be some sort of something at work—magic or God— because she certainly hadn't gained access due to good behavior.

She heard the dog bark and Ty's chatter before she saw them. Doggy nails clattered up the deck steps. Ty popped into view at the far end of a leash, practically dragged by a huge Irish Setter. The woman she'd given her babies to, Mrs. Morgan, clomped up with Katie on her hip, Katie's short legs kicking out like she was saying "Giddy up!" to a horse. Mrs. Morgan just held on and smiled.

"Mama!" Ty called, dropping the leash as he bounded through the door and into her arms.

"Ty-baby. Sweet boy." Annie Mac pulled him close in spite of the twinges in her chest. She ran her hands through his clean, sweet-smelling hair, pressed them to his cheeks. "Let me look at you. Oh, my, you've had a haircut. Aren't you the handsome one?"

"Mama!" Katie lunged out of Mrs. Morgan's arms, almost dropping Agatha in her rush to be there. Fortunately, Mrs. Morgan caught both her and the doll and set them gently on Annie Mac's lap when Annie Mac opened an arm toward them.

"Hey, baby. Come on and sit right here on Mama's lap. How's my little one today? And here's Agatha, all safe and sound."

Katie patted her mama's good cheek and snuggled against her. "Mama," she said, a sigh of contentment on her lips.

Mrs. Barnes came in with a bag of clothes and carried them on through to the children's room. "I set the car seat in the garage, Miss Hannah. I think that's about everything."

"Thank you, Becca."

Annie Mac hadn't known Mrs. Barnes's first name. She wondered if she'd be allowed to use it. Probably not, considering the lieutenant called her Mrs. Barnes. Maybe it had to do with employer/employee relations.

Ty slipped out from her encircling arm. "Mama, did you see our room? All our stuff's there."

"I saw it. Aren't you going to have fun?"

"Can I—I mean, may I go play?"

Well, look at that? Had Mrs. Morgan taught him the word to use? Another thing on the debit scale for Annie Mac: failed teacher, and she with a degree in education.

"I think you have something to say to Mrs. Morgan, don't you?"

Ty turned sheepishly, his hands rubbing down the sides of his shorts. "Thank you for letting us stay with you. It was real fun."

"You're very welcome, Ty. We loved having you and your sister at our house."

"Can Harvey come play with me sometime?" He looked at his mother and back again. "Do you think he could?"

"I don't see why not. Maybe you can watch him for me occasionally. If I have to go somewhere."

"Oh, could I? Could I, Mama?"

"If it's okay with Lieutenant Dougherty. This is his house, remember."

Mrs. Morgan laughed. "Clay won't mind. He and Harvey are great friends."

"O-kay!" Ty said. "Thanks, that'll be swell. You bring him over any time you need me. And maybe I can come see him at your house. You know, to help with that obedience stuff."

"I'll count on it. Now, I guess I'd better get him on home, let you settle in with your mother." She bent to collect Harvey's leash as Ty fled to his room. "Come on, fellow, time to go. No, you can't follow Ty."

Annie Mac spoke to her daughter. "Katie, honey? You need to thank Mrs. Morgan, too. She's been very nice to you both, hasn't she? Taking care of you and letting you stay in her lovely home?"

Katie nodded, clutched Agatha closer, and said, "Thank you for being nice. I like your house."

"Oh, sweetie." Mrs. Morgan grinned at Katie. "You're very welcome. I'm glad you're back with your mother, and you're all going to be fine."

The other woman glanced toward the space Ty had occupied and then back at Katie with what sure seemed like longing. Annie Mac reached out a hand. "I don't know how to thank you. You've done so much, you and Mr. Morgan. I will never forget it."

"We won't forget you either. It's been wonderful having your children with us. You've done a great job with them. They're darlings." She swiped at her eyes, and laughed at herself. "I fell a bit in love with them, I have to admit. We'll miss them, Matt and I."

"Mrs. Morgan, please, if there's ever anything I can do to repay you, not only for taking care of these two, but for the house, for arranging things...."

"Well, you could start by calling me Hannah. This Mrs. Morgan stuff makes me feel ancient." Mrs. Morgan—Hannah—wiped at another tear, but her smile seemed to loosen. "You have to realize your children have been calling me Miss Hannah since we met."

"They have? I'm sorry. I taught them better."

"I didn't give them a choice. I introduced myself as Hannah, and they added the Miss to make it polite." Her hands stayed clasped, almost as if she were fighting the urge to reach out to Katie, before she turned her focus back to Annie Mac. "When you're well again, Matt and I would love to have all three of you come for dinner. Let you see where your children spent some time."

"I'd like that. Thank you. And perhaps you'll visit us here, while I'm waiting for my leg to get free of this weight? I think Ty would like it especially if you brought your dog back. I don't know how we'll live without one now."

"I'll be happy to share Harvey. Any time." Hannah tugged the animal in question up off the floor. "I know you don't want to leave, but leave you must. Come on."

Annie Mac went back to snuggling Katie as the door closed. She'd known Hannah was kind, hadn't she? When Ty had gone on and on about the dog and the house and what they were eating and learning. Ah, but now her precious ones were back with her.

Where they belonged, even if the where of their staying was not home... and was just a little odd. She'd have to see what happened next and try her best not to worry about that until she needed to. For now, she was determined to enjoy this little bit of luxury before she had to slip them all back into a very different reality.

26 CLAY & ANNIE MAC

Clay turned the Jeep out onto Cedar Street. His suddenly full house meant another body ruled in his—emphasis on *his*—kitchen. Maybe Mrs. Barnes cooked well, but she wasn't asking him for the menu, was she? If he went home now, he'd be faced with their leftovers or with having to start from scratch, while all those other bodies would glance sideways at him. What he needed was a little time and a lot of distance between him and his houseguests. Let them get settled in and find a routine that didn't include him.

He pulled into the Chinese place just down from the Piggly Wiggly. Six weeks. Or at most eight. That was all. He could endure anything for eight weeks, and maybe by then they'd have captured Roy.

The news wasn't good from those still searching. The man seemed to have vanished. Could be he'd become gator food.

The weather had cooled enough for Clay to eat his Kung Pao Chicken with his car windows open. He wished he weren't so spoiled. The truth was, he liked his own cooking or his mama's a whole lot more than he liked most others'. He didn't mind eating out when there was a chef worthy of the name, but this place was not on that short list. Dining out alone made him self-conscious, sitting at a table set for two, the only single person there. He'd tried the Front Street Grill with friends. The food was great, but it wasn't the kind of place where he could go for a quick bite. He'd gone to Aqua three times, once with a date. It was too intimate a place to take a woman he didn't really want to pursue.

Aqua would fit right in as a New York restaurant. Hadn't he had some feasts in that city, on vacation to see the museums, the sights. Tadie'd been the one to convince him to go, told him about the incredible food. Hannah had chimed in with her own stories of food delivered to the door.

Still, food was food when the holes need filling. And sitting here used up some of the time he wanted behind him, time for Mrs. Barnes to get the mother settled, the children in bed.

The dark roads were nearly empty as he headed east. By the time he'd reached his drive, the moon was on the point of rising. Almost full, it cast a glow over the marshes and the water. He turned off his headlights at the creek's edge and paused to listen to the nocturnal cacophony that one could hear when people noises ceased.

Light blazed from the large windows of his house. How odd to come home to lit rooms. The doors were locked as he'd instructed, and he let himself in quietly. Mrs. Barnes sat alone in the great room, knitting, low music playing from his stereo. An aria by Puccini.

"Ah, Lieutenant." She folded her needles and rose as he entered. "I hope you don't mind me listenin' to some of this you had on the player. It soothes a body."

"It's good to come home to a house lit and welcoming."

"The children are down for the night. Miss Annie said she'd be readin' one of your books. I fetched her a pile to choose from. And you should be knowin' that those children don't swim." She angled her head toward the water and waited.

"We'll have to see about that."

His answer elicited a smile and a nod. "Is there anything else you'd be wanting?"

"No, thanks, I'm fine. I'll see you in the morning."

He watched her amble to her room off the front of the house before he filled a glass with water and picked up the book he'd been reading. He felt a bit like Papa Bear whose chair had been moved slightly to the left. He fiddled with the position so that it faced into the room instead of out into the black night and settled down to read a few chapters.

And there he sat, turning pages without taking in a single word. It must be all those people filling his house. A stranger lay beyond the wall at his head. Her bed faced that wall, so if he turned, they could be looking at each other if the wall were invisible. It made the back of his neck itch.

Was she sleeping yet or still reading? Had she heard him come in? What was she thinking?

And the children. What if they woke in the night and were afraid? Their mother couldn't help them. Who would hear them? He'd be all the way on the other side of the house.

Annie Mac lay awake, listening. He'd spoken to Mrs. Barnes. Then there'd been a scraping sound, probably the recliner moving. Which of his books would he read, this police lieutenant who was so kind to them?

Who sat just on the other side of the wall from where she lay, helpless. Unable to lock her door. Unable to go to her children if they needed her.

She should ask Rita to bring a monitor so Mrs. Barnes could hear the children. It wasn't safe, no grown-up woman near enough to help.

What if the lieutenant wasn't as nice as he seemed? What if, in reality, he was like Roy … or worse?

It sounded as if he were getting up. Why? It wasn't likely to be his bedtime yet.

She tensed, waiting, ready to scream bloody murder if she heard his footsteps in the hall. This wasn't going to work. She could tell right now she'd never be able to get any sleep. She'd been stupid to agree to move in here. She was too vulnerable. Her children were too vulnerable. Mrs. Barnes might be large enough to take him on, but he could still murder them all without her knowing a thing about it until he'd finished.

And death wasn't the worst thing he could do to her babies.

What had she opened them up to now? She'd been a fool again. Unthinking. Believing what she was told.

He was coming. Those were his footsteps. Should she scream now or wait until she heard footsteps on the wooden floor?

Clay stood at the hall entrance and listened. The lights were off in the bedrooms, but a night-light burned in the hall bath. All was quiet. He waited a few moments, then hit the switch by his chair and wandered into his bedroom.

The shower soothed his tired body. He stood in the glass-enclosed area, leaning forward, one hand on the tiled wall until the water cooled, as he willed his mind to empty.

This was going to be a very long six weeks. All he could see ahead were lumpy seas, with him more prone to seasickness than he'd been in a long time.

27 ROY

Pete kicked the stray hound in its hind quarter, laughing as it yelped and limped off the front porch. Roy watched through the screen door from a corner where he lounged on Pete's second-best bed, a rickety thing with sheets that hadn't seen a washer in months. The place had the look of neglect, one that Pete and his brother Jocko fostered. Around back, though, and through a bit of swampy muck and forest, Pete and Jocko had their little lab where they made enough chicken feed to drive the whole of Carteret plumb crazy.

Roy didn't use the stuff himself. Didn't trust it not to kill him. But old Pete sold what he and Jocko made to folk who liked to zone out, all types these days, even some in-town lawyers, if you could believe Pete.

You'd have thought it would take more smarts to fix up a meth lab, but it seemed almost anyone could do it, according to these two. Anyway, it paid the bills and let Pete keep a right decent place off Ann Street in town. The shack was for nights one of them worked the lab, but Roy figured they used it for other things they didn't want known. It was serving his purpose. He just hoped he wouldn't need it for much longer.

Pete set a couple of bags down and put a kettle on the filthy stove. "Brought you some cans of chili. 'Bout outta stuff around here."

"Thanks."

"Found your girl."

"Annie Mac?"

"No, the tyke."

That got Roy up. "Katie? Where is she?"

"You won't believe this." He turned his skinny face in Roy's direction. "They're all staying with some police lieutenant."

"You gotta be kidding."

Pete shook his head. "Nope. A buddy of mine's married to the sister of one of the officers."

"Pete, you walk on water."

Pete laughed a little hysterically. Roy wondered how much he'd used today.

"So who's this lieutenant, and where does he live?"

"I haven't got that bit yet. The buddy's wife only overheard the reference to a lieutenant. No name. And she didn't want to ask, so it wouldn't look like she was eavesdropping."

"I need to find out."

"I know you do. I'm working on it. All I've got to do is find out how many lieutenants are in Beaufort. Can't be a whole lot, little place like that. I'm thinking one, unless everybody got promoted the same day." Pete headed to the door. "I'll bring you news soon's I have it. And what stuff you need."

"More birdseed would be good."

"Don't be surprised if Jocko shows up."

Roy listened as the car backed out the drive. He sure hoped he wouldn't have to see Pete's brother. As a boy, Jocko had been big and stupid. Growed, he seemed to have even fewer cells in his brain cavity. Muscles, though? A person didn't want to rile Jocko.

Roy's blood heated as he thought how close he was getting to Katie. No police lieutenant or anybody else was going to keep him from his baby girl. No, sir, not this time.

His daddy hadn't done right by him, but he'd do right by Katie if it killed him.

That made him cringe a little. "All right. I know."

The walls didn't make particularly good company, so he went out to sit on the stoop. Leastways, he could sprinkle the last of the seed he had on hand.

He oughtn't to have touched her that way, his own baby. It hadn't been right. But it had just come to him at the moment, and there he was, doing it.

It was on account of him watching that movie the night before. Annie Mac hadn't been much interested in fooling around. Not for a long time. And there he was, up late. He never used to watch things like that, but it had gotten him thinking.

Well, not thinking really. It had just stuck in the back of his mind, and then he'd found himself off work early.

"All right, I was fired. I admit it. But it wasn't for anything real. A stupid misunderstanding."

Much as he'd like to forget it, he remembered that day, the last time he'd held his baby girl. The house had been empty when he got home, so he'd thought to head to the neighbor's to pick up Katie, have a little alone time with her. Maybe feed the birds together.

"You hear?" he said to the robin pecking at the edge of his scattered seed. "I didn't mean nothing."

She'd had to pee, but her overalls were caught, so he'd helped her. Then it had just happened.

A guy messed up. Nobody was perfect, least of all Miss Self-Righteous Mother-of-the-Year Annie Mac. The way she used to rile him! On purpose, it seemed.

Now look at them. And he couldn't even get to his lovely Rachel.

Ever since Annie Mac had thrown him out for that one little mistake things had gone downhill. Well, not for him and Rachel, but for him and his baby.

"I know what you're thinking," he mumbled as he tossed a few more seeds in front of a greedy jay, "but I could have fixed it. I could've made it right if that woman had given me half a chance."

But she wouldn't. She hadn't. Then she'd tried to keep Katie away from him forever. That's what those papers had said. Forever. So Katie would never know her daddy.

That was *not* going to happen.

28 HANNAH

Hannah swept into Tadie's big country kitchen. "Get up off that couch, Mrs. Merritt. We've places to go and people to see."

Jilly danced up to Hannah, those cute little pigtails bouncing. "Who, where?"

"Ty asked for Harvey to come play, so we're going visiting."

Jilly hopped from one foot to the other, her attention focused on her semi-recumbent step-mother. "Can we, can we, Mommy? You're not doing anything."

Hannah raised a brow. "Tadie?"

Tadie brushed damp hair away from her face. "It's hot. I decided to veg out today."

Glancing around at the air-conditioned room, Hannah said, "Hot?" and intercepted a scowl.

"Fine." Tadie groaned as she raised her body up and off the couch. "I was trying to be creative earlier, fill up the jewelry case for Isa. I couldn't. I'm useless."

"Isa will cope. Come on. You can be useful to me."

With Jilly and Harvey settled in the back seat and Tadie riding shotgun, Hannah walked around to the driver's side and buckled in. It took her three tries before the key fit into the ignition, but finally it did, and the engine started, and she could back out onto Front Street.

She turned east, reminding herself that she was an adult and in control of her emotions. She could do this. But, Lord, have mercy, going out there, seeing those children with their mama, felt like a disaster in the making.

"What's up with you?" Tadie shifted her seatbelt strap off her belly.

"Nothing." Everything.

"Come on, Hannah. You're talking to me, your best friend. Let's have it."

She locked the nasties behind shuttered eyes because not even Tadie needed to know everything. Her best friend surely didn't need to see the jealousy that had its fist clamped on Hannah's heart. Maybe she could deflect Tadie's curiosity with this one thing. "Matt wants to take me to Europe."

"Matt? Matt wants to leave Beaufort and go out of the country?"

"That's what he said."

"He must be desperate."

That turned Hannah's head. She glared at her friend. A honk pulled her attention back to the now-clear road.

"Well, it's odd, isn't it? After all these years of being Mr. Stick-in-the-Mud?"

"He said we could go anywhere I wanted."

"And?"

"You know how I've longed to see Italy. Europe."

Jilly piped up with, "Can I come? I want to see Italy, too!"

Hannah laughed without humor. She tried to shape a real smile, at least.

Tadie shushed Jilly. "Not likely, missy. Not until we get this baby raised a bit."

"Oh, right." Jilly leaned back in her seat.

"And when, may I ask, is this trip supposed to take place?"

Hannah didn't look at her friend, but she could imagine Tadie's expression, haughty brows to go with her tone. "You know perfectly well I'm not leaving Beaufort until you've had that baby and we've stood up for its christening."

"You'd better not. I'm expecting some babysitting services, too. I think that goes under the godmother heading." Tadie angled toward the back seat. "Jilly, did you know that Auntie Hannah gets half of my half of this baby?"

"She does?"

"Well, that's what we decided when we were not much older than you are. We'd take turns with any children and share the good and the bad."

"Ahhh," Jilly said knowingly. "That means Auntie Hannah gets to change poopie diapers, doesn't it?" She giggled.

Hannah checked the rearview mirror until she caught Jilly's eye. "I'll let you take care of the diapers, how about that?"

"Me?"

"Yes, ma'am. After all, you're the big sister."

Red hair flapped from side to side. "No way. I'll rock her and help with the feeding stuff. Then I can teach her how to sail when she gets older."

Hannah's brows rose. "Do we know the gender? Something I've perhaps missed?"

"Jilly's hoping. We don't care which it is."

"Auntie Rita already knows she's having a boy. So it would only be fair if we got a girl, don't you think?"

"Whatever we have," Tadie said, "I'm going to need help. Will's got his head in some machinery design, and it feels like he's always on the computer. Matt can't take you anywhere right now, even if it would be good for you both."

"Not being at all selfish about this, are we?"

"I am. But I'm about to pop out a baby, and I'm scared. I need you to help hold my hand."

Hannah reached over. "I'll be there. You know I will."

Jilly sat as far forward as her seatbelt would allow and touched Tadie's shoulder. Hannah saw the small hand out the corner of her eye, saw Tadie reach up to press it. "I'll be there, too, Mommy," Jilly said. "I'll hold your hand."

"I know you will, sweetie. You're always good to me."

"So," Hannah said brightly, hoping to steer the conversation away from subjects that choked her—like holding someone else's baby, even if that someone else was Tadie. Hoping as well that her idea had merit—and that Tadie wouldn't ask any questions about motivations—she said, "I've been thinking. We need to rally 'round the fort here, maybe have a barbecue on Clay's deck. Bring the men and the food and prop Annie Mac up in that recliner."

"Doesn't that seem a bit pushy? Too much, too soon?"

Deep breath, keep the smile lit. "Think about it. Clay's bound to be hiding out, as paranoid as he is about women, and Annie Mac has to be feeling like a burden. Skittish would be my guess from what Rita's said. I figure we'll just change the dynamics. Show her that she and the children are part of the group and drag Clay out of his shell and his bedroom."

Tadie still looked uncertain. "I guess we could suggest it."

"And, Jilly, you and Harvey could be a big help in making them all feel at home."

"I'll be really nice to them," Jilly piped up from the back seat. "And Harvey will, too, right, Mommy?"

"Right, sweetie."

"Clay may be a policeman, but Annie Mac doesn't really know him. This has to be stretching her comfort zone."

"She did get railroaded into the whole thing, didn't she?"

"She did." Hannah turned the car into the long lane leading to the creek and the house. "Clay, too."

"In that case, do we make the plans and tell Clay when to show up, or do we ask him first?"

"Both." She hit the brakes and pointed at three deer who nibbled long weeds at the edge of the field. "You don't usually see them mid-day like this and hardly ever this time of year."

One raised its head and studied them. The other two continued foraging until the first bounded toward the trees.

"I love deer," Jilly said. "I got to pet one at the zoo once. My first mommy was with us. I was little."

"I bet that was fun," Tadie said.

Hannah picked up the conversation where she'd left it as she shifted back into gear. "We'll get Mrs. Barnes involved, see what Clay has to say. I can't think he'll object. After all, we're not asking him to cook. Though, on second thought, he may have a wonderful recipe he'd like to share."

"Okay, you talk to Mrs. Barnes and Clay, and—" Tadie stopped mid-thought. "You are going to include Rita and Martin, aren't you?"

"Rita's been in on this from the beginning."

"And Martin's a pediatrician. That should soothe her."

Hannah parked near the flagstone walkway that led to the deck. "It'll be fun. Jilly, honey, you take Harvey's lead, okay? Hold on tightly, so he doesn't run into the marsh. He'd get real stinky if he did."

"Yuck." Jilly unbuckled her seat belt before wrapping Harvey's leash twice around her wrist. "Let's go find Ty, boy."

Hannah knew what she had to do. It was just the doing that came so hard.

29 HANNAH

She rinsed her mug and added it to the dishwasher before filling the dispenser with soap. This was the first time she'd needed to run the thing in days.

Her eyes snapped closed on a wave of longing. Empty dishwasher, empty laundry hamper, empty rooms. Harvey sidled up and rubbed his snout against her thigh.

She scratched behind his ear. "I know, boy. I know." His whine felt familiar, but the house felt too silent. "Maybe..." But she couldn't finish the thought or actually say the words.

They'd walked west instead of east this morning, south instead of north. It had felt drippy enough for rain. Rain sounded like a good idea. Perhaps a storm was brewing out at sea.

She stared at the phone. She still hadn't called Clay.

She should have done it yesterday before Matt got home, but she'd dropped Tadie and Jilly off at their house after that lovely visit—really, it *had* been—with the children and Annie Mac, and then she'd raced up to her studio, flinging clay on the kneading board and pounding for all she was worth. Her stomach hadn't unknotted even with the physical abuse she gave her arms and hands, and before she'd finished, Matt had walked in the door, ready to take her out for dinner.

Lovely, lovely man. He'd treated her like a queen since the children had left, and she didn't mind it one bit, but sitting down to a meal at Aqua was not the time to let him know she was butting into their lives again.

She remembered breakfast. His words.

He'd sat across from her, shoveling in oatmeal and sipping his coffee. But he had done more staring than usual over his spoon or across the brim of his cup.

"What?" she'd finally asked.

"You keeping busy enough, with the house this quiet?"

Had he been reading her mind? "I'm trying to. Trying to get some work done. You know."

"Anything special for the kiln?"

"Focusing's hard."

He had reached across the table, lifting the fingers of one hand from her mug and rubbing gently across her knuckles. It took a minute or two before he'd spoken. "I was wondering... I mean... " His touch had tickled, but she hadn't wanted to interrupt and lose whatever was working its way out of his mouth. "What do you think," he finally said, "about filling it back up?"

Those were not the words she'd expected. "Filling what back up?" But as soon as she'd asked the question, she'd known. "You mean the house. A baby."

"Or a kid. Doesn't have to be a baby, does it?"

"I've been imagining. I just didn't know you had."

He'd drawn her fingers to his lips. "Think about it. We can resurrect those applications whenever you want."

With a sigh, she had pulled her hand back and used it to pick up her spoon. Unwilling to commit to anything, she'd kept silent.

At the door, they had kissed—a good kiss, a healthy, solid, so-glad-I'm-married-to-you kiss—and now she tried to pull herself together as she cleaned up the kitchen. What, actually, did she want?

Besides Ty and Katie.

Stop it.

Yeah, well, easier said than done. She tried to will herself into a constructive attitude—or at least a positive one. That was what the gathering at Clay's was supposed to be about, wasn't it? A shift in attitudes, rah-rah, the gang's all here?

She picked up the phone, waited for Clay to answer, and told him their plans.

"You want to do *what?*"

"It'll be good, Clay. You'll see."

He didn't answer for a few seconds. "I don't think Ms. Rinehart will welcome this. You ought to just let her recover."

"You know, Clay, you probably ought to call her Annie Mac. Everyone else does." Hannah paused as something occurred to her. "Have you avoided going home evenings? She enjoys company."

"It's easier."

"She won't bite."

"Yeah, well, I'm sure she's afraid I will."

"That's absurd. You're both grown-ups."

"Don't patronize me, Hannah."

She stuck her tongue out. Too bad he couldn't see the gesture. "This party sounds like just the ticket to help you break down some of those walls."

A deep sigh sounded as if he'd aimed it at the phone. Hannah could picture him trying to come up with a good reason why she should leave well enough alone.

"According to Mrs. Barnes," he said, "Ms. Rinehart—okay, Annie Mac—has had to take meds to sleep at night. I'm pretty sure a party will be too much, too soon. Way too soon."

"Not true. The distraction will do her a world of good. Besides, she needs to get to know you."

"You think?"

"Funny." She would not let him irritate her. "The way I see it, your badge is bound to intimidate her. She's a victim; you're a cop. We're hoping to help her feel like part of a group of friends, some of whom happen to be really great men. Might make you feel more comfortable, too."

"Don't start with me. I just want my house back."

"I know."

"You're sure a pushy woman, Hannah Morgan. Matt needs to rein you in."

"He likes me the way I am."

"Well, I don't."

"Oh, come on, Clay. Be a sport."

She heard mumbling. Perhaps he was cursing at the walls so he wouldn't ruin his saintly reputation over the phone. She waited.

"Fine," he said. "Have a barbecue. I'll supply the house."

His tone made her want to laugh aloud. She stifled it. "It'll be fun. Wait and see."

"Hah."

She'd gotten her way, and maybe, just maybe, party planning would help her corral thoughts better left unthought.

She'd been prepared to dislike Annie Mac, to blame her for exposing those sweet children to Roy and making them cringe. But in getting to know the woman, even slightly, she'd seen someone she might actually like.

Maybe liking her would dispel the jealousy that had raised its ugly head again yesterday at the sight of Katie in Annie Mac's arms. She'd likely burn if she didn't shed such an ugly emotion. Here Annie Mac was, mauled and broken and facing penury, and here she was, healthy and with more personal wealth than she deserved. She should be ashamed. She *was* ashamed.

If only a magic wand could wave away nasty emotions. It was fine to tell her heart to cease and desist, but it never obeyed. Maybe the party would help.

And maybe she'd grow a new head.

Okay. Deep breath.

Matt would welcome the festivities now that Clay had agreed. They were going to fix a great dinner, all of them. And have fun, all of them.

All of them. Having Ty and Katie in their home had proved she and Matt could cherish a child not of their own conception, but those two were definitely one-offs, the darlings. Only, not hers. Never hers.

The idea of bringing home a child who wouldn't fit, who'd be hard to love, had made them shy away last time. Could she—they—risk such a possibility now?

30 CLAY

Frustration continued to clog Clay's path to rational thought. He combed fingers through his hair as he leaned back in his desk chair and listened to thunder rumbling offshore. New flashes of disaster, like that lightning, were headed his way. His joints ached.

And wasn't that telling in more ways than one? How old was he again?

Way too young to have joints that spoke to him.

Maybe Hannah, Tadie, and, oh, yeah, Rita thought they were helping. Sure they did. But a group playing couples where three quarters were the real thing and one quarter consisted of a pseudo landlord and an abuse victim? Maybe he could convince Mrs. Barnes to join in. Otherwise, he could picture the scene. The only ones having fun were going to be the children and the dog. The rest would be trying too hard to make something happen and, if he remembered correctly, there wasn't a one of them who'd be drinking anything harder than iced tea—Matt and Hannah because of Matt's health, Tadie and Rita because they were pregnant. Will and

Martin were unknowns. He doubted they'd bring anything with them to produce liquid relaxation. There certainly were times—and this was one of them—when he regretted his vow of abstinence.

Forcing something never worked. They'd all do much better to leave things alone and pay attention to their own issues. Annie Mac wasn't one to be manipulated into looking at any man kindly. That would take time, if it ever happened at all.

A knock interrupted him, for which he should've been grateful. He wasn't.

"Yes?" he asked, and not in the nicest tone, of the officer standing innocently in his doorway.

"Sorry, sir, but there's a guy here says he's Mrs. Bingham's brother."

Clay raised his brows. "Her brother? What name did he give?"

"Kevin Rinehart."

"Kevin Rinehart." He thought a moment. "Can you get a look at the car he's driving? Run the plates for me?"

"Yes, sir."

According to Annie Mac, her brother was dead. Was this some henchman of Bingham's come to find her? Clay wandered out to the front office, took a deep breath, and extended his hand in greeting.

Either this fellow was the brother raised from the dead, or he was some long-lost, very blond, male version of Annie Mac. "Lieutenant Dougherty. How may I help you?"

"Kevin Rinehart," the look-alike said, shaking Clay's hand cautiously. "I'm trying to find my sister."

"Why don't you come on back with me?" Clay led the way to his office and motioned the young man to a chair. "Have a seat. You want anything? Soda? Coffee?"

"Just information, please."

"I didn't think Ms. Rinehart had any relatives."

The young man gave a disgusted snort. "Oh, she's got them all right. Two living parents, plus me, two uncles and aunts, along with assorted cousins."

Clay picked up a pencil and twirled it through his fingers. "You want to explain that? How you only turn up looking for her now?"

There was something about boys who became men and were still prettier than their sisters that didn't sit well. Really, lashes like that? On a man? My sister would die for eyelashes she didn't have to stick on or darken with one of those wands.

Not that Annie Mac—Ms. Rinehart—didn't have those same piercingly blue eyes. And great brows, small chin. She'd probably turn into a fine-looking woman as soon as she finished healing.

A blush rose on the young man's pale face, making him, if possible, even prettier. He must have guessed Clay's reaction. "I know. I hate it." He shrugged. "You try growing up with a face like this and hoping people will take you seriously."

Clay couldn't help a grin. "My sister would kill for your looks."

"Lieutenant, she can have them. Honestly."

"What is it you do? I take it you're not in a line of work where looks count."

The blond head shook. What the fellow needed, Clay decided, were horn rims. Hide those eyes a little.

"I'm a geologist, studying for my doctorate at the University of Colorado."

"Glasses." Clay pointed. "You know, camouflage?"

Kevin waved a hand and grinned. "Glasses, a crew cut. Something." Then he sobered. "Look, Lieutenant. I didn't even know Annie Mac was alive until yesterday. I was visiting my folks before classes start again and found newspaper articles, a series of them, in my mother's chest of drawers. I wasn't snooping. She must have forgotten they were there when she told me to bring her a sweater."

The pencil had stilled in Clay's fingers, but he sure wished he could give Kevin something else to rub so he wouldn't wear out the knees of his khakis.

"They told me my sister was dead. She'd run away and something had happened, I don't know. I was only ten. All I thought about for years was that she'd left without saying good-bye." The remembered hurt showed in Kevin's eyes. "You can imagine my shock when I read she was not only alive, she was a mother and an abuse victim."

"You know her husband is loose somewhere and looking for her?"

Kevin shook his head. "I only know what I read before I confronted my mother." He sounded disgusted. "All she could do was weep. She begged me to find out what I could, insisted I promise not to tell my father she'd kept the articles."

"Did your sister run away, or did he throw her out?"

"It had to be the latter. Why else would my mother be so upset?" Kevin stood and paced in a circle before leaning with both hands on the back of the chair. "What can you tell me? Is she okay? What about her children?" He combed his fingers through that thick hair. "This is driving me crazy. She was the sweetest sister. I adored her. I was always small, and, yeah, had these absurd eyes, but no one was allowed to bully me when Annie Mac was there. Then she was gone."

The pencil snapped. Clay tossed the pieces in the trash and pinched the bridge of his nose as he took a deep, calming breath.

Kevin slid back into the chair. His voice sounded grim. "The newspaper mentioned that she'd been assaulted and her children were being cared for, but it didn't go into detail. Tell me, please."

"She's going to be fine," Clay said. "Her oldest, Ty, is ten. He looks a lot like you."

"Ten." As Kevin again brushed fingers through his hair, Clay inadvertently mirrored the movement.

"She must have been pregnant with him when she left," Kevin said. "Pop wouldn't have stood for that. I'll never forgive him."

"Katie is Royce Bingham's daughter. She's four. Very sweet, very wounded. There was some abuse."

"If only I'd been older."

Clay could second that. "We're trying to protect them all while we look for Royce."

"May I see her? See them? How badly was Annie Mac hurt?"

"She's only recently come out of the hospital. She still wears a cast on her leg and has some broken ribs, lots of bruising. She'll probably have some scarring on her face. He was brutal."

Kevin covered his face. "My God. My God."

Clay cleared his throat, embarrassed by the other man's emotion. Still, Kevin might be exactly what that family needed. A man for Ty. An uncle. Clay pushed back his chair and stood. "I need to talk to her. Find out what she wants."

Kevin looked up, his expression suddenly hopeful.

"How can I get in touch with you?"

Kevin gave him his cell number. "You think she could see me tomorrow? I mean, if she wants to?"

"I don't see why not. You staying at your parents' place?"

"I'll come back any time. Doesn't matter when."

"I'll call you."

After seeing Kevin to the front door of the station house, Clay asked Stella if she'd run the plates.

"Registered to a Dorothea M. Rinehart. You want the rest?"

"Can you get me a hard copy?"

She handed him the printout. He'd like to go tell those parents a thing or two. But what he needed now was to see their daughter.

He was halfway home when he remembered the party the ladies had planned. He slammed his palm against the steering wheel. A houseful of guests was the last thing he wanted.

31 CLAY

Clay stuck his head through his polo shirt, pulled it down, and tucked it in his jeans. He'd done the good-old-boy, back-slapping ritual with Matt and Will and had met Martin, Rita's husband. Just on the other side of his bedroom door, a bunch of women were busy fussing with everything like hens pecking around the yard. His bedroom felt like a sanctuary.

Now they expected him to come out and do the pretty.

Rain had disrupted the plans for a picnic. He located enough chairs for everyone and dug out the card table for the kids. Becca insisted she'd rather eat at the high counter. "I can watch them young'uns best from here. Besides, I got another batch of biscuits to tend. Y'all don't want to run out of my biscuits," she said with twinkling eyes.

"No, ma'am," Clay said. "Wouldn't want that to happen."

Matt and Will helped Annie Mac move from the recliner to the wheelchair. She had to sit sideways at one end of the long table, but she'd declared, with more force than she'd used before in his hearing, that she didn't want to be left out of the conversation and off by herself in the recliner, acting the invalid.

Clay took a seat at the other end. The symbolism wasn't lost on him. Probably wasn't lost on Annie Mac or on any of the others either. Well, he'd pretend everything was normal.

Normal?

Who was he kidding?

"You've done a great job on the chicken, honey." Hannah patted her husband's hand.

Matt seemed to have returned to his jovial self. Well, why not? He'd gotten his way—and kept his den.

Interesting that the thought didn't make Clay grind his teeth this time.

He accepted the chicken platter from Tadie and forked a piece of white meat. Next came the potato salad and baked beans. Mrs. Barnes brought out her biscuits, which were soon devoured. The coleslaw was a close second.

"How're you kids doing over there?" Will called, looking past Tadie to the smaller table where four mouths were chewing.

Annie Mac must have noticed, too. "Best not to feed the dog at the table, Ty. You either, Katie. I'm sure he isn't supposed to beg."

"He's hungry," Katie said, lowering her lashes and grinning.

Ah, thought Clay, so that's where her uncle's lashes went. At least Katie had inherited them and not Ty.

Hannah laughed. "You know he's not. You guys filled his bowl earlier so he wouldn't beg at dinner. If he keeps acting like that, your Uncle Matt's going to shut him up in the garage."

"I am?"

"You are," Hannah said, pretending to scowl.

Tadie spoke softly so the children wouldn't hear. "Did you catch that eye work of Katie's? Annie Mac, you'd better watch that child. She's already learned how to flirt."

"All three of those children have an arsenal of tricks they seem to come by naturally," Hannah said.

Matt saluted with a drumstick. "Amen to that."

The conversation continued to be lively, and Clay tried to keep his attention focused on things Rita said from her place to his right, or things Tadie said at his left, and not on the woman laughing at the other end of the table. It was the first time he'd actually seen her loose more than a meager smile.

The ringing phone startled them all. Mrs. Barnes picked up the portable, answered, and then nodded toward Clay.

"Excuse me," he said, heading toward his bedroom. "I'll get it in here."

Expectant faces greeted his return. He took his seat and lowered his voice to keep it from carrying to the children's table. "That was Chief Bradley. Seems there's been a robbery over near Newport, along with a shooting. The gas station owner was wounded, but he was able to sound the alarm to get the sheriff there in time. He'll live. The Chief said he gave a description that was an awful lot like Royce. They've got patrols scouring that area."

"Did he have a car?" Matt asked. "Did the man know?"

Clay nodded. "He didn't get the license, but he said the car was an old green Chevy. It reminded him of one he'd worked on one not too long ago. Fellow brought it in with alternator trouble."

Will placed his hand over Tadie's to silence her drumming fingers. "Is anyone following that up?"

"I'm sure they are. I'll be doing interviews tomorrow."

"Not tonight?" Annie Mac asked, another worry line etched between her brows.

"Police work isn't usually like you see it on TV," he said. "The county sheriff and his men will follow up tonight. It's their jurisdiction. Tomorrow, we'll share information and continue our plodding way to the answers."

"So he's closer than when he escaped."

"Maybe. It may mean he was trying to get some cash, now that he has a car. And though the car will let him get out of the area, it can be identified. He's got to know that. If it was stolen, it will help us catch him."

"If?"

"He may have friends."

"I can't imagine," Rita said, disgust evident in her voice.

"Oh, he has friends," Annie Mac said, "as awful as he is."

Rita huffed. "Takes all kinds."

"And gives you employment," Matt pointed out to Clay.

He blew out a sigh. "Too much sometimes." To Annie Mac, "If you can come up with any names that you haven't already given us, I'd appreciate it."

"I stayed as far away as possible from people he hung out with."

"Will you let me know if anyone comes to mind? Anyone at all. We'll catch him. Don't you worry."

"I'm trying not to."

So was he.

32 ROY

Roy eased the car down a well-packed dirt lane, the wipers missing beats as they traced an arc across the windshield. Good thing it was solid dirt and gravel instead of the rutted thing going toward Rachel's. This one wouldn't get him stuck. According to the satellite picture and map Pete had printed for him, this lieutenant's place was off a big creek, sorta like a bay. If the picture showed it right, there'd be some woods up a ways on the left that he could sneak into now it was dark. In case someone was driving in or out this time of night. Probably wouldn't be many in this messy weather.

There. That looked like it. He could snug the Chevy back in where somebody'd already made ruts in the tall grasses. Just go on a little farther in, and so what if he scratched the car on low branches? Wouldn't change this junk's value one whit.

He chuckled, patted the faded dash, and inched the car forward as he watched for soft ground. The rain had finally slowed to a drizzle, but that didn't mean the ground hadn't soaked enough to trap him.

Tucking the gun in the back waistband of his jeans, he grabbed a flashlight with his other hand. He'd check things out tonight. See how hard it was gonna be getting Katie out of here. If she was too protected in this place, he could wait for a school-yard heist. They were too dumb to worry at that school. Figured it was safe in a sleepy town like Beaufort. Hadn't learned much from other places and other incidents. Fools, but who was he to complain?

He tried not to make much noise as he sneaked through the woods at the edge of the lane. And there it was, lights blazing. Lots of cars. The fancy, smantzy lieutenant must be having a party.

Annie Mac shouldn't be attending a party without her lawful husband by her side. Shame on her.

Best check out the cars, take down the plate numbers. Good thing he carried a pad with one of those mini pencils stuck in it, along with this penlight. A body never knew when information might come in handy.

He edged around toward the back side and near the deck. And then he eased up to peek in one of those big windows.

My, oh, my. A passel of folk. And just there, his baby. Hey, little lamb.

A big red setter sat next to that fool of a boy. It pointed its snout at him, curled those lips enough to show teeth, and growled.

Pete's source hadn't said a thing about the lieutenant owning a dog.

The boy's head turned. His eyes locked on Roy's.

Roy ducked. And ran.

33 CLAY

Clay felt the boy's hand on his shoulder and smelled that little-boy scent. Got him smiling as he turned. But that smile died at the worry—or something more—in Ty's eyes.

"Can I talk to you, sir? In private?"

"Sure, son." He wiped his hands and pushed his chair back from the table. "Excuse us a minute, will you?"

He'd barely had time to close his bedroom door when Ty's words stopped him cold. "He's here."

"Who? Who's here? Royce?"

"Unhuh. He was staring in the window. I looked up 'cause Harvey growled."

Clay squeezed the boy's shoulder. "Good man. Now I want you to go on back out with the others so nobody worries. Tell them I'll be back in a few minutes." He smiled encouragement. "You can act like you know I need to use the john."

"Yes, sir."

"I'm counting on you, Ty. You've got to act like all's well. Can you do that?"

"Yes, sir."

Once the boy had drawn the door closed, Clay collected his gun and tucked it in his waistband. The deck remained in shadow, but the rain had ceased and a moon slid from behind a cloud.

He edged around to the front of the house, giving his eyes time to adjust to the dark. Nothing moved. Only the black outline of trees showed in that moonlight beyond the house. He paused, listening.

At first, he heard only drips from trees, and then an engine growled to life out on the lane. He dashed toward it, not worrying about cover. He could hear the whine of spinning tires, hear the engine fighting and the sound of the tires grabbing. He knew what he'd see when he got there.

How had Roy found them?

Someone had talked. The folk inside were far too protective of those children. He couldn't even imagine Mrs. Barnes speaking to one of her cronies. No, she'd taken to mothering that crew and knew the risks.

Tail lights taunted him from the far end of the lane just before it curved to the right, and he tossed an expletive into the night air as he returned to the house. Perhaps there'd be tire marks to find when daylight came, but he wasn't sure what good they'd do.

He replaced the gun in his closet, changed shoes, and re-entered the great room, shaking his head at Ty. "I need you to help me out again and take the girls in the bedroom to play for a little while. We don't want them frightened."

"No, sir. I understand."

Everyone had gone silent. Ty grabbed Harvey's collar. "Come on, girls. Let's go."

"But what about dessert?" Jilly directed a stricken look at Tadie.

"It'll keep. You do what the lieutenant wants right now."

Mrs. Barnes brought a damp cloth to wipe Katie's fingers. "Come on, sweet girl, let's go get you cleaned up. And Mrs. Barnes will fix you all some nice ice cream as soon's the lieutenant says so."

Jilly looked worried. "Mommy brought cupcakes."

"Just go on now," Will told her.

"And, Mrs. Barnes, can you come back out as soon as they're settled?" Clay asked.

"Be right back. Jest want to make sure this baby doesn't go playing with sticky hands."

Ty took his little sister's hand. "I'll make sure she's clean."

"I thank you, Ty." Mrs. Barnes watched them go. "That's a good boy you got there, Miss Annie. Now, Lieutenant, what you got to say to us?"

He told them. While they debated back and forth, tossing out various solutions, he stood at the glass doors, watching the trail of moonlight on the short waves. He hated this. He'd brought them here to keep them safe, and yet somehow Royce had found them. Words came into focus behind him as Hannah's voice penetrated his thoughts.

"I say we move Annie Mac and the children to the other side of the state. Find them a safe house until this madman is caught."

"That's a possibility," Matt said. "What do you think, Clay?"

Returning to his place, he braced his hands on the back of his chair and leaned slightly forward. "It's the leak that's worrying me. I'll talk to my chief tomorrow." He checked each face. "What's done is done, but we've got to be extra careful from now on. No discussion of what's happening or of any steps we're taking."

"We haven't been," Rita said. "Only my mama and daddy know, and they wouldn't say a word."

"Of course not. Mrs. Barnes, how about folks at your church? Or your daughter?"

"No, sir. I knowed I wasn't supposed to speak of it, and I haven't. My daughter calls my cell phone. That's all she knows. Not where I am or who I'm carin' for."

Everyone else shook his head. Clay nodded. "Sorry, I had to ask. Which means it's at my end. Someone in the department has been talking out of school."

"That's terrible," Matt said. The others echoed with words or nods.

"It is. But this is a small town. Everyone knows everyone. So, here's what I'm considering. I'll have to check with my chief tomorrow, but I think I'll start a rumor that we've done exactly what Hannah suggested. That we actually did move Annie Mac and the children out of harm's way. It might put Royce off a little."

"Why don't we do it for real?" Hannah asked.

"Because of the difficulty of setting it up and the people we'd have to involve. A real potential for harm exists if the wrong person found out where we'd moved them. I'd like to try throwing out the bait while keeping this thing as controlled as possible."

"What happens next week when the children are supposed to start school?" Annie Mac twisted her napkin, a pleading look in her eyes that Clay didn't think had much to do with the children's education.

".Jilly homeschools," Tadie said. "She and Ty aren't far apart grade-wise, so they could do a lot of their work together. And Katie isn't really in school yet, is she?"

"Would the school board go for it?"

"How can they not? You call and tell them you're moving and not enrolling Ty this year. When this is all over, you can change your mind."

"Will he be behind his class?"

Will smiled. "Annie Mac, I promise you, the only way a homeschooled child is behind is if the parent hasn't been doing his or her job. Jilly tests three grades ahead in everything and works a grade or two ahead in most subjects."

Clay pushed off, too restless to stand in one place. He paced back toward the French doors before turning. "I think Tadie has the answer, Annie Mac. And you're a teacher. Perhaps you two can help each other out, especially with Tadie about to have her baby."

"Oh, I'd love to help," Annie Mac said. "Any way I can."

"Tadie?"

"That sounds ideal. Will could teach Jilly, of course. He always used to, but he's got this big project he's working on, and I've been dreading the thought of failing Jilly while taking care of a new baby." She laughed. "I can't even imagine what it's going to be like, having my first while I'm raising an almost-ten-year-old. I feel ancient merely thinking about it."

"I'm going to call the security people we used at the hospital to get a guard out here."

"And, Clay," said Tadie, "you said Harvey's growl scared Royce off this time, but you may want to think about having a dog here full time."

Matt glanced first at Hannah, then at him. "What do you think, Clay? You mind if Harvey moves in for a while?"

"What's one more?" he said, then hated himself for his rudeness. "Sorry. It'll be fine."

"This is too much of an imposition." Annie Mac seemed suddenly to notice that she'd shredded her napkin. She piled it beside her plate. "I'm sorry. I hate being so helpless."

Rita rose and gave Annie Mac a quick hug. "We know you do. But you're one of us now—"

"Because of Ty and Katie."

Tadie leaned forward, both palms braced in front of her as if she wanted to make a point. "Sure, it started that way. But now we like you for your sake."

The sobs began with a ferocity that startled everyone. Rita left a hand on Annie Mac's back, patting her as Annie Mac buried her face in her hands.

This was his fault. He needed to divert attention so she'd have time to recover, but he couldn't think of a thing to say. At least Mrs. Barnes had the presence of mind to fetch a box of tissues.

He cleared his throat. "Having Harvey here sounds like an excellent idea." Good start, he told himself as his head cleared. Another call to David Brock was in order. "I'll make arrangements to get a couple of guards, set up a security detail. I'd also like to suggest none of the children go outside where they might be seen. Hannah, your van has tinted windows, so if any visiting is to be done, you should do the driving." He let his gaze sweep the group. "There's too much cover here for me to feel comfortable, so no further than the deck, and there only with Harvey and Mrs. Barnes in attendance. At least until we get this guy behind bars."

Annie Mac's shudders lessened. Mrs. Barnes handed her another tissue, and she ducked back down with it.

"I agree," Matt said. "Hannah can pick up the children and get them together with Jilly any time. That way Mrs. Barnes can remain with Annie Mac, and no one will ever be alone."

"Good. I'll get the guard here first thing. The doors will stay locked with the alarm on and remain unanswered unless we know exactly who's there. That needs to happen wherever the children are."

Mrs. Barnes spoke up. "I'm thinking that we should be moving Miss Annie's chair away from the window some, too. Don't want to make no targets."

"Excellent. Thank you. If you can think of anything else, let me know. You're as involved as any of us now. And I'm going to put my cell number on auto-dial in your cell phone."

She nodded. "Thank you, Lieutenant. I aim to make sure none of these dear folk get hurt on my watch. You all going to be wanting coffee or anything?"

Clay looked around. "I think not, though we appreciate it."

The next morning, Clay stood at the basin sink and lathered up. Staring at his upper lip as the razor raked from his nose down, he remembered that he hadn't told Annie Mac about her brother. He glanced at his watch, finished the shave, and slipped into his slacks and shirt before heading across the living area. It was early, but he heard her mutter something, probably from discomfort.

"Yes?" she called in answer to his knock.

"It's Clay. You awake enough for me to speak to you?"

"Of course, come in."

She had pushed herself up and was leaning against her pillows. He stood at the end of her bed, trying not to notice her hands clutching the sheet to her neck. "I'm sorry I forgot to mention this last night, but a young man came into the office yesterday wanting information about you. He said he's your brother Kevin."

"Kevin?" One hand let go and flew to her mouth. "Oh, my. Really? Kevin?"

"That's what he said. About twenty, white-blond hair and killer lashes."

She stared at him a moment before asking, "He was looking for me?"

"According to him, your parents told him you were dead. He only found out you weren't when he came across an article about the assault. Your mother kept clippings."

"Mama? I can't imagine what about."

"Probably births, marriages, that sort of thing. She must have followed pretty closely."

"I wouldn't have thought she'd care. Not after she helped boot me out." She sniffled and reached for a tissue. "Where is he?"

"At your parents' house, but I have his cell phone number. If you'd like, I'll bring you the phone." Clay grinned. "I figure he's so eager to hear from you, he won't mind the hour. Just make sure you caution him not to mention your location to anyone."

"I'll tell him. Oh, and thank you."

Annie Mac's fingers fumbled as she punched in the numbers, and she had to start over. The sheet had fallen to her lap, but she didn't seem to notice. She smiled at him while she waited for an answer. "Kev? Kev, is that you?"

34 ROY

Roy was spitting mad. According to Pete's source, the bird had flown and taken his baby with her. It was that fool boy's fault, having that dog, looking up.

He stamped on the floor, shaking up dust. "Nobody knows where they went? What about the fellow? That lieutenant? You think he's the one drove her out of here?"

"Doesn't seem so." Pete flicked ashes into the sink behind him. He drew on his cigarette and blew lazy smoke rings. "Not when he's the one saying they moved her. No time, you know? Seems one of their friends—you said they had a crowd over there—took her and the kids."

"It was probably the colored gal. Sort of thing one of them would do." Roy would sure like to know what Annie Mac had been doing, sharing a meal with a colored woman. There'd been an older one with a serving bowl in her hand, but that young thing? That woman hadn't been waiting on anyone, just sitting plumb in the middle of that same table. Didn't make sense to him. But one thing he knew, his little girl wasn't going to grow up that way, folk stepping beyond their rightful place in the world. He sure wasn't having any of it, no matter how uppity black folk were getting now they had that fellow elected. What was the world coming to?

"Who was she?"

"I don't know and wouldn't care, 'cept she was fraternizing with my girl." He pulled his little pad out of his shirt pocket and tore off the top sheet. "Got the license numbers of those cars while I was sneaking around. Can you do anything with them?"

"Sure. I get the names and addresses, maybe you can figure which is which."

"It's what I'm aimin' for."

"Maybe they were getting set to leave. Maybe that's why the colored girl was invited."

Roy shook his head, disgust filling him. "Doesn't make sense. She was hired to drive Annie Mac, she wouldn't be sitting down to dinner with her."

"That's true. Well, it's a pretty sure thing it was someone else hauling them, not the lieutenant."

"That's no help, not unless we can get someone talking about where they went. You think it would be on a computer someplace?"

"What?" Pete looked skeptical. "Like a database for protected folk?"

"Sure."

"Don't think they do that in places small as Beaufort."

"But if they've got an open case, won't they write up stuff? Put it in a file?"

"You been watching too much TV," Pete said, grinning as he ground out the cigarette under his boot.

"What's that brother of yours doing these days?"

"Got himself a new woman over toward Cedar Island."

"Wondered why I hadn't seen hide nor hair of him."

"Oh, he'll be back eventually."

"So, you gonna to be able to find out where Annie Mac took Katie?"

"I'll ask around. Someone's bound to know."

Roy chuckled. "Can't keep secrets in Beaufort. No, sirree."

Pete threw his beer can at the recently emptied bucket, swearing when he missed. Yanking a new one from the plastic rings, he flipped the top and took a long swig. When Roy tossed his own empty can and hit the bucket first try, Pete cussed again.

"Ain't fair."

Roy laughed, this time with humor. It was an old joke, but it gave him a leg up. Not many of those left these days. "I've been telling you, it's practice. You never would practice anything."

"I practice what I like. Don't you imagine I don't."

"Got a sweet one you haven't told me about?"

"A sweet one, and this gal's got a sister with an itch. You interested?"

Roy grinned, slugged back more beer. "It's been a while. You let her come here?"

"Why not? We'll say it's your vacation place." Pete looked around, slapping his knee.

"Hilarious," Roy said. "Might as well announce I'm running from the law."

"Listen, that little gal won't care. Most of the time, she's higher than a kite. Makes her itch that much greater."

"Does, huh?"

"Yes, sir. Likely, she won't remember you or here."

"I'd take offense," Roy said, "only I'd prefer she not recognize me. What picture do they have up?"

"Mug shot, and not very flattering. Besides, that beard and your long hair? Nobody, not even your mama, would know you."

Roy pursed his lips. He didn't want to be recognized, except by his baby. Sure didn't want to scare Katie away. Still, a blitzed-out woman? "Make sure the gal is feeling no pain 'fore you bring her here."

"I plan on it."

"And you get a chance, see if that friend of yours can find out anything."

The woman Pete had sent wobbled out to the car the next morning. Hung over, Roy suspected. The man behind the wheel didn't speak, but Roy recognized him as the one who'd brought the Chevy.

Well, no skin off him if the man wanted to play deaf and dumb. Better probably.

He took a shower, spread some peanut butter on white bread, and carried it with a sack of birdseed out to the wooden stoop. The hard surface dug into butt bones that were losing way too much padding, and he wiggled, trying for comfort that had been eluding him since he'd been here. Time to get a move on. Seriously.

He imagined a thick juicy burger. Fries. The smell of salt and oil and onions. Oh, yeah, first on his list once he and Katie were free of this place.

He reached in the sack for another handful of seed and dusted the ground over near a shade tree. Weren't too many going after the feed, but he could hear twittering off in the woods. Maybe they'd come out soon.

Pete had promised to see what secrets his computer could hunt up. Roy rubbed his hands together in anticipation. Pretty soon, he'd know who those folk were at supper with his family. Good old Pete and his computer. Amazing what a man could do, knowing how to control one of those things.

He ruminated on possibilities. Maybe once he'd finished this, he just might find himself one of those little bitty computers, the kind you could carry with you, and figure out how to channel information for himself. Pete had shown him the light, yessir. Things Pete could find out were purely amazing.

He got a computer, got Katie, and set up someplace else? Why, then he'd be ready to send for his Rachel. Wouldn't that be something? No more ladybirds for him, just his own gals, his own place.

A car rumbled up the drive, its engine announcing itself before the old Ford came into sight. He rose and stood waiting near the door. "You got 'em?" he asked as Pete stepped out of his company car.

Pete waved a sheet in the air. "Addresses and all."

"Man, you're good."

"Those scales may be tilting slightly in my direction after this."

"I get out of here and you need something, you only have to ask. You know that."

Pete grinned. "Yeah. I know that. I'll be holding you to it."

He studied the names and addresses. Figured the one he wanted was the colored gal. She had to be the one causing the trouble, so she was the one he'd teach a lesson to.

Front Street Beaufort wouldn't be her address. Not that other one either. Too much old money in those big houses on the waterfront. Could be she was somebody's servant. Only, if so, she'd not have been sitting down at table. No, more than likely, she'd have a place out of town. That's where he'd check first. A lesson to one, maybe they'd all learn and leave things be as far as Katie was concerned.

Pete suggested they do a bit of camouflage work on the Chevy before Roy went driving it again. He grabbed an old set of plates, set them aside, then went around to the shed. Roy didn't know why he was surprised when Pete came out with a paint sprayer.

"Don't work on rainy days, mind you," Pete said, "but it'll last long as you need it."

"Pete, I'm just growing more and more impressed by you, boy."

It didn't take long for the paint to dry. He saw Pete off, then climbed in the now mud-brown car and smiled to himself. Didn't do to show up places he might be recognized in the same old Chevy. Not after that fool attendant had survived to snitch. It was even in the papers, so folk would be looking for the car. Wouldn't see it now.

He drove slowly past the place Pete had marked on the map, parking down the block, well out of sight of the few cars moving real slow so their bellies wouldn't get ripped out by the speed bumps. This development was one of those new areas out the road to Swansboro. Seems there were two cars registered to the same address, one of them to a Martin Levinson, one to a Rita Levinson. The name didn't exactly sound colored, but he'd find out soon enough. That brought a grin to his face when he thought of how easy it was to tell. Little gal would walk out her front door, and he'd know. No mistaking possible.

Pete's source said the husband was a doctor. Profitable job, doctoring. But, hey, he didn't have a squawk with them, unless they were folk who'd moved out of the natural order of things and gotten uppity. From what he'd seen at the dinner table, the only one from the wrong side of the line was female. It was the wife he figured didn't belong with his Katie, and so he'd tell her when he found her.

She was home. Leastways, one of the cars was, most likely hers. So he'd bide a while and see who came out to get in it. He had patience. He could wait.

He was on his fourth toothpick when he caught sight of her locking up her front door. He hadn't quite figured out what he was going to do, but he knew he'd have an inspiration at the right time. He always did.

She got in her car, took her time buckling that seat belt over her belly protrusion, and pulled out. He'd let her get a ways ahead before he eased out behind her to the highway stop sign. It wasn't likely she'd spot a tail. Not like she knew him or anything. He turned out with one car between them, keeping an eye on the little black thing ahead.

She pulled into a turn lane. Yep, there she went onto that old road near the cemetery, obviously planning to cross over to highway 70. "See?" he said to his reflection. He'd known she'd give him an opening. He'd have liked to ask her some questions, but likely she wasn't the one with answers. No, but she'd learn a thing or two.

This was the perfect road. Lots of trees both sides, not much traffic, a good stretch coming up with no houses. He came up on her tail. A little faster, and he bumped the back of the shiny black Mazda she drove. Good color, he thought, grinning. He could almost see her face, scared about now. He imagined her gripping the steering wheel, clinging, not sure what was happening. That pregnant belly of hers had probably hit the wheel on that one.

He did some of his own gripping as he pulled around to her side and slammed the Chevy into her car, ramming the driver's door. He only had to push a little bit harder next time. That little car would land right in the ditch.

He edged up, turned to the right with the force of a big American dominating that pitiful foreign make, and Bam!

There she went, off the road. "Lookee there!" This time he crowed the words aloud as he sped on past. Bet she didn't have a clue what had just happened to her.

35 CLAY & ANNIE MAC

Clay's cell phone rang with a number he didn't recognize. "Martin here," the voice said. "Someone ran Rita off the road."

"Tell me."

Martin did, ending with, "Thank God, she's okay. The baby seems fine, but her obstetrician said we need to watch for changes in blood pressure or for any dizziness."

"You home or still at the hospital?"

"Rita wanted home. I'm here with her. Elvie'll stay with her in the morning."

"What did Rita say about the car? She see anything?"

"It was brown. Older model, American make. How many crazies do we know who would come after Rita deliberately? You think Royce has access to a brown car, too?"

"I'll check with the Highway Patrol. See what they found out."

"Rita says he rammed her three times. The last time was hard enough to push her off the road. There was plenty of passing room on that lonely stretch."

Clay's thoughts ricocheted in different directions. He pulled them back long enough to say, "I'll look into it. Ask her if she's angered anyone recently, maybe the husband or boyfriend of someone from the center."

"That was my first thought. She said it wasn't likely because she doesn't appear in court. She has a point. How would anyone know she was involved in a case?"

"I'll get back to you. If she remembers anything else, call me."

Clay drummed his fingers on the desk, damping down the frustration that grew as he made calls. The Carteret sheriff's department hadn't found a single trace of the car from the robbery, nor any word of a stolen green Chevy. The green car the attendant had mentioned checked out. It sat up on blocks in its owner's driveway and from the look of things hadn't been anywhere recently, certainly not churning up Clay's driveway. The tires and underbody were dirty but not muddy.

He talked to the Highway Patrol. The investigating officer had seen something odd with the paint residue on Rita's car. Said the brown was water-based, and there were flecks of green paint in one of the larger dents in Rita's car. With this next storm coming? The hit-and-run car would be green again by morning unless the owner had a garage.

But why Rita? Unless it had something to do with the party at his house. Bingham would have seen her. But would he have known who she was?

Clay headed home early. The blackening sky would only add to the mood there.

He waved at the guard leaning against a gray sedan parked at the edge of the woods. This was a different man from yesterday. After stopping to identify himself, Clay pulled into his garage.

The fellow approached, his hand extended. "Clive Oliver's the name."

Clay shook it. "Appreciate you keeping watch like this."

"Yes, sir, Lieutenant. Don't want any maniac getting past, that's for sure."

"Noticed anything?"

"Not even much wildlife. Been real quiet today."

"Let's hope it stays that way tonight, though it's likely to get a little messy weather-wise. When's the next guy coming? Have I met him yet?"

Mr. Oliver shook his head. "Those other two were only here temporary like. Dick and me, we're going to be the ones working long as you need us. He's due to come on at five. Five to five, that's what we're working."

"Long shifts."

"Only if you stay sitting. I got a cooler back there," he said, pointing to the backseat. "And I walk the area every so often. Mostly, we just want to let anyone trying to intrude know that you're guarded. We're not trying to catch him for you."

"Have the new guy check in with me when he comes?"

"Yes, sir."

Entering the kitchen by way of the garage door, Clay paused to reset the alarm. "Hey, there, Mrs. Barnes. How's it been today?"

"Just fine, Lieutenant. The children had lunch on the deck so they could get some sunshine, but they had me and Harvey doing the guarding. They're real curious about the man out front, and I told them to wait for you to get home."

"I'll take them out. It might make them feel more secure."

"It might." She wiped her hands on the towel and picked up her stirring spoon again. "Afternoon, after Katie's nap, we all sat down to a game of monopoly. Miss Annie played with us. Kept everyone's mind occupied."

"Where are they now?" He leaned over to sniff what looked like a pot of chili. "Boy, that smells good."

"Corn bread to go along with it."

"Mrs. Barnes, you're an angel."

She poured out a smile that felt like warm chocolate tasted. "I aim to please. Miss Annie's lying in her bed for a while. She walked with me 'round the house some this afternoon, but she got pretty tuckered out. I think it's nerves much as anything, tell you the truth."

"I imagine it could be. And the children?"

"You were nice enough to say they could watch the television in your room, so that's what they're doing. Sesame Street's still on."

"I'll go say hey."

Mrs. Barnes nodded. "Storm's coming."

"It is indeed. We may need candles out. You'll find plenty in the pantry."

"I'll take care of them. Get a bunch ready in case."

"You'll find a couple of flashlights in there, too. Best have them on standby."

"Yes, sir. It'll comfort the children, having a light they can use. And, Lieutenant?"

"Yes?"

"Miss Annie's mighty excited about that brother of hers comin' tomorrow. It's a good thing, isn't it?"

"I think so. I think it will be good for all of them."

Her smile came again, crinkling her eyes, showing white teeth in the dark face. "Glad to hear it."

As soon as he poked his head in the bedroom, Harvey eased himself up and ambled over.

"Hey, boy." Clay scratched where the dog liked it, right behind his ears. "You been watching things for us?"

"Hey, Lieutenant," Ty said.

"Hey, Ty, Katie. What's happening with Big Bird?"

"It's kid stuff. But Katie likes it. I'm mostly listening to music." He showed Clay a little black iPod. Clay had given Annie Mac a white one.

Clay grinned. "Hannah get you that?"

Ty's eyes lit. The boy—unlike old Harvey there, whose joints shimmied when he was excited—obviously didn't know how to show joy, so his smile kind of crept up on him. "It's cool. Miss Hannah let me download a bunch of songs and books. But Katie likes Sesame Street better. It's good for her. Teaches her stuff."

"That's important." He ruffled Katie's hair, smiled when she glanced up and grinned around her thumb. "Excuse me for a minute," he said, heading to his closet to change into cooler clothes.

He waited until the ending credits rolled before he switched off the set. "I understand that you'd like to meet the man standing guard outside."

Ty's head shot up. "Yes, sir!"

They used the front door, shutting off the alarm system on the way. "Hold on to Harvey's lead, Ty. Don't let him get away from you."

Clive Oliver was sitting in his car. He stepped out, gave the children a smile, and extended his hand for Harvey to sniff. "Good looking dog you've got there, young fellow."

"He's a guard dog. He's very smart," Ty said.

"I can see that."

A second car approached, parked next to Clive's, and a large man with sandy hair hauled himself out.

"The children wanted to see who was watching the place," Clay said. "Thought I'd let them make the acquaintance of you both at once."

"Mighty pleased to meet you," Clive said, extending his hand to shake Ty's before he bent toward Katie. "And this lovely young lady, too."

"This is Ty, and that's Katie," Clay said. "The redhead is Harvey."

"Hey, Harvey." Clive turned to his replacement. "This here's Dick Webber. Good man for night work as he prefers sleeping in daylight. Go figure."

Clay extended his hand. "Clay Dougherty. I don't think we've met."

"No, sir. But I've heard about you."

"All good, I hope." Clay shifted to present the children.

"I'll be on call here, Lieutenant," Dick Webber said. "Like Clive told you, I sleep better days, since I got used to being up nights years ago. Don't bother me none, and it's usually a whole lot more peaceful after dark." He glanced around. "Though out here, bound to be right quiet most times."

"Usually is. Do you have everything you'll need? Water, coffee, food?"

"Yes, sir. I stocked up." He handed Clay a business card. "Here's my cell phone number, you need to reach me. Got yours and the house number plugged in so's I can call you."

"Thank you, Mr. Webber. Mr. Oliver." Clay nodded to the other man and turned to the children. "Let's give Harvey a bit of exercise before we go find dinner."

They let Harvey sniff around the house and down by the creek edge. The dog needed a good run, but, after what Hannah'd said, he didn't want to let him loose to go chasing squirrels. Maybe later they could take some exercise together.

Ty was the first to notice his mama's open door. He dodged furniture in his hurry to get to her, followed closely by Katie and Harvey. Annie Mac sat propped up against a stack of pillows with her leg elevated, her smile growing as she reached toward her children. "Hey, guys," she said, ruffling Ty's head and then Katie's.

Katie draped herself forward on the edge of the bed. "Mama, are you better now?"

"I had a nice rest, sweetie. Did you?"

"Uh-huh. So did Agatha. Ty didn't."

"What did Ty do?" She turned to her son with those killer eyes dancing.

Clay's pulse quickened at the sight—a response he did not want to have, ever—as he watched from her doorway. He would not look at those eyes. He just wouldn't.

"I read some," Ty said. "Harvey and I hung out."

"And, Mama," Katie said, "we met the man with the gun."

Ty pushed at his sister's arm. "Katie! He was the guard!"

"But he had a gun. They both did."

Annie Mac touched Katie's head. "They're protecting us, aren't they? So nothing bad can happen."

"That's right," Clay said, hanging onto the lintel with one hand and leaning forward. Casually. "How are you today?"

She blushed. Clay tried not to think her adorable with her pixieish face coloring brightly and those big eyes wide. It took a few moments before she could offer a slight smile in his direction. "I'm much better, thank you. You're home early."

"I thought it best. We're due for a storm before long."

"Oh, my, I hadn't even noticed."

He opened her curtains enough for her to see the gray clouds that had grown heavier in the time he'd been home. A peal of thunder sounded several miles away.

"My, it is darkening, isn't it? Are we ready for it?"

"Candles and flashlights. Would you like to come out into the living room to eat or would you prefer to have a tray?"

"If it wouldn't be too much trouble, I'd love to have a tray. I'm still quite exhausted."

"Can I have a tray with you, Mama?" Katie asked. "I won't spill."

"I know you won't, lovey, but I think it would make too much work for Mrs. Barnes. Why don't you and Ty sit down with the lieutenant, and you can come in here with me later? If you bring one of your books, I'll read it to you."

"Okay, Mama. I'll go pick it out now." She scampered off in search of the promised treat.

"I'll speak to Mrs. Barnes," Clay said.

"Thank you, Lieutenant."

"Clay."

Annie Mac bit her bottom lip before she let it ease into a real smile. "Clay."

"That's better." He smiled back, then patted his thigh. "Come on, boy. One more trip outside before the rain hits."

Rain splattered against the glass, and thunder shook the heavens. Rumbling noises and light splashes were not Annie Mac's friends.

Mrs. Barnes set a flashlight on the bedside table. "I'll be back to help Katie get settled when you all finish your book."

"Thank you, Mrs. Barnes. The dinner was delicious, especially that corn bread. I never can get it to come out that moist. Perhaps you'll give me your recipe."

"It'd be a pleasure, Miss Annie."

Annie Mac smiled to herself and snuggled Katie closer. "Miss Annie," Mrs. Barnes had said. She'd been accepted. She belonged. The ache of it almost brought her to tears.

Clay was out there showing Ty how to unplug appliances and electronics that could be damaged in an electrical surge. They discussed how many candles they might need as they lit two for atmosphere and just to be ready. A man and a boy. A kind man and a boy who needed someone.

When had she started thinking of Clay Dougherty as a man she didn't have to fear? A man who was rapidly becoming a friend?

Ty came for his goodnight hug, followed by Mrs. Barnes. "The lieutenant found us a battery-powered night lamp," Mrs. Barnes said. "I put it in the bathroom so you'll be able to find your way, even if the lights go out."

She'd no more than spoken those words when they lost electricity. "Look at that, will you? Here now," she said, fumbling for the flashlight she'd set down earlier. "There we are, a nice light to lead us. Let's go find yours, Ty. I'll bring this one right back to your mama." Turning toward Annie Mac, she said, "I'll fetch you a candle, too, soon's I can."

"No need, Mrs. Barnes." Clay arrived with two flickering candles. "One for you," he said, placing one on Annie Mac's nightstand before ushering the children out with the second.

As she watched them go, the Pied Piper and his troops, she realized that this was the first storm she'd ever experienced where she hadn't wanted to cower under covers. Her daddy used to say lightning was God's judgment coming on the earth. Since he ranted about her innate wickedness, she was sure God was going to smite her dead one night. Auntie Sim had tried to soothe her, but some things couldn't be talked away. It took belief in something. Or someone.

And believing in safety didn't come easily. At least tonight they didn't need to worry about Roy. He hated storms worse than she did. She couldn't imagine him out on a night like this.

Mrs. Barnes returned to check on her. "The children's all settled in. Ty's got himself a tight hold on that other flashlight so's he can read a while, but that Katie's so tuckered, I don't think she'll last many more minutes."

"Thank you. You're very good with them."

"Children and me, we always get along. They're God's gift."

Annie Mac wiped at the spill-over that flooded her cheeks. Weeping and blushing were going to be the end of her. "They are."

"You need me to help you to the bathroom again before you sleep?"

"I think I'm fine. Thank you."

"Well then, I'll be just a shout away, so you don't need to worry none. The lieutenant's out there, too, where you can call him, you need anything at all." She looked at the candle next to the bed. "I'm wondering how you're going to blow that thing out when you want to sleep. Let me take care of it now, and I'll just leave this flashlight here right next to you. That way, you won't have to do more than turn it off."

Another lightning bolt flashed. She counted the seconds before she heard the rumble of thunder. Not too close.

Please let it stay that way, on the other side of forever. Let the bad flee. *Please.*

36 HANNAH

Hannah stood at the bathroom sink, slathering on face cream, when the house phone rang. Matt, already in bed, growled as he reached for the receiver. "Who on earth? It's almost ten."

She continued to smooth in the moisturizer. His "Oh, God, no" got her full attention.

"What?"

"We'll be right there," he told the caller and swung his legs over the side of the bed. "Get dressed. Will wants us to meet them at the hospital. Martin has taken Rita in. Things don't look good."

They pulled on whatever was close at hand and grabbed raincoats on their way out the door. The rain made visibility difficult, and Matt drove as fast as he dared, dodging the bigger puddles where Morehead's drains couldn't keep up with the deluge.

In the hospital waiting room, Rita's kin, blood and not, had gathered and sat silently waiting. Elvie Mae and James held hands. Tadie leaned into James, clutching his free hand. Jilly, on Will's lap, watched with sleepy eyes.

Hannah draped her coat on an empty chair and crouched next to Rita's mama. "What happened?"

"You hear about the accident?"

Appalled, Hannah shook her head. "What accident?"

"Some fool run Rita off the road, rammed her car smack into a ditch."

"Is she okay? Did it hurt the baby? Did the doctor see her?"

Elvie glanced over at James. He spoke up. "Seems she was a might sore. Doctor examined her, but the baby's heart sounded fine, and she wasn't bleedin' or crampin', so he sent her on home. Said to watch for signs of trouble."

"None much came," Elvie said. "Aches, but doctor said it was normal from being slammed around like that. Still, Martin was watching her. We went over just to check, you know?" Elvie stopped long enough to take a deep breath.

"Yes, ma'am."

James patted Elvie's hands and picked up the story. "So, Elvie here fixed them some dinner, which Rita wouldn't eat. She seemed tetchy, said her skin was cold and she was real thirsty, but there weren't no bleedin'. So we come on home. Martin promised to call if he needed us more tonight."

"When he did call..." Elvie began, then closed her eyes. They could see her lips moving.

James finished for her. "'Round eight-thirty, it was. Martin said she was in bad pain, crampin' all the time. He brought her in."

Hannah's heart hit bottom. Not Rita. Not Rita, too. She hugged them, one and then the other.

"Sweet Hannah-girl," Elvie whispered. "It's gonna be all right. The Lord's here. You know that."

But she didn't know that. She'd like to think so, but where had God been when her own babies had died? She bent over to hug Tadie.

"Lands, Hannah, this can't be happening again, can it?"

"Don't you worry," she whispered back, keeping her lips next to Tadie's ear, the one far from James. She needed to say the words, and she figured Tadie needed to hear them, but James and Elvie didn't. "Don't you even imagine something'll go wrong for that child in there." Hannah touched Tadie's rounded form. "Don't you even imagine it. That's my godchild, and I'm due one."

Tadie sniffled and gave her a lopsided smile. Tadie had to be struggling. Last time they'd been here waiting on a baby, it had been Hannah's second.

The second who had died. Her little boys, perfect little boys, little hands, little feet, little tender faces masked with death. One after the other.

This time platitudes wouldn't work either. If she'd heard them once during and after her pregnancies, she'd heard them a dozen times. "They're in heaven. God must have needed them more than you and Matt. It wasn't meant to be." If she'd believed that about God, she'd have signed up for atheism so fast necks would have snapped.

Tadie hadn't been fool enough to spout nonsense. Tadie'd wept with her, because all she'd wanted then was a shoulder. And her babies.

A shoulder was what she'd give now.

Still, maybe Martin would come through those doors and dispense good news instead of what they all feared. What could possibly go wrong, now that Rita was here, under care? Surely, the baby was near enough to term that they could save him if he'd been hurt. Maybe Rita only had the flu. There was a lot of it going around. Maybe the accident hadn't done any real harm.

She stood, moved toward Will. "Hey, Will."

She touched Jilly's hair, gently pet her head. "Hey, baby. You getting sleepy?"

Jilly nodded. Grunting slightly, Will rearranged the child's weight. Tadie asked if he wanted her to take a turn. He shook his head. "We're fine."

As Matt led Hannah over to another couch, she leaned into him, knowing that he, too, remembered. She closed her eyes. She'd pray. She'd align herself as best she could with Elvie and James over there, with Tadie, with Will and Matt. Surely God would hear their united pleas, even if none spoke them aloud.

The quiet felt funereal. She knew the staff here did their best. But she sure wished Martin could have gotten Rita to Duke or Chapel Hill. Even the hospital in Greenville would be better. They had specialists there. Experts.

Though even those experts in Greenville hadn't saved hers. Some things just happened.

But a body didn't have to like it. *God? Are you listening?*

She helped Tadie huff herself upright. "You need to go?"

"Yes, ma'am."

"Come on, then."

Tadie waddled down the hall, leaning on Hannah's arm. They didn't speak as they entered the restroom or as they each used a stall. Finally, scrubbing their hands, they looked at each other in the mirror.

"What do you think happened?" Tadie asked.

"Maybe something's just worrying the doctors. They could want her on monitored bed rest, you know? To protect the baby?"

"You think so?"

"Probably."

Tadie wiped her eyes. "Okay." She took a deep breath. "If it's something like pre-eclampsia, isn't that life threatening?"

"I think that's treatable. But we don't know, so let's not imagine things." She pulled her best friend into a hug. "You stop this worrying. Right now. Everything's going to be fine."

"As Martin always says, from your mouth to God's ears."

"Amen."

They waited. They paced the hall. Elvie Mae clung to James's hand, Will snuggled Jilly, and Matt moved from resting elbows on his knees, to slouching back, to crossing an ankle over his knee.

When Martin finally appeared, his gray, pinched face brought her up and toward him. He focused on James, who helped Elvie to stand. The rest, all except for Will with a sleeping Jilly on his lap, circled him. He reached one hand to Elvie, one to James.

"The baby was dead when we got here."

"Oh, my lamb, my little lamb." Elvie moaned. Sobs broke forth. She turned into James's arms.

"His heart just stopped beating. The doctors say they think the accident damaged Rita's placenta, causing it to separate from the uterus."

"Oh, no." Elvie started to shake. "Oh, my poor baby." James held her tightly but his eyes also filled.

Martin spoke stoically, obviously trying to hold himself together. Hannah wished she could do something, make this all go away.

"They've punctured her membrane and are giving her Oxytocin and saline, hoping she'll deliver very soon."

"What about bleeding?" Tadie asked the question several of them probably wanted an answer to. Hannah certainly did. "Are they worried? I mean, what's next?"

"All we can do is wait now. They're watching."

"But what about...?"

Martin raised a palm to stop Tadie's next question. "I've got to go back to her. You don't have to stay any longer. I don't know when you'll be able to see her."

"We'll be staying right here," James said. "Her mama and daddy will be holding vigil. You tell her that."

"I will. It'll mean a lot."

Hannah heard his whispered prayer as he turned to leave. "Avinu, Our Father in heaven, I beg of You, G-d of my fathers, have mercy."

She held the door for him. She doubted he even noticed. His last words carried to her before he disappeared down the hall. *"HaShem, Elohim, G-d Who saves, save us."*

Oh, yes, please, she begged silently. Please.

And then she opened her eyes and moved to Tadie's side, circling her with an arm as Will hefted a sleepy Jilly. "You go on home. I'll stay here."

Tadie turned into her embrace. "I hate this," she said, unable to control the tears any longer. "I don't want to leave any of you."

"I know, honey. But there's my godchild to consider. Please."

Nodding as she wiped her eyes with the back of her hand, Tadie said to Will, "Let's go."

Elvie and James slid back down onto the sofa, hands clasped. Elvie's tears had stopped for the moment. She always filled herself up with goodness and strength and passed it on to others. But this time? Would it be as easy for Elvie when it was her own grandson?

Hannah helped Will gather Jilly's bear and reached out for Matt. "You go on home, too. I'll walk you all down to the cars and come back here to wait."

Matt shook his head, his voice filled with sadness and compassion. "We'll both walk down, but I'm waiting with you. We've done this before, you and I. We need to stay together."

She turned away to open the door for Will and his bundle so Matt's words wouldn't be the ones to start her flood. He slipped up behind her and took hold of the door handle. "You help Tadie."

They were silent. Nurses spoke in hushed tones at various stations as they walked to the elevator. Will's rubber soles creaked with each step, Matt's harder ones tapped. The lone guard at the entrance nodded as they passed, but no one else acknowledged them, as if they were already walled off from the rest of the world.

The rain had slowed to a mist. Lights from cars and street lamps danced in the puddles. Objectively, Hannah knew it was beautiful, but not a one of them would appreciate it this night.

Mourning had begun.

37 CLAY

Snuffling and dog nails on the hard floor woke Clay. He heard a whispered, "Shush, Harvey."

"That you, Ty?"

"Yes, sir. Just making sure everything is okay in here."

"You and Harvey doing inside guard duty?"

"We are."

His eyes began to adjust to the dark. "Noises bothering you a bit? I bet that branch cracking off woke you."

"Yes, sir."

"You gonna be able to get back to sleep?"

The boy's doubtful "I guess so" got Clay moving. He pulled on a robe to cover his naked chest. "I'm wondering if maybe you and I need to fetch ourselves something warm to drink. Maybe see if we can ease the worry for both of us."

"You think that might be a good idea?" The boy's voice sounded hopeful.

"Well, we're both awake. And it might help."

"You need the flashlight, sir?"

"I could use someone to point the way."

Clay tightened his sash and followed Ty's light toward the kitchen. "You want to go close the door to your mama's room so we don't disturb her?"

"Yes, sir. I'll tiptoe, but you oughta keep Harvey from following. He makes a lot of racket on the floor."

"I'll do that. And let's light ourselves a candle."

Ty held the flashlight beam on the task and then tiptoed to do Clay's bidding. Good kid there. Thoughtful kid.

Clay poured some milk into a pan and lit the gas under it. Harvey sat near him until Ty returned and then shuffled over to the boy's side.

"Good thing you have a gas stove. Back home, we had to use a little candle thing under a pot when the electricity went off."

"This far out in the country, we lose power often enough that I insisted on gas. Thought I'd make hot chocolate. That sound like a good drink on a night like this?"

"Yes, sir! It sounds great."

They sipped their cocoa at the table, the candle burning between them, Harvey curled up on the floor beside Ty's chair with his head on his crossed paws.

The boy sipped slowly, silently, until he said. "You know something?"

Clay waited.

"You can't be quiet like this with girls."

"True. I've noticed that. But guys don't have to talk."

"Katie always chatters."

"Well, she's a girl. It's expected."

Ty nodded. And then another crash of lightning struck nearby. The boy jumped, and Harvey whined, moving closer to his foot.

Clay eyed them both. "You want to hang out a while more? We could maybe sit on my bed, lie down if one of us wanted to."

"It's a real big bed, isn't it?"

He raised an eyebrow. "You asking if it's big enough for Harvey, too?"

Ty grinned. "He wouldn't be any trouble. He could stay on my side."

"Fine. But if I fall asleep, keeping him still and quiet's your responsibility. No letting him wake me up, not unless there's an emergency."

"Yes, sir!"

"I'll take him in. You run check on your sister first and listen at your mama's door, in case that noise woke either of them."

"I'll be real quiet. I won't shine my light on either of them."

"Maybe you ought to open your mama's door carefully, in case she needs anything. Can you do that?"

"Yes, sir. I'll be right back."

Clay went to his bedroom, donned his pajama top, and had two pillows propped behind him when Ty returned. The boy held his flashlight pointed at the floor. "Everyone's asleep 'cept us. I checked."

"Good man." Clay fluffed one of his pillows and slid deeper into the bed. "Now, you think you and Harvey can crawl up on that side? We'll keep each other company, but tell you the truth, son, I'm tuckered out."

Ty settled himself under the sheet and called to Harvey, who leapt up and found a spot between them. Clay heard a quiet repeat of the word son in his mind as Ty turned off his flashlight.

38 ANNIE MAC & CLAY

A dim light showed around her closed blinds when Annie Mac woke, stiff from being in the same position all night. She stretched her arms first, then her good leg, lifting it as high as she could and as far to each side. She tightened her muscles, one group at a time, relaxed, and repeated the process, all the while longing to be free of the wretched cast. It divorced her from normal activity, which at this moment included a trip to the bathroom. And then wouldn't it be lovely to waltz into the kitchen, put on a pot of coffee, and make breakfast?

Today, she'd see Kev, after all these years. He said he'd arrange it with the lieutenant. The thought made her grin foolishly.

Family. She had family for her babies. A brother was enough. It sure was more than she'd had yesterday morning.

It was awfully quiet in the rest of the house. So, there'd be no help unless she were heartless enough to yell and wake everyone.

At least she had the hoist. She had been working to strengthen the muscles in her arms and stomach to make lifting herself easier, but she'd only achieved nominal success so far. Grabbing the bar, she began the laborious process. Pull-ups had never been her strong suit in school, and unused muscles had a way of shrinking to almost nothing. Granted, hers had bulked considerably in recent days if you compared them to their rope-likeness from before she'd started exercising. But it still exhausted her.

From a sitting position—very awkward because she looked like a stiff, rotated "L"—she swung her cast off the bed and inched her butt toward the edge. Mrs. Barnes had set her crutches within reach if she leaned way to the right. She brought them over, trying to balance and not slide to the floor. With even less grace, she used the hoist to lift herself to a wobbly standing position.

She felt like such a wimp. Her muscles quivered. Her breathing was labored. And she wanted to weep.

Really, Mrs. Barnes wouldn't mind if she called for help. But the electricity wasn't on, so she couldn't use the monitor, and a cry would wake the children as well as the lieutenant. Which would be cruel. And embarrassing.

Suck it up, Annie Mac.

She secured the crutches under her arms and hobbled out her door and down the hall. Pausing at the children's room, she glanced in. Katie slept curled around Agatha, but where was Ty?

In the bathroom, she braced on the handicap bars with her leg stretched out, trying to balance. How on earth did people with permanent handicaps face this day in and day out?

All she wanted to do when she'd finished her ablutions was fall back on her bed and quit for the day, but she had to find her son. If he'd been nearby, he'd have heard the slop/slide of her crutches and slipper on the hall floor, though they made little noise on the thick-piled rug almost as large as the great room.

Gray light filtered through the French doors, revealing neither Ty nor Harvey. He wouldn't be foolish enough to go out, would he? Unless he'd gone just beyond the door with Harvey.

But, no. He wouldn't.

The lieutenant's door stood ajar. Her heart sped from more than exertion as she approached, prepared to wake Clay so he could help her search.

She lifted her hand, glancing at the bed. And every horrible story of men taking advantage of small boys slammed into her. She opened her mouth to scream, to rush in there, crutches flailing, to beat the living daylights out of the man.

And then outlines emerged. Of her baby curled next to the snuffling dog on one side of a huge king-sized bed. Of Clay, far to the other side, out of dog-range, his brown hair mussed, his long body relaxed in sleep.

She closed the door on the sleeping trio and wiped her eyes. She was doing it again, leaking at a sweet sight. That boy of hers was the kindest, gentlest soul she'd ever come across, and he'd suffered so much from her choices. She didn't want to mess up again, but she was so afraid he'd bind his heart up with that man in there, and then they'd leave.

When she crossed to the kitchen, she found additional evidence of the man's kindness. A pan holding the remnants of cocoa and two mugs sat next to the sink. She had thought of putting on a pot of coffee, but felt too overwhelmed to make the effort. Instead, she hobbled over to the recliner, eased awkwardly down, tipped it back, and closed her eyes.

This was the first time in all his short life that her precious son had bonded with a man. She knew he needed one in his life if he were going to learn how to be one, but this was probably not the healthiest choice in the long run.

No, now she had Kev, at least part time. He'd said he was due back in Colorado in a week. He had an assistantship to help pay for his doctorate. Imagine, Kevin becoming a geologist. Well, he always had liked rocks.

He had told her on the phone that if she needed him, he'd drop out of school for a while. Stay here and take care of her.

Wasn't that the sweetest thing? But she couldn't let him.

Holidays, though? They could have holidays together. And he'd be here this afternoon to meet the children.

She felt the wet oozing again from her closed eyes. She pressed both hands against them, hoping to stop the flow. But her fingertips couldn't quell the ache that pressed those tears out. Nothing could.

She needed to learn to live with it. To get strong, get out on her own, and get past being so needy.

Clay awakened slowly and stretched. The boy slept, still snuggled next to the dog.

When Harvey opened an eye to watch his movements, Clay leaned over to pet the dog's head. Harvey's eye flipped closed.

A boy and a dog. In his bed. His stomach did a little lurch.

Stepping into the shower, he ducked his head under the full force of the spray, wishing it were a hair shirt or at least a barbed whip. He braced his hands against the tiled walls and felt the water's sting.

What had he gotten himself into? He knew better. He was the investigating officer, for crying out loud. He had to keep a proper perspective as well as a proper distance. He'd vowed after his first case never to bring his work home with him. Never to get involved on a personal level. A cop in a city had to be careful, but in a town the size of Beaufort? This was career suicide.

But hadn't there been something since he'd first held Katie up to kiss her mama? Since he'd let them give that mama his old iPod?

He'd felt like a hero.

And then he'd tried to run while making it so much more than a job. He just hadn't tried to run fast or far enough.

So, what had happened while he'd dawdled?

Fool!

Maybe it had been sneaking up quietly for a while, and that's part of why he'd fought so hard to keep his distance. Obviously, not hard enough. He cringed, remembering how easily he'd caved.

Did it matter? Maybe, maybe not.

He rubbed the bar of soap on the long loofah and scrubbed at his back.

When her eyes had been all swollen and discolored, he'd thought only of their color. But later, he'd discovered they could laugh. Laugh and fill with light.

Yes, light. They'd glowed with it.

And when that sheet had fallen to her waist, the blue gown, sort of a green-blue, had tinted her eyes and deepened them. He'd handed her the phone to call her brother, and joy had transformed her whole face.

Just last night, she'd gazed at him with a trust he'd never imagined she could feel. He wasn't quite sure why she did.

Then the boy had come to him.

Lord, help him, he was falling for all three of them.

He adjusted the water temperature, grabbed the bar of soap, and attacked his legs and feet, then his arms. As the water cascaded down his face, he whispered, "Impossible." He was a crazy. Or maybe so bored he was imagining things. That had to be it. Bored and needing what? Sex?

That elicited a hoot. He turned off the hot water so he'd cool down. Felt the cold shock his skin.

He wasn't supposed to think that way about a woman dependent on him, living in his house.

Right. Sure. He wasn't human? Only Catholic priests were called to celibacy, and yet wasn't that how he'd been living?

He shivered as he turned off the water and grabbed a towel from the rack. Scrubbing at his skin to redirect his thoughts worked for approximately two minutes.

If he remembered correctly, this had never happened to him before. Oh, yes, he remembered correctly. It must be that he was getting old, or maybe losing his mind was more like it.

Annie Mac Rinehart was still a married woman, even if she used her maiden name. And maybe she was starting to trust him, but that didn't mean she was ready for a relationship. She was bound to be needy. Her kids were bound to be needy. Didn't those words register in his messed up brain? He did not do needy, not after he'd helped raise his siblings. There'd been plenty on his plate, still was, if you considered he was the only one in shouting distance of his mama, who wasn't as young as she used to be. Rescuing folk was part of his day job, not of his personal life. Period. End of story.

For that matter, the last thing Annie Mac would want in her life was another man. Especially one who had to be at least, what? Eight years older... He thought back to her file as he ran a brush through his hair, picturing the dates. Not eight. He tossed the brush on the counter and reached for his tee shirt. He wasn't eight years older, but a whopping twelve years, ancient in comparison. Not that he thought of himself as old, but Annie Mac was closer to his baby sister's age. And he'd changed Dana's diapers, for crying out loud.

The whole thing did not have the makings of a good idea, no matter how you looked at it. It certainly lacked the makings of a happy ever after. If he even believed in those.

He shaved, trying not to notice every one of the nearly forty years etched on his face. He was growing older with a speed that he'd never imagined in his twenties. And now, here he was, yearning like a twenty-year-old for something unattainable. You'd think with age would have come a little more wisdom.

He saw himself as neither particularly handsome nor particularly plain. He was merely an okay-looking guy with a square jaw, a longish nose, a decent smile, and plenty of dark brown hair. Thank God for the hair. Avery, years younger, was already balding. But, let's face it. Nobody's head was going to turn when he walked down the street. So, maybe he believed in happy ever after for his good-looking younger brothers, who were both married to great women. And for their beautiful Dana, who was engaged, happily, to someone he respected. His mother and father had loved each other and been faithful to each other until the day his father had died.

So, yes, happy could work for some people. But it sure wasn't likely in the case of a man like him with a woman who'd been through the mess Annie Mac had.

He wiped out the sink, hung up his towel, and turned off the light. Ty and Harvey still slept. What a picture they made, the two of them snuggled in his big bed.

His brothers had winked at each other with smirks of understanding when they'd helped him set up the bed, making jokes the whole time. He'd raised his brows at their antics, told them a room this size called for a big bed. Even with the huge bed, he had space for a desk, a lounge chair, and a hassock. And, no, he didn't have anyone in mind to share it with, thank you.

Little brothers. Especially married brothers. His two thought they knew everything and wanted to share that everything with him.

As it turned out, Ty and Harvey were the very first to share his bed. Maybe, in the back of his mind, he'd imagined marriage and children and the comfort of being able to bring little ones to snuggle between their parents on stormy nights. Only, he hadn't found anyone he'd wanted to let into his world.

Before now. Before he'd gone and fallen for an impossible woman.

And, oh, how he'd fallen for her son.

He took a deep breath, trying to stick the ache back below the surface so it wouldn't show. Surely, he'd get over this. They'd move on, and he'd be fine.

Someday. Right now, he'd fix a cup of strong coffee. Then he'd rouse Harvey and take him out to do a morning check on the world.

He had a good life, which he'd go back to in a few more weeks. She'd lose the cast, he'd get Royce put away for life, and they'd all go their separate ways.

The sunlight that seeped over the horizon revealed Annie Mac lying in his big chair with her crutches at her side. Her dark red hair—and didn't that hair just make his fingers want to push through it?—waved around her face. She looked so peaceful, her eyes closed, her breathing even. He felt a catch in his throat as he neared. He badly wanted to touch her, to trace a finger along her cheek, across her lips.

As he stood mutely staring, her eyes opened, and she stared back at him, just as mutely.

39 HANNAH

Hannah woke with a start. She'd fallen asleep against Matt, and her neck had a crick in it. She pushed up and away from him. With his head lolling back like that, he wasn't going to feel any more lively than she when he came fully awake.

Elvie nodded at her, woman to woman, as James slept with his gray-fuzzed head in her lap. Hannah pointed to the corridor and headed straight to the nurses station.

"She's still in recovery," the duty nurse said.

A cold dread filled her as she headed to the bathroom. Recovery from what?

The question accompanied her to Elvie's side. She crouched low to whisper, "They said Rita's in recovery. I don't know what that means."

Elvie shook her head. "Martin will come tell us soon's he can."

It was another half hour before they saw him. Matt helped Hannah to her feet and led her over as Martin knelt in front of his mother-in-law. James opened his eyes and sat up, as if he'd been waiting for Martin. He rested a hand on his son-in-law's shoulder. "Tell us."

Martin gulped in a large breath. "She had concealed bleeding."

"What...?" Elvie began.

"Her placenta. It separated from the uterus high up." He paused. Took another sharp breath. "Not all the way at first, so no one knew she was bleeding when she came to the emergency room. But then the placenta separated all the way. They said it was too compromised. They called it a placental abruption."

"Oh, son." This from James.

"If they'd known when she came in the first time, they could have done an emergency C-section and saved the baby, but no one knew. There were no signs except for her rapid pulse. Anxiety, they thought." When his eyes filled, he let the tears overflow down his cheeks.

No one spoke. They weren't quite sure what he was saying, but Hannah felt the shock of it, whatever it was, like a wave of grief washing over the room.

"They... they had to perform a hysterectomy."

"Oh, Martin." Elvie reached out and set her small, gnarled hands on either side of his head, pulling him forward into her lap as his tears turned to sobs. "Oh, honey lamb, I'm so sorry. So very sorry."

He clung to her for another moment as he regained control. Elvie let him go, waiting silently as he used his arms to wipe his face. Hannah handed him a box of tissues.

"They didn't know until the baby's heart stopped," he was finally able to say. "When Daniel was born, he was so perfect, so beautiful, those tiny, perfectly formed hands and feet. We were dealing with the grief of holding him when Rita started hemorrhaging. They tried to stop it, tried everything they knew to do, even packing ice, but they had to take the uterus so she wouldn't go into shock and die."

"Thank the good Lord she's alive, son. And your baby... well," James said, squeezing Martin's shoulder again, "that baby is right in the arms of that same Lord, don't you doubt it for a minute."

Matt took Hannah in his arms. She wanted to spill her own tears, but the shock had dried them. She turned to Martin when he scrambled to his feet. "I'm so sorry. So very sorry."

Martin hugged each of them in turn. "I've got to go," he finally said. "I've got to be with her."

"Tell her how much we love her."

He nodded.

And they waited, for hours, it seemed. When finally Elvie and James were allowed in to see their daughter, Hannah drew them close, one at a time. "Tell her we'll come by later. I ... I'll bring Tadie."

"Yes, sweet girl. I'll tell her," Elvie said. "She'll be glad."

Hannah couldn't imagine Rita being glad of anything for a very long time. She could remember those months. Those years.

They grabbed coffees and eyed scones at the Dunkin' Donuts on their way through Morehead. They weren't hungry, but food seemed to be what one did. Not rejoicing. Slogging through. "Take some to the Merritts?" Matt suggested, his voice the same colorless gray she felt.

"They'll want to hear."

"We won't stay long. I'm so tired I can hardly see."

"No, we won't stay."

Will unlocked his back door, held it open. He looked almost as exhausted as they felt.

"We bear gifts," Matt said, plunking the bag of scones down in front of Tadie, who sipped tea instead of coffee at the kitchen table. They sat down across from her.

Tadie opened the bag and peered inside. Will got plates, poured more coffee for himself, and joined them. "Tell us."

Hannah had taken out an orange cranberry scone, but she merely held it. "Martin, well, Martin..." The pastry crumbled between her fingers.

Matt cleared his throat before the words could come. "They had to perform a hysterectomy so she wouldn't bleed out."

Tadie's chin fell toward her chest. She clutched her hands so tightly that her knuckles whitened. "She lost her baby *and* her womb?" Her voice barely whispered the words.

Will slid next to her and placed one hand over hers. He didn't speak. None of them did. Obviously, now was not the time to go into detail. Hannah sniffed, wiped her eyes, gestured to have Tadie call her, and then she and Matt left.

In the car again, she said, "Knowing what Rita is going through..." Her throat closed, and it was a minute before she could force out the rest of the words she needed to say. "Knowing what it's going to be like for them for the next while..."

Tears finally broke free. Matt reached across the seat to clasp her hand.

"I know."

"For forever. It'll hurt. Maybe not this..." She paused on a broken sob. Matt pulled a tissue from the box in the center console. She put it over her mouth, dabbed it on all the wet places. "Maybe not so badly, but it'll hurt. Oh, yes. It'll be there. Forever."

"I know, love. I know."

Matt hugged her again when they got home. "Go take a warm bath. And then it's into bed."

"You, too?"

"I'll be along shortly. I'm going to call Roland, see if he can keep the appointment I had today."

Afraid she'd fall asleep in the tub, she opted for a shower. As she dropped into bed, she heard Matt coming up the stairs. "Everything set?" she asked drowsily.

"Mmm..." He climbed in next to her, pulled her toward him, and circled her waist with his arm.

The comfort. Oh, the comfort. With the ache still acute, she let go and slept.

The picture slammed into her and repeated, rewinding, those lines and lines of perfect babies, all silent, all dead. She knew they were dead, but they were pink-cheeked and rosy, as if they merely slept. Why didn't they cry? Or breathe?

No mothers mourned them. Oh, God, where were the mothers? She searched everywhere, but she couldn't find any. Why wasn't there someone to cry over the lost babies?

Where were the mothers?

She woke, thrashing, crying.

"What?" Matt mumbled.

Oh, thank God. It was just a dream. "Nothing. A dream. Go back to sleep."

"Love you, Mrs. Morgan," he said into her hair. "Love you. Forever."

She edged against him, let him pull her close. "Forever."

Still, the tears fell for the lost babies. For all the lines of babies.

40 HANNAH

Bed was seductive. It had claimed her for months after the loss of her own babies. It claimed her again now and had for days.

She smoothed her fingers over the sheet, cool now where Matt had lain with her late into the morning. But he was gone, and she was here. Alone in her big, too-quiet house, where the only sounds came from the air conditioner as it cycled on.

Where had Matt said he'd be? The phone had rung. He'd gotten up, showered, and then kissed her cheek.

Work? No, it was the weekend. Wasn't it still the weekend? She glanced at her clock, surprised that it read one thirty-four. In the afternoon.

She'd brushed Tadie off yesterday, said she was busy, but when she'd tried to work in her studio, she'd smashed every single piece. Or it had flattened on its own.

She pushed up and off the bed and shuffled into the bathroom. By the time she came out, the message light was blinking on her bedside phone. She dialed in and heard Matt's voice.

"Hey, honey, I saw Will and Jilly outside Ace Marine a little while ago. They're headed up to the boat, but he looked kind of peaked. And Jilly, well, she wasn't her bubbly self. Seems to me like you may want to stop by Tadie's, see what's going on there."

Something more than the loss of Rita's baby? For heaven's sake, Tadie still had her own baby safely tucked in the womb.

Okay. Not nice.

She'd been trying to work on her attitude, hadn't she? Be kind. Be thoughtful.

Cow. That's what she was. A cow.

A mean-spirited shrew.

Cow, shrew—either fit.

She pulled on a sundress, not because it was a dress. It was just easier than two pieces of anything. If she had to find pants and a top, she'd have to coordinate. Then she slipped into sandals, grabbed a purse, and headed out the door.

No, she wouldn't stop to eat. She could scavenge from Tadie's refrigerator if hunger overwhelmed her. Right now, she just wanted to stop thinking.

And, yes, she'd walk. Exercise was supposed to clear the head.

Okay, she probably should have worn walking shoes instead of sandals that slapped against the concrete. But she'd come three blocks, which put her closer to Tadie's than home. She kept going.

When Tadie didn't answer her knock, Hannah checked the knob, which was supposed to be locked. She had a key, but all she had to do was waltz right in. Anyone could have opened that door. Including a murderer.

Set to yell at her best friend, she climbed the stairs. And found Tadie curled in a lump on her bed, still in her nightgown. Hannah eased herself down by Tadie's knees.

"You sick?"

"No."

"You need help getting up?"

"No."

"You want to talk about it?"

That seemed to open Tadie's faucets, but she ignored the tears that spilled toward her pillow. Hannah yanked a tissue from the nearly empty box by the bed and wiped at a few trying to climb the bridge of her friend's nose.

Tadie snuffled and grabbed her own tissue. "I'm a disaster."

"Yeah, well, join the crowd."

"No, I mean really."

"You mean more 'really' than I can see? More than the rest of us?"

Tadie snuffled again. Her head bobbed once.

"Ah."

"I'm a wicked step-mother and a horrible wife."

"Oh, pooh. You're thirty-nine weeks pregnant."

"Jilly went wailing to her room last night. I'm supposed to be her mother, to be loving and kind and a good influence, and what was I? A miserable cow who barked at that sweet little girl. Again!"

"A cow, huh? I think that's what I called myself about twenty minutes ago. Oh, and I mentioned shrew, which has to be worse than cow. Just cuddle your sweet girl when she gets home. She'll forgive you."

"And then I made Will finish cooking."

"I bet he did a good job."

"That wasn't the big thing." Another snuffle and more tears.

Hannah waited.

"I took a bath."

Ah, a bath. That would account for it. But Hannah kept her mouth shut.

"I locked the hall door. To get away."

"Um." An um was the best she could do, because really?

"Then all I did was sit in a full tub, worrying about my varicose veins and my belly button, if it will ever be an innie again. And how far down my breasts will sag, or if I'd end up with wrinkly, horrid skin. And, oh, Hannah! Rita had just lost her baby!" Tadie curled her legs right up to her abdomen and her sobs turned guttural as she covered her face with her hands.

Eventually, the sobs evolved into hiccups. "I'm such a... a mess."

Well, yes, she was, but Hannah knew better than to say so. She didn't want to get to comparing messiness, because, honey, she'd win.

"And it... it just got worse." Tadie blew her nose. It came out as a honk. "And... and Will tried to soothe me. He was wonderful. But I... I snapped his head off."

"I'm sure he understood."

Tadie's eyes flashed at that, and she wailed out, "Of course he did! He always understands!"

Okay, time to intervene. "Honey, you've got to stop this. You're working yourself up to a frenzy."

Tadie glared but didn't answer.

"I know you're miserable. And that it's your pregnancy speaking. But you've got to get a grip, really, because there's not a one of us who isn't broken up about Rita's baby." Hannah plucked at her wedding ring. "Besides, this stress isn't good for my godchild."

She waited. Either Tadie would yell or get over herself.

Her friend grabbed another tissue and blew hard. "I know. I'm sorry."

"Lands, girl, I know you are, but get up now and let me fix you something to eat. Fix us both something. I'm starving. You probably didn't even have lunch, did you?"

"Or breakfast." Tadie's voice was still small, but she showed teeth in the beginnings of a grin.

"What can I do?" Hannah extended a hand as Tadie pressed on the mattress, struggling to move her bulk.

"Pull?"

Together they got the fat lady up, on her feet, and waddling to the bathroom. "There's chicken salad in the fridge."

She had the sandwiches on the table and drinks poured by the time Tadie made her way into the kitchen. "You're looking better."

"I feel almost human, but I'll be a whole lot happier once that food hits what space is available in here." Tadie patted her mound and picked up a sandwich half. "Thanks."

"You're welcome." She bit into a chunk of chicken, keeping her eyes on the sandwich in her hands as she chewed. She needed half a glass of water to get the food down.

Maybe telling Tadie was premature. Maybe she should wait.

And maybe the words would prove a distraction. For them both. "Matt suggested we adopt."

Tadie spluttered past her own mouthful. "Adopt?" She held up a hand until she'd swallowed. "Now? Oh, Hannah, yes!"

"You think?"

"I do. But won't it take a long time?"

"It might. I guess it depends on whether we want a baby or an older child."

"Oh, a baby, if you can get one soon. Think about ours growing up together."

Hannah turned away for a moment. "You and Rita thought you'd be sharing this. How do you think she'll feel if it's the two of us instead?"

Tadie sobered. "Whether you adopt or not won't give her back her baby. I know Rita. She'll be thrilled for you, just like you were thrilled for us."

"I was jealous."

Her friend took another bite and didn't speak, but her expressive eyes made Hannah wince. She didn't want pity.

"I hated myself for it."

"No, no, I can see it. I'm sorry. I should have been more sensitive."

"And then I fell in love with Annie Mac's children. I was jealous of her, too."

Tadie reached across the table. "True confession time?"

"I'm tired of me. Tired of making things about me when they're not. You know?"

"I do. And now you're going to be one busy lady, playing auntie, traveling to Europe, and then hunting up a baby. No time for much else."

Hannah barked out a laugh. Trust Tadie to put things in perspective. "I am. I guess we'd better get busy on that paperwork so I can concentrate on the auntie part and then on the Italy part, while the agency checks on a match."

On her walk home, the beat of her sandals made Hannah smile as her thoughts leapt ahead. She couldn't wait for Matt to get home so they could discuss strategies. This time, her silent house felt expectant.

Talking. A best friend. Being honest.

Who knew it would make her feel so much lighter?

She kicked off her shoes, grabbed a glass of ice water, and hunted for something constructive to do until he got home. Dirty laundry waited in the washer. That could be first.

She poured in a measure of detergent and started the machine. The vacuum sat where she'd left it, so she ran it over the still-clean floors. When the washer shut off, she loaded the dryer and headed upstairs.

On a roll, she tackled the master bath, because they'd used it a few times, she and Matt, since the last time she'd spritzed and wiped. The guest bathroom hadn't been used since ... well, fine, it was clean.

The dryer pinged. She removed and folded the laundry.

This time, when she pictured the small shirts, the little girl socks, the young boy underwear, she imagined a child of her own, not borrowed, but hers. And Matt's. A child who needed them, who needed a forever home. Katie and Ty had always been meant to go, but they'd left a gift. They'd shown her—and Matt—the possibility of children, their own children.

41 CLAY

Avery strolled into the office, a cup of coffee in one hand and a paper sack in the other. Collapsing in his chair, he glanced over at Clay. "Brought you one," he said, extending the bag of donuts.

Clay shifted his paperwork to one side. "What kind?"

"Chocolate covered, powdered, and cinnamon."

"I'll take cinnamon."

Avery bit into his and spoke around a mouthful. "Mandy'd kill me if she knew I had these. I promised I'd lose ten pounds." He stared at the starch and sugar in his hand. "Guess this isn't exactly the best diet plan." Grinning, he finished it, then licked chocolate off his fingertips.

Clay ate his more slowly, washing the doughy sugar down with slugs of water. He'd returned to his paperwork when Avery interrupted with, "You've been working with Dr. Levinson's wife, haven't you? On the Royce Bingham case?"

Clay glanced up. "Yeah?"

"Some folks were talking over to Morgan's. Seems Dr. Levinson's wife lost her baby sometime Friday night."

Clay felt the cold hit him right in the pit of his stomach. "How?"

"The details seemed a little sketchy, you know how guys are. I guess she got to the hospital, they found it was dead. Seems she can't have any more either, and him, a baby doctor. Doesn't seem right."

Clay stood up, excused himself, and stuck his head in the chief's office, telling first Chief Bradley and then Stella that he had to go out. His words got him a nod from the first, a "When you think you'll be back?" from the second.

"Soon as I can," he said. "You need me, use my cell."

At the hospital, he asked for Rita's room. Halfway there he realized he should have stopped for flowers or something. But he kept walking.

He knocked at the open doorway to her room. She was awake, her mama sitting in the chair next to her bed. "Come on in, Lieutenant," Elvie Mae said.

"I just heard. I can't tell you how sorry I am." He took Rita's hand, noting the effort she made to smile at him.

She thanked him. "How's Annie Mac?"

"Doing well. She's going to be devastated about your baby."

Elvie Mae spoke up. "You hear anything more 'bout that man? He still loose?"

"Yes, ma'am, I'm afraid he is. We've got men from Brock's watching my place day and night. Thank you so much for recommending Mrs. Barnes. She's a treasure."

Elvie nodded. "She's a good woman."

"The children have really taken to her, and I think her presence has soothed Annie Mac."

"Clay," Rita said, "do they know if it was his car hit me?"

He hesitated, but only for a few seconds. "It may have been. Seems it had green paint under all that brown muck, same as the one that robbed the convenience store."

She sent her mama a pained look. At Elvie's nod, she said, "You need to know. They..." She seemed to choke on the words.

Elvie handed over another tissue. While Rita used it, Elvie turned to him. "The doctors told us it was the accident did this bad thing."

Rita dashed away the tears. "Murder. He's... he's done murder twice we know of."

Clay sighed. This hurt. "Rita, I'm so sorry." He should have stopped this. Caught Bingham before he could do this thing.

She jerked her chin up. "I don't want you telling Annie Mac. I don't want her having more guilt than she's already carrying."

"I won't. But you can be sure I'm doing everything in my power to stop him."

"Martin figures if it was him, he must have gotten plate numbers at the house that night. What we can't figure out is how he matched mine up with me and who he might try to get to next. Everybody's a target if we imagine I was."

"I'll need to call the Morgans and the Merritts," Clay said. "To warn them."

"Please. I'd rather it came from you. I know Hannah and Tadie will visit again this afternoon, so you might want to give them a call."

"I'll go do that now. Soon as I inform Chief Bradley. We're going to have to get someone in to figure out how Royce is getting his information. Somebody has access to what we know. We need to find out who." He glanced from one to the other, hoping they'd want to know the latest. "I do have some good news. At least Annie Mac thinks it is."

They waited.

"Her brother's in town. He's staying at the house for a short visit before he has to go back to school in Colorado."

"Didn't we think he was dead?" Rita asked.

"We did. She hadn't spoken to him since her father threw her out for being pregnant. Kevin found out she was still alive quite by accident."

"I'm so glad."

"He seems like a good man. Good for the kids and Annie Mac." And probably for Clay as well. Having the young man around might let him plug a little distance back into his world.

"Family's important." Elvie Mae patted her daughter's hand.

He left them with a nod. Elvie was right about families, as long as they were in working order. But those parents who'd thrown out their daughter? Or those who abused kids or tried to take from family members, from the aging? Who let greed take over? Not so much.

Back at the station, he opened his folder and laid out the evidence for Chief Bradley. The man was a good cop who would take this seriously and find help at the state level if need be.

The chief said, "You had any luck finding more on Bingham's history? Who he hung out with?" He waved at the computer screen. "Whoever is tapping into these databases either has a PI's license or a relationship to the police force. Or he's darn good at hacking. It'd be good to find a relationship somewhere, because this is making me mighty angry."

Clay raked his fingers through his hair in frustration. "Bingham didn't have many friends, not as a kid or when he returned to Beaufort to work at Morgan's. We've interviewed co-workers there, and they don't have anything good to say—or much, other than that he was an angry drunk. Morgan's fired him over a year ago." Clay shuffled through the folder, hunting up the news article he'd printed out.

"Did they find out anything more from that girlfriend up in...where was it? Alligator?"

"She's sticking by her story that he couldn't have done any of these things, not the Roy she knew. Claims he was always good to her and all he wanted was access to his baby girl. They just wanted to share custody with Annie Mac."

"Right. So he beats up his wife to show good intentions."

Clay nodded, pulled out the sheet he'd been looking for. "And he kills in cold blood. But take a look at this, will you?" He slid the copy toward the chief. "Seems our Mr. Bingham performed at least one heroic act when he was a kid."

"Heroic?"

"If you believe the article from the *Sun Journal*. His name came up as the nine-year-old kid who rescued another boy from a pond. The younger boy, Peter Rasman, was drowning. Bingham went in and pulled him out."

"So what happened between nine and now to turn him into a madman?"

"Same old story, from what I've been able to piece together. Abusive alcoholic father. He beat Royce so Royce beats up on others." Disgusted, Clay said, "Except, it seems, when he's with that Rachel woman."

The chief shook his head. "When does it end, that cycle?"

"Let's see that it ends here and now. We're going to catch this man, and we're also going to catch the person helping him."

"See to it, Clay."

"I'm going to ask Ms. Rinehart if she's ever heard of a Peter Rasman. Maybe we can find a connection."

After phoning Will and Matt to warn them that Bingham might know where they live, he headed home. He had questions to ask.

It was good for Annie Mac to have her brother there. That first day, Clay had pulled the younger man aside. Said he was welcome to visit any time he wanted, but they had to make sure no one followed him. Granted, Bingham probably didn't have any idea Kevin existed, but the fact remained, the folks at the station knew, and if they did, word might filter back to Bingham.

"You think I could endanger them?" Kevin had asked.

"I don't know. We've put out word that they're gone from here, but I'm not sure what this man's capable of. How long do you plan to be in town?"

"I've got a week before I ought to leave." He'd looked around the yard. "I've already told Annie Mac I'll cancel my classes, give up my assistantship, if either of you thinks I can help more here. I sure don't want to lose my sister or her kids. Not when I've just found them."

Clay had put his hand on the young man's shoulder. "Why don't you stay here at the house? It would mean the couch, but I imagine you're still young enough not to mind camping."

The joy on Kevin's face had been reward enough. "Could I? That would be great."

"You checked in any place?"

"Not yet. I was going to ask for recommendations."

"Pull your car in the other space in the garage, out of sight. I take it you don't have to return the car to your folks right away?"

"Nope. It's Mama's." Kevin pumped his hand. "I can't thank you enough. Really."

"Go tell your sister. She could use some cheering up."

Clay drove into the yard now and waved at the guard, then entered the house via the garage door. Mrs. Barnes glanced up from putting clothes in the dryer and gave him one of her gentle smiles.

"Evening," he said. "Everybody well?"

"Um-hmm. Every last one of us. Good to have that young man here."

Clay walked toward the great room, pausing at the entrance to take in the homey scene.

Annie Mac reclined in the big chair, her eyes closed and a smile on her face. Across from her, Kevin listened to Ty chat about his action figures, while Katie lay on her stomach, intently coloring on a pad of paper. Harvey seemed focused on Katie's hands as they scribbled across the page.

Harvey stuck his nose up and turned his head to Clay, which caught Katie's attention. The smile that lit her face was seconded on Annie Mac's and nearly did him in.

"Hey, all," he said, walking into the room. He bent to touch Katie's head, reached to pet Harvey. "Ty, Kevin," he said, gaining a grin and a "hey" from Ty.

Kevin saluted. "Lieutenant."

"Clay, remember?" Then to Annie Mac, "How're you all doin'?"

"Fine." Annie Mac waved her hand across the room. "As you can see. What brings you here this early?"

"Thought I'd stop to check on things. All seems well outside. I'm thinking our ruse may have worked."

"Oh, I hope so."

He pulled up a chair so he could sit near her. "You don't need to fret any, Annie Mac. We're going to take good care of you and yours."

She reached out a hand, which he took and cradled between his two much larger ones. "You are," she said softly. "I thank you." And then, as if realizing their hands touched, she carefully withdrew hers.

Mrs. Barnes, carrying folded towels to the guest bath, said, "I think it's time that dog went for a walk, and I'm needing a short one myself. Anyone want to join me?" She looked pointedly at Kevin, who nodded and got to his feet.

"Yes, ma'am. Can't sit around too long. Let's go, kids."

"Ty," Mrs. Barnes said, "while I put these up, you go fetch the dog's leash, and Katie, honey, run collect your shoes."

In the aftermath of the mass exodus, Annie Mac turned back to Clay. "She's such a gem. I don't know what I'm going to do without her."

"I feel the same way. Maybe I can bribe her to stay forever."

"Don't I wish I could."

Annie Mac's laugh warmed him, but Clay didn't say what he was thinking, what he'd have liked to tell her. Still, it took a minute for him to swallow those words before speaking again. "How's it been having Kevin here?"

"Wonderful. I like him so much."

"Were you afraid you wouldn't?"

"It's been a long time."

"And he grew up under that father of yours."

Annie Mac nodded. "That has worried me ever since I left. But it seems Kevin's stronger than he looks. He told me our uncles helped out. One teaches at the high school."

"He the one who influenced Kevin to be a geologist?"

"Must be. I had him for earth science, but it wasn't my thing. I didn't see him a whole lot out of school."

"But Kevin did."

"I don't think Uncle Nate believed the story of my running away. After all, he knew my dad. So, he went all out for Kev."

"Good for him. You said there was another uncle?"

"My mother's younger brother. He wasn't approved of at all because he was rough around the edges, a farmer with hordes of children. Our house was near enough that Kev got to spend a lot of time there, riding tractors, messing around in dirt. My uncle and aunt pulled him right into the fold. Dad may not have liked it, but he didn't stop Kev from going."

"They didn't include you?"

Annie Mac sighed. "They tried to, but their children were babies then. I babysat occasionally, but once I met Ty's father, I wasn't content doing that any longer." She blushed. "I thought I was in love. Obviously, I was merely a fool."

"You were young."

"Yes, well." She paused, then said, "Thank you again for Kevin."

"He did it. As soon as he found out you were here, he came running."

"I'm just so grateful."

Clay cleared his throat before he launched into the news he'd brought. "I've been by to see Rita."

"Oh?"

"It's not good news." He told her the story, leaving out Bingham's probable involvement.

"Oh, Clay, no."

She glanced outside toward where the children played with the dog. "I can't imagine not having either of them." He held out a hand. She stared at it blankly before letting hers fall into place. When he tightened his grip, her fingers responded.

"No possibility of more," she said. "How must she feel?"

Clay shook his head, remembering an agony, the worst he'd known. "Like I did when my dad was killed." Her mouth opened in surprise, so he nodded and told her more, adding, "I was in the truck with him."

"I'm so sorry."

"This limp I have?" With his free hand, he pointed to his leg, but she just looked puzzled. "You haven't noticed?"

"I haven't."

"I guess I've gotten better at compensating. I've set off metal detectors with all the pins and plates in there." He hoped for a grin in response and got a shy one, but it seemed as if giving her a moment of levity let her notice where her hand lay. Again she took it back, but this time was more of a snatch than a slide from under.

"How old were you?" Her voiced trembled. From the subject under discussion or from the hand-holding?

A man wanted to know these things.

"Sixteen. My brothers were thirteen and ten, my sister only five."

"Your poor family. What did you do?"

"What could we do? We carried on."

"And you became the surrogate father." She didn't make it a question.

He shrugged and gave a short laugh. "Sort of."

"Tell me about them. Is your mother still alive?"

Finding a lighter tone wasn't hard, not when talking about his family. "She is. She lives not far from here on the old homestead. You know, one of those houses that came through so many generations you can almost tell the family history—certainly its size increase—by the years of room additions."

"I bet you all love it."

"Yeah, but I don't know who will take it over when Mom's too old to live there alone."

"It would be sad to let it go, wouldn't it?" She sounded wistful.

"I'm hoping one of my brothers will move east. Alan and his wife might. He's in Raleigh now, but an electrical engineer ought to be able to live anywhere. At least, that's what we tell him. John is in construction, which has him in Cary. So, we'll see. There's time. My little sister, Dana, is engaged to a fellow who teaches at State, so she's probably destined to stay there."

"You sound proud of them."

He smiled more fully this time. "I am. They've done well for themselves."

"As you have." Her face was so expressive. The blush that rose made his stomach do little flips.

"It was hard losing my father, but the community was good to us. So, I give a little back."

"Instead of going to a city?"

"I graduated from UNC, same as Tadie, as a matter of fact, and enjoyed Chapel Hill. I did a stint in Raleigh, got started in police work there, and finished my master's degree at State. But it wasn't home."

Her eyes seemed to find a moment of humor. He waited to see what that meant. Finally, she let a grin spread, and her arm swung in an arc. "Ty, Katie, and I sure are glad you picked here to live. This place. You've been so generous with your beautiful home, and if you hadn't been here, we wouldn't have been able to be your guests."

He laughed, as she obviously meant him to. *"Mi casa es tu casa."*

"Your house is mine?" Her laugh degenerated to a giggle, which was hugely appealing. "You want to trade?"

He grinned. "Don't you wish!"

Before the others came closer than the deck, he changed the subject. "I need you to think again, dig a little deeper to help us catch Royce. Did he ever mention someone named Peter Rasman? Or anyone else he might have gone drinking with? I'm grasping at straws here, but we need something, anything that might help us find who could be aiding him now. Someone has to be."

"I've told you all I remember."

He leaned forward, rested his elbows on his knees as he concentrated his attention on her. "I know you have. But I'd like you to do it once more. Just cast your thoughts back to the beginning. When you met him, perhaps. Those first years. Before things got bad between you."

She closed her eyes. He waited, enjoying the play of emotion on her face. Finally, she looked up. "We didn't go places with anyone, even in the beginning. I suppose I should have known that said something about him. There has to be a reason a man has no friends he wants to show you." Her hands plucked at her shirt. "I didn't pay any attention. I was a fool."

"Not a fool."

"I was. I thought he was trying to make me feel special, taking me out to nice meals, bringing me flowers. I never thought to ask about any friends."

"You couldn't have known."

"I should have."

Clay agreed, but he didn't like her berating herself.

"I've been wracking my brain." She shook her head. "Nothing."

He sighed and was about to let it go, when she said, "Wait a minute. He got to drinking heavily one night and he did mention somebody named Pete. He said Pete owed him. He was always saying things like that. I owed him, his dad owed him, his boss owed him. Pete was the only real name he used that I can think of. The rest were random people, like the local mechanic who'd overcharged him." She raised her hands to cover her cheeks. "If you'd heard how he talked."

Clay rose, dragging his chair back out of the way as the children pressed toward her, the dog at their heels. "Once upon a time, Royce rescued a boy named Peter Rasman from drowning."

42 ANNIE MAC

With the lieutenant headed back to work, Annie Mac asked Mrs. Barnes to help her hobble to the bathroom. "And then maybe to bed for a little while?"

"That's right, Miss Annie. Do your back good. You been sittin' in that same position too long now."

The bedroom cocooned her and gave her time to think. She couldn't quite believe that she'd actually joked with the lieutenant. Actually let him hold her hand for a moment. No flinching, no heart going thwack, thwack against her ribs.

That look? There'd been a gleam in those eyes of his.

But he couldn't find her attractive. She'd been at her worst in his presence, her absolute ugliest. And she still wasn't much to look at.

That elicited a chuckle. Put Kevin next to her, and it was Beauty alongside the Beast with the wrong gender attached. Her smile widened. It was a good thing she loved her brother so much, or jealousy would be licking at her right now. The same genetic input and look at the results.

At least, she was no longer shorn or quite so raggedly looking. She could even pull her hair so the short parts and scar weren't so noticeable. The doctor had done a good job on her cheek. That one probably wouldn't show nearly as much as she'd imagined, not once it healed completely. She'd never been and never would be as gorgeous as her baby brother, even at her best, and her best was far from her present state.

So, what did Clay's reaction to her mean? Unless she was very much mistaken, the lieutenant liked her. And not just any old liking either. He liked her as a man liked a woman.

If truth be told, she rather liked him, too.

Lord, have mercy. She was just going to die. Plain and simply die. She could not like a man. Or let one like her.

Her track record was abysmal. How could she trust emotions? She certainly couldn't trust attraction—not hers and not a man's. That whole neediness thing had to be got past. Better, really, that she figure out how to be strong on her own than go imagining romance with anyone. Even if that anyone did have twinkly eyes and hair that mussed. Even if he did have a kind and brave heart.

She let herself remember the news he'd brought. Rita must be in such terrible pain right now. If only there were some way to help. But she'd never lost a child. Any pain she'd experienced had to be so much less than the loss of a baby.

Kevin poked his head in her room. "Hey, how're you feeling?"

"Okay. Just a little tired."

"I thought I'd take these two back outside. Ty's still about to bounce out of his skin. I'm figuring they need more exercise than they've been getting, and truth be told, so do I."

"Not near the water."

"We're just going to explore the marsh. I'll take care of them. Harvey'll be with us, so no one's going to come snatch them."

"They don't swim."

"You've told me, but I'm not taking them far. Stop fretting." He glanced over his shoulder. "You know, you'd better do something about them and water. Get them some lessons."

She sighed and nodded. But every time she thought of swimming, she remembered her father tossing her in the deep end of the pool, saying she was old enough to learn and all she had to do was try. She'd almost drowned before he'd hauled her out, yelled at her, and the next day sent her to the YMCA for swimming lessons. It had been cold and miserable and smelly and the other kids had called her a chicken. She'd learned, sort of. But she'd never gotten over the feeling that the water wanted to suck her under. And no water was going to have her babies.

She was intelligent enough to know her fear was irrational. But she wasn't smart enough to know how to fix it.

She closed her eyes.

Bad move. With eyes shut, a quick image hit of heavy water closing overhead, choking her. She heard her father's jeers, his disappointment. Always disappointment.

She turned toward the window and looked out at the bright sky. At sunshine. She couldn't see it, but she knew the creek was beautiful to look at, its color changing as it reflected light. She had nothing to fear. Her father was not here.

And she was a grown-up woman. Who was going to take control of her own life. Her own emotions.

But, you know what? Sometimes, like now, she just wanted to release the pent-up feelings, the ones she'd kept stuffed under wraps for as long as she could remember.

Yeah, and as soon as she did, Mrs. Barnes would run in to hand her a tissue or give her a hug or maybe croon at her. If the lieutenant were here, he'd hold her hand, for heaven's sake. Kev would laugh, say he was glad to have her back, Lord, love him.

She could almost understand Ty's certainty that magic existed. Maybe it did. Or maybe Auntie Sim's God was at work here.

That was surely something to think about.

Clay said they'd talk again when he got home. Listen to her: thinking of this as home. It hadn't been all that long ago she'd been horrified at the thought of anything *en famille*.

Mrs. Barnes wandered in with a glass of water. "Got to keep your fluids up." She waved toward the back yard. "My, that brother of yours is a nice boy. It's real healing for those children, having more family loving up on them."

Annie Mac emptied the glass and handed it back with a thank-you. "Did you know about Rita's baby?"

"I heard yesterday morning. They had prayer for her at church, so my daughter called me."

"I wish I could do something."

Mrs. Barnes shook her head. "I put her and hers on my prayer list, and that's probably the best place they could be 'bout now."

"I think I ought to call Hannah. What do you think?"

"That's a fine thing to do. I'll bring you the phone and the number."

Annie Mac had never phoned the Morgans' house, but she punched the buttons, hoping Hannah would be there.

A woman answered, and Annie Mac said, "Hannah?"

"No, it's Tadie. Hannah's still outside. Is this Annie Mac?"

"Hey, Tadie. I heard about Rita."

A space of seconds passed before Tadie spoke. "It's hard."

"Is there anything I can do? I don't want to bother her, but she's done so much for me."

"I don't know." Tadie sounded upset herself, making Annie Mac wish she hadn't called. "A card maybe? Clay will have her address."

"Yes, thank you. I'll write a card. I'm sorry to have bothered you."

"Bothered? Oh, no, you're not bothering me. I'm just not myself right now."

"Are you well? I mean, your baby...?"

"Rolling and kicking. No, no, I was out of sorts even before this happened. Snapping at the world."

"I did that when I was pregnant with Ty."

"You did?"

"I think, well, I'm sure it's normal."

"It may be normal, but it's making me hate myself. Especially when I'm still pregnant, and Rita can't have another. All because of some fool driver. Hold on, I hear Hannah coming."

Annie Mac held on.

"Hey, there." Hannah's voice had a pleased lilt to it.

She relaxed marginally. "Hey. I wanted to talk to someone, offer condolences, you know, after Clay told me what had happened."

"It's pretty bad."

"I'm so sorry. But what's this about a driver?"

"They think it might be Roy."

"Roy? How?"

"They don't know for sure. But there was green paint left on Rita's car from when he pushed her off the road. Matt said—"

It sounded like Tadie called Hannah's name. "What?" Hannah said before she muffled the phone. When she came back on, she said, "Seems I wasn't supposed to tell you that. I wasn't thinking. I'm sorry."

Annie Mac squeezed shut her eyes. No, no, no.

"Annie Mac?"

"I... I'm here. It's okay."

"No, it's not. I shouldn't have said anything. Me and my big mouth."

"If that's what happened, I need to know." But she wished she didn't. She wished there weren't another debit on her account. Another thing she might have prevented if she'd only stopped him sooner. Gotten the madman behind bars before he killed anyone.

"You all okay out there? Ty and Katie?"

"We're... we're fine. My brother's here."

"Rita said he'd found you. I'd like to meet him. I don't know if it'll work, but maybe Tadie and I can bring Jilly out while he's there."

"That would be nice. If you can."

"I think Tadie's trying to get some books together for Ty. The same things she's using for Jilly."

The conversation wound down. Annie Mac stared at the phone after she'd disconnected, turning when Kevin and the children clomped up the deck steps, full of laughter and giggles. "We need towels!" Ty called.

She looked out her window at her now-ragged crew. Kevin held up dripping shoes, Ty was covered in wet and mud, and Katie, her pristine Katie, waved at her mama with smudged hands and face. Annie Mac waved back.

Mrs. Barnes pointed them all to the hose at the side of the house. "You get yourselves cleaned up and dried afore you come trooping in here."

"Landsakes, Miss Annie," she said, poking her head in the bedroom with an armful of towels, "that brother of yours is something else. I haven't heard them young'uns laugh so much since they got here."

"I wish he could stay."

"I know you do, honey. But now he's found you, he'll be back. You can count on it."

She wouldn't let him come back, not if she had any say in the matter. Not until Roy was locked up or dead.

Dead sounded best. Then he couldn't hurt anyone else she cared about.

She sighed. She probably shouldn't hope for dead. But honestly? It was hard not to. Auntie Sim would tell her to pray for Roy. Good idea, hard—maybe even impossible—to execute.

43 CLAY

While the station's computer guru checked for unauthorized access to their database, Clay searched for information on Peter Rasman. He eventually learned that Rasman lived on Ann Street and drove a fancy Corvette that had to have cost a whole lot more than someone with a declared income of $31K should be able to afford. His 1040 claimed only money from rents and the small gas station he and his brother had inherited. Wells Fargo held the mortgage on the house he lived in. His business rental out on Highway 70 brought in some cash, not a whole lot. But, and here's where Clay's grin broadened, it housed a computer shop. And wouldn't you know it? The computer shop happened to be run by the brother-in-law of one of Beaufort's finest.

Ookaay. Clay rubbed his hands together. Now they were getting somewhere.

He headed to the chief's office. "You got a sec?"

When the chief invited him in, Clay shut the door and gave him the news. "Officer McKinley, eh?" Chief Bradley sounded disgusted. "Guess I'm gonna need to have a little chat with that boy."

"You might want to wait on that, sir. I'm thinking we might be able to use that pipeline a while longer."

"Who're you going to put watching Rasman's house?"

"Avery. He's the only other one I want knowing about this."

"Fine. Keep me posted."

Avery was off duty and obviously napping when Clay called. He answered with a "What's up?"

"We've got a lead on the person who may be helping Bingham. The house is on Ann Street." Clay gave him the number.

"I'll go check it out."

Avery called back in less than thirty minutes. The Corvette sat in the driveway. "What do you want me to do?"

"How about you watch until midnight, then go on to bed. I'll get there around dawn."

He made one stop at the drug store to pick up some children's movies. By the time he made it home, everyone else had eaten.

"Sorry I'm late," he called to Annie Mac and Kevin. He waved the DVD's at the children. "Brought some things for you two."

Ty marked his place in his book and bounded up. "For us? Movies? Can we see one now? Mom, can we?"

When Katie started jabbering at her mother, Clay left the negotiations. He had his head inside a clean shirt when Ty skidded to a halt outside the walk-in closet. "She said yes!"

His head freed and the shirt on, Clay nodded to the bed. "Why don't you climb up there to watch."

"Oh, yeah!"

Katie mimicked her brother, a pillow at her back and her legs crossed on the bed. Clay grinned at the picture they made as he set up *The Lion King* in the player and handed Ty the remote.

Following his nose to the kitchen, he eyed the plate Mrs. Barnes had readied. "It looks great, and I'll get to it in a minute. Don't you worry about clean-up either."

"Thank you. I've got some reading to catch up on."

He poured himself a glass of water and joined Kevin on the couch. When he glanced over at Annie Mac, he couldn't help noticing the rose that tinted her cheeks. Ah.

"How'd things go today?" He directed the question at her to get them both thinking of something else.

"Kevin took kids and dog into the muck, which means they've been having a good time."

He nodded at Kevin. "Muck's good for kids."

"My thoughts exactly." Kevin grinned.

Good thing there weren't any susceptible young women around to see that smile.

Annie Mac said, "I hear it was Roy's car that hit Rita."

Clay tried to school his face. He wondered whose big mouth had opened. "We don't know that for sure. Whoever it was, we're trying to catch him."

Her big eyes watched, but she didn't speak.

"We found out where Peter Rasman lives. That may be the lead we need."

"I was thinking about that name, how Roy claimed he was a hero and nobody was going to say differently." She let out a long breath. "His words, said when he was slapping me around."

".Just you?" Kevin's hands balled into fists.

She nodded. "I taught the children to hide." Tears welled. She tried wiping them away before they could fall. "How could I have done that to them? He didn't use his fists often, but it should never have been more than the first time. I should have locked the doors then. What kind of mother was I?"

"Shush," Clay said. "Don't." He'd asked himself the same question more than a few times in the beginning, but he also knew abused women often felt trapped.

Kevin knelt by the side of her chair, taking her in his arms. "Hush, honey. Hush."

Clay studied his hands, wanting to give them some privacy.

"You did your best," Kevin said. "You were trying to keep him away. Divorcing him."

"But I never should have let him in to start with."

"Think about Katie. What a beautiful child she is." Kevin voiced the words Clay would have, given half a chance. He looked up when Kevin said, "You wouldn't have had Katie. Be grateful for her. Be grateful and know you're all going to be fine."

She stared over her brother's shoulder through her tears, drawing Clay closer as eloquently as if she'd spoken. He smiled at her. "Remember, a man like that doesn't take a 'no' very well. You kicked him out, and you were trying to make a new life. You're a strong woman, Annie Mac. You are strong and beautiful and a fine mother. Don't let that …" And, oh, wouldn't he have liked a curse word about now. "Don't let that creature win."

Kevin whooped. "Creature?"

"Yeah, well, I was thinking something a whole lot worse."

"Creature works. Conjures lots of interesting images."

Clay let the silliness ease him. "Lots of words in my head for his moral deficiency, but they were too crude for mixed company."

"Your mama tell you cursing displays your limited vocabulary?" Kevin's eyes held a twinkle as he stood, keeping Annie Mac's hand clasped in his.

"Yours too?"

"Every time. Stifling now."

Tear-streaked, Annie Mac stared from one to the other.

"I think we've shocked my sister." Kevin patted the hand he held with his free one. "You okay?"

She nodded.

"I like your lieutenant," Kevin said, his expression reminding Clay of Ty's when the boy held in a laugh.

She sniffled. "I do, too." And there was that blush again. "Oh!" Her hands flew to her cheeks. "I didn't mean..."

Kevin pinched her cheek. "Of course, you did. But it's okay. I don't think Clay minds." He turned to Clay, who was now on his feet and ready to flee. "Do you?"

Go on and hike up those jeans, tuck in that shirt, Clay told himself, thinking how he used to use those gestures to distract his mama when she got upset with his antics. Now, he wiped his hands down the side of his legs because his palms suddenly felt clammy.

"If you two will excuse me," he said, not looking at either of them as he turned toward the kitchen. "I'm going to grab that plate and then get myself to bed. I won't be here when you wake up. We're taking turns watching Rasman's house."

Sleep eluded Clay as the clock clicked over to 2:57. He must have dozed eventually, because the next thing he heard was the alarm at five. He pulled on his clothes, crept past a sleeping Kevin, and headed for town.

From the police-issue van parked half a block away, Clay studied the first rays of sunlight that glittered off the silver Corvette. About now, he sure wished for some big-city electronics equipment, but Beaufort hadn't the budget for fancy surveillance toys. So, he waited, and he watched. Around eight, he called Avery and asked him to pick up coffee and bagels. Told him to park around the block and come up on the sidewalk side of the van.

Avery did that all right and moseyed straight on past when a jogger ran toward him. He gave a negligent salute to a woman shaking her small rag rug and bent to retie the running shoes he'd put on for the day's work. When he stood, he slapped his forehead as if he'd forgotten something before turning back to the van. Clay opened the side door to let him slip inside.

"Having fun?"

Avery grinned. "Makes me feel like a real cop. So, yeah." He handed over the breakfast supplies.

Clay laughed. "I almost believed that pantomime."

"Hey, I never had this much fun in Durham." Avery hunched down on the side bench in the van's rear. "Seen anything?"

"All's quiet so far."

"Did you get a tap on his phone yet?"

"Chief's taking care of that, though Rasman probably uses a cell. We'd need to be NSA for that." Clay pulled the top off his coffee and took a sip. "Thanks for this. Sleep deprivation is taking a toll."

Avery pointed to the bag. "You don't want both those bagels, I'll be happy to help."

Clay took one, held out the other.

They'd taken a last bite when the front door opened, a man headed to the car, and that powerful engine roared to life. "Looks like our friend is going for a ride. You wanna come?"

"I'll follow in the Explorer." Avery opened the door and climbed down. "You might need something with a few more horses under the hood to keep up with that baby."

Clay settled in the driver's seat, watching to see which way the Corvette headed before he eased out onto the street. At the intersection with Live Oak, he called Avery. "He's heading east. See if you can get closer than I do. We'll play a little tag."

"I'll pick him up... at the..."

"You're cutting out."

"Wh...t?" And then there was only static, which didn't make sense. Not when Clay had five bars on his phone.

The Corvette angled onto 101 at the Ace Hardware, then shot down the highway, slowing just shy of a Highway Patrol car. Avery, ahead of the Corvette, turned into a driveway.

What on earth? Clay glanced in his rearview mirror, a smile curving his lips when Avery pulled back out behind the van. Avery had taken him literally: tag it was.

The chase continued past Parker Boats, where Avery zipped on ahead. Clay drove at a more sedate pace, allowing Avery to do the fancy maneuvering. The Corvette took off out of sight. Clay sped up to keep an eye on Avery. They were nearing the Craven County line when the Corvette made a sharp turn to the right.

Clay's palms began to sweat. He just knew Pete was leading them straight to Bingham. He let Avery make the turn, while he continued on 101 until he could safely park. Making Pete suspicious of the van would not be a good idea.

It was painful to wait around when they were this close. But wait he did. And wait. Finally, he called Avery's cell phone. It went straight to voicemail.

44 HANNAH

Hannah checked the rearview mirrors for the umpteenth time. "I haven't seen a soul," she said in an undertone to Tadie. "I'm glad I can say that literally. Finding out that what's his name can change car colors at will makes me a little paranoid."

In the back seat, Jilly sang a ditty and fidgeted, her feet hitting the center console. "Calm down back there." Tadie leaned between the bucket seats, her left hand grabbing Jilly's bouncing sneaker. "You keep that up, you'll end up going through the roof."

Hannah grinned as she listened to the interchange between the two strong-willed females. The child seemed to be winning, especially when Tadie turned back and murmured, "How much longer, O Lord?"

It was Hannah's turn to pat a knee. "Relax. She's fine."

"But I'm not."

"I know. This will be a good distraction for both of us."

"I can barely move at faster than a snail's pace. I want to weep all the time. I just can't get past hurting for Rita." Tadie paused and on a deep sigh said, "I'm sorry. You must feel as if it's happening all over again."

Well, yeah, but she would not go there. "I never, ever would wish that pain on another person."

"It scares me."

Hannah glanced over to see why her friend's words sounded muffled. Tadie turned from staring out the side window but kept her voice low so her words wouldn't carry to the backseat.

"I have yet to get through a day without jumping down Will's throat, not to mention Jilly's. I can't help but fret."

Fretting wouldn't do that baby any good. Hannah corralled images leftover from her own lost babies and tucked them low and out of sight. She took a deep, cleansing breath and said, "I know, love. But you mustn't get yourself worked up. If you can't trust, at least consider the percentages."

"Interesting that you mention percentages. I've been considering them."

"And?" Hannah slowed the car to give Tadie time to say what was on her mind before they had to turn into Clay's lane.

"How often do you hear of someone having lupus? Not often, right? As a matter of fact, I don't know of a single person in Beaufort who has it, at least in our circle. But Will and I met another cruiser when we were docked in Baltimore whose sister has lupus, whose best friend's wife has lupus, and who went to a church in Delaware with two women who suffer from it. One of the women lives in northern Delaware, two live in the border area of Pennsylvania, and the other lives slightly south of them, all within a radius of about fifteen miles. What are the odds? Is it something in the water up there? Something from all those chemical plants or the munitions factories they had a hundred years ago?"

Hannah glanced over at her. "You're comparing the loss of babies in our small group to lupus up north?"

"Well? It's a tragic and terrible thing to have my best friend lose her two children. Then my second closest friend, who grew up practically in the same house as I did, loses hers, too. And neither of you can try again..." She reached over to give Hannah's forearm a quick squeeze. "Except, of course, through adoption, and I'm so proud of you for going ahead with that."

Hannah ignored the aside. "So, you think we've got a water issue in Beaufort or some chemical thing that's going to kill my godchild as well?" She threw one hand in the air. "Tadie!"

"I know, but I'm scared."

"Of course, you are. But let's get real here. Please."

"I'm trying."

"Look, you know perfectly well that recessive genes caused issues for our sons. Rita's was killed by a madman who ran her car into a ditch. You are not going to have either of those things happen to you. You don't drive yourself anywhere, and we're prepared now if we see any suspicious car. Right? And neither you nor Will is related to us, which makes the likelihood of you carrying the same genetic defect so remote as to be a non-issue. Do you hear me?" Hannah felt as if she were asking herself the same question. She turned into Clay's drive as she waited for Tadie's response. Instead, her friend crossed her arms over her belly. Hannah could picture her lower lip forming a straight line. "Sara Longworth Merritt, do you hear me?"

"Auntie Hannah, is Mommy in trouble?" Jilly asked from the back seat.

"Out of the mouths." Tadie sighed.

Jilly leaned forward and placed a hand on each of the front bucket seats. "Daddy and Mommy call me Gillian Grace Merritt when I'm in trouble."

Hannah reached back between the seats to pat Jilly's knee. "No, sweetie, your mommy's not in trouble. I wanted to get her attention." To Tadie, she said, "Do I have it?"

"Yes, ma'am. I hear you."

"Good." She steered them to a stop behind a car she didn't recognize. "Oh, I forgot we had this to look forward to." At least the guard wasn't in uniform or showing his gun. One more degree of separation from the reality of danger worked for her.

Harvey barked from the deck before racing down the steps toward them. He circled Jilly, barked again, and dashed around to greet Hannah, where he only lingered for a quick pat before bounding back to Ty and Katie, then hurtling once again toward the car. The children laughed, called to each other, and danced right along with the dog.

Mrs. Barnes offered her hand to Tadie. "Just grab hold, Miss Tadie."

"The fat lady descends," Tadie said, groaning as she heaved herself out.

The guard called, "Y'all need help?"

Hannah waved. "Thanks. I'll put the kids to work. Ty, Jilly, come carry these things." She doled out a sack to each child. "Becca, how's it going?"

"Just fine, Miss Hannah. Especially with Mr. Kevin here."

They followed her up the deck stairs and into the house, and then Hannah stopped. Standing next to Annie Mac's wheelchair was one of the best looking individuals Hannah had ever seen, male or female. She tried not to gawk, but she had to slam her mouth closed so it wouldn't flop open and show her tonsils. She set the bags down on the dining room table.

"Good morning." Annie Mac encompassed them all with a look of pure pleasure. "I want you to meet my brother."

As she was making the introductions, Ty skidded up to the big table with his armload. "Mama, look! We've got lots and lots of books. Jilly and me can do school now!"

"Jilly and I," his mother corrected.

"We've been looking forward to meeting you, Kevin," Hannah said as Ty bent over his new treasures.

"And I've wanted to thank you both for all you've done for my sister and her children. I wish I'd been around to help or had even known they needed it." He laid a hand on Annie Mac's shoulder, clasping hers when she raised it. "It's still hard to believe she's only been a few hours away all these years."

"Uncle Kev, look at these," Ty called.

Ty pointed to the stacks, flipping through a couple to show his uncle. Jilly pushed Katie's pile of alphabet and number recognition books to the end of the table.

Katie beamed. "Mama, see, I can do school, too."

"Aren't we going to have fun?"

Tadie slid down into a straight chair. "I'm getting too fat to move."

Annie Mac laughed. "You look like you're going to pop any minute. Have you had any Braxton-Hicks yet?"

"Daily. The doctor said things are going along well. He figures I'm probably right on schedule, but what do doctors know?" She shook her head. "I'm sorry. I can't seem to be anything but grumpy."

"It'll pass. I told you I chewed off everyone's head, especially with Ty." Annie Mac looked toward the children, who chatted among themselves. "To be honest, when I was pregnant with Katie, I didn't dare let my discomfort show."

"Because of Roy."

"Things were hard by then. Poor Auntie Sim."

Hannah took glasses of sweet tea from Becca and passed one to Annie Mac, set another on the table for Kevin.

"I'll have water," Tadie said. "Oh, thank you, Becca. You anticipated me."

"Caffeine won't do that baby a bit of good."

"No, ma'am. I'm really looking forward to a cup of coffee and some sweet tea when this is all over."

"Just you watch yourself while you nurse that young'un. Don't want him awake from your coffee."

"Oh, lands, I forgot about that. Good thing I like water."

"Yes, ma'am. I've been giving Miss Annie tall glasses of it."

Annie Mac smiled fondly at the housekeeper. "She's flooding me."

"So, tell us, is there any—oh, my!" Tadie said, placing both hands on her stomach. "Ooooh."

"Miss Tadie?"

Hannah and Annie Mac glanced at each other. Mrs. Barnes checked her watch. Loud breaths whooshed between Tadie's lips.

"Don't think that's a Braxton-Hicks," Hannah said.

"Best to move around when that one ends, Miss Tadie. Get yourself walking, see whether they last or quicken sudden like." Mrs. Barnes bent down and helped Tadie to stand, holding her arm while Tadie paced slowly around the room.

Kevin responded to his sister's nod. "Come on, kids. Bring some of those books and Harvey." He corralled them toward the back bedroom. "Let's get out of the ladies' way."

Just shy of ten minutes later, the next contraction slammed into Tadie. Mrs. Barnes stayed at her side, monitoring the time. Annie Mac reminded Tadie to breathe.

Hannah collected her purse and Tadie's. "I'm thinking I ought to get us back to town. Mrs. Barnes, would you call Will and Matt? Will's at the house. Matt's at Morgan's."

"Be happy to, Miss Hannah. I'll help get you to the car first. You just leave Jilly here. We'll take good care of the child."

"Thank you," Tadie said as her breathing calmed. "I need to say good-bye to her."

Jilly's voice separated from the others as she raced in and came to a stop in front of Tadie. "Mommy? You okay?"

"She's having what are called contractions, Jilly," Annie Mac said. "Her muscles are working to bring your baby into the world."

"Now?"

Hannah nodded. "Yes, I'd say she's about to have another one. Becca, aren't these coming rather quickly?"

Mrs. Barnes consulted her watch. "Down to eight minutes, looks like. Best get to town."

Jilly stared hard at Tadie's face. "Why's she breathing like that?"

"It's so the muscles can work better," Hannah said. "Now as soon as that's over, give your mommy a hug so I can take her to the hospital."

"Can't I go?"

Annie Mac reached toward her. "We'd like it if you stayed here to keep Ty and Katie company. It's going to be a whole lot of that breathing going on for a long while. Most babies don't come right away."

Jilly didn't look convinced. Tadie let go of her belly and pulled the child close. "Before you know it, punkin', I'll be calling you and introducing you to your new brother or sister. And we'll all be together."

"Will Daddy be with you?"

"Yes, ma'am. Why don't you help Mrs. Barnes call him? You can tell him what's happening, and I promise we'll let you know as soon as this baby gets here."

"Okay."

"Thank you, sweetie. And you be good for Mrs. Barnes and Miss Annie Mac, will you? Do whatever they say."

Kevin appeared in the doorway. "You need me to drive you?"

"I think we'll be fine. You stay here and help with the crew," Hannah said as she and Becca assisted a waddling Tadie toward the car. "We'll call you soon's we know anything."

45 CLAY

Clay held his temper in check as Avery climbed out of the Explorer and leaned his forearm on the van's open window. "Dang it, Clay, I lost him. One minute, I was behind that fool car. The next minute, two pick-ups pulled out in front of me, one in each lane, like they were purposefully running interference for the guy. I couldn't do a blasted thing!"

"I'm surprised you didn't flash a badge at them."

"Sure." Avery scoffed. "Give the whole game away."

"And you think you didn't?" Raking his fingers through already messed-up hair, he sighed again and said, "So, how far down did you get before you lost him?"

"Four miles, give or take."

"All right. Go on. Get your car over there out of sight and climb in. We'll drive the road together, see if we can spot anything."

"Let me change shirts, put on a cap. What good is undercover if you don't look the part?"

"Just hurry up."

With Avery in the passenger seat, Clay pulled out on the highway. "What happened to your cell phone?"

Avery had the grace to look sheepish. "Battery died. I was sure I put it on charge last night, but I guess not."

"You don't have a car charger?"

"Nope. Never needed one." He pulled the phone out of his pocket. "I've got one of those extended-life batteries."

"That's great if you extend its life by charging it."

"Won't happen again."

"And get a charger for your car."

Back at the station, Clay told a disgusted Chief Bradley what had happened before he went in to write his report. Typing one-fingered, he tried to keep frustration out of the words. They'd been so close to finding Bingham. So close.

He'd about finished when the chief summoned him. "Phoned the sheriff to tell him where his men might keep a lookout. Not exactly a shining moment for us, but it seems that neck of the woods is full of modern-day bootleggers who can smell a cop a mile away. You have to be really swift to get past them, which, I take it, Avery wasn't."

Clay shrugged. "Not much action around town. Avery may have gotten a tad overzealous."

"A tad. You might want to speak with him about caution. If he's tailing someone, flashy doesn't work. Those guys could easily have shot him first, then asked questions."

"Already taken care of." He slouched in a chair next to the chief's desk. "So what's next?"

Chief Bradley glanced at his watch. Right, Clay had forgotten.

Harold Bradley was smart, he was careful, and he was an excellent leader. He was also a brand new grandfather, and his wife had been bugging him to visit the baby. Only, the baby and her parents lived in Myrtle Beach.

"What time is Marlene picking you up?"

"Ten minutes. Sorry to take off on you now, but my life won't be worth a plugged nickel if I tell her I can't go."

Clay sighed, stood up, and raked his hands through his hair for the umpteenth time that day. This afternoon, the barber.

"It's killing me, chief. We need more manpower, but if we put anyone to watch that house, it'll be back to him before the night's out."

"I know it. I've been thinking how we can get around this, and I put in a call to Grayton's sheriff. They're the only ones who feel about this like we do, so I asked him to loan me a man. He's sending one of his better deputies."

Clay sighed. "I hope this one won't lose a prisoner." Or get himself killed. "If we've got someone coming nobody here knows, and we can keep him out of sight so our hand doesn't get tipped, maybe we can set up a sting."

"You figure out how to do that within our budget, I'm game." The chief pushed his chair back, stood up, and began stacking papers. "No cell coverage at my daughter's, so here's her home number." He scribbled on a card and handed it to Clay. "You need me, you call. Just try not to need me before Sunday. We're traveling home Saturday. Hope to miss most of the traffic."

That didn't make much sense to Clay, considering Saturdays at the beach were a disaster, but maybe the chief knew something about that route he didn't. "Yes, sir. What time is the Grayton fellow arriving?"

"He's on his way. Name's Garth Evans." The chief stuffed a batch of papers in his briefcase and another batch in the top drawer, which he locked.

"I've given Evans your number. Keep him busy and off the street, will you? We're putting him up in Morehead at Jane's Motel. I told him to check in, call you, and you'd tell him what to do." Hefting his briefcase, the chief glanced around his office a final time before ushering Clay out the door.

"Have a good trip," Clay said.

"Bring pictures," Stella called to the chief's retreating back. He waved over his head. Stella laughed.

So he'd have Avery and this Evans fellow on his team. If Evans turned out to be as dumb as his predecessor, they were in big trouble.

46 HANNAH

Hannah gripped the steering wheel. She would not panic. "Breathe," she told Tadie as another contraction hit. She sucked and whooshed right along with her best friend. "You're doing great."

"I knew it would hurt. I just knew it. The instructor for those birthing classes said just focus. Just breathe. It wasn't supposed to hurt like this. She lied."

"They do lie. They don't want you to call it off. Or take drugs."

"Drugs sound good."

"You'll be fine."

"Sure, right. Easy for you to say."

"I wanted a knife."

"So get me to a knife. Or that epidural."

Another one slammed into Tadie. She groaned and began the breathing. Hannah didn't bother checking the time. That couldn't have been eight minutes.

"You're doing great," she repeated at its end. "Really. As soon as you hold that baby, you'll forget all this."

"Thanks, Mother."

Hannah laughed. "You're welcome."

The traffic was light enough for them to zip across into Morehead. Will met them at the hospital entrance, Tadie's bag in hand. He bent to help her out of the car, settled her in a wheelchair, and left Hannah to find a parking place.

"Here we go again." Hannah punched in the numbers for the All Saints office. She was not going to wade through this afternoon without reinforcements, especially as her personal access code to God seemed all but blocked. Father Ames's secretary promised to get the message out for prayer. Thanking her, Hannah clicked off the phone, tucked it in her purse, and took a deep breath to steady herself.

She figured they'd have checked in by now and would be in the birthing area, homey rooms where birth was treated as a natural process rather than an illness. Hannah pushed away the worry, the reminders of last week in this same hospital. This time, there'd be a perfect baby as the outcome.

Neither she nor Tadie had eaten, which was probably a good thing for Tadie but was a bad thing for her. Acids floating around in her stomach would only lead to heartburn, which would lead to behavior she'd like to avoid. Tadie needed calm, not caustic. She should have called Matt while she was outside.

On the birthing floor, light filtered in the windows, none of that somber hush-hush from the medical wards. But it was still a hospital. There were still all those beeps and bings of machines, the subdued chatter from medical staff. Oh, and wasn't that someone screaming?

Screaming was not what she wanted to hear. Surely, that wasn't Tadie?

At the nurses' station, she paused to ask for Mrs. Merritt's room. "Around the corner, first door on the left."

Will was massaging his wife's stomach through a contraction, helping her with the breathing while she leaned against a wall. At the end of it, Tadie pushed off and started pacing. "Come on in, Hannah. They said it would go faster if I walk. I need it to go faster."

"I can understand that. What can I do?"

"Nothing. Everything. They didn't give me drugs. Why did I say I didn't want drugs?"

"I'm sorry."

Will looked up from his watch. "Get ready. Another's due soon."

Will helped her lower her body onto the couch and took a position on one side of her with his hand resting on her abdomen. Hannah perched at her other side.

"Now," Will said, as the muscles bunched and tightened. "Shallow breaths, think of these contractions working to get this new life into our arms." He glanced at his stopwatch. "Breathe, that's it. No, slow it down, that's my girl, it's coming to a crest. There, now it's on the down side, coming down, down, good. Relax."

Hannah wiped Tadie's hair back from her forehead and got up to fetch ice. The nurse came in to check her. "You're doing beautifully," she said and gentled Tadie through two more contractions. "It won't be long now. I'll be back soon."

"What does she mean, it won't be long? What's not long?"

"Take it as a good sign. You're obviously dilating well. They say that bouncing along in a car helps push the baby out."

"I hope so. Oh... Ohhhh."

And so it went. When Matt stuck his head in the door to ask if anyone needed anything, Hannah followed him to the hall. "A sandwich? Anything? Will says he's eaten, but he'd like a tea. I'm starving. Tadie gets ice chips."

"Yes, ma'am." He kissed her lightly.

During transition, Tadie barked and demanded, while Will maintained a sense of humor. Good thing. Hannah tried to rise above it but didn't like being growled at. She pasted on a smile and took her cues from Will.

Finally, after eight hours of hard labor, Baby Boy Merritt slid into the world. His jubilant father cut the cord. Tadie grinned as the doctor placed a very red-faced but healthy boy on her slightly less protuberant belly. "Oh, Will. Hannah. Look."

A boy. And red-faced. Red-faced was good, wasn't it? And lusty? Hannah looked over the nurse's shoulder when she took him for a preliminary check under a heat lamp.

"Looks very good," the nurse said. Very good worked. Very good meant he might live. This was her godson. Who. Was. Going. To. Live.

She ran to Matt's hideout in the waiting area and brought him back to the birthing room. When the doctor pronounced a perfect Apgar score, she burst into tears. Matt mopped her wet face, held her until the springs dried up, and turned to give Will a back-slapping hug.

"What are you going to name him?" Matt asked.

Tadie nodded at her husband, opening her eyes just long enough to share a smile with him. Will reached for her hand. "We're calling him Samuel James Longworth Merritt."

"Lord, have mercy." Hannah blew into the tissue. "Honey, that's some handle, but, of course, I can see why you'd do it."

Tadie reached her free hand toward Hannah. "You'll call them? James and Elvie?"

"We'll stop by. James is going to burst."

"Well, he'll have to share billing with my daddy."

"Wouldn't your papa have been proud? I can see him now, him and Miss Caroline. This is a good thing. A very good thing. And I'm to be godmother. I told you it would be fine. You see that? Perfect. Just like I said. We didn't need to worry." She was babbling. Okay, breathe. Suck up that emotion. It would not take her under again. "Landsakes, Mrs. Merritt, what could be finer than that beautiful boy? You did it."

That was all it took. Will backed out of the way quickly as waterworks sloshed from both women. Tadie reached for her, and she fell right into her friend's arms. She heard Will say, "Sound a bit like sheep bleating, don't they?"

"Been behaving this way since they were girls," Matt said. "They'll get over it soon enough."

Tadie sniffled, mumbled into her ear. "Dear, darling, best friend in the world. I love you so much."

"You know I love you. And that boy there. I can't stand how happy I am."

Finally straightening, Hannah reached for a tissue, blew into it, and dried her face. "I'm such a mess."

Matt draped an arm over her shoulder. "But you're a wonderful mess." She punched him in his side before turning into his embrace and tightening her arms around his middle. He said, "Good job, Mrs. Merritt."

Hannah climbed out of the van and waited as Matt parked behind her. "You up for this?" he asked as they climbed the garage apartment stairs.

She nodded. "It'll be okay."

"Come on in." James looked more haggard than he had in years, his eyes puffy from lack of sleep. His graying hair seemed to have lightened in the last week, aging him perceptibly.

A fist clutched Hannah's heart. This had to be so hard for them. She hugged him and then leaned down to kiss Elvie Mae.

"Y'all want some tea? James, bring the pitcher."

"That would be fine, Miss Elvie. We come brimful of good tidings," Matt said, accepting the chair James offered.

"News?" Elvie clasped her hands together. Her eyes glanced eagerly from one to the other. "Good news? We could sure use some of that around here. What is it?"

"Soon as James gets back," Hannah said. "It's for both of you."

"Tadie?" Elvie whispered. "Is it something to do with our Tadie?"

Hannah grinned at her and nodded.

When James came in with the pitcher and glasses and had passed around drinks, Matt raised his in a toast. "To the newest member of our extended family, Master Samuel James Longworth Merritt."

James's eyes rounded, crinkling his brow. Elvie Mae whispered. "Oh, my." She covered her mouth, her eyes misty.

Taking Elvie's hand, Hannah said, "He's so beautiful. He was born at 7:56 PM, after a very short labor, relatively speaking. You've got to see him."

Elvie turned to James, who still sat too stunned to speak. "You hear what that girl of ours did? You hear that, James?"

"I hear'd. I got ears, so I hear'd." His smile spread, but he sounded a bit choked up himself. "She done good, did she?"

"Yes, sir. The labor took us by surprise and went very quickly. He's a beautiful baby. Weighs eight and a half pounds, so no wonder she felt fat."

"Gave us all another generation, our Tadie-girl did." A sigh of pleasure followed Elvie's words.

James nodded, but you could see the pleasure marred by the pain that sneaked back into his eyes. He sighed before saying in a faltering voice, "The Lord giveth and the Lord taketh away, blessed be the Name of the Lord."

Hannah reached over to grab his hand and hold tightly. "I know. It's hard. For all of us."

James returned the squeeze. "Yes, ma'am. I knows you be feelin' it, too."

"It's goin' to be a mite hard for Rita and Martin to learn 'bout this," Elvie said.

"Yes, ma'am. Their Daniel was supposed to be the one carrying on for you. And for them."

"The Lord calls us to praise him, no matter," James said, squaring his shoulders and taking a deep breath. "And this here baby will fill a whole lot of hearts, I knows that." He patted Hannah's hand, then gave it back to her so he could stand up. "They've done me an honor. It's hard for a man like me to cotton to such a thing, being held up next to Mr. Samuel. A rare man was Mr. Samuel. A mighty rare man."

Matt laid his hand on James's shoulder. "So are you, James Whitlock. You'll look at that little boy growing up, and you'll remember how much Tadie and her family love and respect you. You've been here for her most of her life. You were here to help her daddy when he needed you, like Elvie was for her mama. She—and Will—want you to know they're grateful. That they love you. That's a big thing, it's true. But there's not a person who knows you and them who won't think it fitting. It can't make up for the loss of Daniel, but this child will still be family for all of us."

James dashed a hand across his cheeks. As Hannah looked into Elvie's face, they reached for each other and hugged again.

"Ain't we the weepinest women you ever saw?" Elvie tried to smile as she brushed away tears.

"It's been that kind of a week, hasn't it? Full of sadness and full of joy."

They left soon after, pleading exhaustion. It was obvious that they all felt it, the weight of sorrow followed by the joy of new life.

At home, Matt said he'd leave word for Father Ames that the birth had gone well. Hannah thanked him and headed out the back door.

Tadie's baby had been born. There was glory in that, in the fact that their small family of forever friends had at least one new and living child.

When the tears slid silently down her cheeks, she didn't wipe them. She just sat on her stoop, where the cool of the brick could seep through the cotton of her pants and the darkness could hide a certain sadness she'd feel until the end of her days.

47 HANNAH

Hannah owed Rita a visit. Who better to bring comfort than someone who knew the same loss? Courage, she told herself. Courage and daisies from the florist.

Martin accepted her hug and pointed her up the stairs. "She's not doing well."

Hannah wasn't prepared for the drawn curtains, the sight of Rita with stringy hair and dull eyes, propped up against her pillows, her hands clasped on her lap, unmoving. A full glass of water waited on the side table along with a half-sandwich and slice of apple that hadn't been touched.

She set the daisies on the bureau and pulled up a chair. "Hey, girl."

Rita nodded but said nothing. Hannah was tempted to start talking, but if she did, it would come out as babbling. Or tears. So she just eased down and waited.

Eventually, Rita spoke. She still didn't look at Hannah. "He was so perfect, you know? Every time I close my eyes, I see those tiny

314

toes and those fingers that would barely have been able to curl around mine."

"I know." Her own words were a whisper.

Maybe the quiet of them brought Rita's head up. "You do. I know you do." Another pause. "And his expression. It was almost serene."

"Yes."

"Daddy keeps telling me I'm supposed to praise God in spite of the pain. I can't."

"I couldn't either."

Rita's voice remained even, toneless, as if she'd bled out all the tears she had. "I've cried until my tear ducts have shriveled right along with my face. When I go brush my teeth, I cry. When I pee, I cry. When I sit here, I cry. Poor Martin. He gets nothing but tears when he gives me a cup of coffee or tea. Because, you know, I can drink caffeine now that it doesn't matter. And that just sets me off."

"Have you been eating?"

"I can't. I've tried, but I'm just not hungry."

Hannah knew about that too.

"I keep remembering why my breasts have to resize themselves. How I have to heal from the mess of taking out my womb. Why I'm lying in an absolutely still house across the hall from that empty crib and the rocking chair Mama and Daddy gave me. Have you seen it? We decorated the room in blues with yellow and blue rocking horses and teddy bears stenciled across the walls."

"I still hear the music box from their mobile sometimes."

"How long before it gets better, Hannah?"

"Little by little, it will. I'm not going to lie to you. I sometimes still feel the loss like a knife to my gut. But not often and never as sharply cutting as it was just after." Just after each one. Just after times two.

She couldn't say that last. Rita'd lost her womb too. That meant one fell swoop of hopelessness.

Rita said, "While we waited in that hospital room for Daniel to be born, all I could think about was how he was already dead. We prayed that it wouldn't be so, that God would somehow work a miracle in my womb. But all that time, I had this dead baby inside of me, this baby who'd been moving just the day before. We picked his name because of Daniel in the lion's den. We thought it would protect him." A pause, then, "You know what Daniel means in Hebrew?" She shook her head. "God is my judge."

"Oh, honey."

"Perhaps God judged and found us wanting."

"Oh, no, never."

"Mama says God doesn't do that. He didn't kill Daniel."

"She's right. Your mama knows a lot about God."

Rita sighed, wiped at her eye. "She does. She has way more faith than I do."

"Probably more than most folk, if it comes right down to it."

"But this feels like punishment. Like God would have healed me and protected Daniel if I'd been a better person. If I'd done more, prayed more. Gone to church more."

"Oh, Rita." What could she say? Isn't that exactly how she'd felt after? That something had to be lacking in her?

"Mama and Daddy say that God isn't like that. That his nature is love, but we live in a fallen world. Do you believe that?"

She did, didn't she? Wasn't that what she'd tried to hang onto?

Rita didn't wait for an answer. "Even Martin's been whispering that to me. But I think his tears mean something different."

They sat there, unspeaking. What Rita suggested about God punishing her really was unspeakable... if a person were going to hold onto any faith at all.

"I don't know how you had the courage to go on," Rita said, "especially when it happened the second time. They didn't do a hysterectomy, did they?"

Hannah pulled herself back from the edge. "No, they said there was nothing wrong with my uterus. Just our genes. I had my tubes tied."

"You're so brave, Hannah."

"No, I'm not. I've never yet been able to rejoice about the losses."

"Yeah, my folks say rejoice always, in everything." Rita stared at nothing, unless her unfocused look had caught on the far wall. "When Mama told me how Tadie'd named her baby after Daddy, all I saw was red."

Hannah sat back, fiddling with her own tissue. "I was afraid you would."

"I've been trying to convince myself it was really nice of them. I mean, we weren't even going to add James to Daniel's name. It wasn't like they stole it, you know?"

She nodded. There really wasn't anything she could say to make it better.

"I'm trying not to be jealous. Really."

"But you keep imagining her nursing a living baby."

Rita's stricken eyes pooled with tears she didn't bother to dash away. "You do understand. I knew you would."

"I do." She handed Rita another tissue. "I've been plagued with jealousy since the two of you got pregnant. And I've hated myself."

As if she hadn't heard that last, Rita blew her nose and took a deep breath. "Sometimes, I lie here, imagining the silence around me growing, having an actual shape with form and substance. Isn't that a strange thing to think about?" Another sniffle, and then, "I thought my weeping would dissolve it, that the sound of my heart slapping my rib cage would make it go away."

Her next words were dreamy, as if she'd forgotten Hannah sat across from her. "I wondered if this huge thing, this blob of silence would fill up with the sound of my blood. Because I could see its trail, you know, the blood's trail as it flowed from my heart to the rest of my body." She tilted her head and looked directly at Hannah. "I heard it, that thurump, thurump." Another moment's pause. "I figured I was probably going crazy. Hallucinating."

Goose bumps pebbled Hannah's skin. What did Rita mean, the silence looked like a blob? Hannah knew about pounding blood echoing in the ears, but what was this?

As she searched for a response, the doorbell rang. Footsteps followed voices, and Isa entered, carrying a glass bottle of brilliant silk flowers. She set these next to the daisies, nodded at Hannah, and lowered herself on the other side of Rita's bed. With no preamble, no polite greeting, she began. "I'm so very sorry about your baby, but I thought you might like to know you're not alone. I've been through the very same thing. Murder."

Hannah was too stunned to speak. Isa turned to her.

"I know you lost babies and can't have any, Hannah, but a victim of murder has a whole other set of issues to face. Rita's baby was murdered. Mine was too. And because of this, we both lost the chance to have others." Isa's long fingers lay still on her lap, her silver rings for once reflecting nothing. "Rita, your baby and mine were killed by the act of a madman. In my case, he happened to be my husband."

"Oh, Isa." That was Rita's voice. Hannah couldn't speak.

"I never told anyone here. I didn't want to remember. I was six and a half months pregnant. He beat me so hard my unborn daughter died."

"Oh, no."

"I'm older than you by a number of years, but when this happened, I was young. I dreamed of children, my own children, and from the moment I lost that little girl, I haven't stopped missing her and wishing."

"What happened to your husband?"

"I reported what he'd done to the doctors and the police, but no one believed me. He was an important man. They believed him when he said I had fallen and done this to myself and to my baby. I'd been careless. He wept in front of his friends, and they doled out sympathy like it was his due."

Rita reached out a hand. Isa grasped it and took Hannah's with her other. "At least the man who killed your baby will pay," Isa said. "He will be caught."

"My parents say I've got to forgive him."

"How? And why? He doesn't deserve forgiveness."

"For my sake. Because that's what God did for me."

Isa scoffed, dropping both hands. "Ridiculous."

"It's biblical. But it's hard."

"I don't believe in forgiveness for the wicked. I'm certainly not accepting the word of a book that was flogged in my face by that same abuser." Isa stood. Her hands found the pockets of her loose gauze pants and hid there. "Not after what happened—and the way those sanctimonious folk acted. Taking his side."

Hannah finally said, "Did you ever tell them? The church people? Did you tell them how he was? What he'd done?"

"They wouldn't have listened. He convinced the police, and then he assured me that he could make every single person in that church stand and swear to his innocence."

"And you believed him?"

"Why not? They were his friends. They'd picked him as a leader."

That sounded absurd to Hannah. "If you don't speak the truth, it's not likely other people will know it by osmosis because you think they ought to. How can you blame them for an ignorance you wouldn't fix?"

"Okay, time to drop the subject." At the door, Isa spoke to Rita. "I hated when people from work or from the hospital said they knew how I felt. They didn't. They couldn't have. If you ever want to talk about coping with your loss, call me. I won't spout platitudes, but I'll understand."

Hannah rubbed her upper arms against the chill Isa left behind. She suddenly couldn't stand the gloom and got up to pull back the curtains. She needed the light, even if Rita didn't.

"Hannah."

She came back to the chair and took one of her friend's cold hands.

Rita spoke in a strained voice. "Please, please don't let me ever become that bitter."

"You won't. It's not in you."

"I hope not." Rita's eyes filled again. "It's just so hard."

"I know, love. I know."

Rita, Isa, and she together in the no-babies club. Hannah'd never imagined Isa among the ones who'd lost. The can't-haves.

But maybe not forever.

Please, God.

48 ANNIE MAC & CLAY

Annie Mac squeezed her eyes shut as she pulled Kev close. She didn't want to let him go. Ever. He felt so good. Smelled so good. Not the little boy of their childhood, but a man grown.

"You sure you'll be okay?" He leaned back to look at her as he crouched at her side. "I can cancel my plans. Easily."

She touched his dear face, traced her finger to his chin and felt the dimple there. "I'll say it again, because it needs saying. Thank you, from the bottom of my heart, for finding me. For not believing the bad about me."

"I couldn't. You're not—and never have been—who he says you are. No matter what, you hear?"

She nodded, sniffling as she wiped her eyes. She sure hoped tears were cleansing. She'd cried more in the last month than in her entire life. "What... what are you going to tell him when you get home?"

"That his behavior toward you has negated all the good he ever tried to do for me. If he wants a relationship with me again, he's going to have to make some changes."

"Oh, Kev." She blew her nose hard, which brought a smile to his face, one she couldn't match. "Honey, I don't think he can. I really don't think he's capable of changing."

"Then it's on his head." He stood to his feet, but continued to hold her hand.

"And Mama?" Oh, how she wished she had a real mama.

"Mama is going to be so excited to hear about those two," he said, indicating the children with a nod of his head.

Annie Mac sighed. "I don't believe it. You weren't there when she agreed with him and showed me the door."

"But she's had a long ten-plus years of living with that, hasn't she? Ten years to regret her choice. Those news stories in her drawer tell their own tale."

"You'll let her know I'm fine? Let them both know, if they're interested, that I've got friends and a teaching career I can go back to."

Kevin fished in his pocket and pulled out his phone. "Let me get a picture of you three." He waved Ty and Katie over. "Ty, you go stand on that side of your mama. Katie, sweetie, you come right here."

Annie Mac drew them close. "Thumb out," she told Katie. "And smile." To her brother, "Not that I want my present condition immortalized."

"You're beautiful." He tucked the phone away as Katie crawled up in her mama's lap and Ty returned to his book. "I'm so glad you had Auntie Sim."

"She tried to reach you, but they cut her off. He told her if she took me in, she'd be dead to them, too."

Kev kissed her hand. "I've got Christmas. I'll be with you then. I wish I had more time to give you now."

"Honey, we're fine. We're going to be just fine."

He let his gaze roam over the room and out the windows. "You will be if you let yourself. You need to remember, not all men are like the few you've known."

"My head knows that, but not the rest of me."

"Give him a chance. The lieutenant's a good man."

"I'm scared."

"He's worth the challenge. I can tell."

"You can?"

"It's my man radar. Men can tell about other men." He winked at her, gave her another hug, and spoke to the children. "You troops ready to help carry this heavy bag and make sure I get to the car okay?"

"Yes, sir, captain!" Ty saluted him.

Katie giggled. "Yeth!"

At the door, he waved to Mrs. Barnes, who covered her cell phone and called out that she was coming. To Annie Mac, he said, "I love you, Annie Mac. You have my phone number. You need me any time, I'll be here."

"I love you back, you crazy boy. Be safe."

Mrs. Barnes finished her phone call and followed them down the deck steps. What a comfort to know she'd keep them in her sights and bring them safely back inside.

And when they all trooped in, Mrs. Barnes sent them to look again at their schoolbooks. "I need a word with your mama, hear?" She took a chair near Annie Mac. "That was my friend from church on my little phone. Seems Elvie Mae called in, asking for stepped-up prayer for her daughter now that the Merritts have a baby named after Rita's daddy. Said Rita's not been handling things so well. Having a faith struggle. Does your brother know who they're thinking did it to Rita?"

"No. He's got worries enough on account of leaving us."

Mrs. Barnes smoothed her apron over her skirt and got up. "I expect that's true. He's a good boy."

"I'm so glad they didn't ruin him." Annie Mac didn't mean to sound bitter, but she had some of it in her, no doubt about that. They'd told him she was dead. All these years, that's what he'd believed. How could they have done that?

"You hang onto the good things, hear? Let the bad stuff go. Good can fill you, Miss Annie. Let it do that." Mrs. Barnes picked up the empty glass from the table. "You need anything more before I start a load of laundry?"

"Not a thing. Thank you." She lay back in the big chair, her hands fisting.

She had all afternoon to fret. And to try to come up with a way she could help fix things. One idea cropped up, only to be shot down as impractical. Her choices had made the mess. She wanted to help end it.

When Clay finally walked in the front door, he seemed preoccupied. He ruffled the kids' hair, and scratched behind Harvey's ears. He smiled over at Annie Mac and sniffed toward the kitchen where Mrs. Barnes was making pot roast for dinner.

Annie Mac waited for him to change clothes and for the children to go back in to finish the last minutes of a nature program. "Will you come sit a minute?" She motioned him over.

He slid one of the dining chairs near her. "How're you feeling today? Kevin got off without any trouble?"

She nodded. Now she had him there, she didn't quite know what to do with him. She hoped he'd figure the nod covered it all, that it answered same as her saying "fine" or "okay." She wasn't either, of course, but she still hadn't decided how to ask him what she wanted to know.

"Did you finish your book?" He glanced toward the suspense novel she'd been working on for a few days.

"Too distracted."

"Well, that one is pretty slow going in the beginning. It gets better if you can stick with it."

Maybe she would, maybe she wouldn't. Speaking of slow going, best get this over with. "You're pretty sure it was Roy who killed Rita's baby, aren't you?"

Clay did that raking thing of fingers through hair. He had thick brown hair, long enough that finger combing mussed whatever style it might have had, though he'd obviously just had it trimmed. She tried not to find the gesture endearing, that almost shaggy look he got when he was thinking or, like now, uncomfortable.

"We can't say yet, you know that. Suppositions only, when what we need is proof. And we need Roy."

"For whom you're hunting."

"Best we can."

"How do you think he knew to go after her?"

The hand sifted his hair again. She couldn't help smiling, but stilled her lips before he looked up.

"If he's the one who did it," Clay said, "he must have gotten her license plate from the night everyone was here."

"Which means he could have everyone's."

"I've warned them all." He'd finished with his hair and now his fingers tightened as he clasped them so the tips of each bit into the back of the other hand.

Her own went from fisting to flattening at her sides. The tension seemed to ricochet around the room. "I heard Tadie's got a new baby. I'm scared he might hurt more folk." The idea made her insides bubble as if they might come shooting up her throat. "We've got to do something. We've got to stop him."

"We?"

"I've been thinking. What ifs, you know?"

"You don't need to be afraid, Annie Mac." Clay touched her forearm with his long-fingered hand, just for a moment. "I'm not going to let him get you again."

The heat of his hand branded her, and tears gathered. But they didn't cool the blush that heated up at his voice, at his touch. This was so, so unlike her—*wasn't it?*—all these colors and emotions showing up when she didn't want them. Tears spilled onto her cheeks. "It's because of me this happened! Because of me, Rita can't have babies!"

Clay reached for a tissue. "It wasn't your fault. He's a sick individual. You can't blame yourself."

"I can."

"Then don't."

Platitudes, meant to make her feel better. She appreciated his effort, but it didn't work, couldn't work. She should never have let these nice people be her friends. She was a leper, only the danger in touching her wasn't disease. It was death. She blew hard into the tissue and wiped her cheeks. "But I do. And because of that, I want to—I've *got* to—help stop him."

He sat back in that straight chair and stared. She'd obviously shocked him.

"Really, I think I can help." She spoke quickly and with as much force as she could muster. "And if I can, I must."

He seemed to consider this. "How?"

"I've been thinking about it for a while, how you've been waiting for him to do something so you can get him. Only, I find out now, the things he's doing aren't getting him caught. They're hurting folk I care about, and hurting them badly."

"I'm listening."

"You said you had someone in the police force getting word out. What if you used that to help catch Roy and not just to protect us?"

"That's what we're trying to do."

"Well, what if I was to move back into my house—" When he started to object, she raised a palm to stop him. "No, not with the children. Just me and maybe a few policemen watching the place. You could let the word leak that I was back home, make him think the children were there, too. So he'd come. I know he's working so hard at this because he wants Katie. That's what he kept repeating that night between slamming me, blaming me for trying to keep him from his own daughter. Saying I'd better tell him where I'd hid her."

Clay's brows lowered, and he drew a line with his lips, but she didn't stop. "It would work better than us hiding out like this, waiting for him to pounce on someone else."

"You thinking of taking Mrs. Barnes back there with you?"

That stopped her momentarily. She hadn't even considered Mrs. Barnes. Then she remembered why not. She shook her head. "No, you'd need her here to watch out for the children." She looked down at her leg. "I'm getting better all the time. I can't run or even walk fast with the crutches, but if we set up the same thing there you've fixed for me here, the hoist and bars, I could manage. I don't eat much, so maybe I could get some frozen things to pop in the microwave. Or one of the policeman—do you have any police ladies?—maybe one of them could heat the food. I'm betting that Roy won't wait too long if he doesn't see any guards or police around."

Clay flattened his lips and waved that away. "He'd know. He's bound to know we wouldn't let you loose on your own."

"Can't you say I insisted? He already thinks I'm ornery, which seems to be his favorite descriptive. You've spread word that I went out of the county. So maybe that didn't work. I was too much trouble for the folk who said they'd help, and I was tired of moving around, depending on other people." She smoothed her hands over the floppy pants she wore. "Come on, Clay, you know how to work it. You can sound disgusted with me, say I'm a fool when you tell the story, but there doesn't seem to be anything you guys can do if I don't want protection. That's right, isn't it?"

He sighed, but he didn't look pleased. Well, she didn't really want him to, did she? Pleased would mean he wanted her gone.

"Yeah," he said finally.

"Can't you find someone you can trust to watch my place?"

"I guess I could have one of Brock's stay with you. I've got a deputy from Grayton County helping." He stood, did that thing where he wiped his hands down the side of his pants like they were sweaty. "Listen, Annie Mac, you've given me some things to think on. But that's all I'm going to do right now. Think. I don't like the idea one little bit."

"But if it's the best option?"

"I'll have to take it."

He strode away. From the set of his shoulders, he obviously wasn't going to give in without a fight, but he was a reasonable man and would make a decision based on what was best. For everyone.

And how did she feel about that?

Scared all the way down to her toes. With just a smidgen of powerful thrown in.

It's what she'd wanted. To do something. To take responsibility. To quit being a whiner.

The children begged to come with him out to the dock. When their mama nodded her okay, Clay waved them forward.

Evenings had cooled as September slid into place, but since the thunderstorm, the sky had remained clear and the breezes moderate. Right now, the water was doing what it did best about this time of day, flattening. The sun's lowered rays flickered and bounced back as if from diamond facets.

Soft noises over the water sounded just below the children's chatter: the hum of an engine bringing a fishing boat into the harbor across the way, the caw of a gull, the screech of one of his ospreys. He called them his because they nested on an old stand about seventy-five feet off his property. Every year, a pair returned, rebuilt and padded its nest, hatched an egg or two, and flew off for the winter months, returning in March to repeat the cycle.

Fish leapt, mostly mackerel. Katie giggled and pointed. Ty's grin widened. Teaching those two to swim was something he was going to have to work on soon as they got Bingham behind bars. A boy needed to be comfortable near the water so he could learn to mess around in boats. Well, so did a little girl who would grow soon enough and be able to follow that boy. And, yes, a mama had to be soothed into letting the children learn. Into trusting the world with her babies.

Now, though, he had to keep them safe until he could figure out the next step. He hated to admit the truth of what Annie Mac said. He didn't want her to be right. He sure didn't want to put her at risk.

But he just might have to.

He liked Garth Evans, who seemed smart and insightful, so he'd sent him off to gather as much information as possible about Pete Rasman and his movements. If they ended up using Annie Mac, he could put the deputy on the job as well as some of Brock's people.

Would that work? Could they do it and keep her safe?

David Brock would need to make sure one of his best came on board to guard from inside. Maybe David had a woman who could help out. He'd call.

"Lieutenant, look!" Ty waved toward a pelican who'd come up with a fish too big for his bill. Other pelicans skidded to a watery halt and tried to snatch it away. The children giggled at the tug of war.

Until it began to worry Katie. "They won't let him have his dinner."

"Give him a chance. Let's see who wins."

They watched. Clay returned to his internal debate.

What were his options? They could continue with another tail on this Pete fellow, hoping to catch him doing something illegal. They could hope Officer McKinley led them to new evidence. And they could try to set up a sting using policemen and not Annie Mac as a decoy. If they were a big-city police force, they'd even have a policewoman they could put there.

Well, he wasn't going to do anything until the chief got back. He could hope—pray—that Evans came up with something before then.

"He got it!" Katie said, pulling on his pant leg. "He swallowed it!"

It took Clay a moment to shift gears. "Bravo."

Hoisting Katie to his chest, he gave her a swift hug, but when she laced her little arms around his neck and her legs around his middle, he felt a lump in his throat ready to choke him. He turned toward the house with the child still in his arms.

"Let's head back in. Mrs. Barnes has that nice dinner waiting."

He'd worry about tomorrow's ills later. For now, he'd memorize the sensation of small arms tightening on his neck; the perfume of clean, little-girl skin; the sight of a rosebud mouth curled into a grin; and the sound of clattering feet bounding up wooden steps once he put her down, coupled with high-pitched laughter and a dog's bark.

It was enough.

But after a dinner when the mother's laughter had joined theirs, the mother's eyes had sought his, and the mother's blush had rocketed through him, he excused himself. "Work to do," he said, closing his bedroom door to separate himself from temptation.

Too bad he couldn't separate himself from need. That took another shower that began as hot spray slamming into his chest and changed to a cold dousing as he stood with his head bent and his hands splayed on the tile walls.

49 CLAY

In case Garth's efforts led nowhere, which Clay profoundly hoped would not happen, he set to work readying Annie Mac's house, installing the grab bars himself. Grab bars were a good idea anyway.

Garth called with a report early Monday morning. Pete had arrived home around ten Friday night. He'd gone out once on Saturday to the rental property he owned and visited the computer shop—the one that tied him to Officer McKinley. He'd stopped off for groceries and spent some time in a local bar. Most of Sunday he'd stayed home, where he'd been visited by a young woman who stayed until early Monday morning.

"Avery's on duty now. I'll be back in touch when I relieve him," Garth said.

By nine o'clock that same morning, Clay sat in Chief Bradley's office, wishing for some colorful language. It swirled in his brain, but he clamped his teeth together and listened to his boss's response to Annie Mac's proposal. "If she's willing to risk it, I don't know how we can say no."

Clay thought of all sorts of ways he could, but none of them seemed valid. Especially when he got David Brock to assign a woman to stay with Annie Mac at the house. Another of Brock's men would monitor the backyard from inside. Nights, Garth Evans would sit where he could watch the front. Beaufort's finest would do hourly drive-bys in order to make the move seem realistic.

Word would go round the station house Tuesday morning, once Clay had set up the house and installed Annie Mac there. They would pull Evans off Pete as of Tuesday night, but if Pete showed signs of leaving town, Evans would be the one to follow, not Avery. "I can handle it," Garth said. "We'll switch places, Avery and me."

Clay soothed Avery's wounded feelings with promises to let him be in on the action if anything went down at Annie Mac's. Brock's agents were due to arrive after dark.

He went over the scene in his mind as he walked the house, vacillating between pulling Garth to the inside because of his intelligence or moving in there himself. But if either he or Avery disappeared from the station for longer than a day, it would rouse suspicions. They had to remain visible and accessible. He'd stocked a week's worth of easily prepared meals, refusing to consider the chemical additives that made the meals a camper's choice.

Mrs. Barnes had also been busy. As per his instructions, she'd made recordings of the children chattering, squealing, and giggling. It wouldn't do any good to say the children were there if anyone standing outside couldn't hear them. That clapboard house wasn't soundproof. Probably wasn't even well insulated.

Avery drove with him to help fetch Annie Mac and her gear in the van. Katie clung to her mama's lap when Annie Mac tried to say good-bye.

"I'll see you very soon, sweetie. But Mama has something special she has to do so we can go home again, all of us. I need you to be my big, brave girl and help your brother and Mrs. Barnes. Harvey is going to stay here to take care of you, and the lieutenant will come home nights." She took Ty's hand. "Can you do that, sweet boy? Can you take care of Katie for me? This time nothing bad's going to happen. You trust the lieutenant, don't you?"

Ty nodded, but he took back his hand and stuffed both deep in his pockets. His shoulders hunched forward.

Clay rested a hand on one of those shoulders. "We'll get along just fine, won't we, son? Your mama needs to know she can count on you, so she can go off and do this thing to make sure Roy won't ever come to bother you or her again."

Ty looked up at Clay with fear rounding his eyes. "Who'll take care of her?"

"Remember, I told you I've found three really good people. One is a woman who works for the same company as Mr. Oliver and Mr. Webber, another is a friend of theirs, and the third is a deputy sheriff who is a very smart man. Also, Detective Grainger and I are going to be checking up on her all the time." He crouched to eye level. "You know I won't let anything happen to your mama. She's my friend."

Ty stared at him for a long minute before nodding. He took Katie's hand. "We can trust the lieutenant. Mama will be okay."

That nearly killed Clay. One look at Annie Mac and he could see she was biting her lip to keep her own tears from spilling all over them. He picked up her bag and nodded to Avery, who pushed the wheelchair while Mrs. Barnes set Katie on her hip. Ty threw his arms around Harvey's neck, hiding his face.

Under cover of dark, they got Annie Mac settled in her own bed with the hoist and crutches nearby. Bernice Falkner was strong, but she was no Becca Barnes, so Annie Mac was going to have to use the hoist all the time when she wanted to move from one place to another. At least Bernice could roll the hoist into place wherever Annie Mac needed it and help her maneuver to the adjoining bathroom.

Fletcher Peters was an ex-Marine sergeant who had worked for Brock for the last thirteen years. He came equipped with some fancy gadgets Mr. Brock had ordered.

"Borrowed them from his son Ed for this assignment." Sergeant Peters spoke over his shoulder as he set up motion sensors and showed off night vision goggles.

Avery climbed back in the van with Clay. "I want a set of those. Think the chief would spring for some?"

"You could always ask."

"The department is paying for all these extras, aren't they? I mean, you're not footing this bill, too?"

"They're paying, but we'd better hope something happens soon, because I doubt the budget will stretch to more than a week."

"What do you want me to do?"

"Tomorrow, you come in to the office to tell me about getting the call from the contact out where we stashed Annie Mac. Act all disgusted that she moved back home with the kids. I don't know. You're good at this. You can get into character. The thing we've got to do is make sure Brand McKinley is on duty when you begin the charade. We want word to get to Bingham as soon as possible."

"Got it. I'd hate to be in Officer McKinley's shoes when this all goes down. What do you think? Crossing guard duty for the next six months?"

Clay laughed. "Or for life."

They eased past Pete's house on the way back to Avery's car. The Corvette sat in the driveway.

"If Garth goes chasing Pete out of town, you'll be on night watch. And not in your own car."

"I'm your man."

Back at his place, the children had had their baths, and Katie snuggled with Mrs. Barnes as she read a story. Ty lolled on the floor of Clay's room, watching a movie.

"Hey," Clay said, as he sat down to remove his shoes. "Mind if I join you?"

Ty smiled shyly. "If you want to. It's your room."

"It's big enough to share. Come on up and get comfortable."

Ty scurried onto the bed and leaned back against a heap of pillows next to Clay. He crossed his ankles, much as Clay had done, and set the remote control between them. Harvey hadn't moved from his post on the floor, though he eyed Clay before going back to sleep.

"Looks like you tuckered Harvey out."

"We wrestled."

"Good. He probably needed it."

"Yeah."

The story they watched was about an Irish setter and a young boy, one Clay had seen at least twice when his brothers were young enough to get a kick out of it. "I got your mama settled," he said. "The woman guard has figured out a way to help your mama move around. And the man brought night vision goggles."

"Really? You mean those things that make people look like green things moving around in the dark?"

"They ought to help him see anything bad."

"Like Roy."

"Yes, like Roy or anyone who comes near the place."

"Has he got a gun?"

"Everyone taking care of your mama is fully prepared to deal with anything that comes up. They're trained and capable."

When Ty asked why the woman guard couldn't pretend to be his mother, Clay said he'd wondered the same thing, until they reminded him it would be like Roy to call the house and expect Annie Mac to answer. If someone else did, the game would be up. He didn't tell Ty, but he'd also suggested they could have calls forwarded to his house, but that was shot down when he admitted Annie Mac wasn't the only person who answered the phone here.

"I'm going to take Harvey for a last bathroom walk while you finish the movie."

Big Red and his boy faced a climactic moment. Ty flipped around to get closer to the screen and propped himself on his elbows. "Sure."

By the time Clay had settled Harvey at his water bowl, the credits rolled, and Ty lay curled with his head on a pillow, asleep. Clay debated moving him to his own bed. Instead, he just tucked the boy in where he'd slept before. He told Harvey to lie down on the floor and went to check on Katie. Mrs. Barnes had her hand on the light switch.

"The child's asleep. I stayed with her 'til her eyes closed, considerin' her worries."

"Ty collapsed in my bed. I hated to move him."

"Well, I've got the monitor goin', so if this child wakes, I'll hear her. What you want me to do if'n she asks for Ty?"

Clay grinned. "Bring her on in, I guess. The bed's big enough for a crowd. You stick her in between, I probably wouldn't even notice."

Mrs. Barnes chuckled. "Wouldn't that be a sight. Yes, sir. That it would be. And she's not been wetting the bed—"

"She used to?"

"Yes, sir. But it's been a few nights now she's stayed dry. If I bring her to you, I'll make sure she goes first."

Horrified, he said, "Yes, please."

50   HANNAH

As she drove home after dropping Jilly back at Tadie's, the thought hit her. She, Hannah Morgan, was the one holding things together in their little circle, a job that usually fell to Tadie. Or, more recently, to Rita. Now, she was the one driving and teaching and shopping for everyone.

The warm glow lasted about five minutes, long enough to park the van at her back door, climb out, and grab the bag of apples she and Jilly had bought at that stand in Otway. By the time she had her key in the lock, that nasty bit of self-congratulation had withered. All she had to do was let herself puff up about something and her face would have mud smeared over it.

She blew a stray hair off her cheek. Marching into the kitchen, she washed her hands, gathered ingredients for a stir-fry, and started chopping.

Matt would be home soon. He wasn't the best vegetable eater in history, so she hid them in interesting sauces. He did like rice. Tonight she'd flavor the meal with a little soy and honey, a dash of lemon and a pinch of Korean pepper. She and Jilly had picked up mangoes at Harris Teeter over in Morehead a couple of days ago. One of them ought to be ripe. Her mouth watered as she decided on the salad course of sliced mango, a few dried cranberries, and some chopped walnuts on lettuce, drizzled with raspberry vinaigrette. Yes, sir. He was going to love that.

He loved it so much he nuzzled her all the way upstairs to bed. She swatted at him, but playfully. "Once again, Mr. Morgan, the way to your heart has proved to be your stomach."

He laughed and pinched her backside lightly. "Yes, ma'am. Your cooking and you. You're making me young again."

Oooh, and wasn't he doing the same to her? As he slowly undressed her, tingles wiggled down to the soles of her feet—and straight up her front, tightening all sorts of lovely places. And then he nipped at the back of her neck.

Oh, yeah.

There was something decidedly delicious about a man who knew what you needed even before you did. In bed, she curled toward him, her hand splaying on his chest where a sprinkle of hair dusted the firm skin.

"Thank you," she whispered.

"There's one thing more I have for you tonight, Mrs. Morgan."

He turned slightly toward the far side and dropped his long arm toward the floor as if reaching for something. When the hand resurfaced, it held a little blue jeweler's box.

"I was going to wait until our anniversary next month, but I can't. Do you mind?"

Hannah stared at the box. Did she mind? "Um, no. Delayed gratification has never been big with me."

As he slid the box toward her, she uncurled and sat up next to him. He turned on his side to watch. The box was velvet-covered. Expensive. Her heartbeat, which had slowed after lovemaking, now sped with the excitement of a fast train coming out of a curve.

"Open it."

"I am." But she was almost afraid to. The box was so gorgeous. How could the contents improve on it?

That was stupid.

She held her breath and lifted the lid. "Matt." And that's all she could say because her throat clogged and her eyes filled. The ring nestled inside was the most beautiful thing she'd ever seen.

"I thought it time." He eased up against the headboard until he sat next to her. "Your eyes, my love, are so beautiful, so perfect and expressive. I don't think I've told you often enough how you captured my heart with them, how you've kept my heart yours, only yours, for more than twenty years."

She sniffed and reached for a tissue to blow her nose.

"The sapphires are for your eyes. The diamonds for your heart, multifaceted, shining... mine."

"But..."

He took the ring from her hand and slid it next to her wedding band. "This is to remind you every single day that nothing you do, nothing you think or say or feel can ever stop me loving you. You have all of me, and I am yours."

"Oh, Matt."

He drew her toward him and circled her with his arms, reaching across her to grab a wad of tissues and pressing them into her hand.

She blew. Well, she honked, which produced a bark of laughter. Thank God he loved her, in spite of her unromantic noises. "I... I love you so much."

"I know. But a little romance in our life sounds like a good prescription for these aging bodies, doesn't it?"

She pushed up to look at him. "Would you quit talking about aging? I'm not even forty."

"But I'll soon be pushing forty-five, and you've got to admit, we were living rather staid lives before those children showed up." He pinched her chin and pulled her back against him. "So, Mrs. Morgan, we're going to kick up our heels, and I'm going to take your young body and my older body gallivanting around Europe." Picking up her hand, he kissed the tips of her fingers and then touched the new ring. "New memories, my love. And when we come back, another new adventure." He traced the outline of her jaw. "One more thing."

"More?"

"I sent in the redrafted paperwork."

"For the adoption?"

"And I talked to the service. We're scheduled for an interview next week."

"Oh, Matt." And that's all she could say as she listened to the thump of his heart and felt the slight rise and fall of his chest. Oh, Matt.

The next afternoon, Jilly didn't stop chattering until Hannah pulled up next to the Merritts' back door. After a full day of children, Hannah's ears buzzed, and she longed for silence, please. Blessed silence. And home. Where she could dream and plan. And admire her new ring.

Tadie's kitchen was one of those huge rooms with sink and stove and a slew of cupboards against the back wall and with more cupboards, a refrigerator, and a breakfast table across the way. Next came the doorway into the dining room. There used to be a butler's pantry in between, but that wall had come down to give better access to the breakfast table, and the only pantry now opened off the far end of the room, past a living area with a couch and chairs. Tadie's mama, Caroline Longworth, used to sit in one of those big old chairs to watch the goings-on in her kitchen. Caroline had been a sweet soul who lived in her own world. Which was why Elvie Mae had taken over mothering and doing for Tadie and her little brother.

Hannah loved the way everyone could congregate in this kitchen. She could smell something delicious as she and Jilly stepped through the back door. Yep, there was Elvie Mae, stirring what looked very much like her ham-and-bean soup.

"Hey, doll baby," Elvie said, catching Jilly in a one-armed hug. "And, Hannah, how're you doing?"

Hannah smiled in answer. And then looked past Elvie to the living area where Rita sat next to Tadie, holding baby Samuel.

"My girl's here, you see?" Elvie said. "She said she needed to get out of the house, so I brung her to see Sammy."

How had this happened? Last Hannah'd heard, Rita was still hiding out at home and talking about blobs. And now here she sat, tears streaming down her face.

Jilly climbed on her mama's lap. "What's wrong, Auntie Rita? Don't you like our baby?"

"I do, Jilly-bear. He's the sweetest thing." Rita dashed the tears away with the back of one hand. "Almost as sweet as you."

"Then why …," but she didn't finish her question. "Oh, I'm sorry. I forgot."

Rita nodded and opened her mouth as if to speak, but the words didn't come.

"I'm really, really sorry about your baby."

That increased the torrent. Tadie set a box of tissues between them and reached out to take Samuel. "Run on in and speak to your daddy, Jilly."

The child fled.

"Sorry about that," Tadie said.

Rita nodded again, obviously trying to control her emotions. "No, I'm sorry. I didn't come here to weep all over you."

"It's good to see you again." Hannah sat down opposite the other two, not quite sure what to say. Nothing would be enough, as she well knew.

"You, too, Hannah. I thought I was past the constant flooding." Rita waved across her face. "Seems I'm not."

"It takes a while."

Rita dabbed away tears. "Probably a really long while."

"Seems that way." Hannah's ring finger itched. Or maybe it burned. She twisted her wedding band, around and back again.

Elvie turned off the stove and checked the oven before looking their way. "You want something cold, any of you?"

"I could use a glass of water, Mama," Rita said, "but I hate you to be bothering."

"No trouble at all, you know that. Anyone else?"

"While you're at it, I'd love one." Hannah'd like to put her head under ice or slap something cold over her thoughts so she could be in the moment with Rita's pain, instead of wanting only to kiss that sweet baby's fat cheeks and flash her new ring—and her other news—around.

"Tadie-girl? You're nursing. You need lots of liquid."

Elvie brought over the glasses, set them down, and said she was just going to check on Jilly.

"Thanks, Elvie." Tadie settled Samuel at her breast. Still watching the baby, she said, "Rita spoke to Annie Mac this morning."

"And?" Hannah asked. "Any news?"

"You won't believe it." Rita brandished another tissue to wrap around the icy glass. "Annie Mac has decided that all this, including Daniel's death, is her fault." Her eyes dropped at the mention of her lost baby.

"Oh, man, you're kidding." What was this guilt thing, an infectious disease hopping from one to the other?

"Can you believe it? She thinks her bad feelings, along with the fact that she didn't fix everything to get Roy locked up earlier, made me lose Daniel."

"What bad feelings?" Tadie asked, glancing up from studying her son.

Hannah clamped her mouth shut. She didn't want to know. Nope, no thank you.

"She was actually jealous of me." Rita blew out a breath. "Imagine. Me."

"Jealous?" Tadie brought Samuel to her shoulder for a burp. She patted his back, laughing when he emitted a lusty burp. "My, I bet you feel better now, kiddo." A couple more pats and she lowered him to her other breast.

Rita touched the baby's tiny foot. "Annie Mac said she wished she'd made the same choices I had so that she could have had a life more like mine."

Oh, my. Hannah looked over her shoulder, willing either Elvie or Jilly to return. She needed to become invisible. Beam me up, Scotty. It was one thing having Tadie know she'd harbored pettiness. Tadie had Sammy. And, in a weak moment, she'd mentioned them to Rita, but she didn't think Rita remembered. She didn't want Rita to remember.

"I guess I can understand that," Tadie said. "Considering."

"Sure, but those feelings had nothing to do with the accident," Rita said.

"Of course they didn't."

Rita sipped her water, trailing fingers over the condensation the tissue hadn't absorbed. "I told her she was being absurd, that Roy was responsible—assuming Roy was the driver. She feels guilty for being friends with me, for letting us hold that barbecue at Clay's where Roy probably got the license numbers. She needs to get over herself."

"Yes, of course." Tadie cooed at her baby.

Get over herself. Good idea, hard to execute. Hannah's sympathy lay with Annie Mac on this one. Besides, she'd like to know how Rita had seemingly gotten over her own self—and her blob of silence. That was one Hannah wasn't likely to forget any time soon.

Elvie slipped back into the room. "Jilly's fine in there with her daddy. He set her up next to his desk so they can work together, so I'm going to take some of this soup up to James. Rita love, you gonna come with me to see your daddy?"

Rita stood carefully, holding her stomach as she rose as if she still felt fragile there. "Yes, ma'am, coming." She reached a hand toward Tadie. "He's precious. Forgive my tears?"

"Oh, honey, you don't need to apologize. I love you."

"I love you back. And you know I'm going to love that baby."

"I know you are. I'm so glad you came today. I needed to see you."

Rita swiped at new tears, waved at Hannah with a "Talk to you later?" and fled.

Her mama bent to kiss Samuel's fingers, Tadie's cheek. "You need me, call, hear?"

"Yes, ma'am, I sure will."

"And Hannah-girl, give me a hug, too. I don't know what we'd have done without you these days."

Hannah hugged Elvie fiercely and then took Rita's seat next to Tadie. Sammy glanced up from the breast before suckling again.

"You sweet thing." His mama cooed and traced a finger down his cheek, around his baby ear. "Look at him, Hannah."

"I'm looking. He's so perfect."

Still watching her son, Tadie said, "It's rather self-indulgent of Annie Mac to blame herself, don't you think?"

Hannah's head shot up. "Why?"

"I don't know. Maybe because it gives her more power than she actually has."

Hannah squinted Tadie's way. Was her friend talking about Annie Mac still? Or was she remembering Hannah's confession? "Aren't you the one who figured all our babies were in some sort of cosmic cycle or something? Even cursed?"

"I was scared," Tadie said. "You know that. And it wasn't a cosmic anything. I was more worried about some chemical anomaly, like that lupus epidemic in the Delaware area."

"And how did that connect to Rita's Daniel?"

"It didn't. You know I wasn't making a whole lot of sense."

"So now Annie Mac is being self-indulgent because she feels guilty for not having that man thrown in jail a long time ago?"

"That's not what Rita said."

Hannah threw up her hands. "Of course, it is."

Samuel fussed. "You're upsetting the baby," Tadie said. "Shhh, sweet boy. Your Auntie Hannah didn't mean to sound angry."

"Sorry, Sammy. But that fussing may mean he wants to burp again."

"Oh. Maybe so." Tadie hefted him back to her shoulder, kissing his soft head. He let out a loud belch. "All better?" Settling a rooting Sammy once again at her other breast, she looked up at Hannah. "Rita also said Annie Mac felt guilty for envying Rita's choices and Rita's life. You know, pregnancy after marriage, happy home life, career?"

Hannah nodded.

"That's self-pity, isn't it?" Tadie said. "In the guise of guilt? But it didn't cause Rita's crash. Or the loss of her baby."

"I know." Hannah carried her glass to the sink. "I've been telling myself that all things work out for good, but sometimes it's just a hard message to hold onto."

"It is. And I've been fighting it myself."

"Fighting what?"

"Guilt that I'm the only one of us with a healthy baby. Rita's pain right now? It's killing me."

"Yeah. I get that. Me, too."

Samuel had nodded off. Tadie eased him to a blanket on the couch beside her.

"I want to show you something," Hannah said, flashing her bauble near Tadie's face.

Tadie pulled her hand close. "That's some distraction, Mrs. Morgan."

"My pre-anniversary gift."

"This new Matt is fascinating me. First, he wants to take you to Europe, then he talks adoption, and now this? Lands, Hannah, what's gotten into him?"

Hannah grinned. "Whatever it is, I'm very happy about it. And last night he told me we have an appointment next week at the adoption agency."

"A baby for you. Finally. It's such a perfect gift for all of us."

"Maybe not for Rita."

"Not yet. But look how far she's come in such a short time. She'll get there. I wouldn't be surprised if she and Martin adopt. Maybe even one of those children they support."

"Maybe. But it shocked me, seeing her here already. I'm not sure I'd have been that brave."

"Nor I."

"Well, I need to get on home. Fix something delicious for that husband of mine."

Tadie tucked a pillow next to Sammy and stood. "Elvie cooked for all of us. You're to take home enough for you two."

"Really? What a sweetheart."

"The biscuits are in the oven," Tadie said, pulling out plastic containers and spooning soup into one. "Did Elvie take her share of those?"

"Two full cookie sheets here."

"You take some, and Jilly can run theirs up. She loves the excuse to visit."

"I'll get this on home while it's hot. Please thank Elvie for me." At the door, she spoke over her shoulder. "And make sure Jilly works on her math. Ty won the speed drill this morning."

"Speaking of Ty and schooling out there. You sure those guards are up to the job?"

"It would be nearly impossible for Roy to get by unseen."

"Unless he figured out how to come by water."

"Glory, Tadie, I hadn't thought of that."

"Talk to Clay?"

"I will." But she wouldn't tell Matt. He'd keep her from going near the place, and she couldn't let him do that.

51 ROY

Roy basked in sunlight, watching his birds do their little dances. When Pete's brother Jocko roared up the lane in his souped-up truck with its huge tires, the birds scattered.

Jocko climbed out, swishing more than Roy remembered as he approached the cabin. His eyes looked loopy. "Good to see you, buddy."

Boy had obviously been living hard. He sure hadn't been out here working or doing much of anything that Roy'd seen.

What had Pete said? Something about a new lady friend?

Roy decided to play it friendly. "How're you doing, man? Heard you've been busy down east. A new filly?"

Jocko flicked off an imaginary speck from his shirtfront. "Heard you been busy yourself. Run into a bit of trouble?"

"Yeah, well, stuff happens."

"You got that right. It sure does." Jocko brushed past him into the cabin.

Roy followed.

Jocko opened a few cupboards, shut them without taking anything. "Pete said to tell you your missus moved back to the house. They've got a cop driving by every hour. He's gonna check it out."

"That's good. That's really good news." Roy rubbed his palms up his thighs. "Grateful you told me."

"Well, I gotta go check on stuff. You're not to go back there. You know that?"

"Sure, man. Not with them gators and cats guarding that place. I don't go no further than that there outhouse."

That set Jocko to howling. He trotted off, still laughing, in the direction of the swamp. It was a long forty-five minutes before he stumbled back toward his car. This time, the man had a grin on his face fit to be tied. He also had a lump in his front pocket that looked a lot like a roll of cash.

Roy stayed where he was on the porch. Jocko stopped momentarily as if surprised to see him, but then he saluted good-bye and took off.

Staring after the rock-spitting tires, Roy considered Jocko's slurs added to Pete's skittish behavior about the cops tailing him. It was time, past time, to move on. He figured on biding his time until tomorrow, long enough for Pete to say what the police were up to. Long enough to figure how to get hold of some cash. He didn't really believe the line Pete had been fed about them just letting her move home on her own. Nope. They were set on catchin' him. He could feel it.

Annie Mac and that bratty boy of hers didn't matter a hoot. But knowing his baby girl was back in town, waiting for him, was a different story entirely.

The next day, Pete headed straight from his car to the woods. On his way out again, he stopped to poke his head in the screen door. "Thought I'd let you know, I've checked things in town. Drove past your old place twice. Heard the television one time, kids laughing and cutting up the other."

Roy rubbed his hands together. "You've done good, yessir. I just need to rescue that sweet little girl, and I'll be outta your hair."

Pete saluted him. "I'm taking off for a few days. Got a meeting set up in Wilson that should be good for business. You do something about fetchin' her and I miss seeing you off, well, I'll catch up with you next time."

Roy watched from the porch as Pete started up the Corvette. Then Pete stuck his head out the window. "Listen, I know I promised you a loan. You can't think of another source, I'll spot you when I get back from Wilson. Don't exactly have much on me now. You know how it is, bills and all. But I know you, buddy. No one more resourceful than you. Grab that little gal and go find yourself a sucker!" Laughing, he raised the window, gunned the engine, and sped off down the lane.

Roy wandered back inside, pulled a beer out of the fridge, and started cogitating. Something was definitely going on with Pete, so he'd best be outta here before Pete returned, loan or no.

First things first. He had to figure out how to sneak in the house without tipping off the police or having to mess with Annie Mac or the boy. Got unpleasant that way and took too much out of a man.

Besides, it would only upset Katie.

52 ANNIE MAC

Annie Mac readjusted her pillows as she held the phone to her ear and listened to Ty chatter about his school work. He'd memorized his times tables up to thirteen so he could do division and keep up with Jilly. "She's real smart for a girl, but I can still read better. Is that okay to say, Mama?"

"You can say it to me, but I think Jilly's really proud to be doing math and history with you because you're a year older. We don't want to hurt her feelings, okay?"

That seemed to satisfy him. She knew Ty felt intimidated by how far ahead Jilly was in a number of subjects. He'd settle down once he saw the progress he made with all this one-on-one tutoring.

She pictured him, this sweet son of hers, as he told her about the new things Harvey had learned and how Mr. Clay had promised to take him sailing soon as he could swim. "You're gonna let me learn, aren't you Mama?"

Kev had been right. She had to do this. "We'll make it a priority as soon as we're together again."

"Thanks. That'll be swell." After he told about the fish they'd seen under the dock yesterday when Mr. Clay took them out, he asked, "Mama, you think I'm gonna grow some more? I want to be tall like the lieutenant. D'you think I will?"

"Your daddy was tall and so is mine, so I don't see why not."

"But Uncle Kevin isn't very big."

"He takes after my mama's side."

"Do I?"

She couldn't help smiling at that, but she could understand his fears. Kevin hated being only five-eight. "Not from what I can see. Don't you worry, honey, you'll grow. It just takes time."

"Seems everything takes time. Way too much, and I sure would like it to pass, you know? For me, so I can get tall and strong, and for you, so you'll be all better."

"I know. You and I, we'll each do our part, and pretty soon, we'll all be together without anything to fear."

His sigh went straight to her heart. "I sure hope so." After a pause, he said, "Mama, I've been talking to God about this stuff."

That choked her right up. "You have? That's a good thing to do." She had to pause a moment herself so she wouldn't worry him by sounding tearful. "You keep it up. You and Katie. I'm sure God really likes to hear from you."

"You think so? Miss Becca said it was needful. Isn't that a funny word? Right after we finished math yesterday, Miss Hannah started saying something to Miss Becca, and then Jilly said how sad it was Miss Rita's baby was dead, and that's when Miss Hannah got all upset. Miss Becca hugged on Miss Hannah and told us to come hug on her, too. It was too mushy for a guy, you know? But Katie? You shoulda seen her, Mama. She just climbed on in there and put her arms around Miss Hannah. Told her she loved her and she was sad about the baby too. And Jilly took hold from the back."

"And what did Mrs. Morgan do?"

"She hugged on back, first Katie, then Jilly. She said she knew Miss Rita would be grateful for our prayers and that she loved Katie and me and Jilly and Miss Becca. We prayed for you, too, Mama, and for Mr. Clay to catch Roy soon so we can see you."

"That's pretty special. Thank you."

"You're welcome. Anyway, here's Katie. She's yanking on me."

Katie sang her alphabet song, melting her mama's heart. "I'm learning to read my letters, and Miss Hannah's going to help with numbers next. It's fun, only, Mommy, you promised to be my teacher."

And didn't that just make Annie Mac choke up again? "I know, sweetie. And as soon as we get together again, I will be. Just a little longer."

"You promise?"

"I'm doing my best, sweet girl. You keep on doing your best, too, okay?"

"Okay." Annie Mac heard Mrs. Barnes in the background. "Mommy, I gotta go. Miss Becca says Harvey needs to go out. So we get to go to the deck and watch. Okay?"

"I love you, sweetheart. 'Bye."

Annie Mac disconnected. Her focus had certainly adjusted down in size so the highlight of her day was chatting with her babies. That thought made her smile. As did the memory of Katie's words from, was it yesterday or the day before?

"Guess what, Mommy!" Katie had said. "Ty and me both got to sleep in Mr. Clay's bed!"

"You did?"

"Yeth. Ty was already there when I woke up and I couldn't find him, but Miss Becca heard me so she came and got me. I asked where he was and she knew and said it was okay for me climb in, too, but first I had to go potty. Did you know it's a really, really big bed? Miss Becca just scooted Ty to the middle and I got to be on the outside, 'cause she couldn't lift me over him. Mr. Clay sorta woke up, but not enough to help Miss Becca, only to smile sorta with his eyes closed, so she told Ty to scoot. She told Harvey first, 'cause he was lying right in the way and she didn't want to trip on him, but he moved. And then he came right back so he could keep guard."

How quickly things changed. Something about the scene, with Mrs. Barnes—Miss Becca—doing the shifting made Annie Mac smile at something that would have sent her over the edge into panic only a couple of weeks ago. It would have sent Katie and Ty right along with her into screaming, wouldn't it?

They were happy, her two. Mrs. Barnes was a jewel, and Clay would guard the children with his life. She wasn't sure how she knew this or when she'd decided she could trust him completely. Maybe it had begun the night of the storm. But if she knew anything, she knew he loved Ty and Katie.

She fidgeted, trying to push herself up in the lumpy bed. The thought of going back into the living room to play another card game with Bernice sure didn't appeal. Fletcher occasionally joined them when he wasn't acting macho-guard or moving that recording of the children's noises from room to room.

She'd reread a couple of books that were in the house and had seen two old movies. Clay—was there ever a more thoughtful man?—had Time Warner set up cable, Internet, and phone service, so Bernice could mess around with her computer and they could take turns picking a television program. Fletcher gravitated to police and courtroom dramas. She preferred British mysteries. Bernice liked sitcoms, which made Annie Mac so twitchy that she opted for alone-time in her room.

But lying here was hard. The room had seen too much. Sometimes in the night, she heard a replay of her past, as if the walls remembered Roy's shouts and her tears. As if the house—and she—had forgotten the good years with Auntie Sim.

But even if the house felt wrong, it looked really good. Those lovely folk had fixed everything. Not just fixed, but upgraded. And they'd painted the interior of all the rooms a lovely, bright cream.

Sure, the furniture remained the same, except for what Roy had torn or broken. The replacement couch had come from the Salvation Army store, so it was used, but clean. Rita explained that they wanted to let her pick out a permanent one later.

Annie Mac would never be able to repay a single thing they'd done for her and hers, but this odd group of new friends didn't seem to tie up good works with strings. Her parents and their puckered-up friends used to go out to do good works, lacing every little deed not only with scripture preaching but also with fear-of-God-hell-fire rantings. If the recipients weren't properly appreciative, well, they'd soon discover which direction they were heading come Judgment Day. As if the hell-fire folk were on the list of prophets sent to usher others in or out with their finger-pointing.

Her world, from her youngest days until she moved in with Auntie Sim, had been about deserving. One was either deserving or one wasn't. One obeyed the rules and found love and acceptance, or one disobeyed and was ostracized. Even Auntie Sim's unconditional love hadn't quite erased that early training, though Auntie Sim sure had tried.

Annie Mac shifted again. She needed to do some lifting exercises and change position or she'd end up with bedsores and weak legs.

Auntie Sim had said she needed to find healing from the inside out. She'd been willing, if indeed one could choose to be healed or not. Considering things from the perspective of her broken body and all these Auntie Sim-clones who'd barged into her life—a lot like Auntie Sim had done in saving her the first time—well, looking at it now, it sure seemed to Annie Mac that Kev was right. She'd been a sucker for Roy because her expectations had been so low. Her dad. Ty's dad. Her brother's words and his coming to find her, along with the kindness of all these new friends, might help her raise the bar.

She let her fingers trail over the upper portion of her cast. Rita had become childless because of their friendship. And, yet, what had Rita said? "We're friends, Annie Mac, and that doesn't change because some crazy man hurt me and mine. Quit thinking this is your fault. If Roy did it, it's because of who he is. Period."

Rita's attitude seemed unbelievable. Oh, she knew Rita wasn't intentionally lying, but maybe Rita said what she thought she ought to say. What her faith—or her parents' faith, or somebody's faith—demanded she say.

Twice now, Rita had phoned. The first time had been to thank Annie Mac for her condolences. She'd been upfront and honest about her own grief. When they'd talked about Roy, Rita had said, "Martin and I want him caught and punished, but we've been working really hard on letting it go. I had a visitor the other day, a friend whose husband beat her so bad she lost her baby and her chance to have others. She's so bitter, it hurt just listening to her, and, honey, I don't want to be that way."

"You and your Martin deserve happiness."

"It can't be about deserving, can it? Not when the undeserving get and the deserving don't."

"Then what is it about?"

"Honey, if I had those answers, I'd be thrilled to share them. My mama says everything good comes to us as a gift. Fine. I know intellectually that she's right. I'm just working to get it past my head to my heart. So I can find peace."

Rita paused, and Annie Mac just waited, afraid she'd say the wrong thing.

"Anyway, we're trying to believe that some good will come out of it all."

"That's surely a... I don't know... a positive attitude."

"I hear an 'only' in your voice." Rita laughed, but it sounded humorless. "I've got them a-plenty, so I recognize it."

She sighed. "I don't see how a person gets to that place."

"I'm not there. But I... I'm trying." There was a crack in Rita's voice. "Sorry, I've got to go."

She was so far from being at the place Rita talked about and pretty far from even trying to arrive at it. It would take a lot more than words to make her feel positive about Roy or about Rita's loss. Positive wasn't in her. Not by a long shot.

Grateful for the good? Sure. For the bad?

No, thank you.

But maybe she could do this one thing right. Maybe she could help catch Roy.

53 ROY

Roy rested his arms over a chair back, a fourth can of Bud in his hand. Yessir, old Pete had set off on his little jaunt knowing he wasn't gonna give his buddy Roy a blessed cent. He'd tossed out a message there, one Roy would be a fool to miss. Pete wanted him gone and out of his hair for good. Period.

Was that any way to treat someone who saved your life? Send him off penniless?

Pete had money. He just didn't want to share it.

What had Pete done for him, really? Let him stay in this dump? So what? Roy had paid for it by watching out for trespassers. Pete had helped him with some chili and beans when Roy's cash ran out? Big whoop. Helped him find a car? It was a junk heap. Roy'd be lucky if it got him and Katie as far as Fayetteville. Sure, Pete had shared the beer and brought a couple of fake driver's licenses, but that didn't even up the scales.

Nope. Pete wouldn't even be alive if it hadn't been for one Royce T. Bingham back in the day. Pete wouldn't have that 'vette or that house in town or this business. Pete would be worm food.

Roy paced. He hated things not being equal. And didn't Pete have a whole lot these days while Pete's good buddy had next to nothing?

There was that lab tucked away in back. Why was Pete so all fired worried he might head in there? Jocko had helped himself to something and sure looked happier when he came out. And with a pocketful of cash, too.

Maybe Pete had a stash of stuff in that lab that he hadn't taken to sell. And maybe he had his bankroll hidden there.

Roy scratched his belly, bare while his shirt and pants dried. Wouldn't take much longer, he figured, and then maybe it would be time to go hunting.

But hunting in which direction, the lab or the road? He wandered to the porch and looked around. The last of the bird seed had vanished yesterday, but maybe one of his little buddies would be there, give him a sign.

Lookee there, a robin. Fat little thing, hopping down the drive. Driveway. "That's it."

He grinned and said, "Thanks, little buddy," to the robin who hopped a couple more feet and took off to a nearby bush.

He was supposed to take the car and go get his girl. Yep. First things first.

It was still daylight. If they'd set a trap, more than likely they'd fixed it for night. Nobody'd expect him to come looking while it was light, would they?

He slipped on his jeans and buttoned his shirt. Took a look in the mirror. He'd keep the beard, but the hair? Using Pete's clippers, he gave himself a clean cut. Wouldn't do to attract attention, no, sir.

All the way to town, he schemed. Things usually came to him as he needed them. And look, there was the perfect place to park just a block up from Pete's. He could mosey on over. Surely, Pete wouldn't mind him borrowing a set of decent clothes.

He knew Pete hid the key for the back door under a rock, third bush from the stoop. And there it was. Easy to break in. Pete didn't even have an alarm system, but Roy guessed that was because here in town old Pete owned a legitimate business. Nothing to hide.

That set him laughing.

A storehouse of fine clothes filled Pete's closet. He pulled out a good-looking pair of slacks, sort of khaki colored but made of some non-wrinkly stuff. Felt good. And a good-looking tailored shirt in a sort of yellow. Reminded him of a canary. Katie would like it. Good thing Pete was about the same size, except for the shoes. Pete had the muscles, just didn't have the feet.

Okay, so maybe his boots looked odd, but, hey, not much he could do about it now. He grabbed a light jacket and a tie, for after he got Katie. It would be a heck of a lot easier getting money if he looked like he didn't need it.

Back in Pete's kitchen, he rifled in the pantry and grabbed a couple of fruity snack bars to tide him over. And there on a hook was a key ring. Didn't that look like the one for the truck sitting out in Pete's drive?

Cops might be looking for the Chevy, but they wouldn't know about the Dodge. His company truck, Pete called it. Far as Roy knew, Pete usually kept this out at Jocko's. So, see, life was favoring him. 'Bout time, too. He'd just drive it a couple of blocks closer to Annie Mac's. Park it where he wouldn't have so far to carry Katie.

He stashed his old clothes in a plastic sack and dumped them behind the passenger seat. Good truck, started on the first turn. He backed out, went the long way around, and pulled into a space just a block away from his quarry. He climbed out and began moseying down the street.

A car easing down the road behind him set his heart to racing. Best look like he knew what he was doing and where he was going. He grabbed a newspaper tucked in its slot by a mailbox and headed up the sidewalk. Goin' home, that's all he was up to.

The car rolled on by, one of Beaufort's. Maybe on his way to Annie Mac's.

Leastways, the cop hadn't stopped to question him. More than likely because of the clothes and the haircut. Made him look real respectable. He watched the cruiser turn left, waited a few minutes, and set the newspaper on the porch.

This daytime idea wasn't so brilliant, but no one could say Roy Bingham couldn't think on his feet and admit when he'd made a judgment error. All right. Where could he wait out the dusk?

He thought about Annie Mac's open backyard and the shed right next door. Old man who lived there was stone deaf.

He got to it easy enough. The shed was full of old stuff, but not so full he couldn't find a perch on a couple of boxes. He dusted the tops with a rag that was lying on the shelf next to some stinky cans. Looked to him like no one had been in here in years.

He had a candy bar in his pocket he'd been saving for Katie, but he was the one needed it now. He peeled back the wrapper and bit into the chewy candy. Too bad he hadn't thought to bring a bottle of water.

A picture of Rachel came to mind. "Won't be long now, honey. Not long before we'll all be together, you, me, and our baby."

Rachel would smile that soft smile and take his hand. And he'd bend down, touch her lips with his, and give her the moon. Her and Katie. Oh, yeah. His girls.

54 ANNIE MAC & ROY

Annie Mac held her hand up in the late afternoon light, studying the minute wrinkles between her palm and wrist. Here she was, not even thirty, and she had a wrinkly wrist.

Bernice stuck her head in. "Something wrong?"

"Boredom. Wrinkles. I want out of this bed and out of this house."

"I get that. But right now, you need anything? I'm thinking of taking a nap while it's so quiet."

"If you could help me up here, I'll—"

She was interrupted when the phone rang. Bernice motioned to say she'd be in the other room.

"Hello," Annie Mac said, her heart quickening as it did each time she heard the ring, thinking this time it could be Roy.

"Hey," Clay said. He'd taken to calling her at odd times. Each time, his words eased things in her and gave her hope.

"Hey, back."

"What exciting things have you and Bernice been up to recently?"

"Exciting? Us? I'm afraid this idea of mine is going nowhere fast. Poor Bernice and Fletcher must be bored to tears."

"Hey, where's the intrepid woman who volunteered for hazardous duty?"

"Gone to sleep. Somewhere else."

She hadn't imagined you could actually hear a smile until he said, "Nah. I don't believe it."

"Do. We've played Gin, Gin Rummy, Hearts, and Black Jack until the rules swim together, and I don't remember whether I'm supposed to draw or ask to be hit."

That elicited the hoped-for laugh. "Who's winning?"

"Depends on the game. When Fletcher joins in, I'm really glad we only play for matchsticks. Bernice and I are about tied in piles that dwindle and increase, depending on the game."

"I have a bit of news to pass on. Nothing concrete, but I thought you'd like an update."

"What?"

"It seems that Garth Evans followed Roy's old friend Pete out of town to a dirt lane that just may be where our boy has been hiding. It's not our jurisdiction, but Chief Bradley has been in touch with Craven County authorities. They'll check it out."

Annie's breath felt like it would gallump right out of her. "You think?" She paused to slow the words, the breaths. "You think maybe you'll catch him?"

"I think we're closer, Annie Mac. A whole lot closer."

She couldn't speak. She closed her eyes and bit her lip, wanting Roy behind bars so much it hurt.

Clay cleared his throat. "On another subject. I thought I might bring you all a treat this evening. I'll sneak in the back if you tell me what you most want to eat."

"Really?" Oh, the blessed thought of something different, something not fixed in the microwave. "You know what we've been eating, so I'll take anything. Chinese sounds good. Let me ask."

She called out to Bernice, asked her to check with Fletcher. The consensus was that Chinese would work, and he could surprise them. "Only nothing too hot for Bernice, she said. For me, I'm game for hot, medium, or plain, I just don't like a lot of fried food."

"A woman after my own heart. You're on, Annie Mac. I've got some things to tend to, so it'll be late. Can you wait? Maybe have a snack so you don't faint from hunger?"

"Yes, sir. For something different, we can wait."

She hung up and felt her cheeks relax as a small smile settled, lasting into Bernice's return to the room.

"You look cheerful," Bernice said, easing down onto the far side of the bed.

"Good food's coming. Not for a while, but it's coming."

Bernice's eyes held a gleam when she pointed out that Annie Mac's smile might have more to do with who was bringing the food than the food itself. The heat of that unwelcome blush suffused Annie Mac's cheeks again, and she couldn't stop the smile that grew at the thought of how easily he brought about a reaction in her. How was she going to convince anyone she didn't care if her face kept betraying her? Instead of trying, she asked, "You going to get that nap or not?"

Bernice stood back up and laughed. "I'm going. You might want to get one, too."

"What I'd really like is to wash up before dinner. After your nap, I could use a hand with this silly hoist."

"Sure. Why don't we both sleep for an hour or so, then I'll heat up some of that leftover soup to tide us over." She gestured toward the adjoining bathroom. "After that, a wash?"

"Thanks." She longed to take a long, hot shower. Or soak in the tub for an hour with bubbles up to her chin. In the meantime, she could only do her best.

Dusk held enough of the dark to hide him, and it would be full-on night soon. Roy studied the house and the yard from his access point. If he came in on the west side, he'd be able to ease up to one of the back windows without being noticed. He stood behind the old man's shed and reconnoitered. There was a big light off the stoop he didn't remember. Looked like one of those motion sensors.

That would take some considering. He knew something about motion sensor things, how they worked fine but had blind spots. He just had to figure out where those were.

A cat slunk out from a hedge. There it went, meandering across the yard, right in front of where that light should have been flashing on. Well, hello. A malfunction or a blind spot? Dumb of Annie Mac not to check.

Dumb to put security in and leave it to chance.

He wouldn't be so stupid. Not when it came to protecting his girl.

He left his boots next to a tree and scooted across in the footsteps of that cat. Well, leastways, as best he could, straight up to the back of the house.

What on earth were they watching, the television blaring with something that didn't sound much like a kids' program? Maybe his baby was already asleep. He sidled closer, tried to pick a window, but all the blinds were closed.

Katie didn't usually go to bed so early, and, anyway, how would she get her rest with all that noise going on? Good thing her daddy was going to get her out of there.

"Here I come, little lamb."

Somebody laughed. Didn't sound like Annie Mac. He eased toward the edge of the kidlet's bedroom window, thinking he'd kill Annie Mac with his bare hands if she'd brought some boyfriend home, some man in the same house with Katie.

The windows were locked. He didn't want to scare his baby. And who knew? They might have those security sensors that would start up a siren if glass broke.

A smidgen of light showed behind the blinds in Annie Mac's bedroom. He squinted through the crack between the blinds and the window. There was her bed. Empty. Now, if he could jimmy her window open without messing up the glass ...

What was the woman thinking?

She'd left the ceiling fan on, lights on, no one in the room, and the top window open. He growled, furious at her for taking risks like that.

Well, he'd always known who had the brains in the family. It sure wasn't Annie Mac.

He cut through the screen with his knife, undid its latches, and removed it, setting it out of the way. Next, he eased the window open. When it creaked, he ducked, taking slow, quiet breaths.

Still, no one came. Must not be able to hear him, all that noise they had going on in the living room. Good thing they didn't have a dog like that nasty piece of work at the police lieutenant's.

Tucking the gun in his waistband at the small of his back, he slithered over the windowsill into the house. Water ran in the bathroom. He listened to see if somebody was bathing or only washing hands.

When it kept splashing, he checked the hall. Not a one of those voices was his Katie's. Or the boy's. It looked instead like Annie Mac had company staying, and at least one was a man. Maybe she'd brought in cops, trying to trick him.

Annie Mac was dead meat.

Softly, he locked the door to the hallway and hid behind the closet entrance. Wasn't long before the water stopped. Shuffling sounded, a scraping noise, and a grunt or two followed by a tap-tap. The bathroom door opened. Annie Mac dragged herself forward on crutches.

Wasn't that convenient?

He waited until she got right opposite him before he sprang out at her back, cupped a hand over her mouth, and stuck the gun upside her head.

Annie Mac gasped under the foul stench and the taste of his hand as he jammed her lips against her teeth. But she didn't wiggle. She steadied herself. This time, she'd wait. This time, she would not let him win.

But she'd like to know how he'd gotten in? Where was the guard on duty outside? What about Bernice and Fletcher? The doors and windows were supposed to be locked. The alarm working.

Had Roy killed everyone?

He growled in her ear. "Where is she?"

She shook her head as much as his grip allowed.

"You don't give her to me now, I'm going to kill you. Right here, right now. Bang, you'll be dead."

His hand over her mouth, all she could do was grunt. And try, this time, to think.

"Seems you've got company staying with you. Is Katie out there with them or not?"

Okay, Bernice and Fletcher weren't dead. If she could keep him occupied long enough, Bernice would be in to see if she was ready for the hoist to get back on the bed. The closed door would alert her. Wouldn't it?

"You leave those kids up in the hills someplace? Come home without them?" He paused. "No, you wouldn't do that. They've got to be stashed nearby."

He chuckled, low and soft. "Trying to catch me, are you? This supposed to be a trap?" Another soft laugh. "Figured as much. But, lady, that ain't gonna happen."

He dragged her toward the window. "Now, here's how it's gonna go down. You're gonna climb through that there window and come along with me. You hear?"

She pointed to her leg.

"No problem. You make it a problem, I'll break the other and leave you hurting instead of dead. Hurting sounds better anyway, all the grief you put me through."

Annie Mac tried not to move her head as she scanned the room for something, some weapon. She had her crutches, but they were holding her up, and she wouldn't be able to get enough force behind one with him hanging on at her back.

And then he moved to the side so that he straddled one crutch. It happened in a flash: he was trying to move her and himself, trying to get a better purchase as he propelled her toward the window. She used his position, let go of one crutch, and grabbed the other with both hands and smacked it up hard between his legs.

He howled, dropped his hands to his crotch, and curled forward. As she fell, she kicked the gun away with her cast and reached toward the bed post, flinging herself forward and screaming as she went.

Auntie Sim's antique bed post held her as pounding sounded in the hall, at her door. Fletcher yelled, Bernice, too. Roy loosed his hold on his genitals as he searched frantically for his gun. Just as he bent and grabbed it, she aimed at his shoulder with her cast, slamming it into him and grazing the side of his head. A blinding flash of pain shot through her leg as it connected with Roy.

Another scream rent its way out her throat.

She lost track of what happened next beyond the effort to keep from breaking her head open when she landed. She heard Bernice shout something, felt Bernice's hands touch her. But that was all.

55 CLAY & ANNIE MAC

Clay had the Chinese tucked securely on the floor of the Jeep and had finished his conversation with Garth when his phone rang again. After Bernice told him what had happened, his heart beat hard enough to break ribs, and sweat drenched his shirt as he set his magnetic flashing light on the roof of his car, turned on his siren, and sped back to Annie Mac's.

He redialed Garth, explained that Roy was on the run, heading out of Beaufort. Garth said, "It's going to take me close to twenty minutes to make it back to Rasman's. You really think he'll return there?"

"Don't have a clue, but I'm pulling up in front of Annie Mac's now. Give county your ETA. Let's not lose him again if he's fool enough to go back to that house. If I were Bingham, I'd be headed far away just as fast as my car would take me, but who knows how that man thinks?"

Dick Webber would be the guard on duty now. At a stoplight, Clay dialed the man's cell phone, waited for him to answer, and said, "Bingham just tried to take down Ms. Rinehart, but she got the better of him. He could be headed your way."

"I'll keep a lookout."

"Far as we know, he's driving an old Chevy. Can you take your car back up the lane, maybe keep anyone from getting as far as the house? You remember the place where the lane curves so it's close enough to the creek to let you see a boat coming in. Lots of moonlight, plus you've got all of Marshallberg's lights. No telling if he's smart enough to come by water. But I'm tired of losing this man."

"Yes, sir. I can stand watch where I'll see both ways."

"Good man."

Clay slammed on his brakes in front of Annie Mac's. Avery waited for him in the driveway.

"I was watching the whole time," Avery said, keeping pace with Clay's long legs. "Just like we agreed, same spot, as soon as it started to get dark. You've got to believe me. There was nothing out here."

"Yeah, there was. Just not where you looked." Clay balled his fists at his sides. "Have you spoken with the chief?"

"He's on his way in—and not happy."

Clay opened the screen door. "I'm going to need to talk to all of you, but first I'll check on Annie Mac."

"She says she did the man some damage," Avery said. "There's blood on the sill."

Fletcher sat hunched on the couch with his head in his hands. He looked up as Clay entered. "Shoot me now."

Clay raised his brow and headed straight to the back bedroom, where Bernice sat next to Annie Mac.

She stood as he entered. "I'm so sorry, Lieutenant."

He only nodded as she left the room. "Tell me." He took Bernice's place and clasped Annie Mac's hand in his. "Tell me before I kill every one of those bumbling fools."

His unprofessional statement elicited a weak smile, but her voice shook as she told the story. She grinned again, this time sheepishly, when she mentioned the crutch to Roy's sensitive spot, and that lovely blush suffused her face.

"He climbed back out the window?"

She finished the story. "I'm sorry. I did my best."

He traced a line down her cheek. "Annie Mac, I've lost years in the time it took me to drive here, imagining you wounded and headed back to the hospital. Instead, look at you. You beat him."

She waved off his words. "But I didn't."

"Sure you did. You stood up to him. He didn't hurt you. He left with some damage to his body. I'd say you did a great job."

"He got away."

"Who had the gun? Did you?" She shook her head. He angled his. "You used what you had, and you saved yourself. It doesn't matter that he got away. He didn't get Katie, he didn't hurt you, and we will get him. He's going to make another mistake."

She clutched his hand in hers and stared through tear-drenched lashes. "I wanted to maim him enough so Fletcher could stop him. Poor Fletcher. He's not taking this well."

"I'm afraid our good marine must have gotten a mite careless if Royce could get in here without him knowing it. Was the window unlocked?"

Annie Mac nodded. "It was hot today. We forgot."

"I can understand you forgetting, but either Bernice or Fletcher should have made their rounds as soon as dusk hit."

"I know. We should have thought."

"They should have. That's what they're paid to do. Think. Act." He stood, still holding her hand. "You going to be all right?"

She nodded again. He lifted their joined fingers and kissed hers. He didn't care what she thought of the gesture. He needed to make it.

She sucked in a breath, but that's all. Okaaay … good to know.

"I'm heading home. I don't think you have to worry about Roy returning here. Besides, I've left Avery as backup for Bernice and Fletcher. We've got roadblocks set up, but just in case he goes hunting at my place, I want to be there."

Tears filled her eyes. "Do you think he will? Oh, Clay. My babies."

He leaned over to kiss her forehead. "I'll call you."

Back in the living room, he waved Avery outside. "See what else you can discover, including any neighbor who might have seen something."

"On it."

Fletcher and Bernice looked like bookends on the couch, perched at the edge, their fingers laced, their backs bent. When they both spoke at once, Clay held up his hand. "Let me ask the questions." He waited for their nod. "What happened to the motion sensor?"

"It must have malfunctioned." This from Fletcher.

"Have you checked it every day? Twice a day?" Fletcher shook his head. Clay didn't belabor the point. "And the window was partially opened. Unlocked and begging for entry."

"Yes." The word came from both of them, as it should have.

"And you were doing what? Watching television that was loud enough so you didn't hear him?" They nodded. "Annie Mac says he knew Katie wasn't here. Does that mean he walked down the hall to check her room before going after Annie Mac?"

"I can't believe he could have done that. The TV wasn't that loud, and I was listening for Annie Mac. Maybe he just figured it out?" Bernice's cheeks turned ashen under the white light shining overhead.

"I've already called Mr. Brock and made a full disclosure," Fletcher said.

"And?"

"He wants to see us first thing in the morning."

Clay looked from one to the other. "I wouldn't want to be in your shoes tomorrow."

"No, sir. We're not looking forward to it."

Clay brushed his hands on his slacks and left them to their misery. Outside, he asked Avery, "Any news?"

"They've got roadblocks on Highway 101 and the Highway Patrol is on the lookout both directions on 70 and up on 24. The chief got through to the county boys, so they're on their way to see what's what."

"I'm heading back to my place in case he goes after the children. You come get the food out of my car. And do not leave this house." He sounded disgusted, because that's how he felt. He handed the food to Avery. "You know how to reach me."

Annie Mac was safe. That worry gone, Clay had to focus on Bingham's next move. Roy knew the children weren't with their mama, so he might go looking at the last place he'd seen Katie.

Annie Mac couldn't do it. She couldn't lie here in this bed knowing her babies were out there, possibly in danger. Clay was headed home, but this was *Roy*, a madman.

She closed her eyes, tried to pray, but even that got confused with worry. Maybe she couldn't be much help, but there were three people in her living room who could, who had guns and could be backup for Clay.

And if Roy didn't show up there, fine. Better, even, because she'd be back with her babies. And her part in this thing would be over.

She called into the other room. "Bernice, I need you."

Bernice came running. Amazing what a little fright could do for a person. Annie Mac pointed to her crutches. "I need to get dressed and I need to get up." Good thing she had on her loose-fitting pants. She just needed a different top.

Bernice didn't move. "The blue top," Annie Mac said. "Bring it here, please."

When Bernice handed it to her, Annie Mac thanked her and changed. Then she tucked her mass of hair into a ponytail band and reached for the crutches.

Bernice handed them to her. "You need to use the bathroom?"

Annie Mac eased her leg off the bed and stood. She didn't answer, only headed into the hall and out to the living room. Fletcher and Avery looked up.

"Avery, I want to go out to the creek house."

Avery's expression would have seemed comical if she hadn't been so determined. "You can't. We're supposed to keep you safe here."

"That worked so well last time, didn't it?" At their guilty expressions, she relented. "You did your best. But Roy is not coming back to this house, so we don't need all three of you lined up in protect mode. Clay needs help. And my babies need me."

Bernice had come up behind her. "Annie Mac, you're not thinking here. If Clay needs help, there are deputies who can be his backup. Roy won't get to them. Besides, he's probably headed into the next county by now."

Annie Mac shook her head. "That's fine. The entire county can have Roy. Twenty counties can have Roy." She looked from one to the other. "But I want to be there for Ty and Katie. They need their mama, and I need them—and not tomorrow morning."

"Now look," Avery said, "as soon as Roy is in custody, I'll take you to Clay's."

Annie Mac started to the door. "We're going now. Unless you want me to call a taxi instead."

"Really, Annie Mac—" Three voices rose in protest. She unlocked her front door and turned to glare at Avery. "Are you going to help me down these steps and take me out there, or are you going to make me do this the hard way?"

"But we might get in Clay's way," Avery said.

"I promise I won't stir from the car until you assure me the coast is clear. And you can go help if Clay needs you—instead of playing babysitter to me."

She could tell he was wavering. He glanced over at Bernice and Fletcher. Fletcher nodded. "We'll come too."

Bernice shook her head. "We won't fit in Avery's car. Annie Mac needs the entire back seat."

"Fine, then we'll take mine."

"Let's go, Avery," Annie Mac said.

He shrugged and helped her to the stoop. Then Fletcher was there to assist in getting her down to the sidewalk, over to Avery's vehicle, and into the back seat.

"We'll be right behind you," Fletcher said. "You sure there's room for all these cars at Clay's?"

"Plenty," Avery said. "But he's not going to be happy."

Annie Mac smiled. "Yes, but I'm your charge. And I'll be happy."

56 ROY

He'd left all sorts of ruckus behind him as he'd fled Annie Mac's, the back door slamming, lights coming on. A little late on that one, boys.

He snorted. He'd knotted that silk tie around his head to staunch the bleeding—what a waste of good silk—and pulled his cap low over it. The whack to his shoulder had distracted him from killing Annie Mac, and all he'd been able to think about was getting out of there before sirens showed up from every direction.

His blood stayed past boiling. He should have shot her in the gut and let her lie there. Finished what he'd been stupid enough to leave undone the first time.

The pounding on Annie Mac's door had pushed him into retreat mode. You found yourself outnumbered, you regrouped. Figured out another way to get what you wanted. He hadn't fired a shot. That was the good news. The bad news was, he didn't have Katie, he didn't have any money, and he'd had to waste that expensive tie. It had either been the tie or the sports coat, and he could find another tie sooner than he'd land another coat like this one.

All right. So maybe he hadn't read the signs right. And maybe he'd wasted a whole lot of time hunkered down here when he could have been out of the state by now, figuring out life somewhere else.

But that just didn't feel like the right thing to do. Not with Rachel waiting for him. And for Katie. He needed to get his girls together. His family.

He just bet Annie Mac had left the kids stashed at that creek place. The whole police force had lied, coming on like Annie Mac had moved them all back to her house. Maybe there were a few guards. And maybe there weren't. He'd go in slow. Be on the alert.

He drove the speed limit east out of town. Wasn't long before he was turning toward North River. Hard to believe he'd made it this far without a glitch.

He checked his rearview mirror. Ah, there they were, flashing lights all over the intersection. He checked behind him as he continued on across the causeway and to the bridge. The lights didn't follow. Must be setting up a roadblock.

"A little slow, a little late." He slapped the steering wheel. Those cops were such fools.

He turned on Harkers Island Road, kept going to the fork. A left here. Good thing he had a memory for roads. It took him another eleven minutes to get to the lane. He drove down it, taking his time. And there, in front of him, was a car, half blocking the way.

He crept up, looking like he belonged so as not to alert the guy. Smart to have brought this truck. Nobody'd be expecting him when he looked like one of the neighbors come to visit.

A man stood just behind his vehicle on the creek side. Plenty of room for Roy to drive up next to him, take out the car without having to shoot. Gunfire would alert other cops, who'd have time to come flying out of the bushes.

He waved out the window like he was a friendly, then he gunned the engine. Big truck versus little car? Oh, yeah. The Dodge pushed that piece of tin smack into the man, sending him under it or off into the marsh. Either way, he was toast.

Roy didn't waste time. He kept a lookout for anyone else to come running and doused his headlights, pulling off closer to the house this time, ready for a quick getaway. He grabbed his flashlight and palmed his gun.

He could figure on maybe one more guard here and so kept to the trees and behind big bushes. All those lights shining from across the creek and that rising moon sure brightened up the place. He'd have to be careful he didn't get seen.

He smacked a mosquito against his neck. He should have sprayed himself with that stuff Pete kept. Nasty bugs.

He could see the creek and anything silhouetted against it, but it would be a whole lot harder for anyone to pick him out against the woods. Keeping low, he crept toward the house.

57 CLAY

Clay made it in record time, his light flashing and siren blazing when he needed them on the highways. He'd called Mrs. Barnes, told her to hide the children and keep the dog close to her.

He dialed Webber's cell after he turned into his drive. The call went to voicemail. He slowed his Jeep to a crawl.

There up ahead was Webber's car in the bushes toward the marsh, battered. No sign of Webber or another vehicle.

Clay eased out of the driver's side, kept under cover as he approached the damaged car. A moan came from the marsh side.

The guard lay half under his vehicle. As Clay leaned over him, Webber opened his eyes and said, "Go. Just call it in. I'll live."

Clay left the Jeep, phoned the dispatcher for an ambulance and back-up. "We've got a man down, and Bingham's here."

58 ROY

When no one came for him with guns blazing, Roy stayed in the shadows and eased up the deck steps toward the back of the house. It was windless tonight and quiet, inside and out.

He hated to scare Katie, but he didn't want some gun-happy guard taking aim at him. He angled his weapon downward and shot that pathetic excuse for a lock off those French doors. The glass spiderwebbed.

Again he waited, but only the fool dog set up a racket. He pushed open the door, paused, and then peeked around. He couldn't believe they'd left his baby with no one but that man outside to keep guard. Must be someone in here, too. First, he'd find whoever it was. Then he'd find his baby.

Behind what looked like a bedroom door came snuffling and scratching. Then a woman's voice.

Roy reached for the handle, keeping well away from the door in case the woman was armed. He didn't want to risk shooting at that lock, not when bullets could hit his Katie. Besides, he'd already made too much noise. It only took two hard shoves with his boot, and the lock broke. Some policeman, having locks that gave way like they were made of aluminum foil.

He readied his pistol to shoot that dog if it came after him. Instead, a big colored lady held tight to the dog's collar.

She stared straight at Roy. "What you be wantin' here? You got no call to go shootin' at folk."

Hoity-toity, wasn't she? Roy looked her up and down. "I only come for my baby, so don't you go getting' your panties in a wad. You hand her over, and we'll be outta here. I don't mean no harm to you or the boy." Though the boy better not come too close.

"She's not here."

Roy squinted at her. "Of course she's here. Where else would she be with a guard keeping watch outside?"

"I sent them to the garage. They were to wait for my signal and then go on out to the woods. I imagine they're hiding real good about now."

Roy raised the gun, pointed it straight at her big waistline. The dog growled low in his throat. She shushed it again. Called it Harvey.

Harvey? "What kind of fool name is that to give a dog?" But he was getting off track. "You tell me where they are, or I'm going to shoot you."

"I told you. They're in the woods. Hiding. You don't think I'd have been stupid enough to let them stay in this house for you to hurt, do you? So why don't you just put that gun away and let me fetch a bandage for that cut on your head."

Was she crazy? He was demanding his Katie, and she wanted to dress his wound? "Woman, you're a piece of work. But you'd better be telling me the truth about those kids."

"Yes, sir."

"Fine. Then we'll all go find them. I bet that dog would lead me to the boy, you give him his head."

"Sure enough." She started forward, still holding the whining dog. "'Course, I could fix your cut and then we could go."

There she went again. Trying to distract him. "You just want to give them a chance to get clean away. No. You show me where they went. I'm right on your heels."

"I need the dog's leash. It's by the back door."

He kept her in sight as he collected the leash. Then he held it out to her. She hooked it to the dog's collar and was heading toward the kitchen when he heard a sound from the deck. A board creaked.

"Stop," he said. "Hold that dog still."

But the dog wouldn't shut up. The more the woman tried to hush it, the more it whined and danced around, its nails loud on the hardwood floor near the kitchen.

Roy grabbed her fat arm and pulled her in front of him, his gun smack in the middle of her back. "You hold that dog, and when I say so, you're gonna walk to that deck. You want me to shoot the dog, try something. You want me to shoot you, try something. I got plenty of bullets in here."

The woman started to walk, but it occurred to Roy that maybe this wasn't such a good idea. "Wait." In a fight that dog would be likely to turn on him and double his chances of losing. Good thing he was using his head.

"Changed my mind." He kept his voice low. "You gotta lock that dog up. We're going to back up here. Slowly." He pointed to the door across from where he'd found her. "Where's that go?"

"A hallway and two bedrooms. A bath."

Well, hello. Maybe she'd stashed his baby back there.

He kept her between him and the glass doors. When he got her over to the hallway, he opened its door. "Okay, we're going in there. You come right on in with that dog."

The dog sat on its haunches, whining before it let out another bark.

Now, would a dog do that if the kids were there? No. "Get that dog in there and close the door."

That fool dog's barking was giving Roy a headache. He had half a mind to go ahead and waste a bullet on the mutt, but that would really upset his baby. And Rachel loved dogs.

Focus, Roy. Focus.

The dog finally went in after a little prodding from the woman. Roy shut the door, kept hold of her arm. And pushed her toward the outside.

59 CLAY

Clay had stayed hidden in the bushes at the deck's edge before creeping up into the shadows next to the barbecue and arming himself with the spatula that hung there, a foot-and-a-half long instrument of heavy-duty steel. He carried his gun in his other hand, but he wanted to avoid a firefight if at all possible. He peeked in the window in time to see Roy close Harvey up in the guest hall and push Mrs. Barnes toward the deck.

Mrs. Barnes shuffled forward. Pressing into the dark against the wall, Clay waited, spatula raised. The door opened, and the housekeeper stepped out. As Roy exited in her wake, Clay brought the metal spatula down hard on the man's gun arm with the flat end turned like a blade. Roy's pistol fell and slid across the deck. Roy screamed as he shoved Mrs. Barnes toward Clay. To keep her out of his line of fire, Clay turned his weapon away, but her flailing arm knocked his gun from his hand. He pushed her off and bent over to retrieve his weapon. Roy lunged.

Even with one hurt arm, the man slammed his fist hard enough into Clay's stomach to double him over. When Roy followed through with his shoulder to Clay's chest, they both went down. Clay shielded his face and landed a punch to the other man's side, but it didn't carry enough force to slow Roy.

The man pushed off and sprang to his feet. "I'm gonna kill you."

Clay grabbed Roy's foot and yanked, but Roy managed to keep upright and jerk free. He slammed his booted toe into Clay's leg. Clay's bad leg.

Pain sledgehammered Clay. He curled toward it, unable to stifle a scream. Roy grabbed Clay's shirt, hefted him, and took aim with his fist. Suddenly, a furious Ty and a growling dog joined the melee. Ty landed on Roy's back and pummeled him with boy-fists, while Harvey's teeth caught the ankle of Roy's boot.

Roy, cursing loudly, threw the boy off and kicked free of Harvey, then went for Clay's gun, closer than his own. Clay bit hard on his cheek to redirect his pain and reached for the ankle Harvey'd been chewing on, yanking Roy off balance and sending him face-first to the deck. Clay tried to take advantage of the other man's fall, but even as he pushed through the pain, his leg wouldn't cooperate.

Clay's hesitation gave Roy a chance to reach for his own gun, but by then both Ty and Harvey were back in the fray. This time, Harvey caught Roy's extended wrist, and Ty grabbed the spatula from the deck and swung it toward Roy's head.

As the spatula connected and the dog's fangs drew blood, Roy screamed. He tried to jerk his arm free and protect his head from Ty.

In the background, Mrs. Barnes was making a whole lot of noise, calling for Ty, crying out to God, telling Ty to come away. "Come on, honey, you're gonna get yourself hurt."

Sirens yowled down the drive, and tires skidded in gravel. The cavalry.

Clay couldn't wait for them. He scrambled over, grabbed his gun, and pointed it at the man's head, away from the boy and the dog. Harvey held on, blood oozing around his bared teeth.

"Enough," Clay commanded in as powerful a voice as he could muster while he struggled to stand.

"Get that dog off me!" Roy punched at Harvey with his free hand, but Harvey held on.

Clay braced himself on the big barbecue. "Ty, son, step back. Now."

Mrs. Barnes was already there, drawing Ty off. They both backed away. "Good dog," Ty said. "Good Harvey."

Clay kept his gun and attention focused on Roy. "Now call off Harvey, Ty."

"Come on, boy. Enough." Ty grabbed Harvey's collar and pulled. But the dog only snarled. "Harvey, let go." Ty put his body into it.

Suddenly the dog obeyed, throwing Ty in front of Clay's gun.

In that instant, Roy grabbed the boy and yanked him close, even as he dove again for his weapon. His curses mingled with cries of "You're dead meat."

Clay knew a moment of sheer panic. All he could think about was the boy. Ty. In that madman's clutches.

As Roy scooped up the other weapon, Clay pushed Ty to the side and raised his pistol. The muzzle of Roy's Glock made an arc toward him.

Clay fired.

Roy, his eyes wide and his jaw dropping, collapsed, his head falling within inches of Clay's feet. His gun skittered away, and there he lay, motionless, his blood pooling on the wooden deck.

Ty buried his face in the dog's fur. Clay holstered his gun and leaned over the boy. "Son, go on in with your sister, please. Don't let her come out here."

Ty looked up, his eyes huge. "She won't. She's too scared."

"I need you to take Harvey and go inside." Clay glanced at Mrs. Barnes, who seemed rooted in place.

"I'm sorry. Yes, of course," she said to Clay. "Ty, baby, come on in with Miss Becca. We need to see to Katie."

Clay felt as if needles pierced his leg. He needed to get an ice pack on it. And then some heat. Or vice versa.

Feet stomped up the deck steps. Avery was first on the scene, his gun drawn and ready. Two deputies followed, also at the ready. Behind them came two of Beaufort's finest.

"Lieutenant," one said. "Sir," said the other.

Clay acknowledged them and nodded toward the body. "See to him, will you?"

A chorus of "yes, sirs" followed.

Clay steadied himself and hobbled up to Avery.

"You okay?" one of the deputies asked. "You're limping."

Clay acknowledged him. "Bingham kicked me where it hurt."

"You might want to see to that."

"I will." To Avery, he said, "Aren't you supposed to be in Beaufort with Annie Mac?"

Avery angled his head toward the parking lot, which had grown very crowded, including the addition of Fletcher's car. He and Bernice climbed out, one on each side, their doors open as they waited.

"What on earth?" Clay grabbed the railing and eased himself down the steps.

"Had to, Clay. There was no shutting her up otherwise. She was ready to call a taxi."

Clay limped over to the back door of Avery's car and yanked it open. The overhead light revealed Annie Mac with her leg stretched out on the seat next to her, fluttering fingers at him, her bottom lip caught between her teeth.

"You're killing me." Clay raked his fingers through his hair. "You couldn't have waited?"

Her lips curled up at the edges in an almost-smile. "Not once you said Roy might come here. Avery and the others took a little convincing, but I promised I'd stay out of the way."

Clay raised a brow at Avery before turning back to Annie Mac. "Well, let's get you inside while the boys clean up the mess we've made." Clay waved to Bernice and Fletcher. "Why don't you come make yourselves useful."

He handed Avery his keys. "You all go in the front. Bernice can help Annie Mac. I imagine Mrs. Barnes has her hands full."

"Thank you," Annie Mac said as Clay returned to deal with the men on the deck.

It was a good two hours before the coroner's men had come and gone and all the troops had left with their crime-scene tape intact and a promise to return in the daylight. One of the local boys said he'd have his brother—who'd installed the original French doors—head to Safrits in the morning to get a replacement.

Another reason to like living here. Besides the fact that one rarely had to shoot anyone, help was just around the corner when you needed it.

He headed inside and found Annie Mac sitting up in bed, one child on either side. "Glad to have your mama back?"

Katie, whose eyelids drooped, popped her thumb out. "Mama."

Clay ruffled Ty's hair. "You should have seen this boy of yours. He and Harvey were real heroes."

"Heroes? Really?" She shifted Katie to her shoulder. "I want to hear all about it. And then it's bed time. For all of us."

Clay thought of how much Ty might actually be able to describe. "Son, I'm thinking you might want to be careful how you tell the story. Mindful of little ears?" At this, he nodded toward Katie.

"Yes, sir. I won't say it all."

While the children settled in to tell their story—or rather Ty's story—Clay took a much needed shower, standing for a very long time under the hot spray. Then he popped two extra-strength acetaminophen in his mouth and took ice packs from the freezer for his bruises. Mrs. Barnes saw him limping to his chair with these.

"You want me to wrap those on your poor leg, Mr. Clay?"

"No thank you, Mrs. Barnes. You were great tonight. A cool head."

"Sorry I lost it for a bit there. But I was prayed up, so I knew the good Lord would be helping me and those babies and would bring that man to justice."

"Too bad God doesn't just send lightning bolts for people like Roy before they do all that damage. It was hard on Ty having to see justice dispensed. And by me."

"Yes, sir, I knows it was. And I'm real sorry about all the things Roy did. But we can't be making God out to be a genie who shows up just 'cause we ask for something, you know? He looks at eternity a whole lot different from the way we do, and he knows the end from the beginning for each of us. For some, he's got to let us get to the Red Sea, hoping we'll look at those waves and those soldiers and hang onto him, this side of the water. Praise him, you know? While we're doing that, he parts that sea."

"Hope you're right."

"Now, I'm going to get Miss Annie settled. The children are in bed. They'd fallen to sleep before I moved them. So don't you worry yourself about any of us."

Clay closed his eyes and waited for the pain relievers to do their work.

He woke to the sound of Mrs. Barnes closing her bedroom door. It took him a minute to realize that he was in his chair and the night's trauma had ended. He was about to head to his room when his cell phone rang.

It was the chief. After praising the work Clay and Avery had done, he said, "The county boys found enough evidence out at that property where Bingham had been staying to make them do a little searching. Garth Evans said a couple of the deputies got a little nervous about following the path out back, claiming they thought it best to wait for morning. But Garth wanted to catch his man, so off he went. The locals had to follow." Chief Bradley laughed. "And he said it was worth it. They came to a cinderblock house back in the woods. Bars on the windows. Undergrowth all around. Except there was that path. Well-worn to and from."

"A lab?"

"That's what they were thinking. But they didn't want to go breaking in the place, so they called the experts. Knowing Roy was still loose, the sheriff sent in one of his detectives and a couple of certified meth lab technicians."

"Bet they weren't happy to have to go out there this time of night."

"Probably not. But it's a good thing they were called in. The owner of the lab, undoubtedly our friend Rasman, had rigged a trip line. Once the boys disarmed that, they were able to document and fingerprint. Won't take long to catch Mr. Rasman."

"What did you hear about the wounded guard, Dick Webber? Anything?"

"Bruised ribs, a broken leg. He'll be hurting for a while, but he's not in any danger."

"Good news all around. Thanks for calling, Chief."

Clay hung up and headed toward Annie Mac's bedroom. Her light was still on and her door ajar. At his knock, she waved him in.

"How're you doing?"

"More relieved than I can say." She tucked hair behind her ear with hands that didn't look very steady. "I'm just sorry you all had to go through that. And Ty..."

He approached the bed and sat by her side. "He's strong. We'll get him past it."

"You saved him. He told me."

"I probably lost ten years when Roy grabbed him."

"You saved us all."

Clay looked into her eyes and couldn't move. Finally, he cleared his throat and said, "The chief called. They found where Roy had been staying. His buddy Pete ran a meth lab out there."

She didn't speak, but her eyes had widened, and now tears filled them.

"That will take Pete off the streets for a good while."

"Oh, Clay." Her hand covered her mouth as a sob choked out. "I just wish it could have ended before all the other. Before that deputy and then Rita."

Clay took her in his arms while she grabbed hold of his shirt front. With one hand, he cradled her head. With the other, he gently rubbed her back. "I know. I know. But it's finally over."

"I... I can't believe it," she said on the heels of another sob.

He brushed her hair back from her face when she eased away. Her eyes remained downcast, and she sniffled. He reached for a tissue, used it to wipe her cheeks. When she sniffled again and almost choked on a partial laugh, he gave her another tissue so she could blow her nose.

Her eyes glistened as she lifted her head to look at him. A small smile spread her lips, and she turned her head into one of his hands. His fingers splayed over her cheek, caressing her as gently as he might a frightened bird. He was petrified that she'd realize what he was doing and be appalled.

"Clay," she whispered, not sounding at all appalled.

"I'm here."

He couldn't help himself. He leaned toward her and let his lips gently touch hers, a feather kiss, brushing softly as he waited for her to back away. She didn't. Instead she moaned under his touch, emboldening him. Before long, both were breathing heavily. He broke contact with her lips, leaving his forehead braced against hers as he whispered her name, trying all the while to quiet his rapid-fire breathing.

"Did you know, Annie Mac, that I've quite fallen in love with you?"

Foreheads still touching, her eyes closed, she murmured, "Mmm."

He waited a few moments, whispered, "Do you think you could ever love me back?"

She hesitated. Then, "Maybe. Someday. I might."

He kissed her once more, backed away, and grinned. "I suppose I'll have to work harder at convincing you."

She smiled back as she wiped her eyes. "You've been doing a good job of it."

"I take it that's an encouragement to keep on as I have been?"

Which elicited a laugh and a "Yes, sir, please."

He stood. "We both need to get some sleep. Good night, Annie Mac. Sweet dreams of safety and peace."

"Good night."

60 CLAY

By the time Clay returned home three evenings later, the party was in full swing. So many things had changed since their last group dinner, but after hearing the news of Roy and the meth lab, Hannah and Tadie had organized a gathering to help everyone find closure.

"We've got to get all of us past this mess and into a new place emotionally," Hannah had said when she called to tell him they'd be out, laden with food. "Especially Annie Mac, you know, so she can start over again. And make good memories for that deck of yours. Ty's bound to need that."

He stood in the great room's entrance, taking in the scene. Hannah and Tadie laughed with Mrs. Barnes as they messed about in what used to be his kitchen. Matt, Martin, and Will manned the grill, doing the barbecue thing again, while the children ran around the yard with Harvey. And Rita sat with Tadie's baby on her lap, pulled up next to Annie Mac.

He still limped slightly as he strode into the room. "Smelling mighty good in here. Hey, all."

"Clay." Tadie nodded his way. "Glad you could make it."

He laughed. "Glad I could, too. I see the other working males lost no time in getting to the trough."

"More's coming," Hannah said. "This time, we're going to enjoy your deck. And I hear you got yourself a new door. Not bad. You have any more chairs we can set up?"

"In the garage. Why don't you see if some of those hangers-on outside can fetch them while I go change into something more comfortable?"

"Yes, sir."

Clay waved at Annie Mac and Rita as he ducked into his room and closed the door. He doused water on his face and then got into a clean shirt. He was still in there when a tentative knock sounded. "Come on in," he called.

Ty stepped into the room.

Clay waited for the boy to speak, but all Ty did was bounce from foot to foot. "Got something on your mind?"

"Roy."

"I'm sorry you had to witness that."

"Yeah, well, he shoulda died. He deserved it. And I just wanted to say thank you again. For, you know, saving my life."

"Oh, son." Clay sat down at the foot of his bed at eye level with the boy. "I'm glad it's over. But can you understand that killing a man is never something we should enjoy or even be proud of?" Clay paused to let that sink in. "Roy died because he wouldn't quit. And because he was trying to kill you and all of us."

Ty's head was lowered, but his thin shoulders shook. Clay pulled him close. "No matter how it happened, you're safe. You, your mama, and Katie are safe. And you were so brave when you fought Roy. I'm mighty proud of you."

Ty's arms flew to Clay's neck.

"Okay now. You go on out, and I'll be there in a minute." Clay ushered the boy to the door.

And when Clay walked back out into the great room, only Annie Mac and Rita—with Sammy still in her lap—remained inside. They didn't seem to notice him.

He decided to sneak on past and let them have their girl-time, but when Annie Mac wiped her eyes and touched Sammy's little back as he gurgled in Rita's arms, Clay stood rooted. Oh, man. Rita's loss had to be raw still, and yet there she sat, smiling at the baby, bonding with Annie Mac. Clay shook his head.

Sammy would probably grow up spending a whole lot of time with his Auntie Rita and his non-blood-greats, Elvie and James. Family to Tadie, no matter what their skin said.

He could see how good it would be for Annie Mac to have a friend like Rita. Good all the way around, in his mind. He didn't know Martin very well, but he'd like to. Seemed like the man had a really good head on his shoulders and a fine heart, if what Clay had heard tell of him was true—all those international kids he'd been supporting for years.

He skirted past the women toward the deck, but Rita called. "Clay, hey. You want to help get Annie Mac into her chair so we can go eat?" She rose. "I'm going to give this love-bug back to his mama."

Mrs. Barnes wandered in. "Your leg better today, Mr. Clay?"

"It is, thank you." He turned to Annie Mac. "You ready?" She nodded.

Together they got Annie Mac into her chair and to the table. This time, she sat next to him.

Martin asked to lead the prayer of thanksgiving before they ate. Knowing Martin's pain, Clay felt the man's words hit with a gut-wrenching force.

Martin called them to trust and find faith. He ended with, "Avinu, Our Father in heaven, G-d of my fathers, have mercy on us."

And no one moved.

Finally, Martin lifted his glass of sweet tea. "As it is written in Psalm 92, the enemies of the Lord perish and all evildoers are scattered. We have seen his work in delivering us from the evil in our midst. Now we must rejoice and trust in his goodness from now and forevermore. To deliverance! To justice and peace!"

They raised their glasses and said in unison, "To justice and peace!"

"Jus-thus!" Katie lisped around her thumb, and everyone laughed.

Clay leaned toward Annie Mac as the rest busied themselves with food. "Justice and peace, my dear. And love," he whispered. "To you and yours."

She smiled up at him. "And to you." She pulled his hand toward her lips. And there, publicly, she kissed it. "Thank you. For everything."

Katie came up and leaned on her mama's good side. "Can we live here forever, Mommy? With Mr. Clay and Miss Becca?"

Clay's attention was riveted on Annie Mac as she turned that delightful beet color. And then he noticed that Ty hovered nearby, just beyond his shoulder. The boy must want an answer just as much as he did.

"Sweetheart, let's see what happens, okay?"

"But I like it here. Ty does, too."

Clay figured he'd better intervene. He set his plate down and lifted the child into his lap. "You know what, Katie? This place and I love having you all here. Your mama has some more healing to do before she can go anywhere, so why don't we help her get well and worry about the future when it comes? Does that make sense?"

"The fu-tur?"

"Tomorrow and the next day and the next. Let's focus on getting your mama well, okay? And, you know what? Harvey's going to get to stay here when Miss Hannah and Mr. Matt go on a trip in a couple of weeks. Won't that be fun?"

Hannah must have heard that last. "He's never going to want to come home after all this spoiling."

"Really? You mean, we could keep him?" Ty asked.

Annie Mac laughed. "No, honey. Miss Hannah would miss him too much. But I'm sure she'll let you play with him even after he goes home."

He sidled closer to his mother. "Maybe we could get a dog too. Maybe a wife for Harvey. Then he could have kids."

Hannah hooted. "As long as you're doing the puppy raising. That won't be happening at my house."

"Probably not at mine either," Annie Mac said.

"Aw, Mom."

"Look. Let's just get through dinner tonight. And then let me get out of this cast before you go obligating me to more work. I've got to find a job—"

Matt entered the conversation. "I was at Rotary last night. Seems the wife of one of the guys, who happens to be the local elementary school principal, is going on long-term maternity leave come November. Sorry I didn't think of it when he told me, but you want me to put in a word for you?"

Annie Mac's mouth might have caught a fly if she hadn't snapped it closed. Clay cupped a hand on her arm when he saw the tears form and gave it a quick squeeze.

"Why don't you do that?" Hannah said, coming to Annie Mac's rescue.

Tadie leaned toward the crew at Clay's end of the deck. "Get used to it, Annie Mac. This is the way friends are."

Annie Mac shook her head. "I'm sorry. It's still overwhelming."

Matt excused himself. Clay glanced through the new French doors to see him pull out a cell phone. The chatter continued, and Annie Mac shooed the children back to their food on the steps with a "You'd better finish your dinner or Harvey will be after it. Look there. You're making Jilly do all the work keeping Harvey off."

Katie giggled and bounced forward. Ty stared hard from his mama to Clay and also retreated.

When Matt returned, he stopped near Annie Mac's chair. "Jim Brevard said you're to call him tomorrow. He said the job is yours if you want it."

"Oh, my," Annie Mac said as her hand flew to her mouth. "Mine?"

"Well, I told him you were certified. I'm right, aren't I?"

She nodded.

"When he heard about what you'd gone through and how you're our good friend, he said he'd be honored if you'd consider stepping in to take his wife's place. It's not a permanent position, mind you, but it will get your foot in the door."

Ty called out, "So, I get to go back to school?"

"What?" Hannah said, as if shocked. "You don't like homeschooling with us?"

"I do. I mean, I've learned a whole bunch. But I kinda miss Andy. And playing ball."

Jilly's voice was next. "Can I go to school too?"

"May I," Tadie said.

"Wow, your mama does that, too?" Ty asked.

Jilly shrugged. "They all do. My daddy's even worse."

"Really?"

"So, Mommy, Daddy, may I go to school with Ty?"

Hannah laughed. "Tenacious, isn't she?"

"Always. How about we talk about it later, young lady? We don't need to solve all the world's problems over dinner tonight."

Clay, from his post in listening distance of the steps, heard Jilly's lowered voice. "I bet I'll get to if you do."

Ty nodded as if he had experience getting around parents. As he watched the children, all Clay could think about was how much he hoped Annie Mac would let them stay. How much he longed to parent her two. How much he longed to love her.

Ty leaned over the dog and whispered something in Harvey's ear that was too low for Clay to hear. When Harvey's tail hit the deck three times, Ty made a power jab with his fist and turned to Jilly, looking furtively around and catching Clay's focus.

Next thing Clay knew, the two older children had scampered off the steps, out of earshot. Katie climbed down to follow and pulled on Ty's shirt so he'd lean down and tell her. He wagged his head, but that just got her little feet stomping.

And wasn't that a good sign? When he'd first met Katie, she'd been too afraid of her shadow to have a tantrum and had only waited to know how high when Ty told her to jump.

Ty seemed surprised at his sister's outburst, but he put his big-brother hands on her shoulders, said something very serious, and at Katie's nod, leaned in to whisper to her. That did it. Katie threw her arms around her brother's middle and hugged until he unwrapped her and backed away.

Clay seemed doomed not to know what the children had discussed. He joined in some of the adult conversation, especially when everyone quizzed Matt and Hannah about their travel plans. He'd heard they had restarted the adoption quest, which sounded like a really good idea, but probably not one they wanted to talk about in front of Rita yet.

Mrs. Barnes helped collect the dishes, and the occasional pause in conversation let the evening noises filter across the creek. Katie curled in her mommy's lap and snuggled with her thumb working its magic.

He noticed one little-girl hand touch Annie Mac's cheek. The thumb came out and Katie said, "Mommy, you remember what I asked for?"

"Which time?"

"About you-know-what." Her voice turned to a hissing whisper, which traveled very conveniently in Clay's direction. "About staying here."

"Oh, right. That. The thing we said we'd discuss later."

"Well, Harvey said we'd get to. Ty told me he thumped his tail three times. You're gonna have to guess about the other two things. I'm not s'posed to say."

"And Harvey knows?"

The thumb had retreated between Katie's lips. "Un-huh."

Annie Mac hugged her daughter closer and did not glance in Clay's direction. He knew this because his attention didn't shift, in spite of the laughter and fun all the others seemed to be having as the ladies returned from the kitchen.

Four was obviously too young to be trusted with secrets. Only a few minutes passed before Katie removed the thumb, pulled her mama's head down, and spoke into Annie Mac's ear, the ear nearest Clay, so he heard the words all right.

"It's about a dad." She pulled Annie Mac around so they were almost nose to nose. "For us. You know who."

Oh, man. A dad. The kids (and Harvey) wanted him for a dad.

No, he would *not* get sappy. He wasn't by himself out here.

But, man, this was gonna tip him right off his chair if he didn't watch out.

Now it was his turn to look away. The last thing he wanted was for Annie Mac to feel pressured. He stood and wandered inside. Maybe they needed refills on something. Tea? He could bring out another jug of tea. Or a pitcher of water. He got as far as the other side of his recliner when he turned—and met Annie Mac's stare.

He waited, frozen.

And then she grinned. A big, sappy, isn't-that-a-great-idea grin.

And he grinned right back at her.

AUTHOR'S NOTE

Heavy Weather is my second Beaufort book and picks up two years after *Becalmed* ended. *Becalmed* told Tadie's story and introduced you to many of the folk in *Heavy Weather*. I hope you enjoyed catching up with them. If you haven't yet read *Becalmed*, you can pick a copy in print or e-book wherever books are sold, or you can request it from your local library.

The folk you meet in this story (and some of the places) come solely from my imagination. I wish I could say that men like Roy don't exist in Beaufort or elsewhere, but they do—and they come from every economic and social class. Please, please, if you ever become involved in an abusive relationship, run fast and far. Seek help. There are people waiting to help you find a way out. No one should be allowed to mistreat you. Ever. You're a precious child of God, created in His image. Don't listen to anyone who says you're not.

If you don't know where to turn, write to me, and I'll put you in touch with someone in your area who cares.

And if you're ever in Beaufort, let me know. I'd love to meet you. You can catch up with me at any of these:

> normandiefischer.com.
> Facebook.com/NormandieFischer
> Twitter @WritingOnBoard

I'd love to hear from you.
Blessings, Normandie

ACKNOWLEDGEMENTS

So many people had a hand in helping me get this story from concept to reality. Huge thanks to my critique partners, Jane Lebak and Robin Patchen, and to readers John Pelkey, Linda Glaz, and Regina Smeltzer. Donald Maass, writing teacher extraordinaire, had a hand at one point in making this the best it could be. Don't hold it against these good folk if my follow-through remains imperfect.

After Robin, Jane, and Don poked and prodded, Ray Rhamey of Flogging the Quill took on the task of editing the story. In the proofreading stage, Jane Shealy, Tracie Heskett, and John Pelkey offered their eagle eyes. I'm so grateful to them and to all my beta readers. Thank you. My books wouldn't be what they are without your input and encouragement.

I'm indebted to the following folk for their technical assistance: Chief Steve Lewis of Beaufort Police Department who gave generously of his time to show me the station and talk shop with me; Frank (who only wanted his first name used) at the Carteret County Sheriff's Department who helped in writing about Roy's transfer between counties by saying that yes, it could have happened the way I wrote it. I'm certain none of our local deputies would have ever made the mistakes of that deputy from my fictional county. The Carteret County deputies are wonderful—full of humor and sensitivity. Steven Phifer, Detective Lieutenant over Narcotics and Canine, Carteret County Sheriff's Department, gave me some pointers on the crew who might be called in to see about a meth lab. I talked to one of the women at the Tyrrell County Sheriff's department, who helped with details of the area, and I'm grateful. Sea Venture sailed the Alligator River on our trip with my mama in 2013. My cousin Cora McKnight, a nurse anesthetist, and Regina Smeltzer, nursing instructor, were my medical consultants. And my brilliant and beloved Mr. Fischer helped with the fight scene and recommended I watch more action movies. Sigh.

My mama and husband have been so patient in the days and months and years I've taken to write each of my stories. Thank you so much for putting up with hurried meals and my flying retreat to my novel's world.

What Others Are Saying

About *Becalmed*

It's a rare book that draws you in from the first page, wraps its cover around you, and warmly envelops you in its unfolding tale. This book did that for me... ~Lita Smith-Mines, Boating Times of Long Island

Normandie Fischer can illustrate loneliness as if she has lived through it herself. ~Linda Yezak, Author/Editor 777 Peppermint Place

This book and the lovely writing truly transported me into the world of Southern charm... ~Patricia's Wisdom

Normandie Fischer's spirited tale enchants in the tradition of Maeve Binchy and Anne Rivers Siddons. Her Southern charm pours over the page like warm honey on a sweet bun. Each delicious morsel leaves you longing for more. ~D.D. Falvo,

With a voice that sings and characters that sail right into your heart, Fischer has crafted a story that will keep the pages turning, the heart twisting, and stick with you long after The End. ~ Roseanna White, author and editor

About *Sailing out of Darkness*

Sailing out of Darkness took me traveling beyond my expectations. Normandie Fischer has a way of writing that made me feel like I was moving through time with her characters as they went from place to place. The transitions between scenes, the way that we were in Sam's mind, or were watching her ... all of these were fluid and strong. ~Andrea Bates, Girl Good Gone Redneck

What I loved most about Sailing Out of Darkness was its ability to touch on a lot of tough issues while still being an accessible and somewhat light read. ~The Book Barn

...beautiful, gorgeous imagery... It is take your breath away awesomeness. The storyline could absolutely suck and I wouldn't care half as much because I just wanted to read more descriptions of people, places, feelings and thoughts. This is true writing talent here. And she's a wonderful storyteller too. ~Samantha Coville, Sammy the Bookworm

This is a book with mature conversations, romance that is raw, emotional, and truly real. ~Spiced Latte Reviews

I recommend this book for those that enjoy second chances, sailing, Italy, faith, and true love. ~Italian Brat's Obsessions

Fischer is a master at transporting the reader into the scene. I found myself reading over many passages again and again to enjoy the images and emotion they evoke. The beauty and foreignness of exploring new places is captured pitch perfect in Sam's ponderings as she makes her way through Italy. ~ Lynne Hinkey

CPSIA information can be obtained at www.ICGtesting.com
Printed in the USA
BVOW05s0244170815

413628BV00001B/99/P